Praise for *The Witch of W*

"*The Witch of Willow Hall* offers a fascinating location, a great plot with history and twists, and characters that live and breathe. I love the novel, and will be looking forward to all new works by this talented author!"

—Heather Graham, *New York Times* bestselling author

"Beautifully written, skillfully plotted, and filled with quiet terror... Perfect for fans of Simone St. James and Kate Morton."

—Anna Lee Huber, bestselling author of the Lady Darby mysteries

"*The Witch of Willow Hall* will cast a spell over every reader."

—Lisa Hall, author of *Tell Me No Lies* and *Between You and Me*

"I was entranced by this intriguing and spellbinding novel... I hope Hester Fox goes on to write many more such novels—I for one will be buying them."

—Kathleen McGurl, author of *The Girl from Ballymor*

"This compelling story had me gripped from the first page. The vividly drawn characters cast their spell so convincingly, I couldn't stop reading until I discovered what happened to them. A wonderful debut novel."

—Linda Finlay, author of *The Flower Seller*

"Steeped in Gothic eeriness, it's spine-tingling and very atmospheric. I love the character of Lydia and the way she learns and grows into her powers."

—Nicola Cornick, *USA TODAY* bestselling author of *House of Shadows*

"*The Witch of Willow Hall* is so spookily good I felt haunted by it. Totally obsessed with Lydia's story... I absolutely loved it from start to finish."

—Sarah Bennett, author of the Lavender Bay series

"A creepy estate, juicy scandal, family secrets, ghosts and a handsome yet mysterious suitor make this a satisfying and quietly foreboding tale."

—*BookPage*

"Fox spins a satisfying debut yarn that includes witchcraft, tragedy, and love... The inclusion of gothic elements adds a visceral feel that fans of historical fiction with a dash of the supernatural will enjoy."

—*Publishers Weekly*

Also by Hester Fox

The Witch of Willow Hall

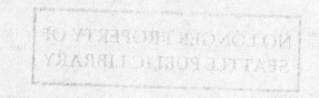

GRAYDON HOUSE

Recycling programs for this product may not exist in your area.

ISBN-13: 978-1-525-83426-4

The Widow of Pale Harbor

GraydonHouseBooks.com
BookClubbish.com

Printed in U.S.A.

The
WIDOW
of
PALE
HARBOR

HESTER FOX

GRAYDON
HOUSE

To Mike

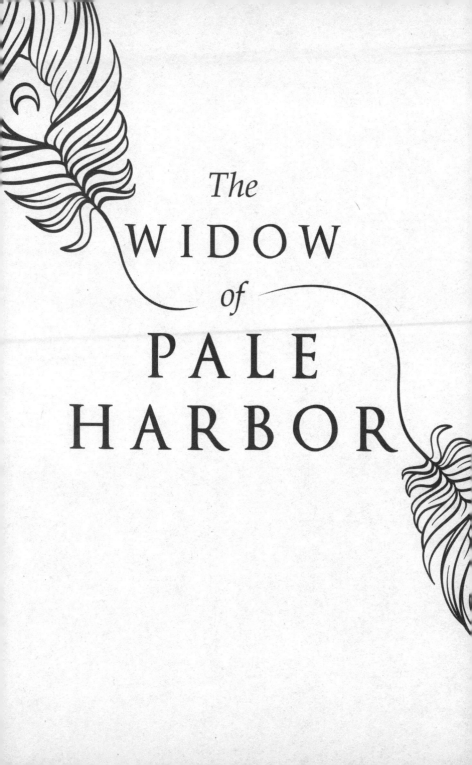

The
WIDOW
of
PALE
HARBOR

"And this was the reason that, long ago,
In this kingdom by the sea,
A wind blew out of a cloud, chilling
My beautiful Annabel Lee;
So that her highborn kinsmen came
And bore her away from me,
To shut her up in a sepulchre
In this kingdom by the sea."

—EDGAR ALLAN POE, "ANNABEL LEE"

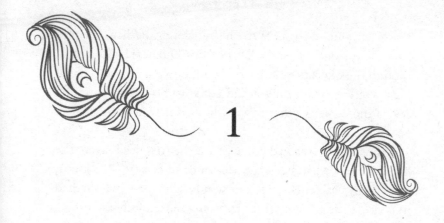

1

This was the fourth dead raven to appear on Sophronia Carver's front path in as many weeks, and there was no explaining it away as coincidence this time.

Except that this one wasn't dead, not quite.

Sophronia had never killed a living creature before, but as she stared down at the raven and its crooked, twitching wings on her front path, she got the queasy feeling that the most humane course of action might be to snap the poor thing's neck.

Tugging her shawl tighter against the chill, salty air, she crouched down to peer at the bird. Its feathers were blue and black—darker even than her own inky hair—and as iridescent as the ocean on a moonless night. The bird stared back at her, unmoving except for the slow blink of its glassy eye. She wanted very much to reach out a finger and stroke its slick feathers, but that somehow felt like a breach of confidence, like telling a secret that did not belong to her.

"Helen?" she called, without tearing her gaze away from the bird. "Helen, come quickly."

Slowly rising to her feet, she gazed about the estate grounds and craned her neck to squint at the roof of the great old house, silhouetted against the heavy clouds. Perhaps the bird had fallen from the eaves. Or perhaps Duchess had felled it, though the old cat could barely bring down a mouse. That at least would explain how it had come to be lain so carefully across the center of the front path, as if it were some sort of pagan offering.

When Sophronia had come across the first dead raven, she had assumed it had been the victim of some sort of sickness, or perhaps weakened by storm winds. The next two she had likewise justified, but with a growing sense of uneasiness.

A prickle of cold blossomed down her spine as she realized that she could no longer dismiss the dead and injured birds. Someone—or something—was leaving them for her to find.

She stiffened, with a darting glance about her, as if someone might be lurking just beyond the broad lawn or out past the gate, watching her. But there was no one—the only movement the breeze through the flaming autumn trees, the only sound the faraway cry of a gull.

The path was supposed to be Safe. The entire grounds of the estate were supposed to be Safe. It was only out past the wrought-iron gate and into the town beyond that chaos and uncertainty reigned. Better to stay inside the grounds, where she had control. Sophronia had long ago learned to push all the bad memories and specters out of the house and into the world beyond, firmly shutting her heart and mind against them. So to see a creature in distress, so close to death—well, that was not Safe.

"Helen?" Sophronia called, louder this time, her voice carrying up the path to where the front door stood open. A moment later, a pale woman of about forty, her dark hair pulled severely back from her face, appeared in the doorway. She frowned at the sight of her mistress standing over the bird.

"Duchess must have caught it," Sophronia said with a shake

of her head as the woman stepped briskly over to where she was standing.

Helen gave her a skeptical look, and then leaned down to examine the bird for herself. "Duchess couldn't catch her own tail," she said, scorn edging her husky voice. "It's the town brats making trouble again, I'd wager."

Sophronia pressed her lips together tightly. They'd certainly had their share of children from the town coming up to the house, peeking through the windows and knocking at the door, all so that they could earn the distinction among their friends for glimpsing the infamous widow.

Suddenly, it was too unbearable to look at the exposed and broken bird a moment longer. Sophronia might have called for Garrett, the groundskeeper, but he was out on the far end of the property, cutting back the grass. Helen was capable and strong, though, and had a way with animals. "You'll try to save it, won't you? And if you can't, you'll make it…" Her words trailed off, but her meaning was unmistakable. *Quick.*

Carefully, Helen positioned her hands under the motionless bird, holding it slightly away from her as she lifted it. She ran a practiced hand along its wings, her dark brows furrowing in a mixture of concern and anger, as if the cruelty of human-kind never ceased to surprise her. "Wings are both broken. And there's something wrong with its foot." But then she caught Sophronia's anxious look and softened. "I'll see what I can do, Sophy."

Sophronia gave her a warm smile and watched Helen whisk the raven off to the carriage house, her movements brisk and efficient, her posture as neat as a pin. She had taken Helen on as a servant and companion during her early days as a lonely young bride, but over the years, the older woman had proved herself to be a true friend in every sense. Now it was just the two of them against the world, as Helen was so often wont to remind her.

The first raindrops were starting to fall when Sophronia finally allowed herself to stop thinking of the crooked bird and what it might mean and return indoors. Before the thump of the raven landing on the path had startled her from her reverie, Sophronia had been watching the storm roll in upstairs. Her late husband had always pompously referred to the large room lined with bay windows as the "upper piazza," taking the big old house's name, Castle Carver, to heart. Sophronia liked to watch storms approach from there; it was a sort of entertainment, drawing back the curtains like those in a theater, the harbor and endless gray sky a stage on which the rowdy gulls acted their plays.

She wandered through the house, unsettled. There were submissions to her late husband's magazine piling up, submissions for which she was now responsible. Usually she enjoyed curling up in the parlor, tucked under a warm quilt with a cup of tea as she read through the stories and essays, curating which ones she would send along to the board for publication. But the raven had rattled her, and Sophronia was too anxious to read.

Instead, she continued back upstairs and threw the windows open. The rain was picking up now, the clouds building into something even heavier and more expectant. There was no moment so promising, so exciting, as the moment before a storm broke. Living on the Maine harbor, with naught but a finger of land to separate her home from the gray Atlantic, she had the opportunity to witness many storms, all from the safety of her window. On clear days, she could see the old lighthouse jutting out on the rocky promontory outside of town, winking back at her from its empty windows, an ally in her solitude. In the other direction lay a lonesome expanse of trees, dark and wild. It was a deceptively beautiful landscape, the sheer scale of woods and ocean promising endless possibilities, but in reality, it only swallowed up the hopes and dreams of young brides. At least on stormy days, the mist softened the harsh realities of the world, cloaked its darkness.

But today's storm was different; she could feel it reverberating in her bones. Perhaps the raven had been a harbinger of things to come, an omen. Or perhaps it was just as Helen said—children from the town playing their cruel tricks on her, just like they had for years since her husband had died so violently and suddenly.

Sophronia sighed, drumming her fingers against the windowsill. God, she was so weary of it all. Weary of the solitude, weary of the little town, its people and their narrow minds, weary of the shell she had become. Tonight, she and Helen would eat a small supper in silence—they had few words left to say that weren't old and stale, used up over the years—and then they would sit in the parlor, play a game of cards, and perhaps Sophronia would read a book or philosophical pamphlet while Helen plucked away at the old pianoforte. Tomorrow the laundry girl, Fanny, would come, and hopefully bring some gossip or news with her. They would chat for a little, and then Fanny would leave, and stillness would settle back over the house. It would be the same as every other day, but monotony was the price of safety. If the grand old house was indeed a castle, then Sophronia was its ghost, forever trapped, restless and roaming the halls.

She leaned out to close the window, but paused, letting the wind sweep up around her in an invigorating embrace. The building energy of the storm electrified her bones and caused tears to prick her eyes. Yes, there was something different about this storm. Change was sweeping toward Pale Harbor, and God knew, she needed it.

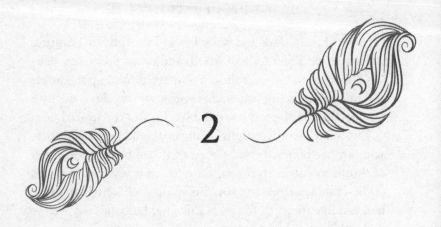

2

If Gabriel Stone had known what was inside the dilapidated old church and what it would lead to, he might have turned around, climbed back on the boat and returned to Concord immediately. But the rain was coming down in unforgiving sheets, and after days of travel, the time for reservations had long since passed.

Wiping the rain from his eyes, he stepped back, craning his neck, and turned his face up into the stormy night, taking in the church that he had trekked halfway up the east coast to reach. It was made of unassuming white clapboard, and its steeple barely peeked above the thrashing trees, as if in humble deference to this wild terrain in which it was an outsider, a latecomer, just like him.

It had taken him two coaches, a rail and finally a ship to arrive in Pale Harbor, only to find that no one was awaiting him at the dock. When it had become obvious that it was too dark even to locate his new lodgings, Gabriel had decided to go to the only other place he knew of in the town: his new church. He had followed the sight of the steeple, slogging through muddy roads that weren't much more than old cow paths, lit only with the occasional lamplight from a lonely cottage window. But when he'd finally arrived at the church, the doors were locked. He was a sopping wet, hungry, short-tempered outsider and damn it, churches were supposed to be a refuge. Putting his shoulder against the old wood door, Gabriel gave another push, and cursed when it would not budge.

The wind howled around him. He shrugged the collar of his coat up in vain, trying to keep the slicing rain from penetrating any farther down his back. He would get in, spend the night, and then, in the light of day, find his lodgings and hopefully the trunks that he had sent ahead.

A glint of shattered glass in the fleeting moonlight caught his eye. A broken window. Gabriel peeled off his sopping wet overcoat, balled it around his fist and punched out the rest of the glass. With all the grace of a wet cat, he shimmied himself through the opening.

The musty air hit him like the release of a breath held in for too long, and he landed awkwardly on his ankle. "God-damn it," he muttered, and then, remembering where he was, grumbled an apology. It was as cool as a mausoleum inside, the air untouched for who knew how many years. The only light came from the brief flashes of lightning, and the occasional gasp of moonlight through the racing clouds. His wet clothes clung to him, chilling him down to his bones. It was not an auspicious beginning to his new venture.

"Anyone here?"

His voice echoed off the empty pews and hollow nave. There was no reason anyone would be in the old church, but one never knew if a lost soul had seen the steeple and wandered inside, looking for shelter or religious succor.

Gabriel let his gaze wander over the dark, indistinct shapes of the crumbling interior. It was not a large church—he could have reached the altar in less than twenty paces—but the rows of pews gaping with expectation gave it a sense of restless hunger, repelling and beckoning him at the same time.

So, this was to be his, then. Good God, what business did he have leading a congregation? It had always been Anna's dream to found a spiritual community, to bring to life the ideals and values about which she so voraciously read and that had surrounded them in Concord. But now she was gone, and the fulfillment of her dreams was left to him. Perhaps he could make her proud in death where he had so often failed in life, but he rather doubted it. He had not been the intellectual, the enlightened thinker that she had so wished of him. This whole plan was madness; he was counterfeiting a version of himself that had never existed, all in the hopes of redeeming himself in the eyes of a woman who was gone. It was pathetic. He was pathetic.

He shook out his hat and pushed the wet hair out of his eyes. Cobwebs hung from the exposed rafters and dust grimed the stained glass, thick and dark. Gabriel cursed again as he tripped over a loose floorboard, steadying himself on the back of a dusty pew. The idea that he could make this a welcoming space was nearly as daunting as the thought of leading a flock to transcendental enlightenment. "Damn," he murmured again, before he could stop himself. If he was going to be an even half-convincing minister, he was going to have to curb his vulgar habit of cursing.

Discarding his dripping coat, Gabriel cast his eye around for something that would make a suitable bed for the night. An old splintered pew couldn't be any worse than the coach he had shared with six other gentlemen on his journey, all of whom had apparently been ill-acquainted with the concept of soap. He was just about to lower himself down onto the sturdiest-looking pew when a sound rose above the howling wind outside. Gabriel froze.

Someone was trying to get in. The door at the far end of the aisle was rattling, thumping, as if someone were pushing on it, just as Gabriel had tried at first. Without thinking, he grabbed the first thing that might reasonably serve as a weapon—a tarnished and cobwebbed brass candlestick—and crept to the door, where the latch was jiggling violently. It might have been a decrepit old church, and he might have been there only for a matter of minutes, but it was *his* decrepit old church, and by God, he would defend it.

Gabriel reached the door, held his breath and waited. His heart was beating in his ears, his mouth suddenly as dry as cotton. He wasn't scared—he'd long ago lost the capacity for that when he'd lost everything that he held dear—but he didn't particularly relish any more excitement for the day either. All he wanted was to close his eyes and get as dry as possible.

Just as the door swung open, he raised the candlestick above his head and lunged at the dark shape silhouetted against the rainy night.

"Sweet Jesus, don't hurt me!" The figure dropped to the ground in a huddling mound. "I—I'm the sexton," the man said, his voice muffled and pathetic.

Cursing, Gabriel stopped his swing. The candlestick dropped from his grasp, clattering to the floor. Of course it was the sexton. Who else would be interested in this rotting old church?

"Gabriel Stone," he said, offering his hand to help the man up. "The new minister." The words tasted strange on his tongue, and he realized it was the first time he had said them out loud.

The man staggered to his feet, wide-eyed and dripping wet. He regarded Gabriel with lingering panic. He was slight, with stooping shoulders and, at about thirty, was only a couple of years younger than Gabriel.

He knew what the man saw: Gabriel was too tall, too broad, too much like a lumbering giant. People glanced cautiously at him out the side of their eyes, as if he were a criminal, a tough. His voice, low and raspy, didn't help. He was used to the reaction, but it never eased the pang of annoyance—and self-consciousness—that he felt. "I'm not going to hurt you," he bit off, unable to keep the irritation from his voice. Then he raised his hands, palms up, in a gesture of pacification.

The sexton gave a hesitant nod and swallowed, extending his hand. "Ezekiel Lewis, but folks just call me Lewis. That's quite the grip you have," he said, rubbing his hand and warily eyeing the discarded candlestick.

Gabriel had corresponded with someone before coming to Pale Harbor, but as with all things concerning this new venture, he had been unsure of his footing, of exactly what he was supposed to say. Now he wasn't sure if it was Lewis he'd written to, or someone else in the town when he'd sent ahead notice that the minister who was supposed to come to Pale Harbor had died and that Gabriel was his replacement. That wasn't strictly true, but it wasn't a lie, either. When the brilliant Reverend Joshua Whipple of Concord had died in a carriage accident, Gabriel had seized on his chance to be the man that Anna would have wanted. It had all moved so quickly after he'd set the plan in motion, and then there had been no going back.

Gabriel regarded the nervous man and decided to take a gamble.

"I believe you were expecting me?"

Lewis nodded. "I was meant to meet you at the dock, but my cart got stuck in the mud and delayed me. When I couldn't find you, I figured you might have come up to the church.

I don't suppose you'll be wanting me to take you to the cottage now, after all?"

The poor man might have been even more soaked than himself, and he had only a threadbare coat to protect him from the elements. "Might as well bide here for a while yet. No use in going back out into the storm," Gabriel said.

Lewis nodded his agreement, looking grateful. He had closed the door behind him and was rubbing his arms to get warm. "It's a wonder the ship was even able to make dock in this weather," he said, after a particularly harsh clap of thunder.

It had been a bumpy ride, the dark water endlessly churning like a witch's cauldron, and Gabriel had watched more than one of his fellow passengers be sick over the rail. The two men lapsed into silence, the pounding storm outside making the church feel somehow smaller, more intimate. Gabriel, though never one for small talk, somehow found himself falling into conversation easily in the dark.

"Have you been the sexton long?" Lewis was decades younger than Gabriel would have thought someone in his position would be, and it was hardly a trade for an ambitious young man.

"No, sir. That is, there isn't much need for a sexton these days," Lewis said, jutting his chin vaguely into the shadowy church. "I work at the cemetery, digging graves and groundskeeping and the like. I come around here a couple of times a month to cut the grass and make sure no one has broken in." His look grew sheepish. "Might have been a few months since I last came inside."

Gabriel had begun to move away from the door and farther into the church, inspecting his new domain as much as he could in the near blackness.

Lewis followed him, swallowing. "I'd wanted it cleaned up

before you saw it…" he said, trailing off, as he dashed a cob-
web away from his face.

"I'll see to all the cleaning later." Gabriel squinted into the
darkness. The last of the moon had long since slid behind a heavy
bank of clouds. "You don't have a match, by chance?"

Lewis fumbled in his pocket, miraculously producing a dry
matchbox, and struck a match. He touched it to a piece of
wood, throwing light onto the empty pews and casting grotesque shadows from the forgotten saints.

The cross at the altar would have to go, and Mary stared at
him with accusing eyes, as if she knew that her tenure would
be short-lived. The stained glass might stay, but everything
else was the vestige of an outdated religion and had no place
in a home for transcendentalism. Or so he assumed, though
he wasn't quite sure. Anna would have known; she had been
so smart, so clever. Unitarianism—with its strict interpretation
of monotheism and all things scientific and rational—might
have taken root in Boston, but it was transcendentalism, with
its wild abandon to the spiritual, that had so enamored her in
Concord. *Stop thinking about her*, he chided himself. *Do this for
her, but for God's sake don't wallow in self-pity*.

A flash of movement snapped Gabriel from his thoughts.
"What was that?" He put his hand out to stop Lewis.

Lewis swung the light back around toward the altar and
took a sharp breath. Something was moving, rustling about
in the debris under the cross.

Without thinking, Gabriel began making his way up the
aisle, pushing aside detritus. There was something at the altar,
a shape blacker than the rest of its dark surroundings. And it
was moving.

His skin prickled and despite his cold, wet clothes, sweat
beaded along Gabriel's neck. The walls danced with quivering shadows, the wind howling and gripping the creak-

ing church tighter. He swallowed. It was not a particularly welcoming place, but now a sense of wrongness took hold of him, as if he were not supposed to be here. As if something did not want him here.

A crash and fluttering broke the stillness. Lewis fell to his knees, and Gabriel flinched as something disturbed the air over their heads.

"What the—"

Taking the torch from Lewis, Gabriel held it up, dimly illuminating the rafters. From the darkness above, a pair of gleaming black eyes blinked down at him.

"It's a bird," he said, feeling foolish that his heart was still racing, his palms sweating. Lewis, who had lost about three shades from his already pale face, let out a shaky breath. "There are holes in the roof. It must have come through one to get out of the storm."

The bird—a raven or a crow, something big and black—cocked its head and blinked down at them with vague interest. Then it shuffled its wings a few times and settled down to roost.

Suddenly, Gabriel just wanted to sleep, even if his new lodgings were cold and empty. He'd had enough of the dank church and its accusing shadows. He was just about to broach the idea of plunging out into the storm when he caught a hint of a strange odor.

The whole church had a musty, unused smell about it, but this was different. Pungent, sweet. Acrid to the point of making his eyes water, and only growing stronger. Curiosity overcame apprehension, and he drew closer to the altar.

He jerked backward. "Oh, God." Gabriel buried his nose in his handkerchief, fighting the rising gag in his throat. Beside him, Lewis made the sign of the cross over his chest.

This must have been what had attracted the carrion bird, why it had been pecking about the altar. It was a wonder he hadn't smelled it right away. Bones and fur lay before them, strips of rancid flesh. It was such a mess that it was impossible to tell what the animal might have been in life, or even if it had been a single animal.

"What the hell is that doing here?"

Maybe some forest creature had found its way into the church and then perished after it was unable to get out. But something about its position on the altar sent a chill down Gabriel's spine. Why wasn't it nearer a door, or window, if it had died trying to get out of the church? How had it come to lie on the most conspicuous feature of the building?

Lewis shifted uncomfortably. "I can't say I've seen anything particularly like this, but—"

Just then a loud crack of thunder rang out, swallowing his words. Lewis jumped back and the light stuttered out, leaving them in darkness.

Gabriel had had enough. The church was in ruins and clearly would need to be addressed in the light of day. The animal remains weren't going anywhere, and there wasn't anything they could do about them in the middle of the night anyway.

"All right. Let's leave it for now."

A hiss of relief came from the darkness behind him. "Very good, Reverend."

They gingerly made their way back to the door, and Gabriel shoved his wet hat back on his head. A pang of melancholy ran through him at the thought of arriving at an empty house. He was running away from a painfully empty home in Concord; had he really done all this only to exchange it for another, and in an unfamiliar place, no less?

Between the unsettling discovery at the altar and the icy impassiveness of the church, what little luster his plans had

had now faded to a dull and miserable gray. Gabriel was cold, weary and utterly alone. And it was only a matter of time before the town of Pale Harbor discovered him for the fraud he was.

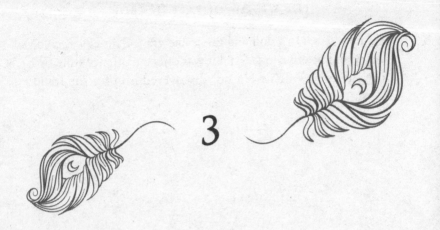

3

The invitations began almost immediately.

If Gabriel had thought that his arrival would be quiet, that he could slip into Pale Harbor unnoticed, then he had been sorely mistaken. It was a small town—Lewis had informed him that their police force consisted of one constable, and the nearest schoolhouse was ten miles away, in the next town—and the arrival of a new transcendentalist minister from Massachusetts had set everyone talking. If he had been a true minister, he would have relished the chance to recruit fresh faces and gather up a flock for his church. But he was not a true minister, and every time he thought of espousing universal truths to a church full of trusting, upturned faces, his heart twisted with guilt. He had thought that doing it for Anna, for making her dream come true, would have been enough, but he was quickly learning that it was not. Without her by his side, his actions were meaningless, his words hollow.

The first invitation came from the Marshalls, who—Lewis had explained in admiring tones—were the foremost family of Pale Harbor, having made a small fortune in the shipment of granite down the east coast. If Gabriel could persuade them to join his congregation, Lewis had assured him, then the whole town would follow. Whether Gabriel wanted a robust congregation was another story, but he would play his part, and at the very least enjoy a hot meal.

He slogged through the dusky little town, the scent of damp fallen leaves and wood smoke filling his lungs. Most of the homes he passed were modest, weather-beaten cottages like his, but old captains' mansions with stately pillars punctuated the main thoroughfare, reminders of the town's once-thriving whaling and trading industries. These could have been Anna's streets, her soft footsteps evaporating into the yawning gray sky. She would have delighted in the tall pines creaking in the wind, the hawks that sat sentry in the spindly boughs far above. The ever-present roll and crash of the ocean would have been her nightly lullaby. Gabriel shook his head, trying to dislodge the painful thoughts.

The road ended abruptly at a steep-gabled house, painted a lush pink and trimmed with white latticework. Rosebushes, nearing the end of their season, climbed defiantly up either side of the porch. Among all the weathered clapboard and peeling paint of the other homes, the house looked like something dropped straight out of the pages of a fairy tale.

As Gabriel climbed the front porch steps, a rosy, stout woman came out and greeted him at the door, beaming at him from under a frilly cap. His melancholy thoughts evaporated, replaced by an anxious knot in his stomach that always formed when mixing with anyone of higher social standing than him.

But Mrs. Marshall put him at ease immediately. "Come in, you poor darling," she said, tutting at his coat, which had never dried properly from the night before. "You must be the minister. I'm Clara Marshall and I'm so pleased to meet you."

Gabriel glanced to his side, half-expecting to see a black-frocked minister to whom Mrs. Marshall had addressed her greeting. But, of course, she meant him.

"Er, yes," he said, recovering. "Gabriel Stone."

"Mr. Stone, then. Come in, come in. Here, give me that damp coat."

No sooner had Gabriel stepped into the hall and surrendered his coat to a maidservant than Mrs. Marshall called out, "Girls!" and ushered forth two identical, golden-haired little girls. "Cora and Flora," she said proudly.

Gabriel dipped his head. "A pleasure."

"You're tall," said Cora, or maybe it was Flora. The other hid her giggles behind her hand.

"Girls, manners!" Mrs. Marshall shot Gabriel an apologetic look, and then passed the twins off to a servant with instructions to have them wash before dinner, and this time make sure they didn't just pass their hands under water, but to really scrub them.

Throughout the harried introductions, a small, wiry man with graying whiskers was hovering in the hallway, fiddling with a cigar case. "Mr. Stone," he said, pocketing the case and sticking his hand out. "Horace Marshall. A pleasure to meet you. Come, will you join me for a drink before dinner is called?"

Before Gabriel had a chance to respond, Mr. Marshall was thrusting a cigar into his hand and leading him into a dim parlor, brimming with expensive furniture and fussy ornaments. It was just the kind of place that made Gabriel nervous, as if all it would take was one careless movement to send a priceless figurine crashing over. He held his breath as he followed Mr. Marshall past a stuffed owl under a glass dome and a vase quivering with silk flowers and feathers.

"I can't tell you how good it will be to have that church

cleaned up and full of parishioners," Mr. Marshall said, lowering himself into an overstuffed chair. "Not just because it's a shame to let that old building rot away, either. Did you know it used to be a Quaker meeting house back in the last century? One of the oldest in Maine, if not New England. More recently, the Irish here were using it as a Catholic church, but they hadn't the funds to keep it up."

Gabriel murmured that he had not known. Perching gingerly on a precarious-looking settee, he searched for an ashtray in which to snuff out his cigar. He'd never liked the things, and the ash was growing long and threatening to spill onto his sleeve.

Oblivious to his predicament, Mr. Marshall tugged at his mustache and continued with his line of thought. "Might do the town good to have more of a godly presence, too."

Gabriel commandeered a vase and discreetly tapped out his ash. "Oh?"

When Mr. Marshall didn't respond immediately, Gabriel asked, "And why is that?"

"Hmm?" Mr. Marshall looked at him as if coming out of some deep private thought. "Oh, nothing. It's only we've had some troublemakers lately, and a bit of fire and brimstone might be just the thing to keep them in line."

"I see." Gabriel frowned. "Well, transcendentalism generally doesn't go in for that kind of thing." That much he knew, at least. That's what Anna had loved about the spiritual movement, "the exquisite freedom" of it, as she had once told him. There was no good and bad, no heaven and hell, only a beautiful energy that permeated the universe, connecting each and every soul. It was a nice way to look at the world, but it simply wasn't true. There was good and evil—he had seen so for himself.

Mr. Marshall looked a little disappointed and cleared his

throat before taking another puff of his cigar. "Well, I suppose you know what you're doing. You're the big city man, but I think hellfire would go a sight farther around Pale Harbor than any of this wishy-washy transcendental business."

Gabriel choked on his cigar smoke but was spared the need to respond by the maidservant sticking her head into the parlor and announcing dinner.

He hadn't realized how hungry he was until the covers were lifted off the dishes, revealing steaming platters of buttery fish and fried potatoes, roast beef, succulent green beans and thick chowder. He shifted in his seat so that his hosts wouldn't hear the rolling growl of his stomach.

Mr. Marshall clapped his hands and rubbed them together in anticipation. "You won't find food better than this anywhere in Pale Harbor," he said. "Tell me, have you employed a cook yet?"

"Er, no," Gabriel said as he helped himself to a heap of potatoes. He'd barely opened his trunks yet, let alone found domestic help.

The twins, who couldn't have been more than ten, had apparently been deemed mature enough to dine with their parents at the table, and were in the process of trying to wriggle out of their starched smocks. Their whispers and giggles were a constant backdrop to the conversation, and more than once Gabriel glanced up to see them sharing secret conversations behind their hands while staring at him.

With a careful glance at them, Gabriel swallowed his food. "Mr. Marshall—" he started, only to be waved off.

"Please, we don't stand on ceremony here. Horace."

If the wealthy businessman had known who Gabriel truly was, would he still have allowed Gabriel to address him so informally? He shifted a little in his seat. "Horace," he began again, "you mentioned something in the parlor." He chose his words carefully, mindful of the young girls seated at the table. "When I first went to look at the church, there was…" He cleared his throat. "There was some sort of…" How to describe the pile of remains that had left him so unsettled and had lurked at the back of his mind since the night before? "Some sort of…animal at the altar. A dead one."

Despite his best efforts, Gabriel had attracted the attention of the twins, who immediately left off their whispers and regarded him with eyes the size of saucers.

Mr. and Mrs. Marshall shared a look. "I expect you will have heard something of the troubles that are plaguing the town?" asked Mr. Marshall cautiously, after a long pause.

"Troubles?"

"Horace!" Mrs. Marshall's ruddy cheeks pinkened further. "That is not a conversation for the dinner table."

Unperturbed, Mr. Marshall gave her a dismissive wave and settled back into his chair, swirling his wine around in his glass. "Well, he's going to hear it sooner or later. He might as well hear it from us without all the embroidery some of the other townsfolk will give the story."

Mrs. Marshall pressed her lips together before snapping at the twins to cease their giggling.

"Troubles?" Gabriel prompted again.

"Just last week Maggie Duncan found a pile of skinned squirrels in the woods behind her house," Mr. Marshall said. "At first she thought it was the work of a fox, but what fox eats just the fur and leaves the meat? Then there was some sort of…of effigy. Crude little doll with all manner of buttons and strings sewed about it and stuffed into the hollow of the old elm tree in town."

Gabriel stiffened in his seat at the descriptions that were eerily similar to what he had found just the other night. This must have been why Mr. Marshall had wanted his church to preach crime and punishment.

A thick silence had settled over the table. Gabriel put down his glass and looked between Mr. and Mrs. Marshall. "What is it?"

A meaningful look passed between the husband and wife. "No one has been apprehended," Mrs. Marshall said tightly. "But most people around here know who's behind it without a signed confession."

Gabriel looked at them blankly, waiting for one of them to elaborate.

"Sophronia Carver," said Mr. Marshall, as if it cost him something just to say the name. "Nathaniel Carver's widow."

"She killed her husband," Mrs. Marshall added. "And lives in…an unsavory manner that I won't expound upon in front of the children."

Gabriel barely had time to ask what constituted an unsavory manner, when the children in question piped up.

"She's a witch," said one of the twins.

"It's true," said the other twin, nodding gravely. "Lucy Warren looked through her window and saw her stirring at a great pot. And what do you think was sticking out the bottom of her dress?"

Gabriel opened his mouth to say he was sure he had no idea, but the twins were too fast.

"A tail!" they exclaimed in joyful unison.

Neither Mr. nor Mrs. Marshall seemed particularly taken aback by this outburst, Mr. Marshall continuing to saw away at his beef, and Mrs. Marshall only saying indulgently, "A tail! I don't know where you girls get such stories."

The twins dissolved into giggles again. "And she has the most horrid scar running down her face."

"Probably from one of her victims trying to escape!"

"Well, tail or no," said Mr. Marshall, taking the accusation against Mrs. Carver in stride, "the woman is queer and you can lay your last nickel on the fact that she's behind all this unpleasant business."

The dinner was taking on a decidedly peculiar slant and, unused to drinking so much rich wine, Gabriel's temple was starting to throb. The widow in question would have to be a queer woman indeed to go traipsing about in abandoned churches, setting out dead, mutilated animals. It seemed more likely that it was, as the Marshalls had first suggested, the work of some cruel youngster.

The conversation continued in that vein for a while longer, but Gabriel was no longer listening. He was tired and on edge from trying to say the right things, to sit the right way on these damned uncomfortable chairs. All he wanted was to stand up, thank the Marshalls for the hospitality, and then go back to his empty little house and fall into bed. But then the conversation took an even more horrifying turn.

"Are you married, Gabriel?"

He froze, his fork hovering over his plate. It had been nearly a year, but the question still made him feel as if the carpet had been ripped out from under him, the breath stolen straight from his lungs. He put down his fork, hoping to appear composed in his answer. "My wife passed away. Childbirth," he added, knowing that if he didn't provide the cause now he would only be asked later anyway. "The baby died, as well."

Mrs. Marshall's face creased and fell. "Oh, dear, I am sorry to hear that."

Gabriel waved off her concern, but it took a considerable amount of effort to keep himself in the present. It seemed that no matter how far he ran from Concord, Anna would haunt him, never mind that he had hungered for her ghost to follow him here.

"Well, I don't like to impose where it isn't my business, but Pale Harbor has any number of good, capable young women who would make good wives to a minister."

"Clara!" Mr. Marshall exclaimed.

"Well, it's true," she said in an injured tone. "I don't pretend to be a matchmaker, but there's no hurt in him considering his options."

Mr. Marshall gave Gabriel an apologetic look as if to say they both knew how women could be. Gabriel dropped his gaze to his plate, his appetite gone.

They finished dinner in silence, even the twins apparently content to be quiet. Afterward, the girls were sent up to bed while the adults retired to the parlor for dessert. Gabriel drank the coffee that was offered to him and ate the fruitcake, nodding politely along at the depthless conversation about the weather and the new portrait studio in Rockport.

Coming here had been a mistake. Why did he think he could converse with prominent, wealthy families? Social graces and etiquette had never been his strong point. What need had a man like him, from his background, for social graces? He'd had to learn everything painstakingly from Anna, and even now he was more suited to enjoying a good story in a tavern than polite small talk over delicate china cups of coffee.

"I should be going," Gabriel said, standing abruptly.

Mrs. Marshall's brows drew quizzically together, but she pasted on a bright smile. "Of course, I hadn't realized how late it was getting. Horace?"

"Mmm? Oh, right, right," said Mr. Marshall, standing with a grunt.

"Thank you," Gabriel said, giving Mrs. Marshall a stiff bow of his head. "Dinner was delicious."

Gabriel's coat had almost completely dried after the benefit of being on a stove, and the men went out to the porch, where Mr. Marshall lit another cigar. The storm of the previous night had rolled off, leaving in its wake a steady drizzle and crisp breeze.

"You'll think all it does is rain here," Mr. Marshall said with a hint of chagrin. "We seem to be stuck in some sort of weather pattern, with storms from the sea rolling into the harbor every few days."

Gabriel welcomed the rain. Every drop that chilled him to the bone was a penance, a reminder. He deserved to be wet and cold for the role he had played in Anna's death. If he hadn't gotten her with child, she would still be here. She had been too delicate, too fragile, for childbearing, and he hadn't protected her. God, he was doing it again. *Stop thinking about her, you dolt.*

Mr. Marshall reached for something in his waistcoat pocket, pulling Gabriel from his thoughts. "I hope you won't mind the presumption, but I've taken the liberty of drawing up a list of all the families in town for you." He handed Gabriel a folded sheet of paper. "Thought you might want to make the rounds and introduce yourself."

Gabriel took the list and scanned the jumble of names, unable to fathom actually having to put faces to them. "Thank you. I'm sure this will be very useful."

But Mr. Marshall wasn't listening. He was worrying at his mustache, staring out into the gray dusk. "There is one name I omitted from that list." He paused. "You would do well to steer far and clear of Sophronia Carver."

"The widow?"

Nodding, Mr. Marshall took a slow puff from his cigar. "My wife has a flair for the dramatic, but there's no getting around the fact that something's not quite right about what goes on in that house."

Gabriel followed Mr. Marshall's gaze to the tip of a white

cupola that just showed above the treetops in the distance. His heart grew heavy and his gut churned at the thought of meeting with anyone on the list, least of all the odd widow who had so captured their imaginations.

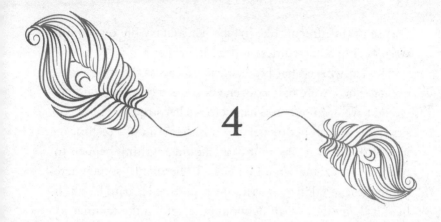

4

Sophronia looked down at the deluge of ink slowly spreading across her desk and bit back a curse; nothing had gone right that morning. First, she had taken out her favorite wool shawl for the winter, only to find that moths had eaten the fringe clean off. Then the magazine's board had delivered a stern missive, warning that subscriptions were down from last year and that if she couldn't bring in a higher caliber of submissions, then the magazine's future would be in grave jeopardy. It was all bluster on their part, but it still was never a good sign when the board was unhappy. The last straw had been when Duchess had knocked a bottle of ink over a stack of unread submissions. Now half of them were stained and stuck together, and would be unreadable. If the next brilliant submission to save the magazine had been in that pile, she would never know.

But even on the hard days like this, she relished her role as owner and editor of the magazine, and wouldn't give it up for anything. All the work could be done from her desk in the parlor, and then Garrett would take her packets of papers and notes and mail them to the office in Portland. It gave her a sense of fulfillment, like maybe her solitary life on the hill wasn't completely fruitless and without merit.

She had worked hard to achieve success as the magazine's owner. There were half a dozen editors and businessmen who would have been only too happy to see her stripped of her position. So what if her ownership was the result of a technicality? Nathaniel had thought that, should anything happen to him, the magazine would be safest in her name, somewhere competitors couldn't get at it. She suppressed a grim laugh. If he'd had any idea when he would die, and in the manner he had, no less, he never would have taken the liberty.

"Duchess, you may have cost us the next Shelley or Byron," Sophronia muttered as she tried to peel the inky pages apart in vain. Duchess gave her an unapologetic glare from the windowsill.

Crouching down, she set all the salvageable pages in front of the grate to dry, and rocked back on her heels. Her vision began to swim as she stared down at her hands, and for a moment they were not stained in black ink, but crimson blood. So much blood…beneath her nails, crusted into her cuticles, smeared across her face. Just like on that fateful night.

The smell of damp earth filled her nostrils, and she could feel the unforgiving wind biting at her cheeks, though the fire was licking away in the grate. Clean, clean… She had to wash her hands, scrub them until they were pink and innocent again before anyone saw and realized what she had done. Heart racing, she rushed to the kitchen sink, pouring scalding water out from the kettle and mercilessly scouring the offending flesh.

The waking nightmare didn't break until her hands were raw and burned, the skin singing with pain. She jumped back from the sink, trembling with how quickly the chimera had come on. A nervous laugh threatened to erupt, but she held it in. God, what a foolish creature she could be.

A breath of fresh air would revive her and clear away the bad memories. She gave her hands one last harsh wipe on a towel, and then went and fetched her cloak and bonnet and steeled herself to face the outside world.

She pushed the door open. The first few steps outside the house were always the hardest, but if she could just get a little momentum, then by the time she was out the door she could keep going, at least a little ways.

If it wasn't for the quiver of movement from the breeze, she would have completely missed the sliver of black marking the door. Slowly, she took a step back into the foyer, her gaze trained on the door and the alien object attached to it.

Below the elaborate brass knocker, a long, black feather hung from a nail.

With a trembling hand, Sophronia slowly reached out and touched it, half-hoping that it would be as fleeting and insubstantial as the delusion that had just gripped her in the kitchen. But the soft bristles met her fingers with heart-sinking solidity.

Sophronia's blood ran cold as she jerked her hand back. It had been still and quiet in the house all morning. How had someone managed to hammer in the nail without her hearing anything?

It was as if whoever had left the ravens had read the doubts in her mind and wanted to make certain that she understood none of this was coincidence or an accident. This was as bold a statement as Martin Luther nailing his theses to the church door. This was a declaration, but of what?

In a fit of panic, Sophronia tried to pry the nail from the door. When it wouldn't budge, she snatched at the feather, sending torn black filaments floating to the ground. But the quill would not budge.

"Blast it." She would have to ask Garrett to pry out the nail and patch the hole. At least it could be easily fixed, and Garrett was nothing if not discreet.

But that was little comfort to Sophronia, who felt as if the world were pressing in around her. Felt as if eyes watched her every movement, even through the walls of the house. If she had thought that the change she had felt coming to Pale Harbor was to be positive, then it seemed she was sorely mistaken. Now it was a growing sense of dread that hung over her, as if a predator was circling just beyond her line of sight, slowly closing in on her.

With a letter in his pocket, Gabriel wandered down toward the harbor, looking for the post. It was a small town, with most of the homes and buildings rising up from the edges of the water, clinging to the salty lifeblood that provided its food and industry. His walk took him past the same run-down houses he had seen the previous week, now benevolently gilded in gentle sunlight. He had been in Pale Harbor for a week now, meeting with the townspeople, cleaning out the church and generally gathering his bearings. But it still felt wrong, and he no more felt that he belonged in Pale Harbor than he had in Concord without Anna.

Restless and a little homesick, the night before he had written to the only person in Concord he considered a friend, Tom Ellroy. Tom, who he had known since they were both boys running wild through the Massachusetts countryside, had stuck by him through thick and thin, and there had been plenty of thin, especially when they'd both joined the navy on a boyish whim. Gabriel had four older sisters, and Tom was the brother he'd never had. Tom alone was privy to Gabriel's reasons for coming to Pale Harbor and the deception he had practiced in getting here.

The morning dawned dry and warm, a crystal-clear September day. Dirt mingled with sand, and every breath carried with it the faint promise of the great ocean beyond. Gabriel was small and inconsequential, a drop of salt water among many in the seaside town, and how liberating it was. In the light of day, the dark discovery in the church seemed far away, and his awkward dinner with the Marshalls insignificant. Maybe he would not be a success as a minister, but he had come this far, and if nothing else, it would be the fresh start he so desperately needed.

Despite the fair weather, the waterfront was quiet, subdued. Only a few small boats bobbed in the placid water, and a handful of dockworkers leisurely unloaded nets full of fish. Mr. Marshall had told Gabriel that twenty-five years ago, Pale Harbor would have been a bustling port, with all sorts of languages being spoken as ships unloaded their goods from lands as far away as China. But the war with the British in 1812 and the subsequent closing of trade routes had strangled the cosmopolitan breath from the town, leaving it choked and withered.

Gabriel ambled down to the water, watching seagulls squabble over a dropped fish. Despite his pledge to take all the rain as a penance, he was enjoying the early autumn sun on his face.

He found two young men taking a rest from unloading crates on the dock, their shirts stuck to their backs with perspiration, their sleeves rolled to the elbows. When he asked them where he could post a letter, they directed him to the dry goods store on the other side of town.

He thanked them and was about to turn to leave. He knew he should introduce himself, tell them about the new church.

That's what a minister was supposed to do. But the idea of proselytizing made him shrink into his skin, and despite days of practicing in front of the mirror, he still tripped over his words and came across as a fool. They would probably scoff at him, just as the Marshalls surely had as soon as Gabriel had left their home, and he couldn't bear to hear Anna's dearest beliefs disparaged.

"Not from around here, are you?"

Stopping in his tracks, Gabriel reluctantly turned back. He took a fortifying breath. "No, not from around here."

The man who spoke had light brown skin and a musical voice with an island lilt. "Thought you might not be local," he said. "Not with that accent."

Gabriel hadn't bothered trying to disguise the brusqueness of his lower-class voice; he felt comfortable here on the docks in a way he hadn't in the Marshalls' dining room. But apparently he had been found out as an outsider anyway.

"Might as well be from Dixie," rejoined the other man.

"Concord," Gabriel told them, and then added, "Massachusetts. My name is Gabriel Stone."

"Well, Gabriel Stone from Concord, I'm Manuel," said the man with the lilting voice. "And this useless lug is Jasper."

Jasper nodded his introduction. He was young, red-haired and pale, with a smattering of freckles. "You're the one taking over the old church, then?" he asked Gabriel without preamble.

"That's right." Gabriel hoped that his curt response would be the end of it, but Jasper was giving him an assessing look, and both of the men's curiosity seemed to be piqued.

Manuel raised a brow. "What is it you'll be preaching?"

Damn it. Gabriel had memorized his little speech, which he had given some dozen or so times in the past week. Unsurprisingly, it came out mechanical and dry.

"Transcendentalism. It's the belief that God is in nature, and that the answers of the universe can be found within man instead of without. The spirit comes from nature and so knows more than our minds. It's, uh…" He paused, trying to remember all the correct words. "It's very popular in Concord," he finished lamely.

There was painful silence until Manuel finally said, "Meaning no disrespect, but you don't do much in the way of putting a polish on your creed. If Saint Peter had been as ho-hum in his preaching, then I doubt Jesus would have had a church to name him the rock of."

The man was right, of course. Without conviction in his words, Gabriel came off as a charlatan. "Well, if you change your minds, you're always welcome." He was just about to turn to leave when Jasper stopped him again.

"Seeing as you're new here, you wouldn't happen to be looking for some help around the house, would you? A cook, maybe?"

"I might. Why?" Gabriel had imagined that he would keep his own council, moving about an empty house as a monk might a cell, reveling in the solitude. But the mundane day-to-day tasks of keeping a house were proving a drudgery, and the night crept in so close and thick that he longed for some sound other than the groaning of the wind. A light footstep around the house would be welcome, and that was to say nothing of a hot meal. For the past week, he'd been subsisting entirely on bread and molasses and the charity of the townsfolk, the latter of which he was eager to stop using.

"My sister, Fanny, she needs a new position."

"Does she have references?"

Jasper's sharp green eyes darkened. "She works up at the castle for that *woman*," he said, barely able to choke out the last word.

Gabriel looked between the two men, brow raised. "Woman?"

Manuel gave a jerk of his head toward the hill. "Mrs. Carver," he said. "The widow."

Her name had now made its way to his ears several times over the course of the past week, usually in conjunction with the shaking of heads and disdainful grimaces. The people here spoke as if the devil himself was in their midst, and Gabriel was growing more and more curious about this almost mythical figure.

"It's not a fit place for a young lady of her birth to work," Jasper continued, his jaw tight. "Me and my sister might be fallen on hard times, but we're of good stock, and it's beneath her to be scrubbing away and laundering for the likes of *her*."

Mr. Marshall's warning came back to him. "People here really believe she killed her husband, then?"

Manuel spat in the dirt and went back to unloading crates without a word.

"She's as guilty as sin," Jasper said, his gaze still trained somewhere past the hill. "She's the worst sort of fraud, living in her grand house like a lady, as if she's better than the rest of us. Meanwhile, her hands are stained with blood."

"I see," Gabriel said, surprised at the force of the young man's words.

"She doesn't leave her grounds, thinks she's too good to mix with the likes of us. But she's not too good to work Fanny like a slave."

Gabriel rubbed at his jaw, considering the proposition. "Send your sister to the church cottage tomorrow, and I'll see what I can do."

The distant, steely look in Jasper's eyes softened into genuine relief and gratitude, and he took Gabriel's hand, shaking it heartily. "I will. Thank you, sir."

Gabriel said goodbye to the men and left them to their work. But instead of continuing to the post, he looped the long way around from the docks so Jasper wouldn't see where he was going.

He wasn't sure why he found himself drawn to the house on the hill, but his feet carried him there as if they knew the answer. For the first time in months, Gabriel's mind was preoccupied with something other than his loss, his restless heart. He wanted to know why everyone here seemed so very determined to keep him away from the widow who lived on the hill. And if the people of Pale Harbor would give him only fairy stories and gossip about the notorious Mrs. Carver, then he would get the real story himself.

The trees hid what a grand house it really was, with its two-story facade of glass windows facing the harbor, flanked with ostentatious turrets in the Gothic style. The confusion of architectural styles and additions gave it a certain vernacular charm, but it was far from the secluded, ramshackle estate he had envisioned. The grounds teemed with activity: a squirrel chittered nervously in a tree, the grass had been raked free of fallen leaves, and the garden beds were mulched and fresh. From somewhere around back came the rhythmic pounding of an ax. For a house that had created such unease in the town, it was remarkably benign in all appearances.

A movement flickered above him from the windows, and Gabriel stopped short, craning his head up. The curtain in the window stirred, and then fell back into place, but not before he'd glimpsed the sliver of a face.

If Gabriel had thought the Marshalls wealthy and above him, their home was nothing compared to the scale of Castle Carver. What in the hell was he thinking? What would he possibly say to this woman? But he had come this far, and his curiosity had reached a peak. Gabriel took the five shallow brick steps that led up to the front door and knocked.

There was no answer. He stepped back to crane his head up to the windows again, but it was still, and no one peered back down at him. Perhaps it was true what they said: not that she was a witch, of course, but that she was a recluse, a madwoman.

The sound of the ax splitting wood had stopped, and just as Gabriel was reluctantly going back down the steps, he ran into a weathered old man, clutching an ax in his meaty hands.

"Excuse me. I'm looking for—"

"Mrs. Carver don't take callers," the man said. "You're wasting your time knocking."

Everything in the man's posture indicated that he didn't want Gabriel to linger for a second longer on the grounds. But Gabriel wasn't in a hurry. He crossed his arms and squinted up into the cloudless sky. "Unnaturally warm weather, isn't it?"

"Don't bother me," the man said with a scowl.

Ignoring the man's contempt, Gabriel asked, "So you work for Mrs. Carver, then?"

The man tilted his bristled chin up defiantly. "That's right. And she wouldn't want some busybody skulking 'bout her property."

There was something about the imposing house that tugged at Gabriel, beckoned him. "A bandage," he said, lifting his hand and showing off a miniscule scrape on the palm. He had gotten it while hauling debris from the church and had all but forgotten about it. "I cut myself and need a bandage." He was sure that if he could just get inside that he would see her, that he could put his curiosity to rest.

The man stared at him with incredulous scorn. "This ain't a hospital!"

This was maddening. He was a minister trying to call on

an old widow, not a thief walking up to a jewel vault in broad daylight. But before Gabriel could let his temper get the better of him, there was a rattle at the door, and then it opened, revealing the widow herself.

Now here was a woman who might have been the picture of widowhood in an illustrated encyclopedia. From her high-necked black dress to the tightly pulled-back hair to the disapproving pucker in her brow, she radiated severity. Though at about forty, she was younger than the white-haired and bent-backed old woman that he had been imagining.

"What do you want?" she snapped, her voice husky and brittle with irritation.

Clearing his throat, Gabriel stepped forward. "Mrs. Carver, my name is Gabriel Stone. I'm the new minister and—"

She said something that he couldn't hear, and Gabriel stopped. "What?"

The lines around her mouth tightened. "I *said*, I'm not Mrs. Carver."

"I..." Gabriel looked around at the vast, rolling grounds of the estate, the unmistakable cupola atop the great house. This was Castle Carver, he was sure of it. If this stern woman in dark dress wasn't the infamous widow, who was she?

"Do you know where I might find her?"

"She doesn't take callers," the woman said, echoing the groundskeeper's pronouncement, and moving to close the door. "Now be off with you."

Too stunned to say anything, Gabriel just stood there as the door started to swing shut. Perhaps everything he had heard about Mrs. Carver was an exaggeration. She wasn't a murderous witch, but was probably old and infirm, cared for by this brusque nurse. In the absence of regular sightings, the townspeople must have built up a legend around her.

Coming to Castle Carver had been a distraction, but now

it was over and he would have to go back to his cottage and sit alone with his memories. Gabriel was just about to leave when a voice stopped him. It was light and feminine, musical.

"All right, Helen, that's enough," the voice said as the door swung back open. "I'll not have a man collapse on my front step for want of a bandage."

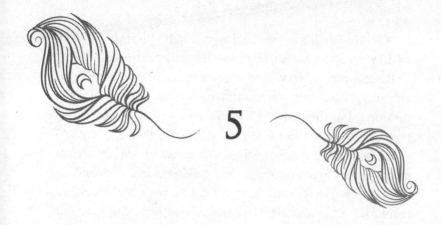

5

"I**...** Excuse me, but I was looking for a Mrs. Carver?"

The man was huge: tall, with broad shoulders, a gently squared jaw and a low, gravelly voice. She had only hesitated a moment before deciding to go to the door; if whoever had been leaving her the nasty surprises had decided to show up on her doorstep, they certainly wouldn't have announced themselves. Beyond that, only one other kind of person would call on her, and that was someone who wasn't from Pale Harbor. And *that* had to be the new minister that Helen said everyone was talking about. But with a dusting of light brown beard and shadowed eyes, he looked as if he had just lumbered off the docks, not come from a church. Suppressing her own surprise at the man who looked more like a sailor than a minister, Sophronia raised a brow.

"And you have found her," she said with a gracious smile.

The man opened and closed his mouth a few times, and then looked behind him, as if checking to make sure that he had indeed come to the right house.

"I... My name is Gabriel Stone. The new minister." He paused, and she let him stew in his confusion for another moment. "I'm sorry, but I thought that you..." He trailed off.

"Oh, don't tell me," she said with a sigh, "that you've been to dine with the Marshalls or the Wigginses already."

Reddening, he started to explain himself, but she gave an airy wave. "No, no, you mustn't apologize. They're all well-meaning, but they haven't the highest opinion of me. I suppose that goes for most of the town, as well. Please, come in."

He was rather handsome in a rough sort of way, but when he passed her in the doorway, she couldn't help her instinct to shrink back. He was so tall, so...big. Life with Nathaniel had taught her that men were dangerous creatures, and here she was, inviting a giant specimen inside her house. Closing the door behind him, she took a breath and drew herself up to her full height. Garrett was chopping wood in the yard, and Helen was nearby. She had nothing to fear. Besides, he was a man of the church.

"You'll have to forgive Garrett and Helen their manners," Sophronia said, giving him an apologetic smile. "We don't do much entertaining nowadays."

That was an understatement. They had never done much entertaining, even when Nathaniel was alive. But ever since learning that the town was to have a new minister, she had felt her heart lightening, a flicker of hope growing in her chest. People left Pale Harbor, but few came, and even fewer of those were anybody other than a poor fisherman down on his luck. Here was a man who hailed from Concord, the epicenter of all the exciting new schools of thought. If anyone could bring fresh ideas to Pale Harbor and persuade the townspeople to leave off in their superstitious ways, it would be him.

The minister followed her mutely, obediently. It was a strange sensation to feel the presence of a body behind her, in her space. Strange, yet not altogether unpleasant.

She led him to the parlor, her favorite room, with its circular walls studded with paintings and plush furniture upholstered in golds and greens. The parlor was also the Safest room in the house, thanks to the charms Helen insisted on hiding around the threshold, and the salt she was always sprinkling. It occupied the ground floor of the turret, so it was cozy and had only one door leading in and out to the hall. Cozy, beautiful, Safe.

"Please, have a seat." She turned to clear some papers she had been reading off the sofa. When she turned around, the minister was lowering himself into the large armchair. Nathaniel's old chair.

"Oh!" she exclaimed. "Not that one!"

He shot up like a bullet. "Oh... I didn't... I'm so sorry."

His cheeks flamed red and he looked genuinely distressed. What was wrong with her? He couldn't possibly know the rules, and here she was proving the townspeople right in their belief that she was a madwoman. She took a deep breath.

"No, I'm sorry. It's just...that was my husband's chair." She paused, twining her fingers together. "No one sits there anymore."

"Oh." He flicked his gaze to the chair behind him and then cleared his throat. "I didn't realize."

She forced a tight smile. "Of course not. Here," she said, pulling up another chair and patting the back. "This one is more comfortable."

Sophronia seated herself on the sofa, compulsively smoothing out her skirts. It had been so long since anyone besides Helen or Fanny had sat in the parlor, let alone an attractive man around her own age. Her pulse fluttered like a butterfly, but she was determined to be cool and composed. He might be a great thinker, but she had always been an excellent conversationalist, given the chance.

But the minister was silent, clasping his hands on his knees and looking exceedingly uncomfortable. Goodness, she knew the townspeople would have painted her in an unfavorable light, but what exactly had they told him to make the poor man look as if he were about to have a leg amputated?

She would just have to draw him out. "I heard you were making the rounds through Pale Harbor," she said. "I wondered when I would find you at my door."

He had been looking at her with unmasked curiosity, but at this he dipped his head and dropped his gaze under the fringe of his golden-brown hair. "I should have called sooner, but—"

With a wave of the hand she stopped him from having to make some paper-thin excuse. "No matter. I am very glad to meet you now." And then, because she couldn't help herself, she gave him a conspiratorial smile. "I'm not what you were expecting, am I?"

His gaze shot back up to meet hers, his lips parting as if in surprise at her frankness. He had full, sensual lips. They softened some of the roughness of his demeanor, and Sophronia had to force herself not to stare. She rushed on before he had a chance to respond.

"You're not what I was expecting either. For whatever you have heard of me, I confess that when I heard we were to have a new minister, I envisioned a man of quite advanced years, with a gray beard down to his watch fob." She stole a glance at his work-roughened hands, his broad shoulders. "It seems we were both mistaken in our preconceptions, for you must have imagined me quite the specter if the people of this town are to be believed."

The minister looked down at his hands, as if it pained him to admit the truth. "Yes," he murmured. "Something like that."

Satisfied, she sat back a little in the sofa. "Well, I assure you I don't have a tail."

At this, the corner of his full lips quirked up ever so slightly, and an unexpected jolt of warmth ran through her. His face lost some of its hardness and his hazel eyes shone warmly, his smile all the more rewarding because of his reserve. To make a man like this laugh, well, that would be a coup indeed.

Some of the tension from her blunder about the chair lifted, and she saw him relax in his seat as well, crossing his long legs at the ankles. He draped his hands on the chair arms, and she caught a glimpse of the cut on his hand that was so bad that he had supposedly needed medical attention. She bit the inside of her lip to keep from smiling…it was tiny, hardly more than a scratch, and all at once she understood his game.

"Oh! Your cut. I nearly forgot," she said, moving to the door. "I'll ask Helen to bring some linen and hot water."

"I really don't need anything. It's nothing."

Sophronia blinked at him with big, innocent eyes. "Oh, but I thought you were injured?"

The tips of his ears pinkened. "It's not so bad as all that," he mumbled.

Just then Helen materialized in the door. "You called?"

"Yes," Sophronia said, trying not to enjoy herself too much. "Our guest has *quite* the injury, and I was wondering if you would be a dear and fetch us some dressings for his wound?"

Helen's sharp gaze darted to the minister and she scowled. But she dipped her head, murmuring, "As you wish."

She stalked back out into the hallway, and Sophronia felt her cheeks flushing. Helen's dislike of the minister was obvious, and terribly rude. "I apologize. She's always been protective of me, but especially lately since—"

The minister's gaze sharpened and Sophronia clamped her mouth shut. He didn't need to know about the ravens, the feather, the sensation that she was being watched.

Sitting back down, Sophronia finally broached the subject

that had been keeping her awake with excitement for the past week. "So, tell me about this new church."

The minister opened his mouth and then closed it again. It might have been her imagination, but something like panic momentarily clouded his eyes and she thought he might leap out of his chair again. But then he cleared his throat and the look passed. "It's... It will be transcendentalist. Similar to Unitarianism, if you are familiar with it?"

Transcendentalist! She had always admired the Unitarian school of thought, but the churches themselves were rather somber affairs. Transcendentalism, on the other hand, incorporated all the most progressive tenets of Unitarianism, such as the rejection of original sin and predestination, and then soared even higher with the idea that society and politics were corrupting forces to the purity of the individual. With transcendentalism, there was no need for society, and that suited her just fine.

She waited for him to elaborate, but nothing more came. She gave him an encouraging smile. "Well, I think it's splendid. You must know Emerson, of course. I absolutely loved his first series of essays, and am anxious to get my hands on his second series. I devour everything I can from the leading minds on transcendentalism."

"Emerson? Oh, yes." He knotted his fingers together, not meeting her eye. "He's very good."

Sophronia frowned. He had not looked like she was expecting him to, and now it seemed that he would not converse easily on the subjects to which she had so looked forward. She tried again.

"I'd be curious to know what you think of his concept of the oversoul." The essay explored the fascinating idea of the human soul and its relationship to other souls and how every person, alive and gone before, was connected. It was unlike anything Sophronia had ever read. "I found the theories intriguing and very much wanted to believe that Emerson's beautiful prose held the truth, but it was difficult to do so when he gives us only anecdotes and stories. Perhaps, as a spiritual man, you need no such proof, but surely the purpose of an essay is to persuade?"

The minister looked like a fish out of water; he opened his mouth, but no sound came out. Just as Sophronia was about to repeat herself, Helen appeared with the tea, and whatever he had been about to say was forgotten.

"Thank you, Helen," Sophronia said as she set the tray down. "You're a treasure."

"It's nothing," Helen said brusquely, but there was a faint glow of pride in her eyes. "Will there be anything else?"

"That will be all, thank you."

The minister didn't say anything as she poured out two cups of tea, just absently rolled some of the linen that Helen had brought around the cut on his palm. She hazarded a glance at him, and wondered what she looked like to him, with her scar, silver and smooth from time, tracing a path from her temple down to her jaw. Did he see a poised, well-spoken woman of means? Or was he able to see beneath her mask, to the scared, haunted ghost of a woman underneath?

When she looked up, she realized she had not been the only one studying the other. He had been staring at her hands as she prepared the tea. He cleared his throat, as if aware he had been caught, and took the china cup from her. He nodded to the paintings on the wall behind her. "You're a collector," he said.

She craned her head around and followed his gaze. Turning back, she gave him a shy smile. "Oh, yes. Are you an admirer of art?"

He nodded. Standing, he moved carefully to the wall. Sophronia knew her collection was exquisite, rivaling some of the best in places like the Athenaeum in Boston. But whereas the walls there were covered in somber portraits and classical allegories, her collection skewed toward the wild, with lots of rugged landscapes and people who were no more than tiny smudges against the grandeur of nature.

He must have been so lost in a world of turbulent waterfalls and sun-soaked valleys that he hadn't turned when she stood to join him. Her sleeve brushed against his wrist as she pointed to a large watercolor in an elaborate gilt frame. "That's a Turner," she said, unable to keep the pride from her voice.

"It's…beautiful," he murmured.

It really was. A tempest of black waves swirled about an achingly fragile ship, shafts of light fighting to break through the cocoon of dark clouds. The painting was alive, full of movement, yet somehow peaceful; the ship was just one element of the storm, one little drama among the greater backdrop of nature. It was her favorite piece.

They moved along the wall as she pointed out some of her finer pieces, transfixed by the animation in his eyes as she discussed the merits of each.

He stopped in front of a small-framed article, illustrated with a lithograph, and nodded toward it. "Was your husband a writer?"

Pressing her lips together, she paused before answering. Why were men always so quick to attribute accomplishments to other men? "He owned a magazine," she said. "That was Nathaniel's one great kindness—he left me his magazine when he died. This was the front page from the first printing I oversaw as owner and submissions editor."

He peered closer at the yellowed paper under glass and looked up at her in surprise. "What, you own *Carver's Monthly*?"

"The one and only."

He gave a long, low whistle and rocked back on his heels. "Damn."

She raised a brow at the unexpected profanity, and he immediately colored. "Sorry. Only that I used to read it every week."

"Then you have exceedingly good taste," she said with a broad smile, finding herself unable to take offense. "It's funny how for all their distrust of me, as soon as the townspeople think I can help them with something, they're more than happy to put aside their prejudice and knock on my door. Just last month, Jasper Gibbs came to me with a volume of stories he had written, asking me to publish them in the magazine."

"And did you?"

"Goodness, no. They were awful."

Sun was coming through the windows in a low, hazy slant. They sat back down as the clock in the corner struck three. He'd been in her parlor for almost an hour, and though he was quiet, he was a good listener and she found herself wishing he would stay for hours more.

But before she knew it, he was rising to his feet and setting aside the tea, which he had hardly touched. "I'm afraid I've imposed on your hospitality long enough."

"You did no such thing," she said, trying not to let her disappointment show. "As you can imagine, visitors are few and far between, and I always welcome good conversation."

Her hand paused on the doorknob before she released him out into the chill evening. "Do come again, Reverend. I believe we have much more to discuss."

6

Gabriel emerged from the house in a haze. Nothing was as it seemed. Dark, abandoned churches in the middle of a roof-shaking thunderstorm didn't scare him, but the erudite widow thinking him simple horrified him. Damn, but he had made a fool of himself when he had sat in her dead husband's chair. Of course she wouldn't want a hulking man like him breaking a beloved relic. She had seen right through him, he was sure of it, saw his charade, his roughness, his deficiencies. It was as if she could read every piece of ugly gossip in the town printed on his face.

There had been something comforting and cozy about the room, not to mention the enigmatic woman who had sat across from him, her silver eyes trained on him as if he were the most interesting person in the world, her smile as warm and honey-mellow as the late-afternoon light. And those hands, those lovely hands. He could no more imagine them taking the life of a man than he could them snapping the necks of birds and building a macabre altar in an abandoned church. He felt a sudden rush of guilt for even entertaining the idea that she could have been responsible for such a thing.

The sun was sinking fast, and the cold air roused him from his reveries. He looked up to find the other woman, Helen, standing on the front path. She was holding something black and sleek in her arms. Was that... Was she holding a bird?

As he grew closer, he saw it was a raven. It was large and sleek, and apparently docile. As carefully as if she was cradling a newborn, Helen crouched down and let the raven hop from her hands. There was something wrong with its leg, and it bobbled uncertainly before gaining its balance and pecking at the ground.

The crunch of gravel under Gabriel's shoes gave him away. Helen stood back up, her expression turning stony as she watched him approach.

"Helen, was it?" Perhaps she could answer the questions that Gabriel had been too diffident to ask Mrs. Carver.

She scowled, an expression that he would have thought permanent on her face, if he had not seen her light up when Mrs. Carver spoke to her. He kept one eye trained on the raven; could it be one of those he had seen his first night in the church?

"You'll forgive me for asking, but do you know about all the dead animals, the strange things that people have been finding around town?" The tack might have been too direct, but he had nothing to lose by asking her; she already clearly disliked him.

Helen gave him a measured look, answering him slowly, as if he were a small child. "I know that folk like to make a fuss out of nothing."

"But you work for Mrs. Carver...you don't share their opinion of her?"

In an instant, the closed, suspicious look evaporated from her face, and her dark eyes misted. "Never," she said. "Sophy saved me."

"Saved you?"

"That's right," she said, jutting her chin.

"How do you mean?"

Helen heaved a sigh and crossed her arms. "If you must know, after my husband left, I ended up in the poorhouse."

She was staring at him with unnerving intensity. "I'm sorry to hear that," he said.

Her scowl deepened. "I don't need your pity. She took me on as a housemaid, and I haven't left her side ever since. We saved each other," she said, her eyes frighteningly bright.

"Saved each other?"

"You wouldn't understand," she snapped at him, apparently done with her nostalgic reminiscing. "Now, if that will be all?"

She didn't give him a chance to respond before she was scooping the raven back up and briskly making her way to the house.

Gabriel walked slowly back toward the road, Helen's story swirling in his mind. He could picture the gentle and elegant Mrs. Carver, basket on her arm, leaning over women in their sickbeds in the poorhouse and doling out comforting words. But good God, what was he missing? How could that same woman be painted as a witch, a murderer?

When he reached the gate, he stopped and glanced up to the windows, but again, no face stared back down at him.

Helen stood in the carriage house window, watching the interfering minister finally turn and leave the grounds. She let out a breath.

What right did he have to come in here, dredging up painful memories and upsetting Sophronia? Sophy would never say as much, of course, but Helen could tell that the visit had taken its toll on her.

The raven let out a soft squawk in her arms, and she absently stroked its head. She still remembered the day Sophronia had come to the poorhouse. She had been like an angel with her bright blue dress and ready, sympathetic smile. She'd come armed with charity baskets for the women, God bless her soul. When she passed by Helen's bed, she'd asked her in the kindest, gentlest voice what ailed her. Helen had told her it was a chest complaint, though in truth it was so much more than that. It was a broken spirit from being abandoned by the man who had sworn to protect her, a broken heart for the children she would never have.

Sophronia had come back the next day with a bottle of medicine. Helen had taken her hand to thank her, and it was then that she knew that their destinies were intertwined. She felt something pass between them, like a flame leaping from the match to tinder. When she was well enough to leave, Sopronia had taken her on as a maid, and since then they had grown as close as sisters, as dependent on each other as mother and child. But no matter how close they were, Helen knew from experience that pretty words and promises were not enough.

She hadn't been resorting to hyperbole when she'd told the minister that she and Sophronia had saved each other. When Sophronia had whisked her away from that wretched poorhouse, Helen had felt forever in Sophronia's debt. But Helen had since returned the favor.

Sophronia would never know how much Helen had done for her, would never know the lengths to which she had gone to keep her safe, and Helen would not burden her with that. But a childhood spent learning herb-craft and spells from the woman on the farm next to her family's in Vermont meant that Helen had the tools to protect Sophronia in a powerful, binding way.

Moving away from the window, she let the raven down onto its wood perch. She paced about the empty carriage house. Sophronia hadn't stepped foot in here since that night four years ago, and Helen was glad for it. It gave her a private place where she could come to practice her craft. Sweeping up and down the dusty room, she recited the words that she had muttered so many times that they might as well have been engraved on her heart.

"Love me well and bind the spell,
I cast the charm against those who mean thee harm,
But should another love thee, untethered ye shall be."

It was a strong charm; once undone it could not be done again. She could give her mistress protective herbs, sprinkle salt at the threshold, but it was the spell that bound her. No, she would not let that minister tempt Sophronia away from her. For if he did, it was more than just Sophronia's heart that would be in jeopardy—it would be her very life.

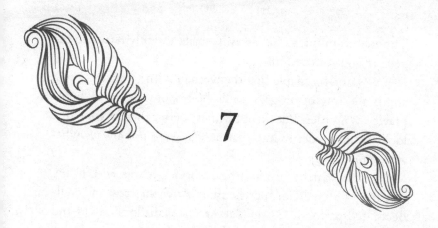

7

Gabriel ought to have gone to the church and continued in his work of clearing away the debris and rubbish. He'd long since undertaken the unpleasant task of disposing of the animal remains, but there was still dust caking the windows and splintered pews that needed repairing. If he was going to have the church up and running anytime soon, he needed to stop procrastinating and embrace this new life that he had forged for himself and Anna's memory.

But instead of going to the church, after he left Castle Carver, he found himself meandering down the wide, tree-lined road to the water. He was caught between being disappointed that Mrs. Carver hadn't been an old crone or a witch—because that certainly would have been very interesting—and uneasy that she was so charming and gracious. Even more disturbing was that he was able to find a woman charming at all. After Anna, how could he even think such things?

When the trees gave way to the broad vista of gray water, Gabriel stopped, hands in pockets, and breathed in the sharp, salty air. A little boat loaded with fishnets slid by, the boy in back raising a hand in greeting to Gabriel as he sailed past.

Though his mind was far away, Gabriel absently returned the gesture and watched him go.

It was unfathomable that the woman with clear silver eyes and frank, intelligent gaze could be responsible for such depravity as murder. But then, he knew better than anyone that looks could be deceiving, that people were not always what appearances suggested.

When he finally turned toward home, it was with heavy feet and a dull sense of apprehension. After the cozy and well-decorated parlor at Castle Carver, his walls looked sad and barren in comparison. He'd thought that he would do his penance of living alone with grace and forbearance, but perhaps his heart wasn't as dead as he had once thought if he was capable of such pressing loneliness.

Prying open one of the two trunks into which he'd piled all his possessions, Gabriel began lifting out the artwork in their chipped gilded frames and wiping the dust off them with his sleeve. The art that had hung in their little cottage in Concord looked lost and out of place on the walls here. Like Mrs. Carver, Anna had loved art and the collecting of it. She had been drawn to amateur sketches, small pieces found in dusty old shops or given to her by friends. It was her imagination and eye that had imbued the artwork with meaning. But without their benefactress, they were simply trifles, not particularly attractive, and without substance. Perhaps he shouldn't have stripped them from the only home they had ever known and taken them to this lonely place.

With a grunt, Gabriel lowered the trunk lid and stood. He didn't want to think about Anna and the mementos she had left behind. He didn't really want to think about anything. He was just about to see if either of the crates contained a bottle of whiskey he thought he remembered packing, when there was a knock at the door.

For some reason, as he put his hand to the latch, he fancied that it was Mrs. Carver on the opposite side, come to continue their conversation. So when his gaze landed not on Mrs. Carver, but on a girl of a few years younger and with bright red hair, he couldn't help his disappointed exhalation. Then he remembered that someone had told him Mrs. Carver did not leave her house. Quickly regaining himself, he coughed and tried to look polite and nonthreatening. "May I help you?"

"Begging your pardon, sir; my name is Fanny Gibbs. My brother sent me, said you were looking for some house help?"

Gabriel stared at the girl blankly until he remembered his conversation with the young man named Jasper that very morning, and the promise that he would send his sister around. How long ago that already seemed since meeting Mrs. Carver. "Of course," he said, holding the door open for her.

With a little sigh of relief, the girl stepped inside. Except for a rounder face and a brighter, gentler demeanor, she was the spitting image of her brother, right down to her sharp green eyes and generous smattering of freckles. She must have caught his look, because she smiled and said, "We're twins, Jasper and me."

She turned her attention to the modest entryway with wide eyes, and Gabriel ushered her into the front room.

He offered her a seat on the only piece of furniture—a threadbare sofa that the previous owners had left—while he stood, leaning against the door frame. "Jasper tells me you work for Mrs. Carver. What makes you want to leave?" He was more than a little curious about what she thought of her notorious employer. "Are you unhappy with your position there?"

Fanny Gibbs was small and plump, and Gabriel couldn't picture her elbow-deep in laundry, or lugging buckets of water up and down stairs. He couldn't even imagine her in Castle Carver; the house would swallow her up.

At his questions, the girl's brow puckered in confusion and she stopped scanning the room to meet Gabriel's gaze. "Leave? Oh, no. I've no intention of leaving Mrs. Carver."

"But Jasper said you were looking for a new position."

Something like anger flickered briefly in the girl's green eyes. "I'm sure he did, but I'm more than capable of taking on more work while keeping my place at Castle Carver."

Gabriel didn't have experience with interviews, or anything to do with domestic help, for that matter. He wasn't sure what he ought to ask, or what was a normal amount of work for a girl like Fanny. "What is it exactly you do for Mrs. Carver?"

"Well, I help around the house with light chores, and I do the laundry once a week. She needs me," Fanny added with a stubborn jut of her chin.

"There aren't other girls that she could hire?"

Fanny shook her head in exasperation. "I *can't* leave Mrs. Carver, not after everything she's done for me. She's my friend. She knew that Jasper and I needed the money, and she hired me on to help."

For a woman who claimed that the whole town was against her—and by his own accounts, Gabriel had found this to be true—here was someone who not only didn't revile Sophronia Carver, but claimed to be her friend.

"Why did Jasper say you needed a new position then?"

She gave a sigh, fiddling at her worn cuffs. "Because Jasper hates her," she said simply. "But she's been kind to me, very kind. I know what her reputation is in the town, and I don't share their poor opinions of her."

There was so much more Gabriel wanted to ask her, but he couldn't very well endlessly interrogate the girl. "Well," he said, "if you're already employed then I don't suppose you'll want the job."

"Oh, no," she said, sitting up straighter, her face becoming animated and her eyes shining. "I can do both. I only go over to Castle Carver a few times a week, and aside from laundry days, I'm only there for a couple of hours. I can do both," she repeated, as if trying to convince herself as much as she was Gabriel.

"Well, I'm not looking for much. I can manage my own breakfasts, but you would be responsible for preparing dinners. Maybe some dusting. What do you think?"

"I think that would suit very well," she said, smiling eagerly.

A weight that Gabriel hadn't realized had been pressing on his shoulders suddenly lifted. He need not be completely alone in his exile, and Fanny was a good-natured, cheerful girl who would help keep the melancholy at bay. "Good," he said. "If you're ready, you can start today. But first, maybe something to eat?"

He'd heard the gurgle of her stomach, seen her slightly abashed expression and recognized the signs of hunger from his own youth. He vaguely wondered what Jasper earned on the docks, and onto what kind of hard times their family had fallen.

Fanny followed him to the kitchen and sat on one of the rickety stools while Gabriel scrounged up some leftover bread and hard cheese. "All I have," he said apologetically as he laid it on the tabletop.

But Fanny eagerly broke off a piece of the bread, piled the cheese on top and chewed contentedly. "It's perfect."

They sat in comfortable silence while Fanny devoured the little meal and Gabriel let his thoughts wander. He'd spent so long fortifying his mind and his heart, forcing himself not to think of Anna or the events of the past year, and inevitably failing miserably. But since meeting Mrs. Carver that afternoon, his thoughts kept turning to the gentle curve of her neck, the quickness of her smile, and her generosity and warmth to the likes of him.

"I know what you're thinking," Fanny said, breaking the silence.

Gabriel realized he'd been staring at her as his thoughts ran away from him. "I'm sorry?"

She gave him a chastising look, a trace of hurt in her voice. "You're wondering what someone like Mrs. Carver would want with someone like me."

He hastened to deny it, but he *was* curious. Mrs. Carver was the wealthiest person in town, pariah or not. She need not associate with the likes of poor ministers or serving girls. "I've heard a lot about Mrs. Carver, and I'm curious," he said, opting for honesty. "How did you meet her? Your brother couldn't have been too happy when you accepted a position with her."

Fanny shifted in her seat, her expression suddenly uncomfortable. "Jasper and me, we needed money. Castle Carver was the finest house in town, so I took it upon myself to inquire about a position there. Everyone warned me about her, but she was nothing but kind to me. Pays me well, and I go over not just on working days now, but other days too just to talk and keep her company."

"All those rumors, though. Weren't you afraid they might be true?"

She crossed her arms and looked affronted. "'Course not."

"And what about the strange happenings around town?"

She surprised Gabriel by smiling, wide and slow. "Oh, I think it's wonderful," she said breathlessly.

"Wonderful?"

"You wouldn't understand what it's like, coming from a big city like you do."

Gabriel didn't bother correcting her. Everyone here conflated Concord with Boston or envisioned it as a bustling city in its own right, neither of which was even remotely close to the truth.

"Pale Harbor is so poky and boring," she continued. "Nothing ever happens here. Oh, it's probably just some troublemaker, but you can't imagine the thrill it gives us. It's like a riddle, but no one understands the meaning. Or hidden treasure…things seem to be found in the most surprising of places. Jane Fisher's sister found the strangest little doll stuffed into a tree."

"I see." Recalling the stories he'd heard from Lewis and the Marshalls, Gabriel doubted as to whether the rest of the town shared in Fanny's enthusiasm. It seemed that everything that had been found had been hidden, secreted away out of sight: the remains left in an abandoned church, a doll hidden in a tree, skinned squirrels in the woods.

He rubbed at the two-day growth on his jaw, not wanting to speak of such things anymore. "So you knew Mr. Carver?"

If Fanny was caught by surprise by the change in subject, she didn't let it show. Indeed, she seemed to be enjoying the gossip. "No, he died before I came on."

"She's so young to be a widow," he murmured.

Fanny shrugged. "She's better off without him, if you ask me. Anyway, when he was alive, they had a cook and a whole score of help. But when he died, Mrs. Carver sent them all away."

"All except for Helen," he said.

"That's right. Helen is so kind to her. She takes good care of Mrs. Carver, even if she is a tough old thing."

"I'm sure she's lucky to have you both," Gabriel said diplomatically. His curiosity about Mrs. Carver had already been piqued, but as he spoke with Fanny, it had flared into an insatiable hunger for answers. He had sat across from the elegant woman herself, listened to her proclaim her innocence in her silky-smooth voice. He couldn't explain why, but he was desperate to see her again, to peel off the rumors surrounding her and discover the person underneath.

Fanny gave a little sigh, though whether of contentment or sorrow he couldn't tell. "And Pale Harbor is lucky to have her."

8

Sophronia rubbed at her throbbing temple, willing the impending headache to hold off just a little longer. She had been editing a submission all day, and the author's penmanship was particularly atrocious, cramped and hard to read. She had only a handful more pages to get through, but they seemed to multiply every time she turned the page, the tight lines of text stretching on forever. As she closed her eyes to give them a respite, her thoughts turned to her unlikely visitor the other day.

The minister had not been what she was expecting, but she had liked him all the same. She had been prepared for a genial older man with kind eyes and a white beard. She had been prepared for polite conversation, tiptoeing around the lies and suspicions planted by the townspeople. What she had not been prepared for was the racing heart, the trembling hands and the sensation that she had known him all her life. And that's what made it all the harder to have to look him in the face and refute all the horrible rumors about herself. What would the reserved man with the watchful hazel eyes think about her if he knew the truth?

Yet she could still hardly believe her luck. How she had prayed, watching that storm roll in, feeling the change that was coming to Pale Harbor. And here it was, packaged in a young minister—a little rough around the edges perhaps—but as fresh as sea-salt air.

Her thoughts were interrupted when Helen came in, bearing a tray with a steaming pot of tea. Sophronia glanced up over the top of her desk, watching as Helen set the tray on the table. Putting her pen down, Sophronia stretched her aching back and yawned deeply. "Is that for me?" she asked with a hopeful smile.

After the minister had left, Helen had not been shy about letting her feelings for him be known. She didn't trust him, didn't like outsiders coming and sniffing around. But she must have forgotten that she was supposed to be sulking, because the tray was decadently laden with all Sophronia's favorite tea cakes.

Bristling, Helen didn't look up as she poured out the tea. "Of course it is. Who else would it be for?" But her bad mood was clearly already dissipating; a smile tugged at her lips.

Sophronia's heart lightened in relief and she sprang up, sending her papers fluttering to the floor. "There's a dear! I knew you couldn't stay angry with me. Now," she said, clasping her hands together as she surveyed the tray of cakes, "which shall we have first?"

Helen took a butter biscuit and sat down. She looked worn and tired, older than her forty years, and a twinge of guilt ran through Sophronia that she had been so short with Helen yesterday. But they settled into an easy conversation as if they had never had a disagreement. They had lived together too long, too closely, for such a trivial matter to come between them. Like two cogs grinding along in the same clock, it would take far more than a tiny, stray pebble to bring them to a halt.

"How is our patient doing?" Sophronia asked as she poured out another cup of sweet, milky tea. She had seen Helen going in and out of the carriage house with the raven, making splints and removing the old bandages.

The little lines at the corners of Helen's eyes softened. "A real fighter, that one," she said. "Had him eating grizzle out of my hand today."

Helen had the touch when it came to animals, though Sophronia suspected some of it had to do with the craft she claimed to practice. Over the years, she had rescued seagulls that blew in from storms, an orphaned litter of kittens and even a fox cub that had found itself the worse for wear after a tussle with a dog.

"You're a wonder," Sophronia said indulgently as her gaze swept over the tempting tray of cakes. She'd been working without pause since breakfast, and she was famished. Just as she was selecting a little honey cake with lemon icing, there was a knock at the door and her hand froze. She caught Helen's eye. It couldn't possibly be the minister again so soon, could it?

As if reading her mind, Helen's face darkened. "Probably that nosy minister come back," she said, and she stalked out of the room to answer the door.

Sophronia hastily swept her hair up, tucking it back into its chignon. Her heart beat a little faster as she followed Helen to the door.

Helen yanked open the door and hissed, "What do you want now?"

But there was only darkness there, and nothing more. Helen stepped back as the door swung the rest of the way open, and Sophronia heard the sharp intake of her friend's breath. "What?" she whispered, afraid that she already knew the answer.

Helen shot out an arm to keep her from going any farther. "Go inside, Sophy," she murmured.

"What? No! Let me see!" Sophronia craned her neck, trying to see past her to the bottom of the steps.

"I'll take care of it. Go inside."

"Helen!" The force of her voice surprised them both, and with a reluctant sigh, Helen dropped her arm and stood to the side.

Sophronia blinked into the darkness, trying to make sense of the dots of light that danced before her.

Candles. Seven white candles stood in the middle of the path, their flames gently guttering in the night's thin breeze.

A chill ran down her spine and rooted itself in her gut. They were laid out so...precisely, so deliberately. Not ten minutes before, someone had been on her front path, carefully arranging the candles and setting flame to each one. Just as the day with the raven, her neck prickled at the thought that someone might be watching her at that very moment.

Darting her tongue over her dry lips, Sophronia finally dared to break the taut silence. "Is...is it some sort of witchcraft?" There was something sinister about the way in which the candles stood, as if they were a jury, judging her, damning her to some dark fate. One of the most popular myths in town was that she was a witch; was this someone's way of accusing her?

After sweeping down the steps, Helen began pinching out the flames with wetted fingertips. Sophronia's chest tightened in fear as she watched her friend descend into the darkness, away from the safety and warmth of the house.

"No, not witchcraft," Helen called back with authority. Then she paused, opening her mouth as if she was going to add something else but had thought better of it.

"What? What is it?"

Carefully, Helen plucked up a little white rectangle from amid the candles. "It's addressed to you." Coming back, she held the note out to Sophronia, who took it and unfolded the paper with shaking hands.

The two words were black and stark against the paper and sent an arrow of cold dread straight into her heart. "I know."

9

I know. I know. I know.
Sophronia's footsteps clipped along in time to the words. They spun through her head, imprinting themselves on the back of her eyelids. How could anyone know? They could have their rumors and suspicions all they liked, but the people of Pale Harbor did not know the truth, or her version of the truth, at any rate. The note with the candles was meant to scare her, rattle her. Well, it had succeeded. The question was, why now? Suspicion had followed her about like a cloud threatening rain in the four years since Nathaniel had died, so why send her this now?

After Sophronia had ordered Garrett to dispose of the candles somewhere out of sight, she had paced about the house, as restless and on edge as a caged animal. By the time dawn had broken, some of her fear had faded, replaced by anger and indignation. How dare somehow violate her Safe space? How dare they threaten her with their cryptic messages?

When she couldn't take the racing thoughts anymore, Sophronia had told Helen that she needed to go for a walk to clear her head. Helen had pressed her lips tight as if she wanted to caution her against it, but ultimately let her go without a fight.

It had been ages since Sophronia had taken a walk by herself without Helen insisting on trailing behind her like some sort of medieval lady-in-waiting. But Sophronia was only going up to the hill anyway.

The hill—which was really more of a gentle slope—was Safe because no one else ever went there, and Helen had told her that she'd designated it as the outer edge of the ring of protection. It rose up alongside Castle Carver, and while it was part of the parcel of Carver land, it was so ambling and expansive that it could hardly be considered private property. It was the farthest that Sophronia would ever go, and at the top she would still be able to see Castle Carver, safe and snug, tucked into the surrounding trees.

The leaves under her boots were satisfyingly crunchy, and it felt good to let her legs stretch out under her layers of petticoats. The September breeze was crisp and cool, holding the promise of colder winds to come. Soon, the candles and the reason for her walk in the first place faded from her mind.

She walked without a bonnet, relishing the wind in her hair. Nathaniel had disapproved of her walking, especially without all the gloves and hats and cloaks that kept her proper. Without them, she'd be no better than a common housemaid in the eyes of the townspeople, he'd said, and it was their job as the most prominent family to set the standard for polite living.

Oh, everyone had loved Nathaniel. He'd been tall and just aloof enough that people deferred to him, but had penetrating blue eyes that made one eager to please him, to win one of his rare smiles. He was distinguished and well dressed, and everything that a wealthy man should be. Sophronia alone was privy to the streak of cruelty that had made him a monster to live with.

Now that she was free of him, she could walk without any time spent fussing over her appearance. But her world had shrunk down since his death. The people of Pale Harbor had worshipped Nathaniel, the wealthy businessman who had donated generously to charity and had given their little town a cosmopolitan flare. The first time she had ventured out into town after his funeral, there had been hissing, spitting and even whispered threats. The cold looks, the eyes flared with hatred, had eventually driven her back to the house, where she took sanctuary. Helen had cossetted her, making spells and charms that she claimed would keep Sophronia safe. It was all right, though; she had no need of the world beyond the grounds of Castle Carver. For all the bad memories that those walls held, there were a thousand more outside.

But when she got to the top of the hill, Sophronia found that she was not alone. She stopped in her tracks, her heart freezing in her chest like a rabbit stumbling across a fox. A man stood with his back to her, hands in his pockets, staring off across the misty landscape.

Sweat sprang to her palms and her throat tightened. What if it was the writer of the note, come to attack her somewhere no one would hear her scream? She turned to run back the way she had come, but tripped on a branch, snapping it. The sound rang out in the hollow air, giving her away. Unable to regain her balance, she went sprawling face-first and landed hard on her hands.

The man's head jerked around at the sound. This was it. Squeezing her eyes shut, Sophronia braced for an attack.

But nothing came.

When she opened her eyes again, she recognized the tall, hatless man striding toward her. Her pulse slowed, but only a little.

"Mrs. Carver," the minister said, his surprise nearly equal

to her own. His coat had been slung over one arm, but when he saw her on the ground, he dropped it and offered her his hand. As he leaned over her, she could see the concern creasing his brow. "Are you all right?"

She let out a long, unsteady breath, and her fear dissipated into embarrassment. Now he would think she was a flighty, clumsy mess of a woman, as well as an eccentric. For all that she was used to being disliked, for some reason it cut her to the core that this man might share in those opinions of her.

Her dress was heavy and cumbersome, but she wouldn't accept his hand, not when she was so vulnerable. With considerable effort, she scrambled to her feet, nearly tripping on her hem.

He stood, hand still out as if he didn't quite trust her to manage on her own. She teetered for a moment, swaying into him before regaining her balance. Before the breeze wound between them, she caught the faint scent of sandalwood and whiskey. It had been so long since she had been touched, at all, by anyone, never mind an astonishingly attractive man. She found herself wishing she could take his hand. "Quite all right," she said briskly when she finally found her voice, taking a good step back.

He gave her a look of lingering concern but only nodded. "I didn't think that you—" He stopped himself, though Sophronia knew what he was going to say: *I didn't think that you ever left your house.* Clearing his throat, he just said, "The path up was overgrown, and I didn't think I'd see another soul."

She pretended she didn't notice. "It's the highest point in Pale Harbor. In the summer, the blueberries will be ripe, and in the winter, when the trees are bare, you can see clear across to the old lighthouse beyond the harbor."

"I should like to see that," he said.

She gave a grim little laugh. "You say that now, but you've

yet to experience a winter here. Bleak doesn't begin to describe it."

"And yet you brave it to come up here."

"Well," she said, bristling, feeling the need to defend her home, "there's a beauty in the bleakness. If there wasn't, the endless months of snow and gray would be enough to make one go mad. Besides, it's part of my property."

She wasn't sure what perversion made her say that, other than she felt he should know that she did exert some control, that she was not a completely ridiculous person.

She waited for him to redden and stammer an apology, but he only leveled a curious look at her. "Is it now?"

"It is."

He nodded without further comment, squinting out into the distance. The shadow on his jaw she had noticed the other day had lengthened into the beginnings of a beard. It became him. Parlors and manners and polite society didn't suit him, and his broad frame looked much more at home here on the rocky hill than it had folded into a chair in her parlor. Unlike her, he was not trapped in a cage of his own construction. He came and went as he pleased, beholden to no one and nothing. An acute pang of envy ran through her.

The breeze was picking up, the sky darkening, and she began to wish she had brought a cloak after all. To change the subject, she asked, "And what brings you here? Gathering inspiration for a sermon?"

He reached into his pocket and held up a notebook, the pages blank. "Something like that." Although he didn't smile, there was just a hint of chagrin in his hazel eyes. "I thought a walk might get the words flowing."

Should she warn him that he might write the most illuminating sermon and it would only fall on indifferent ears? The people of Pale Harbor were not exactly keen for outsiders to come to try to enlighten them. When Mrs. Whittier had come from Rochester and tried to start an abolitionist society, there had been such an uproar that she had been forced to abandon her plans and had eventually left town. The townspeople might fill the pews and listen with upturned faces, but their hearts and minds would not bend from the prejudices that shaped them. Sophronia hadn't the heart to dash the minister's naive hopes, though, and so she bit her tongue.

Pocketing the notebook, he gave a shrug, as if the sermon and the inspiration for it were suddenly unimportant. "And what brings you out here?"

"I was craving some fresh air," she said, omitting the reason for it.

It would be so easy to let her guard down with a man like this. A man who looked at her with eyes as warm as cinnamon, a man who did not judge her or ask anything of her. But neither did he want to offer her anything, as it was becoming clear. He did not wish to engage with her about his church, and he certainly did not seem interested in sharing his thoughts.

"Well, I don't want to frighten away any inspiration," she finally said, turning to leave. She would go and calm her racing mind, seek her solitude elsewhere, and leave him to the privacy he so clearly craved.

"Wait." His hand shot out and he caught her by the elbow. She froze.

"Please," he said without removing his hand, "don't leave on my account. I trespassed on your property. I should be the one to go."

His hand was big and his grip strong, his fingers encircling her arm like a manacle. Panic sluiced through her, and suddenly it was Nathaniel clamping his hand around her in his bruising grip, berating her as if she were a contrary child. She let out an involuntary gasp, wrenching her arm away from him as hard as she could.

At her cry, he released her, dropping her arm like a hot coal. He took a hasty step back. Through her receding panic, she saw the alarm on his face.

Safe. Safe. You are Safe. Just breathe.

She hadn't bothered with a corset today, and she was glad of it as she gulped down the cool, salty air like a tonic. "I…you'll have to excuse me," she said with a shaky laugh. But when she nervously looked up at him, there was no sign of humor or understanding in his expression, only intense scrutiny.

"No excuse necessary," he said, his graveled voice dropping to a soft murmur. "I shouldn't have taken the liberty."

She bit her lip, burning under his level gaze.

"Would…would it be possible, do you think, for us to start over?" She didn't want to be the woman whom he'd heard rumors about, nor the woman who had flown into a panic at an innocent gesture of goodwill. Most of all, she didn't want to be pitied.

For a moment, it seemed like he would not answer. He dipped his head, rubbing at the back of his neck. When he looked up again and met her gaze, his face broke into a dazzling grin. It was glorious, lighting up his whole face and flooding her stomach with warmth. "God, yes."

A weight lifted from her shoulders. His smile was infectious, and she found herself grinning back at him.

He stuck out his hand. "Gabriel Stone," he said. "And you must be Mrs. Carver."

With only a second of hesitation, she put her hand in his and shook it. This time, she did not shrink back from his touch, instead letting the warm strength of his grip envelope her. "A pleasure to make your acquaintance, Mr. Stone."

It seemed silly to cling to such formal conventions when

they were surrounded only by grass and open skies, but she couldn't bring herself to ask him to call her by her given name. But oh, Lord, what would it look like spoken on those sensual lips of his?

"When I come up here I like to sit." She pointed to a little depression in the ground that acted as a natural windbreak. "Will you join me?"

He followed her as she lowered herself to the grass, arranging her skirt and petticoats around her. In a surprisingly fluid motion, he sat down beside her, stretching out his long legs in front of him. How much more at home he seemed out here, what an easy grace he possessed when not confined by parlor walls and social orders. She envied him his ease. Where tea and polite conversation might be confining to him, to her they provided a scaffold of safety, a framework where expectations were clearly delineated. She knew where she stood, and she was Safe. But out here there were no rules, no expectations. It was both intoxicating and terrifying.

Reclining, they rested their heads on the natural pillow the earth provided and stared out over the choppy harbor. Gulls wheeled and cried, sending up the alarm for the coming rain. The familiar tableau was reassuring, but the vastness of it made room in her mind for all the bad thoughts to bubble up again.

"Someone left candles burning on my front path," she blurted without taking her gaze from the diving gulls.

She heard his head turn on the brittle grass and felt his gaze on her. "Oh?"

Her cheeks flushed hot. Why was she telling him this? How did she know she could trust him? She had trouble reconciling this man as the minister he claimed to be, not when he seemed so unwilling to discuss his church or his philosophies. Sophronia did not trust easily, and there was something about the minister, no matter how ruggedly attractive he was, that didn't make sense. Shouldn't ministers be in the business of proselytizing? Shouldn't he at the very least wish to discuss his views and ideas? He was proving a pleasant companion, but that did not make him her friend, her confidant.

She feigned casualness. "I suppose it was some mischief by local children." She didn't tell him about the accompanying note.

He took in a breath, as if he were about to say something else. But nothing came, and they lapsed back into silence.

She was just about to try asking him about the church again when he spoke.

"I've hired your friend, Fanny Gibbs."

Sophronia pushed herself upright and looked at him, unable to keep from smiling. "You did! Oh, I'm so glad to hear that."

He squinted one eye open and looked up at her. "You aren't worried I've stolen her away from you?"

"Worried? Goodness, no. The girl is a treasure and I know she needs the work, though she won't let me give her a dime of charity. Has she made you one of her sweet cheese buns yet?"

His lips curved up in the hint of a smile as he reached into his pocket. "Fresh from the oven this morning. Shall we?"

She'd left in such a fluster, she'd forgotten that she hadn't eaten a bite of the meal Helen had prepared, and her stomach grumbled an unhappy reminder.

Breaking off a piece, he handed it to her and she inhaled the warm aroma of yeast and sweet cheese. It melted in her mouth, and she closed her eyes, savoring it.

When she opened her eyes again, he was regarding her with naked curiosity. "Yes?"

He hesitated. "It's nothing."

She expected that he wanted to ask her something about Fanny, something innocuous about where she had found such a treasure of a girl. "Oh, go on," she said with good humor. "I can see the question practically tripping off your lips."

"Not a question," he said. "Only I think I begin to see why the town thinks you're a witch."

Sophronia's heart seemed to stop. Wetting her suddenly dry lips with her tongue, she tried to make her voice come out light and carefree. "Oh?" Instead, it cracked.

"Mmm. You live in a castle on a hill with an old maid for company. You're rarely, if ever, seen. And it seems you pay no mind to all the stories about you."

Here she had thought they were sharing a pleasant view and a lighthearted conversation, and all he could think of was the petty gossip of the town. He had said he wanted to start over, yet he still seemed to be fixated on first impressions. Was her judgment with men still really so poor? When he had sat in her parlor with her, she had found it so easy to laugh about the rumors because he had seemed so different from what she had been expecting.

His graveled voice held a note of amusement, but there was nothing amusing about the suffocating life she led. Why had she thought she could share this special place with a stranger? Why had she thought he was different?

Abruptly, she sat up and brushed the dead grass from her skirts. "Indeed," she said, her words clipped. "I do hope I've provided you with more fuel for the gossip mill. If you will excuse me, I promised to help Helen in the garden this after-noon and it looks like rain. Good day, Mr. Stone."

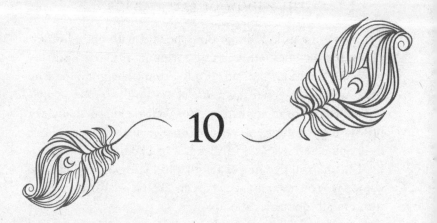

10

Weak light invaded the room through the cracks in the shutters, and from somewhere down the road came the sound of voices, mingling with the early-morning cry of a gull. Gabriel pulled the quilt over his head, not ready to leave the warmth of his bed.

He'd had lain awake all night, unable to find rest. He'd known he wasn't going to be a success as a minister, but for God's sake, shouldn't he at least be able to keep from hurting defenseless widows? And that wasn't even the worst of it. As he lay in bed, unable to settle, his mind had wandered to the sweet curve of her cheek. The way her dark lashes feathered downward against the smoothness of her skin before fluttering up, her flashing silver gaze meeting his. The corresponding jolt of heat that coursed through his body, gathering in his chest and loins.

He'd acted badly when he said he understood why she was such a source of morbid fascination for the town. He'd only meant that he found her intriguing, but it had come out sounding as if he agreed with the townspeople.

Did he believe her innocent of the crime of which everyone

accused her? He didn't know. There was something in the way she carried herself, the defiant jut of her chin and flinty determination in her eyes, as if she challenged the world to accuse her, as if she welcomed it. How *had* her husband died? Had it been an accident? He found himself hoping that Mr. Carver had been old and slovenly, a codger with a strained waistcoat and rheumy eyes. She never would have loved him; it would have been a marriage of convenience, a scheme hatched by poor parents in the hopes of a better future for their pretty daughter. Had life shackled to a sickly old bore proved too much for her? One day after a droning lecture at the dinner table, she might simply have stood up, retrieved a brass candlestick and given him several good whacks to the back of his balding head. But it was impossible to reconcile what he knew of Sophronia Carver with the idea of her committing murder in cold blood.

The vein of guilt that had spread through his chest since Anna had died twisted and throbbed. How easily his thoughts turned to Mrs. Carver, and how easily he forgot all about the church, the penance he was supposed to be serving. He'd hardly thought about Anna at all these past few days. Anna's spirit had been woven into the fabric of Concord, in the gentle cottage gardens, lively churches and the tidy shops carrying the books she so loved. There was nothing of her here in this damp and foggy wilderness on the edge of the world. Whatever he carried of her in his heart was fading fast with time and distance. The church would be an eternal shrine to her memory; he only had to build it. Yet at every step he seemed to find some excuse, some reason why he could not concentrate his energy on it.

The sound of voices outside had grown louder, more excitable. He lay there another minute, hoping that whatever it was would die down, but soon it became apparent that it was more than just the sounds of Pale Harbor waking up and coming to life. Something was happening on the road, drawing more and more attention. He reluctantly got up, dressed and then went outside to investigate.

Down the road toward the town green, a half-dozen men and women huddled about, backs to him, some kneeling, others craning their necks to get a better look at some unseen object in the road. The sun had slid behind a heavy cloud bank and rain was starting to fall, giving the group the somber appearance of a funeral party.

"Everything all right?"

At his voice, a couple of the people turned around, and Gabriel recognized the small, wizened face of Mr. Marshall peering at him from under a dripping hat rim. "Oh, Reverend, it's a good thing you've come," he said, tugging at his mustache and glancing back nervously over his shoulder at the road.

Gabriel strained to see past the group. By now the rain was coming down steadily, sharp and cold. "What happened?"

Mr. Marshall exchanged looks with some men Gabriel didn't recognize. "See for yourself." He gave them a short nod, and they stepped back, revealing the object of their scrutiny.

Taking a step closer, Gabriel frowned. He wasn't sure what he had been expecting, but it hadn't been this. It was a cat. Not a real cat, but some kind of stuffed dummy made to look like one. It was covered in crudely patched fur and had yellow buttons for eyes. Or rather, one yellow button. Where a second button should have been was blank. A cord of rope hung loosely from its neck.

It wasn't real, but it was almost more disturbing than if it had been. There certainly was no shortage of cats in the seaside town, but Gabriel had noticed that the strays that populated the docks were granted an almost elevated status because of their ability to keep the rats away from the daily catches. In either case, whoever had gone to the trouble to construct it and left in the center of town had clearly meant it to be seen. Gabriel was about to stand when he noticed a little slip of paper, tucked under the rope at its neck. Quickly, before anyone could see, he picked it up and slipped it into his pocket.

"Lewis found it hanging from a tree just over the road," Mr. Marshall said, nodding toward a sickly elm.

"Who would do such a thing?" asked a woman with a child bundled on her hip.

"I'll tell you who would do it," said a man with wind-chapped cheeks and small, wary eyes. "A witch. It's some kind of familiar, a voodoo doll. It can only be the work of Sophronia Carver." A murmur of excitement ran through the small crowd.

Oh, for Christ's sake. Mrs. Carver hadn't been exaggerating when she said the town was against her, and as she wasn't there to defend herself, doing so fell to Gabriel.

"It wasn't Mrs. Carver," he said, raising his voice over the rabble.

The murmurs broke off, and a dozen suspicious gazes slid over to him. "And how would you know that?" the man asked, a scowl curling his lip.

Gabriel pushed the wet hair out of his eyes and wrestled to keep irritation from creeping into his voice. "I've spent some time in her company, and I can assure you, the woman is harmless."

Well, not *completely* harmless. She was wreaking havoc on his mind, keeping him up nights, making him moon about on brooding hills like some lovestruck schoolboy. But she certainly didn't pose a threat to *these* people.

An uncomfortable ripple of silence followed, and Gabriel realized too late that he had only damned Mrs. Carver further in their eyes. A respectable woman didn't keep company

with unmarried men, even if the man in question was supposedly a minister.

Mr. Marshall tugged at his mustache again. "I know it's in
your purview as minister to see the good, the godly, in everyone, but with all due respect, you don't know her as we do.
She's taken advantage of the trusting nature of your vocation
and twisted the facts in her favor."

"Mind you don't let her witch you," the woman with the
babe advised him. "You wouldn't be the first love-blind man
to fall prey to her charms. God rest poor Mr. Carver's soul,"
she added with a solemn sniff.

How could they not see what he saw in Mrs. Carver? How
could these people all think her so far from what she really
was? But the rain was picking up, and apparently deciding that
it wasn't worth getting any wetter, the onlookers were losing
interest and wandering back to their homes.

Mr. Marshall was the last to leave, but not before extracting a promise from Gabriel that he would be careful around
the widow and extending another dinner invitation, which
Gabriel had no intention of accepting this time.

Water dripped off Gabriel's cuffs as he sat in his chilly parlor, drumming his fingers against the sofa arm and staring
vacantly out the window. The dampness of his clothes was
seeping into the upholstery, and his throat was hoarse and
scratchy from the cold, but he was too paralyzed by what he
had seen to light a fire or fix himself a drink.

If it weren't for Fanny bringing an armful of wood into
the parlor and humming a tune under her breath, who knew
how long he would have sat there, dripping and drowning in
his thoughts.

"Good afternoon," she said, breaking off in her humming.
"Would you like a cup of tea?" Her gaze shifted to the water

puddling on the floor. "Maybe after you get dried off and into something warm?"

God, that sounded perfect. He hadn't realized what a mess he had made on the sofa, how bone-cold he actually was. "I'll take it in the kitchen with you," he told her. The house was still largely undecorated and underfurnished, and the parlor might as well have been a monastic cell. At least the kitchen was filled with Fanny's bright humming and chatter, and the warm smells of baking bread. Mrs. Carver had been right about Fanny; the girl really was a treasure.

After he'd sloshed up to his room and changed, Gabriel pulled up a stool at the kitchen table and wrapped his hands around the mug of steaming tea. It was good to warm up, listening to Fanny's chatter about nothing and everything as she moved about, preparing supper and cutting thick slices of fresh baked bread. Gradually, the image of the sinister cat dummy and the noose faded into the back of his mind.

She put a plate piled high with buttered bread, sausage and potatoes in front of him. "There we are, a proper meal. You haven't been eating enough, Mr. Stone," she said with a censorious frown.

He gave her the most of a smile he could muster. "I'm lucky to have you to take care of me."

This made her blush and duck her head. "It's only sausage and potatoes, the easiest thing in the world to make." That might have been the case, but good, home-cooked food that was made with love, that was made for *him*, never ceased being something of a novelty.

She made up a plate for herself and joined him. Reaching for one of the magazines that Fanny kept in a stack on the rough wood table, Gabriel began to flick through it as he ate.

It was a copy of a *Carver's Monthly*. Fanny had told him that Mrs. Carver always gave her the old issues to take home and read. She caught him looking at it and nodded toward the table of contents. "Mrs. Carver gave me this one because it's got a Poe story in it. Have you ever read anything by him? He writes so beautifully, so full of pain and heartbreak. His stories are romantic beyond anything."

"One or two, I think," he said. They were a little overly sensational for Gabriel's taste—he preferred adventure stories about men conquering mountains, or sketches of life in tiny tribal villages on the other side of the world—but they were entertaining and had a particular kind of dark appeal.

"Oh, well, you would like this one," she said excitedly. "Mrs. Carver told me that Mr. Carver was proud beyond anything to get it in his magazine. It's about a man who has a black cat and he kills it. First he gouges out the cat's eye because it won't stop staring at him. But then he can't stand the guilt he feels and he kills it. Takes a rope and strangles it, he does. He—"

"Wait, what did you say?"

Frowning, Fanny pushed the paper closer toward him, tapping her finger at the illustration of a bedraggled, one-eyed cat. "The cat. The man hangs it from a tree."

Gabriel stopped chewing, sausage curdling in his mouth. Reaching for the magazine, he hurriedly scanned the lines of the story. There it was, the scene he'd witnessed not an hour before, sketched out neatly in black and white.

When he looked up, he found Fanny studying him, her brow furrowed in puzzlement. "What is it?"

He hesitated. Should he tell her about what he'd seen that morning? It wasn't exactly the kind of thing one shared with young ladies, even if the young lady in question seemed to be morbidly fascinated by ghoulish stories. But she would hear about it eventually, whether he told her or not. Pale Harbor was small and word traveled fast.

"There was a dummy of a cat found near the center of town

today. Just like this one, with one eye and a rope around its neck."

Her green eyes widened as she absorbed the significance of this. "What, just like in the story?"

"Just like in the story."

She considered this. Then her face suddenly brightened. "Do you think any newspapermen will come to write about it? Just think of it, a Poe story come to life!"

Gabriel frowned. He hadn't thought of that. "I'm not sure. I suppose if word gets around they might."

"Wouldn't that be something? It could put Pale Harbor on the map. Why, they might even print our names! Maybe Mrs. Carver can ask someone from the magazine to come up from Portland and write a piece on it."

Gabriel wasn't sure what was more disturbing: the crudely constructed cat, its eerie similarity to the story or Fanny's excitement at the press it might generate. He certainly didn't see Mrs. Carver wanting to have anything to do with it. "I wouldn't trouble Mrs. Carver with such an idea," he said.

But Fanny wasn't listening. He left her to clean up the kitchen, a dreamy, faraway look still in her eyes as she gathered up the plates. Gabriel went upstairs to check the progress of his drying clothes; he had only the one waistcoat, and he couldn't afford to let it get singed. As he plucked it off the grate, a piece of paper fell from the pocket and fluttered to the ground. In the commotion, he had completely forgotten about the note that had been tucked into the noose. It was damp and clingy, but he peeled it open and read the smudged words.

He stared at it for several moments, uncomprehending. Then meaning clicked into place and his blood ran cold. Grabbing his still-wet waistcoat, he pounded down the stairs, and, ignoring Fanny's protests, rushed back out into the rain.

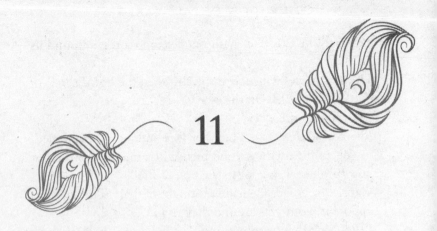

11

No sooner had Sophronia laced her boots and headed to the back door than a foreboding rumble of thunder sounded, and the heavens let loose. Standing in the doorway, she watched as raindrops splattered onto the steps, picking up in intensity until the bricks were stained black and water ran down the path in rivulets.

Before the rain had started, she'd been sitting in the parlor, biting at her lip and warring with indecision. She never walked to the hill so frequently, and certainly not two days in a row. But something in her chest tugged her there all the same, like the needle on a compass swinging toward true north.

She turned around and went back inside, throwing herself down on the sofa and reaching for a book. Duchess jumped up and curled into a ball beside her, as if relieved that the silly human had finally realized it was better to stay warm and dry.

It was no small feat for Sophronia to work up the fortitude to leave the house, and now she was thwarted not by her own anxieties, but the weather. Nervous energy thrummed through her, and she had to force herself to focus on the book, waiting for her heartbeat to gradually slow. Perhaps it was better not to go, not to be disappointed. Who knew if he would be there anyway, and why did she even want to chance seeing him again after his careless words had proved him to be as small and bigoted as everyone else?

Arms full of shopping parcels and water dripping from the brim of her practical bonnet, Helen walked by the parlor door, but doubled back and paused when she saw Sophronia in her walking boots and cloak. "It's raining the devil and pitchforks out there," she said. "You can't possibly be thinking of going out?"

Sophronia gave a sigh, equal parts irritation and disappointment. "No, I'm not going anywhere."

Putting down the parcels and untying her wet cloak, Helen lowered herself carefully onto the chair across from Sophronia. "Probably for the best. You shouldn't be out walking alone," she said. "I took the hack from town and Reuben Reese told me that there's been another unpleasant discovery."

Her curiosity was stronger than her irritation at Helen's oppressive sense of vigilance. "Oh? And what did he say?"

"It was a cat this time...some sort of manikin." Helen paused, pressing her lips tight before continuing. "It was hanging from a tree in town."

Sophronia frowned. "How gruesome." Yet she couldn't help but breathe a small sigh of relief. She had convinced herself that she was the intended audience for the cruelty that kept finding its way to her doorstep, but this latest depravity had happened in the center of town, far away from her.

"We'll have to keep Duchess in the house. I don't want her wandering about outside by herself," Sophronia mused as she ran her fingers down the old cat's silky fur.

"Never mind Duchess," Helen said with a scornful crease of her brows, "*you* shouldn't even think of venturing outside anymore, not even to the hill. We both know whoever is doing this has you in their sights."

Sophronia opened her mouth to argue, but Helen was only getting started. "First it was the nasty looks after Mr. Carver's funeral. Then it was the brick through the dining room window." She was up now, pacing back and forth, ticking off incidents on her fingers that Sophronia would have rather forgotten. "Why, we had to turn down all the lamps, cowering in darkness, so they wouldn't know we were home." Pausing in her pacing, Helen cast a pleading look at her. "So yes, I don't for a moment doubt that this renewed harassment is intended for you."

It might have been true, but Sophronia had no intention of going back to those dark days. "I can only sit about inside for so long," she said. She didn't add, *with only you for company*, because she knew that underneath Helen's brittle exterior beat a very tender, very sentimental heart. But it was true; what had first felt like an inebriating freedom from Nathaniel had been growing ever stagnant and oppressive over the years, and Helen seemed only too happy to languish alongside her.

"I need to get out on occasion, even if it's only up the hill," Sophronia said, standing up and looking out the window longingly at the mantle of fog. How she would love for her Safe place to grow, like a stain spreading on linen. How she would love to have the courage to take a ship and sail out past the horizon, ocean breeze at her back, escaping to the great beyond. But it seemed as if her Safe place was destined to wither and shrink until she could only huddle pitifully in her bedchamber.

The tension in the air thickened around them, the only sound the steady patter of rain on the roof, and the faraway echo of a foghorn. Contrite, Helen came over and stood beside her. She took up Sophronia's hand and gave it an awkward squeeze. "I'm sorry, Sophy," she said, her husky voice pitching higher. "Let me curl your hair tonight. I've got the latest Godey's and you've just the right hair to hold the new sort of ringlets."

Sophronia wasn't in the mood for Helen to fuss over her. What she really needed to do was drown herself in work, read through submissions until her eyes burned and her sinister thoughts were held at bay. But Helen was looking at her with such hopeful expectation that she could no more deny her than she could an orphan begging for food. She sighed and gave Helen a tight smile. "That would be nice."

A knock at the door shattered the moment. Sophronia's body tightened and she locked eyes with Helen, a silent understanding passing between them. It was another raven, more candles, or something worse. She wanted to run upstairs to bed, pull the covers up over her eyes and make the rest of the world outside her door disappear.

Helen reached out and took her by the wrist. "Stay here." But Sophronia pulled free, irritated that once again Helen found the need to play her protector.

A muffled voice rang out from the side of the house. "Mrs. Carver? Are you there?"

She stopped short at the sound of the familiar voice. Shooting Helen a warning look, Sophronia rushed to the door. Opening it, she found a hatless Gabriel Stone standing on her step, wet hair plastered to his brow and his trousers soaked in muddy water up to the knees. Her heart gave a little skip.

"Mr. Stone? But you're drenched!"

One look at his face told her that he hadn't come to discuss the church, or for an evening of polite conversation. One look at the rest of him confirmed it; he had no cape or overcoat, and his soaked linen shirtsleeves were nearly translucent, conformed to the generous muscles of his arms and shoulders.

Whatever had brought him to her door was not good. "What on earth is—"

"Come back to snoop, have you?" Helen said, cutting her off. She crossed her arms as the minister came in and shook his dripping hair out like a wet sheepdog. "And if you've come just to tell us about that nasty business with the cat manikin, then you've wasted a trip and gotten wet for nothing."

He raked his hair back out of his eyes and as soon as his piercing gaze settled on Sophronia, a shiver of excitement ran through her body. To her chagrin, her anger and hurt from his unkind words the other day melted away, replaced with a light, fluttering sensation in her chest.

Without turning from her, his words came out taut and low. "But she doesn't know about the note."

Her relief at finding the minister at her door evaporated, and her stomach dropped in cold anticipation. She looked at Helen and then back to the minister. "What note?"

But Helen seemed as bewildered as she was, her eyes narrowing. "What are you talking about?"

The minister's jaw tightened, but he didn't say anything other than, "May I come in?"

What was wrong with her, letting him stand barely inside the threshold, still sopping wet, with the merciless wind at his back? "Of course," she said, shaking the fog free from her head. She ushered him inside and led him to the parlor, where it was warm and cozy. "Helen, would you be a love and put some tea on for us?"

"I'm not going to go to the trouble of boiling water if he's going to be turning around and leaving in a moment."

"Helen."

Clamping her mouth shut, Helen turned on her heel and disappeared down the hall in a brisk swish of skirts.

Sophronia went over to the grate and poked at the coals.

Her body felt tight and her mouth dry. Behind her she could sense the prickling energy of the minister, waiting for her to say something. When the fire was licking with hot, eager flames, she turned to find him still standing awkwardly where she had left him just inside the doorway.

"Please, won't you sit?"

He looked as if he wanted to say something but made no move to take a seat. "Don't worry about getting the furniture wet. It's only a bit of rain."

Then she remembered with an inward groan the last time he had been in her parlor, and she'd admonished him for sitting in Nathaniel's old chair. Now he probably didn't want to chance offending her again by possibly sitting in the wrong place. Well, they would stand then. Putting aside the poker, she clasped her hands in front of her. "What can I do for you, Mr. Stone?"

Wordlessly, he produced a folded scrap of paper from his pocket and handed it to her. It was wrinkled and damp, and looked as if it had spent some time outside in the rain. He took a step back and looked away, giving her some measure of privacy as she squinted to make out the smudged words.

"You hide in your castle, but I know this will find you. What you took from me, so I shall take from you. All great houses must fall."

She frowned. Something familiar echoed in the words, as if they were lyrics to a song she once knew. The sinister tone held more than a note of foreboding: it held a promise, a threat. Forcing herself to push aside the unpleasant implications, Sophronia pasted a wan smile on her face. "You say this was found with the cat manikin in the middle of town, but I confess I'm not sure why you thought to bring it to me."

The minister's penetrating hazel gaze bore into her, his expression at once incredulous, kind and pitying. "I think you know why," he said gently. "It was written for you."

She swallowed, hard. Of course it was for her. No one else

lived in a castle in Pale Harbor, never mind that Castle Carver wasn't a castle in the true sense. Anyone in town who read this would have known it was meant for her. But she didn't know what to make of the rest of the lines. What did the writer think she had taken from them? What did they want to take from her?

Wordlessly, the minister pulled out two other crumpled pieces of paper. As he unfolded them, she caught a glimpse of typeset and an etched illustration of a large, crumbling house.

Sophronia took the first page and ran her gaze over it. It was one of Mr. Poe's stories; she'd read it when it had come out, but it hadn't made much of an impression on her and she'd subsequently forgotten all about it. Nathaniel had never liked Poe; he'd said the man's stories were too sensationalist and catered to the excitable nerves of women. But that hadn't stopped him from falling all over himself to get one of the macabre stories published in the magazine when the submission landed on his desk. The suspenseful installments kept readers coming back for more, which meant money. And Nathaniel never turned down money.

As she read, the familiar words from the note fell into place. She *had* seen them before. "The Fall of the House of Usher." This particular story had something to do with a house...it collapsed at the end, if she remembered correctly, taking with it twin siblings who were the last two living members of their family line. The second paper was an illustration of a one-eyed cat, another story penned by Mr. Poe.

Her thoughts raced. The birds, the feather nailed to her door...in an instant it came to her. "'The Raven,'" she said, breathless. "There's a poem by Poe called 'The Raven.'" Even she, someone who never left the house, was familiar not just with the poem, but with how fantastically popular it had become. Fashionable families held dinner parties and read the poem aloud around the fire, students recited it in diction classes, and a number of magazines and newspapers had already run parodies of the spine-tingling composition.

Mr. Stone nodded gravely. "I've read it. You said something about candles the other day, as well... I wonder..."

He trailed off, but Sophronia was already scrambling to remember a story or poem by Mr. Poe that included candles. Nothing came to mind.

"Wait here," she said, thrusting the pages back at Mr. Stone. She ran to Nathaniel's study, pushing aside the unpleasant memories that it brought, and forced herself to grab bound copies of the magazines by the armful. When she came back to the parlor, Mr. Stone was just as she left him, one dark brow raised in question.

Laying out the magazines on every surface in the room, Sophronia began to sort through them, separating those that contained stories or poems by Mr. Poe.

"The answers are in here somewhere," she said, a ray of hope breaking through the clouds of despair that had settled over her in the previous weeks. There was a pattern, a riddle—she only had to crack it and perhaps she could put an end to this.

Helen came with the tea, and Sophronia dismissed her without looking up from the magazines. After Helen had gone with a grumble, Sophronia began to scribble a list on a blank piece of paper.

August 29—raven (dead)
September 9—raven (dead)
September 14—raven (dead)
September 20—raven (living)
September 25—Mr. Stone arrives
September 26—feather nailed to door
September 30—seven white candles, note
October 1—hanged cat manikin (in town)

Over her shoulder she could feel Mr. Stone leaning down to read the paper. She tried to ignore the way his breath warmed and tickled the back of her neck, and she shifted away slightly. She had to focus.

"Is there some pattern in the dates?" he asked.

She bit her lip, looking at the incidences that had filled her with so much terror all laid out in black and white. "I haven't the faintest clue."

"What about this author, Poe? What does he have to do with anything?" he asked.

"I don't know," she said. "I suppose his macabre and titillating words are inspiration for someone who already holds a fair bit of malice in their heart. Perhaps they see his stories as a means to frighten me."

She took out a fresh leaf of paper, this time listing the references to Poe stories. The ravens and feather were easy enough to place, and next to them she wrote "The Raven." Then she jotted down the other references next to their respective events or notes: "The Fall of the House of Usher," "The Black Cat."

Pausing, she tapped her pen next to the candles. "This one... I still don't understand what the candles mean."

She couldn't think of a single Poe story or poem that referenced candles in this way. Perhaps they had nothing to do with Poe and had been an invention of her tormentor. But something about the seven dancing flames tickled at her mind. She handed Mr. Stone a stack of magazines. "Here," she instructed him. "Look through these and see if you can find anything to do with candles."

The room grew warm and stale despite the pelting rain outside. Her eyes became dry, her mind filled with the most vivid horrors after reading every ghoulish story in the magazines.

"Here."

Sophronia jumped, the masculine voice piercing her con-

centration. The minister was frowning over a folded magazine. Taking it from his hands, she scanned the lines.

"The Pit and the Pendulum." It was a chilling story of torture during the Spanish Inquisition, full of the most devious
forms of torment. Sentenced to death, the narrator was im-
prisoned in a small room in which seven candles on a table
slowly burn as a razor-sharp pendulum slowly descends toward him. As the candles dwindled down to nothing, so too
did his hopes of survival.

She looked up at him sharply. "Do you think it could be
from this?"

In the dim lamplight, the pronounced contours of his face
were softened, and for the first time, Sophronia realized she
was not afraid to be alone with this man. They had been
working side by side for what must have been hours, and she'd
hardly given a thought to her safety any more than if he had
been Helen.

He gave a one-shouldered shrug. "It must be."

Sophronia shivered. It was more than just the mention of
the candles, it was the familiar feeling of terror that it dredged
up in her. Hastily, she pushed the story away. She would not
succumb to the fear that this person was so clearly trying to
instill in her.

"The real question is, who is behind it all?" Mr. Stone had
pushed aside some of the magazines and was sitting on the
sofa, his elbows braced on his knees as his gaze roamed over
the upturned parlor and scattered papers. Then, as if suddenly
remembering something, he sat up and reached into his pocket,
producing a well-worn piece of paper.

Sophronia got up from her seat on the floor and stood over
him as he smoothed it out on his knee. It was a list of names
of everyone in Pale Harbor. Everyone except her.

"Mr. Marshall gave this to me when I first arrived," he said.

He didn't need to explain his meaning. Sophronia immediately set to work, copying the list to a fresh sheet of paper. Pacing, she rattled off names of everyone she knew it could not be. It couldn't be little Jane Fisher, because a childhood fever had robbed her of her sight. It couldn't be the Marshall twins, for as nasty as they could be, they were only nine and could not have orchestrated such an intricate plot. It couldn't be Jonas Peckham, as he was falling-down drunk most of the time. And so it continued.

When they were finished, they both sat back and looked at the list of more than fifty names; only a handful were crossed out. Looking as if he were weighing his words, the minister scrubbed his hand along the bristled line of his jaw. "It might be a good idea for you to lie low for a while."

Her brows shot up, and she had to bite back the bitter laugh that threatened to erupt. Did he know how little freedom she already had? How tight Safety wound its protective fingers about her? If he did, then he surely would not suggest that she "lie low." For goodness' sake, the farthest she ever went was the hill, and even that was already a rare feat.

Sophronia pressed her fingers against her hammering temples, aware that the minister was looking at her with a burning intensity that hadn't abated since he'd stepped foot inside her house. What, exactly, did those solemn eyes of his see in her? He had already said that he understood why the town condemned her; did he think her guilty, as well?

What was worse was that his nearness did something to her, and even though their task was a dreary one, she couldn't help the thrill that ran through her when his sleeve brushed hers, or he leaned in close. It was all too much, the alternating waves of fear and wanting and physical desire broiling within her. She needed to be alone.

"Thank you, Mr. Stone," she said, turning abruptly toward

the door. "I appreciate your help in this matter, but it is late and I don't think we will find our answers tonight."

He opened his mouth, but then closed it as if he'd thought better of whatever he was about to say. "Of course," he said, with a clipped nod. "If I can help in any way, or..." He trailed off as Sophronia shook her head.

"I'm sure that won't be necessary. Good night."

The sound of his footsteps receded down the hall, and then she heard Helen closing the door heavily behind him. Sophronia stood rooted to the ground, staring out the dark window unseeing as she bit at her thumbnail. Her mind raced with images of broken birds, notes written in a crooked hand, and a man both rough and beautiful who seemed to be able to see right through her.

"I don't trust him," Helen said, sweeping back into the parlor with a fresh pot of hot water. She sat down and poured out a cup of tea, handing it to Sophronia.

Accepting the cup with trembling hands, Sophronia sank down on a chair and closed her eyes, inhaling the comforting scent. "I know you don't." Helen didn't trust anyone, but she had to agree—there was something strange about the minister. He didn't seem concerned with preaching or recruiting, and she hadn't heard much of anything about this new church or when it was supposed to open. It could be no coincidence that he had arrived only weeks after the ravens had begun appearing on her doorstep. Who knew how long he could have been skulking about town before making his arrival known? Nathaniel had never been shy in letting her know that he had all sorts of friends in high places, friends who would relish making her life miserable should she ever try to escape him. Was Gabriel Stone one of these friends, finally come to investigate and avenge Nathaniel's death? And yet despite all that, there was something about the man that made Sophronia *want* to trust him, made her wish more than anything that she could. She wanted those fathomless eyes to look on her with something other than suspicion. Something warm and kind and yearning.

With a weary sigh, Sophronia opened her eyes. "I don't believe I trust him either."

Here was at least one mystery she could perhaps solve. Her body ached with fatigue, but she could not rest until she learned the truth about this man.

Pushing aside the jumble of magazines, Sophronia took out a fresh leaf of paper, dipped her pen in ink and began writing.

To whom it may concern...

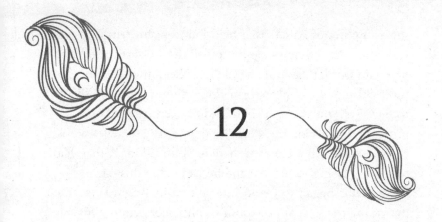

12

It was nearly ten o'clock, and all the pews were mercifully still empty.

Gabriel held his breath as he leaned against the wood pulpit, surveying the small nave with growing hope. The previous day he had posted a notice on a peeling board near the harbor announcing the first service, hoping that the sign would be overlooked and no one would come. Now, with the late autumn sun slanting in through the narrow windows, illuminating every dustless surface, it looked as if he might just get his wish.

It hadn't been easy finally getting the words for a sermon on paper, and harder still to find the will to sit down and banish the memory of Mrs. Carver standing in her parlor, her heart-shaped face drained of color as she read the thinly veiled threat against her.

He hadn't slept a wink all week, unable to think of anything else besides the bizarre evening he had spent with Mrs. Carver, trying to parse out some meaning behind all the vague threats against her. It had almost been a relief to put his mind to the task of writing a sermon. In the end, he'd scraped together a few lukewarm lines, borrowing heavily from an old Emerson pamphlet of Anna's that he'd found in his trunk. It was ridiculous, he'd thought, as he copied the words over to fresh paper, to think that Anna would have been proud of him for such a blatant act of plagiarism. This church was not a shrine to her at all, but an insult. He hadn't even tried to open his mind, to understand the words he'd hurriedly scrawled across the page. But what else was there for him to do? A man had to make a living somehow, and he had come this far.

Just as he began to be optimistic that he might be spared delivering the sermon, the door swung open, ending his stay of execution.

Lewis took a hesitant step inside, eyes nervously scanning the transformed church as if he might be in the wrong place. When he saw Gabriel, he broke into a sheepish smile. "Almost didn't recognize it without all the broken wood and cobwebs." He blinked at the empty pews. "I'm not early, am I?"

"Right on time," Gabriel ground out.

Well, maybe no one else would come, and then he could send Lewis home with an apology and a tepid promise of a service next week. But no sooner had Lewis taken a seat in the center of the front pew than the doors swung open again, and the Marshalls and a handful of other familiar faces shuffled inside.

Gabriel clenched his jaw until it ached. He would have to preach to these people; there was no getting around it. If there was indeed a God, then He wouldn't have been remiss in throwing down a bolt of lightning and sending the whole place up in flames as punishment for this disgraceful charade. But for once, the sky was clear and bright.

As Gabriel forced himself to step up into the pulpit, he tried to picture Anna's face smiling down on him in pride and gratitude. He failed. Lingering conversations gradually died away, throats cleared in polite expectation and bottoms shifted on the creaking wooden pews.

"Friends," he started. His voice cracked like an adolescent boy. Christ. There was a cough from somewhere in the congregation, but otherwise all had fallen deathly silent.

He tried again. "Friends, welcome."

The words on his paper swam and shifted before his eyes. He wet his lips. All he had to do was read them, speak them aloud. He had no conviction, and even less idea about what they actually meant, but it didn't matter. No one here would know, either. They had almost certainly come out of curiosity and nothing more.

As he read off the paper, Gabriel could not help but dart his glance up every few lines and scan the pews for Mrs. Carver. Knowing that she was keenly interested in philosophy after their first meeting, it seemed possible that she had decided to brave the journey into town and come to find enlightenment. But what need had she for spiritual succor? She was a religion unto herself, and if she did not leave the grounds of Castle Carver for social calls or basic errands, he could hardly expect that she would come to the church. Perhaps it was better that she was not here to see what a failure he was proving to be. He could live a little longer in her eyes as a learned man, someone worthy of her esteem.

They stood to sing the psalm. Did transcendentalists sing psalms? He didn't really know, but he had found a pile of moldering hymnals in the office, and if nothing else, singing meant less time sweating in the pulpit.

The last echoing note evaporated and everyone stared expectantly at Gabriel. He cleared his throat compulsively.

"Thank you all for coming. I hope... I hope it was...edifying."

When they realized that he was not going to say anything else, people started to get up to leave, sharing confused murmurs and glancing over their shoulders at Gabriel as they filed out.

It was over. His knees felt like they might give out under him, and he'd never craved a drink so much in his entire life, but it was over. If nothing else, the service had been so underwhelming that perhaps he would not have to worry about anyone ever coming back.

Almost everyone had left when Gabriel looked up to find Mr. Marshall coming toward him. He gave Gabriel a less than enthusiastic handshake. "Well, Gabriel, you've done it. I can't say I understood a word of it, but I suppose that's the way with these lofty ideas and philosophies."

Behind him, the twins rolled their eyes at each other. "What are you talking about, Papa? It was boring," one of them said with a pout.

"More boring than drawing lessons."

"More boring even than math lessons."

Mr. Marshall's cheeks reddened. "All right, that's enough, girls." He gave them a hasty push toward the doors. "Why don't you go wait outside with Sarah?"

Mrs. Marshall had come up beside them and was ushering a young woman by the elbow into the conversation. Good God, why couldn't they all just go home and leave him be?

"Mr. Stone! There's someone I want you to meet," Mrs. Marshall said with a knowing smile. "May I introduce my niece, Miss Harriet Wiggins?"

The young woman gave an unnecessarily deep curtsy. She was petite, blond and very frilly. Her dress was trimmed with lace at every juncture, and her hair was curled into tight ringlets that danced from beneath a ruffled bonnet when she so much as breathed.

There was something in Mrs. Marshall's eyes that Gabriel didn't like. Something suspiciously like scheming.

"Miss Wiggins." He gave her a short bow over her proffered hand. She blushed and fluttered her pale lashes.

"What an *enchanting* sermon. I've heard so much about you from dear Aunt Clara. I had to practically *beg* her for an introduction."

He stifled a groan. "Is that so."

Ignoring his terseness, she smiled up at him with saccharine sweetness. "I'm eagerly awaiting the ball, and hope that you will save a dance for me?"

He looked from Miss Wiggins's expectant face to the Marshalls. "Ball?"

Mr. Marshall tugged at his mustache, looking quite pleased with himself. "I was talking with Clara, and we thought it was time that you were formally welcomed to Pale Harbor. We want to hold a ball with you as guest of honor. Give everyone the chance to properly meet you."

"Oh," Gabriel managed to say. Sweat sprang to his temples and his mouth was suddenly dry. He wet his lips. "I don't know, I…"

He did not dance, and he certainly did not go to balls. Anna had dragged him to more than one town assembly where there had been dancing, but he had only gone on her account. He'd enjoyed watching her dance, standing in the background while she swirled and sparkled, never wanting for partners. She could tempt any man away from the safety of the punch bowl, even Joshua Whipple, the straitlaced minister. She could tempt any man, and all Gabriel could do was watch her.

"I couldn't ask you to do that," he hastily added.

But they wouldn't have any of it. "It's all been settled already," Mrs. Marshall told him with a breezy wave of her gloved hand.

Little wonder that Mrs. Carver kept to herself. He had thought a forgotten town in the middle of nowhere would give him anonymity and peace and quiet, but instead it seemed the opposite. He was an insect under glass, and before this was over, they would see him dissected and his secrets laid bare.

Sophronia perched on the edge of the sofa, dressed in her blue silk afternoon dress and a smart little bonnet pinned into her hair. Fine clothes had always been her weakness, and Nathaniel had been only too happy to indulge her, keeping her in clothing that befitted her position as wife of a distinguished man. And though she had long ago shed her widow's weeds, with nowhere to go and no one to see her, she dressed simply and sensibly in demure shades and modest cuts. All her lovely gowns of silk and taffeta now hung like jewel-toned ghosts in her wardrobe.

But today was different. Today she had a reason to don her favorite dress and to wind girlish ribbons through her bonnet.

Today was the first service at Mr. Stone's church.

Garrett had told her that he'd seen a poster in town advertising the first service this week, and she'd known right then that this was the moment she had been waiting for. What better chance to allay her suspicions about the minister than to see him preaching the ideas he seemed so reluctant to share with her? And if nothing else, forcing herself to go would provide a welcome distraction from the darkness that kept finding its way to her door.

She was going to go to the church and hear Mr. Stone speak; all she had to do was stand up, walk out the door, down the hill and keep going until she got to the church.

It was that simple.

She took a deep breath, stood up and went to open the front door. Then she was outside, the brisk air nipping at her cheeks and tugging at the ribbons in her bonnet. Next came the front path. One foot in front of the other, past the spot where the ravens had lain, past where she had run in a tangle of muddy and bloodstained petticoats that fateful night four years ago.

Her heart lifted, and a little flicker of optimism took root in her chest. She could do this. And why not? She had gone up the hill, after all, and this was only in the other direction, toward town. Perhaps she could be her own lucky charm, her own lantern casting light in a circle about her wherever she went, keeping her Safe.

By the time she reached the front gate, her heart was beating hard and fast. Wrapping her fingers around the iron bars, she leaned her forehead against the cold metal and closed her eyes. She just needed a moment to collect her strength, and then she would step through the gates for the first time in over three years. How the townspeople would gape as she passed by in her fine silk dress, inclining her head in gracious greeting to those who thought they had vanquished her to obscurity. She would walk right past the place where Nathaniel's blood had stained the ground, the soles of her boots treading over it as if it were any other insignificant stretch of road. She took a shaky breath, wrapping her fingers tighter around the bars. *Push. Just push the gate open.*

Her arms turned to stone, her feet equally as stubborn. A chickadee's laughing call taunted her from just beyond the trees. When she thought about it, what was really the point of going to the church? She could invite the minister over to dinner any time, and they could talk for hours. Because if she were being honest with herself, she wasn't going for the sermon or to ferret out the truth about the minister. She was going to see his piercing hazel eyes and to hear the graveled timbre of his voice, to feel that little shiver of excitement that ran through her whenever he was near. That was not a good reason to go. Everyone in town would be only too happy to draw salacious conclusions about her and a possible relationship.

And that was to say nothing of the danger that lurked out-side, just waiting for her to let her guard down. What horrors might she find outside her house? No, there was no need for her to go out, not today.

She let out a nervous laugh that rang hollow in the cold air. Relief made her body light, and she uncurled her fingers, turned around and unpinned the smart little bonnet. Another day. She would go to the church another day.

13

Pounding at the door shook Gabriel from his sleep. Cracking one reluctant eye open, he glanced around the dark room. It took him a moment to remember where he was exactly. Not the snug and tidy cottage he had shared with Anna in Concord, nor the cavernous nave of a church that was so often the setting for his nightmares.

It had to be well past midnight and the room was cold; the fire needed banking. He gave an incoherent moan and pressed his pillow over his ear, hoping that whoever was at the door would go away. But the pounding only came again, harder and more urgent this time.

Goddamn it. Sleep didn't come easily, and once he'd finally slipped into blessed unconsciousness, he didn't want to wrench himself out of it again for anything short of an emergency. Grumbling, he reached for his trousers and stumbled into them, stubbing his toe against the bedpost in the process. This had better be an emergency of the highest order.

"Coming, goddamn it!" he growled as he staggered downstairs amid more urgent banging. It was probably someone come looking for a minister to do whatever it was ministers were supposed to do. Read verses over a sickbed? Assist in the delivery of a baby? Well, they were in for a disappointment. Gabriel didn't make house calls; that's where he drew the line.

When the door swung open, it revealed a breathless man of middle years with dark black skin and a broad-brimmed hat that the wind threatened to carry off. He was wearing an impeccably fitted tailcoat and an uneasy expression. "Mr. Stone?"

Cold air slithered inside, wrapping itself around Gabriel's exposed chest. "Do I know you?" He was still half-asleep, but he was fairly certain he'd never seen this man before.

"Reuben Reese," the man said with a bob of the head. "I run the local coach out of the Chestnut Tavern."

Gabriel vaguely remembered seeing leaflets around town advertising for his service. Then he remembered something else. "But I didn't order a hack."

The man gave him a peevish look. "I know that. You've been sent for."

"Sent for?" Gabriel rubbed at his bleary eyes, the last of his drowsiness evaporating in the cold night air. "Look, you had better tell whoever sent you that they're mistaken—I'm not the sort of minister that makes house calls. Sorry you wasted your time," he added as he moved to close the door.

But the man shot his arm out, stopping the door with a splayed hand. "No, *you're* the one who is mistaken." For the first time since he'd opened the door, Gabriel caught a glint of something like fear in the man's dark eyes. "You've been sent for because they found a body."

As the carriage thundered across town, Gabriel's mind spun out all the possible ways the poor soul could have met their unfortunate end. He didn't know who "they" were, and Mr. Reese had declined to elaborate as Gabriel had shrugged on a coat and grabbed his boots. It was most likely a body washed ashore, some poor soul lost from a shipwreck. Or perhaps an old man who had died in his cups at the tavern. But there was a twinge of unease in Gabriel's gut, and he couldn't help but think of the note that had all but threatened Mrs. Carver's life.

They stopped at the edge of the woods, and Gabriel jumped out before Mr. Reese had a chance to come around and open the door. Unhooking one of the swinging lanterns from the hack, Mr. Reese gestured over his shoulder for Gabriel to follow him. "This way."

Mr. Reese's lamplight cut through the night, illuminating a pale swathe of thick woods. The only other light came from the dim windows of the tavern in the distance. Mr. Reese led Gabriel down a dirt road right to the edge of the woods, where two other men were standing, backs to him. One of the men still clutched a cup of ale, as though he had only stumbled outside to relieve himself and been waylaid by the gory discovery.

Gabriel's mouth went dry at the similarity to the scene that had greeted him around the cat dummy last week. But this time when the men stepped away, it wouldn't be an effigy of a cat, but a real, human body. He gritted his teeth and sent up a silent prayer. *Please, don't be Mrs. Carver. Anyone but her.* At their arrival with the lamp, one of the men turned and Gabriel recognized the pale, freckled face of Fanny's brother. "Jasper?"

"Sorry to wake you, Mr. Stone, but Constable Morris is out on a call for missing cattle and isn't expected back tonight. Thought you might be the best person to come, seeing as you're a man of the cloth."

"A priest, eh?" slurred the man with the ale. He looked Gabriel up and down with dubious, watery eyes. "Heard we were getting some sort of fancy churchman, but you don't look like any priest I've ever seen."

Gabriel didn't recognize the man, but Mr. Reese took him

by the elbow and pulled him away. "Jonas, if you've seen the inside of a church since your mam had you sprinkled by the priest fifty years ago, then I'm Saint Peter himself." He gave him a push in the other direction. "Why don't you go back to the Chestnut and grace them all with your presence there." With a grumble, Jonas took another swig from his cup and stumbled back toward the tavern.

Throughout this exchange, Gabriel had carefully trained his gaze at the tree branches waving in the wind, the fleeting sliver of the moon through the clouds, anything other than the shape on the ground. The body was obscured by shadows, but he didn't want to risk seeing a glimpse of it just yet. What would he do if the pale moonlight revealed Mrs. Carver lying twisted and lifeless on the dead leaves? But Jasper and Mr. Reese were looking at him expectantly, so Gabriel gave them a short nod.

Mr. Reese held the lantern up higher, casting shafts of flickering light onto the form, revealing a man. A very bloody, very dead man.

The overwhelming gratitude Gabriel felt to some unknown power nearly brought him to his knees. It wasn't Mrs. Carver. It wasn't her. He let out a slow breath, closing his eyes.

When he opened them again, he forced himself to take a long, slow look at the body. Blood and the detritus of the leafy ground obscured most of the man's face, yet there was something familiar about him. Gabriel had seen him before. As if reading his mind, Mr. Reese spoke up.

"Garrett Hawkins, Mrs. Carver's groundskeeper."

Jasper raised a brow at Gabriel through the flickering lamplight. "Do you believe us now? She murdered him as sure as she murdered her husband and left him to rot in the street."

Gabriel didn't say anything. No matter who the culprit was, this spelled trouble for Mrs. Carver.

The three men stood gazing down at the corpse, the wind threatening to pull the last of the lamplight into oblivion. For the first time since answering the midnight summons, Gabriel finally felt the cold sink down into his skin, and a shiver rode through his body.

It must have been closing time at the tavern, because across the way men were spilling out into the night, the thin strains of their ribald laughter carrying on the wind. Leading the party of revelers was the man with the ale, gesturing for them to follow him.

They should cover up the body, give Mr. Hawkins some belated measure of respect. But before Gabriel could ask Mr. Reese to fetch a blanket, the men had arrived, amid a cloud of ale fumes and profanities.

A man with a robust beard and a well-worn coat gave a low whistle. "Well, here I thought old Jonas was spinning another tale when he stumbled into the Chestnut, but looks like the old bugger was telling the truth for once."

"He was a good man, was Garrett Hawkins," another man said. "Never could hold his ale, but kept to himself and kept out of trouble."

"It's witch work, isn't it?" someone else added excitedly.

The bearded man shook his head. "That's a demon's doing if I've ever seen it. Same thing happened to MacPherson's dog two years ago. The demons in the woods came out looking for a taste of flesh. She can do that, you know—summon demons."

Gabriel didn't have to ask who they were talking about. He stared at them in disbelief; they sounded like the Marshall twins with all their talk of witchcraft and sorcery. "Surely you don't believe that."

But the men stood firm in their accusations. "You're not from around here," said the bearded man charitably. "But witches and demons is the norm here." The others nodded their agreement.

With a heavy sigh, Gabriel crouched beside the body and held the lantern aloft for closer inspection. He could smell the unmistakable fog of liquor on the man's clothes. Dark, rapidly congealing blood matted his hair, and his head rested on a rock sticky with more blood. Garrett's leg was bent at an unnatural angle, and when Gabriel followed its trajectory, he found his ankle caught in an exposed root. A terrible way to go, but it was a far cry from foul play or "witch work."

Gabriel stood up, keeping the lantern trained on Garrett's leg so that the small crowd could see. "Looks like he had too much to drink, tripped and hit his head on that rock."

Mr. Reese had fetched a large rug from his hack, and he gave it to Gabriel to lay over the lifeless form.

The men shared a look, and the bearded man shifted uncomfortably in his shoes, working the rim of his hat nervously around in his hands.

"Begging your pardon, Mr. Stone," Jasper piped up, "but we've noticed how you've been spending a lot of time in the company of Mrs. Carver. Might it be possible that she's charmed you such that you can't see her handiwork as it lies here before you?"

"Oh, for... You can't be serious." But one look at their grave, slightly apprehensive expressions told him that they were just as serious about this as they were about the demons in the woods. This was the second time someone had suggested that he was under some sort of spell from Mrs. Carver. Gabriel sighed. "I don't suppose Mr. Hawkins has any family, or they would have been sent for?"

A murmur went around the little group and shoulders shrugged, heads shook in unison. If Garrett Hawkins had a family, no one here knew it.

Mrs. Carver and Helen would have to be notified, if they didn't already know. God, that would not be a pleasant conversation.

"And let me guess. Mr. Hawkins wasn't a member of the Baptist church?"

"No, Mr. Stone. Don't believe he was much of a godly man, if I were being honest. How could he be, working for Mrs. Carver?"

Of course his duties as a minister would include funerals, but Gabriel had never considered that when he made his decision to come to Pale Harbor in the heat of passion. He had little enough right to climb up into a pulpit and read off a pamphlet, let alone act as steward for souls of the dead. But he was here now, and he had been tasked with doing just that for old Garrett Hawkins.

When the arrangements had been made to transport the corpse to the church and enlist Lewis to dig a grave, Mr. Reese drove Gabriel home.

This time when Gabriel lay down on his bed—fully dressed—he did not fall asleep.

"Garrett is dead."

Sophronia had been working at her desk while Fanny did mending and helped herself to handfuls of sweets from the tea tray. It was laundry day, which meant that after Fanny had finished the washing downstairs, she stayed for tea, gossiping and sharing all the news from town.

At Helen's bewildering pronouncement, Sophronia put down her pen and Fanny broke off in her story. She couldn't possibly have heard Helen right. "What?"

"Garrett is dead," Helen repeated, and this time there was no mistaking her words.

Fanny let out a little cry and crossed herself.

"Oh, God." Sophronia took a long, dry, swallow. "What... how did it happen?"

"That...minister—" Helen choked out the words "—was just coming up the road to call and tell you. I got it out of him, though, and sent him on his way."

Sophronia's heart sped up. "Well? What did he say?"

"Garrett's body was found last night by some tavern-goers, out by the edge of the woods."

"But what happened? Do they know?"

Helen sat down, matter-of-factly folding her hands in her lap. "They don't know for certain, but it seems as if he had a fall coming out of the Chestnut."

Sophronia closed her eyes; she had been so close to going out *there*, to leaving the Safety behind. Could it have been her if she had found the nerve to go past the gate and into town the other day?

"He was such a nice man," Fanny said between watery sniffles. "He always let me take the roses after he'd pruned them."

Sophronia's mind whirred to make sense of it. Only yesterday Garrett had been out putting sacking cloth over the rosebushes in preparation for winter. The man might have been as rough in speech and appearance as the old burlap sacks, but he'd had a way with plants, and kept the estate in impeccable order. More importantly, he hadn't abandoned her after Nathaniel died, as so many of the serving staff had. He had been at Castle Carver since before Sophronia had come, and she was ashamed to realize she didn't know the first thing about his personal life.

"This is just terrible. Does he have any family?"

Helen shook her head. "Not that I know of. I think he mentioned a niece once, but it was years ago."

"So much blood," Sophronia murmured, more to herself

than to Helen and Fanny. "Sometimes it seems this whole cursed town is steeped in blood."

Helen shot her an alarmed look and then tilted her head to Fanny, an almost imperceptible gesture. They never spoke of Nathaniel's death, even obliquely. Not alone, and certainly not when Fanny was present. It was a taboo topic inside the walls of Castle Carver, and Sophronia had almost come to believe that if they did not talk about it, then perhaps what had transpired wasn't real.

Clearing her throat, Sophronia gave Fanny what she could muster of a smile. "Fanny, why don't you go along home. Don't worry about the mending. I'll pay you for the whole day."

Fanny sniffled back the rest of her tears and nodded. "All right. Thank you, Sophy."

Helen's lips pressed tight in the disapproving grimace she got whenever someone else referred to Sophronia by her nickname. As soon as Fanny was gone, Helen reached for the tray and slowly poured out another cup of tea.

"They'll blame you, you know," she said.

"Oh, come now. Do they think I skulk about at night? Do they think I could take down a big man like Garrett?" But Sophronia knew all too well that Helen was right; if some of the most zealous people of Pale Harbor believed her capable of murdering Nathaniel, then it would take no great leap to suspect her of killing her own groundskeeper. They would be only too gleeful to bring the charges up against her. Taking a long, slow sip of cool tea, Sophronia tried not to imagine iron shackles around her wrists and the red-faced constable leering at her as she stood behind bars.

"They'll blame you, all right," Helen repeated, as if Sophronia hadn't said anything.

Pushing down the rising sense of panic in her chest, she

forced herself to take another sip of cold tea. "I wonder if there will be a funeral service."

Helen looked away, suddenly tight-lipped.

"What is it? Tell me."

She sighed. "Your Mr. Stone is to give a service tomorrow at the new church."

Sophronia flew out of her seat, unable to contain her surprise and exasperation. "What? Were you going to tell me if I hadn't asked?"

"Would it make a difference?" Helen snapped. "We both know that you won't go, that you can't go."

If Helen had slapped her, she couldn't have hurt Sophronia more. Of course, she was speaking no more than the truth, but like Nathaniel's death, they did not talk about Sophronia's self-imposed captivity. At her stunned expression, Helen softened. "Don't worry yourself over it, Sophy. I'll go and make an appearance on your behalf. It will all be very proper."

She couldn't help it. It all came bubbling up: her sadness at Garrett's death, her frustration at her impotence for doing anything about it, her gut-wrenching fear about what would come next. Heat rose to her cheeks. "Proper? *Proper?* Is that all that matters to you? A man is *dead*, a man who worked for me. What need have I for propriety and manners?"

"Oh?" Helen said, raising a brow and remaining maddeningly cool. "And what do you propose?"

Sophronia clamped her mouth shut. She didn't know what she proposed, only that she couldn't abide to do nothing. How would it look to the town if she were absent from the funeral for her own employee? How would it look if she *did* go? Sophronia hated that she was reduced to thinking in such terms, but when she peeled back all the complicated layers of the matter, she found that she wanted to go, needed to, even. Though they had never been close, Garrett had served her well for years, and he had come to an ugly, untimely end. Going to his funeral service was the least she could do for him now.

She wasn't Safe. She had never been Safe. A bird in a cage was no safer than a bird in a bush if someone chose to reach their hand in and pluck it out. At least the bird in the bush had the chance to fly away.

The words slipped out before she could stop herself.

"I'll go."

14

For the second time in a week, Gabriel climbed the wooden steps to his pulpit with leaden feet and a sheen of perspiration on his brow. But this time it was not the prospect of preaching empty words to a congregation that made his chest tight, but the fact that he was responsible for easing the anxious minds of a town on the edge of panic. Never mind that Garrett's death had clearly been accidental—the rumor that Sophronia Carver had had a hand in it had spread quickly and completely, until it was taken as gospel truth.

Lewis had dug a grave in the small cemetery overlooking the harbor, and a local fisherman had donated a stained and tattered sail to use as a shroud. The constable and a physician from the next town over had briefly examined the corpse and concluded that the death was indeed the result of a fall.

As he looked over the sea of expectant faces, Gabriel wondered what he should say to these people. He had already seen how quick they were to judge Mrs. Carver, how hungry for scandal they were. What would happen if their wild fancies about demons and witches were allowed to go unchecked? They believed that they were in danger, and that Mrs. Carver was responsible. Well, Gabriel was not a real minister; why should he give a sermon with all its false comforts and pompous words?

He cleared his throat. "If you've come looking for soothing words or a grand eulogy, then you've come to the wrong place."

A collective murmur of confusion rippled through the congregation.

"I can't offer you any of that." It was the truth, and it felt surprisingly good to admit it. But what *could* he offer these people? Did he have a responsibility to offer them anything? Even if he didn't, there was one person to whom he felt accountable, whether she would agree or not. Every time he thought of Sophronia Carver, the echoing chambers of his heart quivered and his protective instincts flared. He would do anything to protect her, he realized in a flash of clarity. After Anna, when his body had become so listless and empty, there had at least been a freedom to it. He had been a rudderless ship adrift in a sea without land in sight. But to feel something—anything—for Mrs. Carver, well, that alarmed him to his core. The thought was both liberating and terrifying. So when he spoke his next words, it was with only one person in mind.

"What I can give you is peace of mind. Sophronia Carver had nothing to do with this tragedy. She does not leave her property. How do you propose she brought down a man like Garrett Hawkins, at the edge of town, no less?"

Grumbles proliferated through the church at this. He could not assuage them of fears of demons, but in his heart he didn't think they really believed such fancies. It was a way for them to place blame, to make sense of a tragedy. "But we are not here to speak of Mrs. Carver and her innocence," he continued. "We are here to honor Mr. Hawkins's life."

If only he knew something of the man, had been able to speak to Mrs. Carver and learn something of his life. Gabriel spoke in only the broadest terms, drawing conclusions from the little he knew of him, such that he was a hard worker, loyal and had loved his home in Pale Harbor.

It was a few moments before Gabriel realized his words were falling on unhearing ears. All coughing and seat shifting had ceased, leaving the small church in thick silence. He trailed off, and, looking up, saw that all heads were craned back toward the door.

He followed the congregation's collective gaze, and that's when he saw her: Mrs. Carver, resplendent in full mourning complete with a trailing veil, hovering like some sort of dark apparition in the doorway.

Shoulders thrust back, chin held high, her posture itself challenged the congregation to make her leave. Only Gabriel caught the moment of hesitation, manifested in the slight quivering of her veil before she stepped all the way into the nave. But then she was drawing her head up even higher, taking a deep breath and sweeping down the aisle, as erect and graceful as a prima donna gliding across the stage. Behind her trailed a stony-faced Helen, dressed equally somberly in a sensible gown of plain black wool.

There were a few hisses, and an oath spit out in barely concealed undertones. A boy even went so far as to stick his foot out into the aisle, but Mrs. Carver neatly stepped over the trap, and continued her way to the front. Helen bared her teeth at the boy as she passed, sending him shrinking back to his mother's side.

Gabriel finally snapped out of his shock and cleared his throat loudly, drawing attention back to the pulpit.

"Enough," he said, the command and volume of his voice echoing off the church walls. The snickers and whispers immediately died off.

Mrs. Carver, who had dropped gracefully into a seat in the front pew, gave him the smallest of nods.

All his short-lived confidence and bravado fled as soon as he knew her quicksilver eyes were watching him from behind that cursed veil. What else was there to say? He rifled through the old psalm book, rattling off some prayers for the dead and a psalm about the eternal promise of heaven.

When the service was over, a few of the men came up to shake his hand, assuring him that *they* didn't put any stock into the childish fancies of demons and the like. Gabriel murmured that he was glad to hear it, but his mind was already on Mrs. Carver, his eyes scanning the diminishing crowd for her.

But it was Harriet Wiggins, the Marshalls' niece, who found him. She was dressed in black lace and a matching bonnet quivering with feathers. During the sermon, she had loudly and dramatically cried out in great heaving sobs, but now her eyes were dry and sparkling, her black-gloved hands finding his arm and gripping it tightly.

"Oh, Mr. Stone," she said, "*what* a moving service. You are a credit to Pale Harbor and the decent people here like Garrett Hawkins."

Gabriel was spared having to answer, as he looked up to see Mrs. Marshall waving to her niece from the doorway. "Harriet! Won't you walk back with us? The girls are anxious to get home before the rain starts and the sky isn't looking any too accommodating."

Miss Wiggins's lips formed into a pretty pout and she gave Gabriel an apologetic look. "I'm afraid I have to leave, but I hope we'll finish this conversation at the ball next week?"

By the time she was gone, Mrs. Carver was, too.

Sophronia peeled off her satin gloves, unpinned her bonnet and loosened the lace fichu at the neck of her bodice. She kept her movements brisk and purposeful under Helen's disapproving gaze.

"I told you we shouldn't have gone. Look at you, you're shaking."

"It's the cold, that's all." Sophronia went to the grate and poked the dying embers back to life. It was cold, but it was fear that had penetrated her bones and left her with legs like jelly.

Helen gave her a lingering look of concern. "I'm making you some tea." She swept out of the room without giving Sophronia a chance to respond, leaving her in blessed silence. As soon as Helen's footsteps receded down the hall, Sophronia slumped down into her chair, a trembling hand at her temple.

Going to the church had been like plunging into a cold lake; she had steeled herself, and then walked with such purpose and blind determination that she didn't have a chance to talk herself out of it. She had braced herself a hundred times before, though, and had never been able to make the final plunge. What had made today different?

Heat prickled at Sophronia's neck. She could lie to herself all she wanted, but deep down, a rebellious corner of her heart sang the truth: *You went because of that minister. You wanted to see him, to have his gaze fall on you and alight with pleasure. Something pulls you to him, and you can no more keep away from him than a moth can from the flame.*

She sat stock-still, paralyzed by the truths unfolding within her as the fire gradually died again. She didn't regret going. It had been the right thing to do, even if it left her body inside out and her heart racing. Seeing Mr. Stone standing so tall, so implacable behind the pulpit had steadied her, given her the strength to stay. His unflinching gaze had been a rock in the racing current of an icy river. But as much as she might want to cling to him, she had to remind herself to be careful. Men were experts at showing one face to the world, and another behind closed doors. Whatever his motives were, she must be on her guard.

With a sigh, she rose from the sofa and wrapped a shawl around her shoulders. Her stomach was growling, reminding her that she had been too nervous to eat anything that morning. Perhaps a mug of tea and a thick slice of cake would be just what she needed to calm herself before bed.

She was just about to go join Helen in the kitchen when there was a knock at the front door. She froze. Fanny wasn't due until tomorrow, and Helen usually took grocery deliveries in the back. It was too late in the evening for deliveries in any case. If it was another threat or a dead bird, then she didn't want to know. Not today, not when her nerves had almost frayed completely. *Please don't answer it*, she willed Helen. But a moment later the door was unlatching, and Helen's voice floated up to the parlor.

She tensed as footsteps hurried down the hall. But as soon as Helen stuck her scowling face through the doorway to the parlor, she knew who it was. There was only one person who made Helen look like she'd just sucked on a lemon.

"That minister is outside asking for you," she said. "I'll tell him to go away if you—"

But Sophronia was already rising, tucking her fichu back in under her collar and smoothing her hair. "Let him in, please," she said. "And then why don't you retire early for the night? I can bank the fires and turn down the lamps before I go upstairs."

Helen's frown deepened. "But it's Thursday." She gave Sophronia an expectant look, and when Sophronia didn't say anything, added, "I always play the pianoforte for you on Thursday evenings."

She steeled herself against the edge of hurt in Helen's voice. "Tomorrow night, I promise. I'm tired, and after seeing what

Mr. Stone wants, I'm going to bed myself." Her nerves were in tatters already, and now a light, fluttery feeling in her chest was blooming in anticipation of seeing Mr. Stone again.

But Helen didn't move. "You can't think of entertaining a man alone in the parlor, especially at this time of night."

The absurdity of Helen's concern almost made her laugh. Almost. How could her friend think her reputation was anything other than completely and irrevocably ruined?

"I can, and I will." She was so tired, but heat rose to her face. "Who will tell? You? And what would I have to lose if you did anyway?"

Had they always been at each other's throats so much? It seemed that any time the minister came up in conversation, Helen turned prickly and Sophronia defensive.

Helen blinked at her, unmoving. Sophronia thought she was going to spar her word for word, but all she said was, "I don't want to fight, Sophy. See him if you must, but please, have a care for yourself."

Startled that she didn't have to muster the strength to fight, Sophronia watched Helen as she disappeared down the hall. A moment later the minister's heavy tread sounded, and then he was in her doorway, filling the room with his imposing form and silent energy, looking at her with bright, penetrating eyes.

Her heated words with Helen were immediately forgotten. Under his rough overcoat he wore the same suit he had at the church, and for the first time she noticed the slightly frayed cuffs, the worn leather on the toes of his muddy boots. They were his only clothes, she realized. And yet, he was the finest man she had ever seen.

"Mr. Stone," she said. "I wasn't expecting to see you so soon after the service." A knot of dread formed in her stomach. "Is everything all right? Has something happened?"

"No, nothing," he assured her. But he was looking at her queerly, expectantly.

What had brought him here? Perhaps he was angry that she had disrupted his service. Despite his assurance that nothing was amiss, what if he had brought another note meant for her?

"Please, sit," she said, gesturing to a chair. "Would you care for anything to drink?"

"Only if you'll join me."

She rarely drank, but suddenly, a warming glass of brandy to smooth her jagged nerves was all she wanted.

As if reading her mind, he added, "I think this calls for brandy," and before she could respond, he was moving to the sideboard, his large frame gracefully navigating around the furniture.

Grateful to be spared preparing drinks with her trembling hands, she seated herself and watched as he poured out two generous glasses. He handed one to her and then carefully sat down across from her. "Thank you," she said, gripping the glass. Small sips, she told herself. She wasn't sure what had brought him to her parlor, but she must keep her wits about her.

He had no such reservations about imbibing and finished the brandy in one long draft. When the glass was empty, he continued fidgeting with it until he finally put it aside, and, leaning forward, clasped his hands on his knees. "I'm afraid today took a toll on you."

She nearly choked on her brandy. Of all the words she had imagined crossing his full lips, she had not been expecting those. Her masquerade must not have been convincing. Nevertheless, she was determined not to let her fluster show, and arched a brow. "Funerals are never easy."

But she clearly wasn't fooling him. He was looking at her as if she were as easy to read as a page in one of her magazines. "Why did you come?" he asked quietly.

"Why? Garrett was a valued worker, a good man. Why should I not come to pay my respects?"

"No," he said, an uneasy edge to his gruff voice. His gaze fell to his hands, which he studied with a frown. "Of course you must pay your respects," he murmured without looking up. "It was good of you to come."

When he lifted his gaze, the look he gave her was intense, yet unreadable, and she shifted in her seat despite herself. "It was good of you to come," he repeated. Suddenly, he slid forward on his seat and reached out, placing his hand on hers. "You don't leave Castle Carver's grounds. Yet you came today."

Too shocked to pull away, she stared down at her hand in his, resting on her skirt. It was warm—and strong, despite his light hold. A pleasant, numbing heat spread up her arm.

What was she doing? What if Helen walked in? Abruptly, she pulled away. It didn't matter how lovely it felt to have a strong hand around her own; it didn't matter that she couldn't remember the last time someone had touched her like that, if ever. It was wrong, and she couldn't let her physical desires cloud her mind.

Flustered, the minister awkwardly withdrew his hand the rest of the way and sat back down. "Excuse me," he said hastily. "I didn't mean..." He trailed off.

Mean what? To give her comfort? Dare she hope that he longed to reach out and touch her for the sake of touching, just as she found herself wishing she could do with him?

He looked as if he wanted to say something else, but after several moments of silence, Sophronia cleared her throat.

"I would like to pay for the cost of the funeral service, and any other expenses such as the burial."

Without giving him a chance to respond, she went to her writing desk in the corner and unlocked the little drawer.

She came back, check in hand, pen poised. "Well? What was the cost?"

"Mrs. Carver, you can't—"

"I won't brook arguments," she said firmly. "Would a hundred cover it sufficiently?" She knew very well that it would, that it would more than cover the cost of the grave, the coffin, the headstone and then some.

"Mrs. Carver, I can't take your money." He paused, scrubbing his hand through the bristle on his jaw and looking suddenly very tired. "You don't even attend the church."

"And? Your church is a force of good in this town. Please, it's not even up for discussion."

His lips pulled up in the smallest of smiles, and her heart kicked in her chest. "I don't understand," he said.

She gave a weary sigh and put the check aside. "Question my motives all you like, but I only want to do one last thing for a man who served me well over the years."

"It is most kind of you."

A hard lump formed in her throat. She was given so few opportunities to be kind.

In the end, Gabriel had no choice but to accept her money; how could he not, when she looked so determined, yet so fragile and hopeful?

She walked him to the door. Helen was nowhere to be seen, for once, and he wondered how Mrs. Carver had come to find herself alone this evening. He stepped out into the cold, loathe to leave behind the warmth of the parlor and the company of the woman who occupied it.

He had barely opened his mouth to bid her good-night when her words came out in a rush, cutting him off. "You asked me why I came to church today. Now I want to know why you came here tonight to see me." She paused. "The true reason."

He wavered on the doorstep. Something in her tone told him it was not so much a question as it was a challenge. Why *had* he come?

It was cold, but the sharp air made him awake, alive. Jamming his hands in his pockets, he shrugged. "I was worried about you."

The words slipped out before he could moderate them, make them tidy and professional. There was no taking them back, no mistaking his meaning, so he just watched her face carefully, trying to gauge her reaction.

But she gave nothing away, her silver eyes glinting like coins on a scale, weighing his words. She looked so small standing above him on the threshold of the doorway, hands clasped in front of the nipped waist of her mourning gown. He wanted to feel her warm, slender hand in his again. If he were being honest, he wanted much more than that. He wanted to lace his arms around her, pulling her firmly into him and feeling the length of her against his body. He wanted to cup the shape of her under those voluminous petticoats and taste the sweetness of her pink lips. He was standing two steps below her, bringing her just to his eye level. All it would take to bring his lips to hers was the smallest of steps, the merest of suggestions. But Gabriel kept his hands in his pockets and stood his ground.

"I appreciate your concern, Mr. Stone. Thank you for coming."

Relief and disappointment coursed through his body. She was sending him on his way. Giving her a brisk nod, he was just about to go home and douse himself in cold water, when a thought struck him and he turned back. "The Marshalls are hosting a ball next week. I know you don't usually…that is…" He cleared his throat and tried again. "You would be most welcome."

They both knew that she wouldn't be welcome, not by the rest of the town anyway. But he had to let her know that he did not stand with them.

Her lips parted in surprise, and it took every fiber of his being not to lean forward and brush them with his own. Before he could do something that he would regret, he touched his hat and then bolted down the path, to the safety of his cold bed.

15

When Sophronia closed her eyes that night, she saw a road endlessly winding out in front of her. No matter how fast she walked, the road only grew longer, the end just out of sight, until she was running and breathless. But when she opened her dry eyes, crooked ravens and Garrett's bloodied face filled the dark room until she lit the lamp, chasing away the specters.

Swinging her legs out of bed, she padded across the carpet to pour herself a glass of water. But being awake was no easier; all she could think of was the feel of the minister's hand on hers, the compelling pull of his eyes.

Despite the nagging of her brain, her heart blindly tugged her along, wheedling and begging her to trust him. Perhaps she had the capricious heart of a woman, but it *would* be easier to trust him, to believe him when he told her who he was. She did not have copious experience in the ways of men, but she was no fool either; Nathaniel had been an education and then some. Her mind had been the one to agree meekly to his marriage proposal, though every tender nerve in her body had cried out at the idea of being bound to him. Their match had been logical; he had been a prominent newspaperman and would give her a home, stability, his name and all the cache that carried with it. In return he would reap her dowry as a much-needed business investment and have a pretty, young wife to ornament his home. She had known that there would be no love between them, that there was something cold and repellent behind his eyes.

Maybe it was time to stop listening to her brain and start listening to her heart. But even so, the most confident soldier did not go into battle without armor.

Full of restless energy the next day, Sophronia threw herself into all manner of cleaning projects. When was the last time the windows had been scrubbed? The carpets beaten? By evening, her back ached and her hands were raw and stiff, but the exhaustion was satisfying. She felt rejuvenated after her late-night epiphany about the minister, and a fresh outlook required a fresh environment. As the sun dipped lower in the sky, she found herself in the parlor, dusting the last of the picture frames. Helen would have scolded her for not asking Fanny to do it, but running the feathers over the smooth gilding of the frames and watching the dust lift away was relaxing, and she was in desperate need of relaxation.

She hadn't seen Helen since she'd sent her away the night before, and she was feeling badly about the way she had spoken to her. But there was also a little spark of resentment that had been kindled within her; why couldn't Helen let her make her own decisions? Why did she act as if Sophronia only had enough time and regard for either her or the minister, and not both?

The tread of clipped footsteps behind her and the light swish of skirts told her that Helen had come in. She didn't turn around.

"Sophy?"

"Mmm?"

An exasperated sigh. "Put down that duster for a moment and turn around."

Sophronia continued with her cleaning. "I know that Fanny can do it, but really, I just—"

Coming up beside her, Helen gently pried the duster from her hand. "Please."

Something in Helen's voice stopped her, and she put down the duster, wiping her hands on the old apron she'd thrown over her dress.

"I have something for you," Helen said, producing a little velvet box.

Sophronia stared at it. The spark of resentment sputtered and dimmed. Here she had been righteously dwelling on their argument, and all the while Helen sought only reconciliation.

"Go ahead, open it."

"You didn't have to do that." But Sophronia's eyes sparkled, and she held out her hand for her present. She loved surprises and little trinkets, and Helen knew it well.

Carefully, she unclasped the lid, and gasped when she saw what was inside.

"Helen!" she exclaimed, rolling over the exquisite brooch in her hand, marveling at the ruby that was as red as a ripe cherry and as heavy as a diamond. Gold filigree framed the impressive stone, giving it a delicate, feminine feel. It rivaled anything Nathaniel had ever given her.

"It's beautiful! But it's too expensive. You shouldn't have." Helen didn't have any money that Sophronia knew of, but she was thrifty, and perhaps had squirreled something away. She would hate if Helen had squandered all her savings for the sake of a gift. Sophronia was the wealthy mistress; she was the one who should be bestowing gifts on Helen, not the other way around.

A rare smile tugged at Helen's lips. "That's not for you to worry about."

Sophronia gave her one last look of misgiving, and then went about pinning the brooch at her breast. "I love it and you are too good to me. Come here." She held out both hands and pulled Helen into an embrace. But despite the beauty of the gift and the truce it represented, something about it didn't feel right. Why now? They had had more than their share of disagreements, especially recently, and they had never given each other gifts. Sophronia pushed aside her pang of unease. Untying her apron, she gestured to Helen to follow her to the kitchen. "Come, let's make some tea."

She put water on to boil while Helen cut a slice of hard fruitcake she had made the week before. They chatted, Helen telling her about her progress with the raven's rehabilitation—his wings were almost mended, and the legs weren't far behind—and Sophronia listing all the chores she had accomplished around the house. But her mind was on other matters. Matters that had hazel eyes and a broad chest she longed to rest her head upon.

Before she knew why, she was telling Helen about his last visit. "I tried to pay Mr. Stone for the service, but he was hesitant to accept any money." Sophronia didn't tell her that he had eventually relented and accepted her offer.

At this, Helen straightened from the cake, her eyes widening. "I should hope not! Imagine that man coming up here and taking money from a widow. It would be the mark of a scoundrel."

Sophronia smiled faintly at Helen's attempt at gallantry. "He's a minister. I don't think scoundrels generally go in for that line of work."

"No?" Helen dropped the slices of cake onto two plates and slid one in front of Sophronia. Wiping the crumbs from the knife, she sighed. "Well, I suppose not. But if one were to require a guise, they could hardly do better than a minister."

Sophronia's own misgivings about Mr. Stone came bubbling back up. She had yet to receive any response to the letters she had written to every church in Concord inquiring about him, and she was anxious to have her doubts put to rest. She had thought—hoped—that it was only her own wariness making her take notice of all the small details about him that didn't add up, but it seemed Helen had noticed them, as well.

She and Helen drank their tea and ate the cake in silence. It was nice to be back to normal, some of the tension from the past weeks forgotten. But there was something that Sophronia had been putting off telling Helen, and she was not going to like it. She stole a glance at her friend, wishing she didn't have to snap the fragile thread that was holding them together.

"The Marshalls are holding a ball to welcome Mr. Stone formally to the town." Before Helen could protest, she added, "I'm going."

The moment that the minister had invited her, she had made up her mind that she would go. Seeing his usually unreadable eyes fill with hope had stolen her breath. She wanted to see that again. She wanted any little scrap of him that she could get her hands on.

But instead of the outburst Sophronia had anticipated, Helen went completely still, the color draining from her face. She set down her teacup with a jolt, sending tea sloshing over the side. Somehow, seeing her so quietly and completely distraught was worse than a fit of anger.

"Oh?" Helen asked, not looking up from the puddle of tea that was spreading on the table.

The truth was that Sophronia wasn't even sure that she would be able to stage a repeat of her jaunt to town the previous day. In the warm afterglow of her accomplishment, she felt invincible, but she was Safe in the kitchen having tea; who knew if she would be able to find the strength to go to the Marshalls' house when the day came? Perhaps she had already tapped all the courage in her shallow reserve.

Leaning over, she touched a light hand to Helen's cheek. "You know that I value our time together and am so grateful for…for everything you've done for me. But I'm tired of being cooped up in this house." She didn't add that it was Helen's protection that she found suffocating, or that Gabriel Stone's presence had sowed a restlessness deep within her. "Mr. Stone has brought new ideas into Pale Harbor and I think it's time that—"

"New ideas!" Helen let out a huff of irritation. "I was at that sermon, and I can tell you the only new idea was that a minister should bury his nose in his notes and mumble through the psalms."

Sophronia flinched at Helen's harsh assessment of the man she so admired. "Well, I still want to go to the ball. It could be good, a way for the town to see that I am not their enemy, and that I won't be cowed by threats."

Helen's mouth twisted into a petulant frown. "You always laugh at them for their boorish ways and stuffy little parties. Why should you suddenly care what they think?"

"I *don't* care what they think," Sophronia said. "I can still go to funerals and functions, and even balls, without doing so for want of improved public opinion." She let out a breath and weighed her next words carefully. "Why don't you come with me?"

She didn't really want Helen to come. She didn't want another test of her courage dampened by an escort. She didn't want her time with the minister to occur under Helen's disapproving stare. But for the sake of extending the olive branch, she would risk Helen saying yes.

She needn't have worried. Helen's brows nearly flew off her face. "And what would the likes of me do at a ball? Really, Sophy. Can you imagine me fussed up in a silk gown with a dance card dangling from my wrist?"

"Don't be silly." But Helen was right; Sophronia couldn't imagine her dressed up and dancing. She couldn't imagine her anywhere besides Castle Carver, doing anything besides making her charms, tending her herbs and fussing over Sophronia.

"Well, I guess I'm silly, then," Helen said, suddenly scraping back her chair and standing up. "I'm going to the carriage house to change the raven's dressings."

Sophronia watched as she swept out of the room. They had almost gone a full day without fighting. Granted, they hadn't even seen each other most of the day, but now they were right back to where they had left off. Letting out a long breath, she rubbed at the tension in her temple. Why couldn't Helen be happy for her that she was outgrowing her fear?

Her annoyance at Helen was short-lived, though, as she slipped into a reverie about what gown she should dust off. All her dresses were at least five years out-of-date, but Fanny would help her add some new trim and buttons and do something clever with her hair.

Putting the remains of their unfinished tea away, Sophronia went back to the parlor. The stack of submissions on her desk was in danger of toppling over, but she wasn't in the mood for fanciful stories or long-winded essays. Instead, she curled up on the sofa with Hawthorne's *Twice-Told Tales*.

The house was still, the only sounds the fire crackling in the hearth and the crisp turning of pages. She was just starting to lose herself in the story when a sound from somewhere beyond the parlor pulled her from her book. Sitting up straighter, she paused with her thumb holding her place and strained her ear. How cavalier she had felt just an hour ago, sitting snug in the kitchen with Helen, and how easily she had almost forgotten about the unnerving messages that had plagued her for months.

Suddenly, Helen seemed very far away in the carriage house.

With trembling hands, she took up an andiron from the hearth and made her way through the house on tiptoes. The noise came again, a raspy, scraping thud, as if someone were throwing their weight against the door, and then it stopped. When she reached the front door, she closed her eyes and took a deep breath. She threw it open and then stepped back, the andiron raised over her shoulder.

There was nothing except darkness. Sophronia let out a gasp of relief, her hand slackening around the andiron. Perhaps she had imagined the noise; perhaps it was a manifestation of nerves that had been badly tested these past weeks.

But then it came again, louder this time. Upstairs. Maybe Helen hadn't gone to the carriage house after all, and was doing something in one of the bedchambers. Closing the front door, Sophronia grabbed a lamp in her other hand and made her way upstairs. The sound was coming from Nathaniel's bedchamber. What on earth would Helen be doing in there? Then another, more chilling, thought: what if it wasn't Helen at all, but the perpetrator of the notes, the ravens, the candles?

She forced her heavy feet up the stairs, dreading reaching the landing. Heart in her throat, she clasped the doorknob to the bedchamber and turned it.

Nothing. Darkness greeted her. This time the sound came again, almost right in front of her nose.

And that's when she saw the open window casement. Dusky moonlight reflected off the glass as it creaked open and shut in the wind, the purple curtains rustling and billowing into the room. The wind—that's all it had been.

Her body went light with relief. She could have cried, but it was laughter that bubbled up and spilled out of her. God, what was happening to her? Had she conquered her fear of leaving the house only to fall prey to the terror of an old window in the wind? Laughing until tears streamed down her face, she slid down the wall and let the andiron fall from her hand.

16

Gabriel stood on the porch of the Marshalls' house, adjusting his necktie for the umpteenth time. He didn't normally wear the things, but Fanny had balked when he admitted that he was planning on wearing his usual tweed suit with a vest and unpolished boots. This had precipitated a flurry of activity from Fanny that included giving him a good, close shave and rummaging through his unpacked trunks until she'd found his only good waistcoat and tails. The last time he'd worn them was Anna's funeral, and it was a minor miracle the moths hadn't gotten to them first. When he'd looked in the mirror, he had hardly recognized the face reflected back at him.

It was kind of the Marshalls to throw a ball in his honor, but as he finally loosened the tie enough to breathe, he wished they hadn't. There would be stifling small talk, inquiries about the church and gossip about Mrs. Carver. The first bored him, the second unnerved him and the third angered him to his core.

The only thing that kept him from turning around and going home was the slender chance that Mrs. Carver herself might come. Then he thought of the scene at the funeral, and his hopes deflated. She wouldn't come, not after that.

And yet his blood ran a little hotter at the thought of seeing her again.

Taking a deep breath, Gabriel knocked on the door. It opened, but there was no one there. He swung his gaze down and saw the little girl blinking up at him.

"Oh, it's you," said one of the twins. "You're late."

"Flora!" Mrs. Marshall bustled over. "Mr. Stone, come in," she said apologetically, shooing Flora out of the way.

Mr. Marshall intercepted them. "It's good to see you, and under better circumstances than last time."

The faint din of laughter and conversation floated down the hall. "It was kind of you to arrange this," Gabriel said, trying to shore up some sense of gratitude. Without a beard to hide behind, his discomfort was probably writ large on his face.

But if Mr. Marshall noticed, he didn't say anything. "Think nothing of it, the least we could do. Come," he said, leading him into the dining room. "Ah, there's Mr. Cushing. Will you excuse me? Have some punch, enjoy yourself."

He left Gabriel alone in the growing crush of people. It seemed everyone from the dockworkers like Manuel and Jasper, to business acquaintances of the Marshalls' from neighboring towns had been invited. The furniture had been cleared, and a trio of string musicians were tuning their instruments. People clustered at the edges of the room, their chatter competing with the tentative notes. Gabriel turned to make his way to an empty corner where he could watch the dancing from a distance, but he was ambushed by Harriet Wiggins, all dimples and bouncing ringlets.

"Mr. Stone!" She snapped a lace fan and began fanning herself as if it were the height of summer and not a bleak October night. "There you are!"

Just his luck. "Miss Wiggins," he said, "I didn't realize you had arrived."

She gave him a theatrically hurt look. "You naughty man... I've been waiting for you by the refreshments, but you were brooding so intently in the corner I was half afraid to approach you!"

"My apologies," he murmured without looking at her.

Tuned and plucked, the instruments were ready, and the trio struck out the first notes of a country dance. As Gabriel listened to Miss Wiggins chatter, he watched the first children take the floor, giddy at being up so late and twirling each other in dizzying circles. Soon, adult couples were joining them. Was it possible that one of them was responsible for the gruesome events around Pale Harbor? Was one of them Mrs. Carver's tormentor?

He was so lost in his thoughts that he didn't realize that Miss Wiggins had been asking him a question.

"Excuse me?"

"I asked if you would be dancing tonight?"

"No," he said shortly.

Her face fell. "That's too bad. You're still young, and minister or no, a man ought to be able to kick up his heels on occasion. And there are so many nice young ladies in Pale Harbor who would love to dance, I'm sure." She cleared her throat meaningfully, and peeped at him from behind her fan with expectant eyes.

But Gabriel had stopped listening. All the conversations, the music and the buzz of excitement fell away until a pin dropping could have shattered the silence.

She had come.

There in the doorway stood Mrs. Carver, drawn up as tall and elegant as she had been the day of the funeral. Gone was the mourning gown, replaced by purple silk that dipped low across her chest, setting off her slender shoulders and swan's neck. She was an early spring crocus in snow, a burst of brilliant amethyst against the pale shades of the ball.

Miss Wiggins broke off, following his gaze. Her face darkened. "Oh," she said with obvious dismay, "I did not imagine she would come."

Gabriel's attention did not waver away from the magnificent figure in the doorway. "Your uncle said the whole town turned out to welcome me. Surely you would not exclude Mrs. Carver?"

"I suppose, but you must have heard the rumors." Miss Wiggins watched in petulant silence as Mrs. Carver gracefully shed her cloak and smiled at the servant who took it from her, before tugging Gabriel by the arm. "I want to dance," she said playfully. "Come dance with me."

Before he could object, she was latching on to his arm and pulling him onto the dance floor. It would have been nothing for him to unpry her fingers and send her on her way, but even he wasn't so cruel that he would cause a scene. "I don't know the steps," he protested.

"Nonsense. I'll show you."

The music started, and Miss Wiggins tugged and positioned him until he fell into awkward step with her. Gabriel caught Mrs. Carver's eye as Miss Wiggins guided his arm up to her shoulder. Mrs. Carver gave him a small nod of the head, her expression one of mild bemusement.

God, she radiated. Her lips didn't move, but he could hear her calling out to him, pulling him to her like the moon beckoned the wave ashore. It was vital that she not think he had sought Miss Wiggins out, that he was actually enjoying himself in her company when the only woman he wanted to be with was across the room.

"I did so enjoy your sermon the other day," Miss Wiggins said as they took an awkward spin.

"You did?"

"Oh, yes. You speak very well. So many folks around here hardly know their letters, let alone high-minded philosophies and the like."

He barely heard her. Mrs. Carver was sharing a word with the driver Reuben Reese, and he longed to know what they were talking about. She was probably just arranging a time for Mr. Reese to return with the hack, but Gabriel burned with jealousy all the same.

Miss Wiggins gave an impatient cough. "Maybe you aren't as good a listener as you are a speaker."

This brought him back to his manners. "I'm not used to such formal functions. You must forgive me."

She was quick to accept his apology and did so by making a show of smiling up at him so that Mrs. Carver would see. When the music ended, Gabriel gave her a courteous bow, his heart and mind already across the room.

"Oh, won't you dance again?" Miss Wiggins asked.

"I wouldn't deprive the other young men of a chance for your company." Though there were few other men close to her age aside from Jasper and Manuel, who were nursing their drinks in the corner. "Would you excuse me? I must..." Gabriel's words trailed off as he left her on the dance floor, not waiting for a response.

Once he had broken free of the pouting Miss Wiggins, getting to Mrs. Carver was easy; everyone stood an arm's length from her. Mr. Reese had departed, and she stood alone with a crystal glass in her hand.

"You came," he said mildly, his thundering pulse belying his elation at being so close to her.

"I was watching you dance," she said, lifting the glass to her lips. "You seem to have a talent for putting your feet in all the wrong places."

There was a flash of amusement in her eyes, and it sent a corresponding jolt of wanting through him. "And it seems you have a talent for showing up places where you weren't invited." He gave her a challenging lift of his brow, knowing that she would rise to his playful provocation.

The spar was worth it. She pressed her lips, trying to hide a smile, but her eyes were alive with delight. If the journey from Castle Carver had cost her, it did not show on her face. "Now, that's not fair. I received an invitation from the highly esteemed guest of honor himself."

"He's very glad you accepted it."

"Is he?" She held his gaze, searching his face. After the funeral, there had been a shift, an expectation that their next meeting would be different. He had felt it deep within his bones when she'd lingered on the step above him in the descending dusk. He'd seen the glimmer of vulnerability in her eyes, a wall that begged to be torn down. Now as she stood before him, resplendent in her deep cut gown of amethyst, he knew he had not been mistaken.

"And where is the lovely Miss Helen tonight?"

She gave him a warning look and he feigned innocence.

"What? Only a guard dog doesn't usually stray far from its master's heels."

Her face darkened and then she swept her gaze away. "You mustn't poke fun at Helen. She may be as pathetic as a lost puppy, but she is as loyal as one, too."

He didn't want to talk about Helen anyway. He didn't want to talk about anyone or anything other than the woman before him. If only they were alone. He wanted every flick of her gaze, every ounce of her to himself.

"Mrs. Carver, would you do me the honor of dancing with me?" His voice came out remarkably confident, considering he felt as if his heart might burst right through his ribs.

She put down her glass and then pressed her hand into his. "I thought you would never ask." Her arched brow said he was forgiven for teasing her about Helen.

"You may regret that I did," he said. "I don't know any of the steps."

She dipped her head with the hint of a smile. "I'll consider myself warned. But this one isn't difficult. I won't let you get lost."

He didn't ask how she knew the latest dance steps when she had only just set foot outside her house for the first time in years. He was happy enough to give himself over to her, to follow her lead and smell the sweet scent of rosewater in her wake.

He could feel the eyes of every single person in the room on them as if they were needles drilling into his back. Conversations, which had stopped when he had approached her, now started again in whispers. But Mrs. Carver glided onto the dance floor as if she hadn't a care in the world, and so he endeavored to do the same, and pretended she was the only other person in the room. It was easy enough to do with her silver eyes glittering up at him, a half-quirked smile pulling at her lips. She had done something different to her hair that he couldn't really describe, except that the glossy black locks were elaborately braided and twined like a crown atop her heart-shaped face.

They slid easily into the dance, Mrs. Carver gently leading the way. "Mr. Stone," she said, "you are a dreadful liar."

"I am?"

She nodded, eyes sparkling. "You said you could not dance."

"I think," he said, "it has more to do with my partner than anything else."

But she just pursed her lips and looked over his shoulder. When they spun, he saw that she had been looking at Miss

Wiggins, who was seething with a glass of punch in her hands as she watched them from across the room.

"Poor Harriet," Mrs. Carver said. "She's been waiting for an eligible man to come to this town for years. Just her luck that the first one to move here is a minister who lacks all social graces and has two left feet."

He pinched her waist in retribution, and she let out an unbridled laugh, musical and warm, which shot straight through him.

When the music stopped, there was polite applause from the onlookers, and the couples bowed to each other. He loathed to let her go, but he stood back and gave her a little bow. Laughing, she swept a low curtsy. "I can't remember the last time I danced, other than with Helen, of course."

He prickled with jealousy. How quickly territorial feelings sprang up though he had no claim on her.

Leading her away from the hostile stares and whispers, he stationed her next to the punch bowl while he ladled them out a cup each of sparkling pink liquid. They drank in silence until Mrs. Carver asked, "Have you given any more thought to the connections between the…incidents…to Mr. Poe? Try as I might, I cannot understand the correlation."

It took Gabriel a moment to realize what she was talking about. He felt a pang of shame that he had actually given very little thought to the strange connection to Poe they had uncovered since that night. Things had seemed quieter since Garrett's death, with no new threats against Mrs. Carver or strange occurrences in town. "No, I'm afraid not."

"But that's why you're here, isn't it? To pry into the matters of the town?" Her gaze held his, hard, and he had the feeling that perhaps she knew more about him than he would care for her to.

"I'm here to minister to Pale Harbor," he said carefully.

She gave a dismissive shrug, as if she not only didn't believe him, but didn't care what his true motives might be.

The musicians were tuning up again, and soon a waltz started. Gabriel looked around at the small crowd. There was no one else he wanted to talk to. He didn't want to dance with Harriet Wiggins, or suffer through a lecture from Mr. Marshall. He stepped in closer to Mrs. Carver, her rosewater scent intoxicating him more than the strongest punch. "Will you dance again?"

But she didn't seem to hear him. She had gone very pale. "Do you know what song this is?"

Frowning, he listened, trying to pick out the melody. "No, but I don't really know any—"

She gave an impatient shake of her head. "It's 'The Merry Widow Waltz.'"

Oh, Christ. His fist clenched at his side. "Wait here. I'll go talk to them and—"

"No." She stopped him with a hand to his sleeve. "I want to dance it, with you." Her eyes were serious, searching his face for affirmation. She was just as anxious as he was. Without another word, he took her by the hand and led her back out to the middle of the room.

This time there was no laughing over missed steps, no quick smiles when they took a particularly daring turn. This dance was something different entirely. This dance was a question and an answer. Did she want to feel the weight of his hand on her waist as badly as he wanted to feel the warmth of her? She did, she answered by leaning just the smallest bit closer. Would she be able to sleep tonight? he asked. No, she might never be able to sleep again, she answered, with parted lips and a gaze that burned him to his core.

The song ended, another started, and they continued dancing as if the music hadn't even stopped. He had never known how badly he ached for this. Even with Anna he'd never been allowed to be tender before. She had wanted him to be a strong oak tree, a canopy that provided her with shelter, a place against which to rest her back without bending, and he had felt it his duty to oblige. Now, he could feel years of armor crumbling off him.

Guests were starting to leave. Flushed and sparkling, Mrs. Carver finally broke the spell. "I should probably go so that Helen won't have to keep the lamps on for me," she said. "And you have guests to bid thanks to."

Gabriel looked about at the emptying room. He should have been ashamed that this party had been thrown for him, and he had spent the entire time in the company of one person. He felt a pang of guilt, but mostly he was only sorry the music had finally ended. No one had even tried to speak to him after he'd laid claim to Mrs. Carver's dances. "You're right," he said, but did not make a move to leave her side.

She gave him a wistful smile. "Here, I'll make it easier for you." She slipped her hand away from his, breaking the link between them, and dropped a little curtsy. "Mr. Stone, it was a pleasure. You are most welcome in our town, and I look forward to attending your church."

"I hope that I will not have to wait every Sunday to see you?" He spoke lightly, but he already felt as if he were a man given water after a long drought and was afraid it would be snatched away just as quickly.

As an answer, she flashed a disarming smile that lit her soul from within. But just as she was turning toward the hall, Jasper Gibbs came shoving past her, hands in his pockets and elbows out.

Clipped backward, she stumbled into Gabriel. Instinctively his arms clamped around her, steadying her. He could feel the pounding of her heart through her bodice.

"Have a care, Mr. Gibbs," he shouted as Jasper stalked off into the night. "Goddamn brute," he added in a mutter. "Are you all right?"

She forced a smile. "Fine, I'm fine. I'm sure it was an accident."

Gabriel was sure it was no such thing. From behind them in the dining room he could hear hushed titters. Damn them all. And damn him. He'd asked her to come, willed her to come, and now he'd opened her up to yet more abuse.

"Mr. Stone?"

He looked down to see Mrs. Carver studying him as if reading his thoughts. "My hack is here. Thank you for inviting me." She gave his hand a gentle squeeze. "I'm glad I came."

After Sophronia left, Helen stood by the window, knotting her fingers together and losing herself in her thoughts. Her friend wasn't the same anymore. She wandered about with her head in a fog, smiling to herself, humming—singing, even!—as if only her body occupied this world, and her spirit was somewhere else, somewhere secret. Somewhere Helen could not follow.

Helen should have been angry with Sophronia, with the minister, but all she felt was a numbing sense of grief. She had lost her Sophy. It was always supposed to be the two of them together. Helen had envisioned a life of endless summer days stretching on as their hair silvered, picking blueberries together on the hill and laughing over cups of tea in the evening. All her spells and charms couldn't make Sophronia stay.

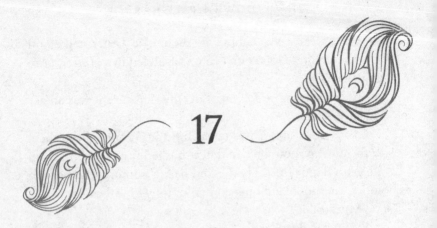

17

Sophronia walked out into the crisp October air, her righteous indignation keeping her warmer than her light cloak. Her fingers curled around the letter she carried at her side, a response to the query she had sent to the churches in Concord after she and Mr. Stone had spent the evening piecing together clues from Mr. Poe's stories. She had still been a bundle of confused feelings about the handsome yet rough young man who claimed to be a minister. Though she was drawn to him, she had still nursed a deep suspicion that he couldn't possibly be a minister, not when he didn't seem to know the first thing about the philosophical school of thought he claimed to preach. Still, she had foolishly hoped that she was wrong.

The walk through town was invigorating, and some of the novelty of being outside the grounds of Castle Carver returned. Now that she had broken through the wall of her fear, the freedom was intoxicating. She wanted to go farther, to walk until her legs could carry her no more, until her lungs burst. She wanted to make up for lost time, smell all the flowers that grew just too far away for her to have ever smelled before, see the hills that lay just out of sight. Most of all, she wanted to feel her heart beat faster and her stomach flip when she laid eyes on the minister. She wanted to feel all the things that she thought had died in her when she married Nathaniel. But she couldn't do any of that until she confronted Gabriel Stone and learned the truth.

At first, Mr. Stone had been a diversion, a fresh face and good conversation in a place where she had grown used to stagnancy. But the more she saw him, the more he had insinuated himself in her thoughts, making her blood run hot and her body ache with wanting.

And then they had danced.

Dancing with the minister had been nothing like the childish fancy in which she and Helen indulged on occasion. His hands on her, the solid warmth of his body, had been an awakening. How extraordinary it seemed that she had been sleeping so long, simply going through the motions, thinking that she was truly alive. And yet, it was not new. When she looked up into his eyes, it felt as if she had always known him and had only been waiting for him to come to her.

And now look where her heart had gotten her. He had made a fool of her. Her newfound freedom, her confidence, all of it she owed to him. She could not even have her own accomplishments; they must be attributed to a man—and a man who would swindle her, no less.

The church door opened easily. Someone had taken the time to sand and polish the ancient door and paint it a crisp, bright red. The churches of her youth in New York had been drafty, forbidding stone affairs with marble columns designed to make one feel small and insignificant. But this little church was warm and welcoming, with flowers pinned to the end of each pew and a simple, whitewashed altar. With the late-afternoon sun shafting in the narrow stained-glass windows, it was breathtaking. How could this man—who was not a minister, as the letter in her pocket told her—accomplish something so special?

She found him out back, sleeves rolled to his elbows, collar open despite the chill in the air, as he brought an ax down and splintered an old wooden beam. When he didn't turn around, she gave an impatient clearing of her throat.

He wasn't a man given to broad smiles, but when he turned and saw her, his lips twitched ever so slightly at the corners of his mouth. "Mrs. Carver," he said, discarding the ax and wiping his hands on a cloth. "To what do I owe the pleasure?"

She'd had a carefully planned speech all laid out, demanding answers and listing all the reasons he ought to be ashamed. But when she saw his hazel eyes light up at the sight of her, her heart lurched. Damn him. She wanted to be angry with him and couldn't be, and that only made her all the more furious.

"Pleasure? I'm not here on *pleasure*," she spat out.

He opened his mouth to say something, but she would not let him get the upper hand in this.

"Who *are* you? I wrote to the minister of the First Church in Concord," she said, waving the crumpled paper at him. "They said the name of the minister they were sending to Pale Harbor was Joshua Whipple, and that he had died. There's no record of a Gabriel Stone ever having preached anywhere in Concord before."

It was quiet behind the church, the only sound in the cold stillness the echo of a foghorn from the harbor. The minister did not move.

"I am who I say I am," he said evenly. "Gabriel Stone."

Oh, but he thought he was cool and clever. She had been ready for him to crumple before her, begging her forgiveness, but he didn't look the least bit perturbed or apologetic. Heat rushed back to her face and she spluttered, "Very well. Who is Gabriel Stone then, if not a minister? Why has he come to Pale

Harbor under such a ruse, and to what purpose? Because I can assure you that neither Pale Harbor nor I have need of you."

She sucked in her breath, stunned at the force of her speech. In the first few months of her marriage, she had been foolish enough to defend herself against Nathaniel, contradicting him when he was in the wrong, and she had paid dearly for it. Why had she let her outrage get the better of her now? Mr. Stone was twice the size of Nathaniel. She waited for him to fly in a rage at her, now that he had been discovered.

But the man named Gabriel Stone just gave a slow nod and lowered himself down onto the stump where he had been chopping wood. "All right," he said. "What do you want to know?"

Caught off guard at his sudden capitulation, Sophronia struggled to put her questions in order. "Why did you come here?"

He leveled a long, unreadable look at her, and then shrugged. "For the same reason anyone has for moving to a new place. A fresh start."

"And your fresh start required you to fabricate a story about yourself? It required that you found a church based on principles in which you hold no belief?"

"Sit down, Mrs. Carver."

Even if she had wanted to, there was nowhere in the overgrown churchyard to sit, save for the crumbling back steps, and she was not about to share the stump with Mr. Stone. "I prefer to stand."

"Very well. My wife died nearly a year ago," he said simply.

The sour words Sophronia had been holding in her throat withered away. "Oh, I'm so—"

He stopped her with a look that said he didn't want to hear it. "It was Anna's dream to be part of the transcendentalist movement. It was all around us in Concord. She loved going to the salons of great thinkers and debating the latest essays. But I, Mrs. Carver, am no great thinker."

She wasn't sure if this was true. After all, he had stood in her parlor discussing the schools of artists on her walls with an eye that was both refined and sensitive. But then, he had so clearly been out of his depth when it came to the most basic tenets of transcendentalism. "No? Then what are you?"

"I'm a nobody. After I left the navy, I became a copyist, transcribing the words of greater men than me for pennies on the page. My wife—" he swallowed, and Sophronia realized that this was not going to be what she had expected "—Anna, that is, she loved reading the pages I was paid to copy, and she developed an infatuation with the minister, Joshua Whipple. They met, and eventually she ran off with him."

Pausing, he squinted up into the clouds as if looking for an answer there. Then he absently rubbed his jaw, sighing. "He was the man I could never be," he continued. "I convinced her to come back to me, and she did. But she was not happy, and she died in childbirth not long after. When I learned Joshua Whipple had died, too—in a carriage accident—I decided to come to Pale Harbor in his place. I decided to be the man Anna had wanted me to be. I came for her."

He went on to tell her that it had not been enough to have him simply writing the words; Anna had wanted him to be the source that produced them, as well. Sophronia could not help but be touched by pity for him, for his ordeal, yet found herself angry at Anna Stone. Why would she marry a man she did not respect, who didn't represent the things that were so clearly important to her?

His gaze was apprehensive, but Sophronia could hardly shepherd her scattered thoughts. Shame, relief and jealousy shot through her. He wasn't here to comb through her past, but he was deceiving people. He wasn't who he said he was, but then again, neither was she. Did he still love his wife? He must have, if he had come here for her. But then what of the dance that they had shared? Surely she had not been imagining the possessive touch of his hand on her lower back, the flare of his pupils when she smiled up at him?

Suddenly, her mouth was very dry. "I thought... That is..."

He stood up, crossing his arms and looking at her with heartbreaking earnestness. "What did you think, Mrs. Carver?"

The naked desire she had seen in his eyes the night of the dance—that had not been pretense, then. He'd nothing to gain by trying to seduce her; there was no information he sought to glean from her. She took a hesitant step closer.

"Would you have told me, eventually?"

The breeze wound around them, sending gooseflesh blossoming down the back of her neck.

"Would you have wanted me to?" His gaze burned through her.

Wordlessly, she nodded. And then, "I want to know everything about you."

As if he had been waiting only for some unknowable signal, he nodded. Then he was moving toward her, his long legs closing the distance between them in two strides. He stopped just short of her, so close that he filled her vision, his body warming the air around her.

She could no more stop herself from reaching out to him than a drowning man could help reaching for a rope thrown into a churning sea. With a tentative finger, she touched his chest, drawing her finger down the rough fabric of his open linen shirt.

His breath caught, his chest muscles tightening beneath her fingers. When Sophronia gathered the courage to look up at him, there was no mistaking the want simmering in his eyes. His hands slid around her waist, warm and firm, drawing her closer to him. They stood like two dancers waiting for the first notes of a song that would never come. Everything else melted away: the veil of fear that had hung over her for the last months, the jealousy and shock of learning of his wife, Helen's disapproval. There was only him and her, the ocean breeze binding them together.

18

His kiss was so warm, and so, so good. Her lips gently parted as she invited him in deeper, his tongue sending shivers of pleasure through her body. She had never been touched like this before, never touched anyone *else* like this before. If her mind had been hungry for fresh ideas, then her body was downright ravenous for the thrill of contact. If only she could give herself fully to him, secrets and all, but there was a part of her she dared not show.

When she finally had to pull away for want of air, Mr. Stone was looking down at her with bright eyes, and lips so deliciously swollen that it took everything in her not to reach up and kiss him again. He seemed to have grown six inches taller, his large frame relaxed, his light brown hair adorably tousled. "You've no idea how long I've wanted to do that," he murmured.

The only reply she could muster was a breathy, "Gabriel."

At his name, his strong hands tightened around her waist, and her body thrummed with joy, every beat of her heart a triumphant cry of *Alive! Alive! Alive!* She didn't tell him that no matter how long he had been waiting, she had been waiting longer. Lifetimes longer.

★ ★ ★

The walk home had been cold and gray, the raspy cry of ravens echoing in the damp air around her. By the time she had reached the drive, dusk was gathering fast. A lamp was burning in the upper window of the carriage house; Helen must have gone to lick her wounds after their spat.

Well, Helen could wait. Sophronia unlocked the front door and made her way inside the house, humming to herself as she shook off her wet cloak and unlaced her boots. Lost in the glowing memories of the kiss that had left her shaking, she almost missed the note tacked above the mirror in the front hall. Fanny must have left it for her after she had done the laundry that afternoon. Removing the tack, she took the note with her into the parlor, where she unfolded it by the light of the dying fire.

Her heart stopped in her chest as she took in the sparse lines. Paralyzed, she read them over again. Then she picked up her skirts and ran through the house, out the door and to the carriage house.

"Helen!" she yelled when she was only halfway there. "Helen, come out here!"

She was barely to the door when Helen appeared, her temple etched with concern. "Sophy?" Taking Sophronia by the shoulders, she peered at her in the gathering dark. "What is it? Are you all right?"

Pulling out of her grasp, Sophronia thrust the note at Helen. "Did you write this? Is this your idea of a joke?"

"What are you talking about?" She took the note from Sophronia's shaking hand. "It's too dark. I can't read it."

With a huff, Sophronia snatched the note back, reciting the message that had already burned itself into her memory. "'A merry widow you may be, but your waltzing days are numbered.'"

She felt Helen stiffen in the darkness at her words. "I didn't write that," she said roughly.

"No? Then would you care to explain why it was waiting for me in the house when I returned from my walk? You were seething with jealousy when I went to the ball, and don't think I haven't noticed the way you look at Mr. Stone like he's evil incarnate. Besides, who else could have left it?"

"This...this was inside of the house?"

Sophronia didn't say anything, but something in Helen's voice told her that she really hadn't known about the note.

"Fanny was here, but she was with me the entire time she was folding the linens."

Of course Fanny couldn't have left it. The girl was too sweet, too simple. But if it wasn't her or Helen, then who could it be, and how did they get inside Castle Carver?

As if she had been following Sophronia's thoughts, Helen sucked in her breath. "Whoever left that...they could still be in the house." Before Sophronia could let the horror of that statement sink in, Helen was striding back down the path. "Wait here," she called over her shoulder.

Sophronia stood still for barely a heartbeat before she hurried to catch up. "I'm coming with you."

Helen stopped and looked like she wanted to say something, but she just nodded. Sophronia allowed Helen to take her by the hand, and they made their way to the house together.

Gabriel stood in the prickly dusk long after Mrs. Carver had gone. Evening settled around him like a heavy mantle, baptizing him in cold, fresh air. He closed his eyes, savoring the faraway sound of the waves, remembering the way she had fit into his arms as if she were made for him.

Then, as if touched by an epiphany, he bolted to the church office, began pawing through papers and writing in a fever of inspiration. If he had been struggling to make sense of the creed he claimed to preach, Sophronia Carver had come and released the dam within him. Sermons that he had struggled to scrape together from other men's ideas suddenly spilled out of him. Words flowed from his pen as if his hand were being guided, as if he were merely a conduit for the breathy song of the universe.

He had never felt anything remotely like this with Anna. Gabriel might have eased the burden of his soul in divulging his true identity to Mrs. Carver, but he had not obliterated the guilt he felt about his wife. Worse still, this was what Anna had wanted from him, a font of enlightenment of which she was the wellspring. He had attained it, but at the expense of her memory.

And what of Mrs. Carver? She knew his secret now, but he couldn't help but feel she wasn't telling him everything of herself. There had been something guarded in her eyes when they'd pulled away from each other. Did she not feel what he felt? Did she not see the same promises in his eyes reflected back at her?

When he got home, there was a letter waiting for him. Perhaps it was from Mrs. Carver, dashed off and delivered after their assignation. Perhaps there were things better communicated through writing, and she had decided to tell him after all. Shrugging off his coat, he retrieved a bottle of wine from the cellar, and settled down in front of the fire to read it.

It wasn't from Mrs. Carver, but his good friend Tom, and the letter was just like Tom himself: teasing, good-humored, and full of gossip and stories from Concord. He asked about the church and the mysterious Mrs. Carver—causing Gabriel to color slightly as he remembered he'd confessed his initial doubt as to her innocence to his friend.

If it would not intrude too much upon your newfound country idyll, I would propose a visit at the end of the month, as business brings me to Manchester, and Pale Harbor is only the matter of a short jaunt by ship from there. I should very much like to see this church you have lovingly built up from ashes and moldering wood, and the congregation that fills it. And, if pressed, I suppose I might just want to see my dear friend, too.

It would be good to see Tom again. Gabriel missed him terribly, and if nothing else, he desperately needed to talk to someone about the building storm of emotions within him.

There was no one in the house. They had gone room to room, Sophronia armed with the andiron, and Helen with Nathaniel's old hunting rifle. But when they had finally reached the piazza and found it empty, it became clear that whoever had left the note had not lingered.

"I'm staying in your dressing room tonight," Helen announced as they returned downstairs. "And tomorrow I'm going to make a new protection charm for you. I have marjoram, but I will have to get cloves from the grocer."

Sophronia opened her mouth to protest, but Helen stopped her. "Sophy, this is more than just the antics of children. Whoever is behind all this is targeting you for something sinister."

She was right, and although Sophronia put little stock into Helen's charms, she wouldn't refuse any form of protection. After they had said good-night and Helen had made up a bed for herself in the small dressing room off the bedchamber, Sophronia closed her eyes. What she wouldn't give to be back in the overgrown churchyard with Mr. Stone's strong arms around her, his hips pressed against hers. Even with the plush carpet under her feet, the floor felt cold, and the windows turned inward on her, watching as she undressed and brushed her hair. Her house had been invaded, and she had been violated. Castle Carver was no longer Safe.

If she were going to be at risk, she might as well be on her own terms.

Following her hadn't been difficult.

Sophronia had been lost in her thoughts, oblivious to the world around her as she marched down the hill. At first it had appeared that she had no intention of going to see that vile Mr. Stone, for she had gone down by the water and spent a good while turning over a piece of paper in her hands as she stared sightlessly out into the harbor. But then she had turned back toward the main road, and Helen's stomach had soured as she realized Sophronia meant to go to the church after all.

After she had disappeared inside, Helen had waited behind the gnarled old elm tree across from the church. Then, as quiet as a mouse, she slipped in behind her. Their voices had led her down the aisle and around the altar to the back door.

Creeping closer to the door, which stood ajar, she pressed herself flat, then peeked in through the gap between the hinges. Sophronia's back was toward her, the vibrant corn-flower blue of her dress shifting subtly in the overcast after-noon. How bright she looked in the overgrown churchyard, and how terribly out of place. If she could have, Helen would have run to her, taken her by the hand and spirited her away from that common minister and his church, back home where she belonged.

They were just out of earshot, but they were arguing. Soph-ronia's color was high as she gestured vehemently at him, but the minister appeared unruffled. When he finally spoke, it was low and soft. Then something shifted in the air, and there was no mistaking the hungry look in his eyes as he moved toward Sophronia.

Would Helen have hated the minister less if he were cold and boorish to her mistress like so many others in the town? Shouldn't she be happy—grateful, even—that Gabriel Stone recognized Sophronia for the extraordinary woman she was? Helen's fingers curled into the quilt. No, nothing would change the fact that he had no right to her company and good opinion. Hadn't Sophronia learned anything? How could she give herself to a man like that? What had it all been for, if she was just going to run off and make the same painful mistakes all over again?

The minister had his arms wrapped around her, as if he had a right to touch her, to even *look* at her, and there he was grasping her and pulling her into his chest. And the thing of it was, Sophronia had clearly *liked* it! She gave herself to him willingly, hungrily, as if she had never wanted anything so badly in her life before. It made Helen sick.

It had been too much. Stumbling back through the church, Helen had just barely made it to the tree, where she doubled over, unable to catch her breath. *But should another love thee, untethered ye shall be.* How on earth would she keep Sophronia safe now?

As she lay on the hard cot in the dressing room, Helen pushed away the memories of similar nights spent in the poorhouse, when all she could think about was how hungry she was and what would become of her. But now, it was not worry for herself that kept her up into the small hours of the morning. If the minister broke the spell, then Sophronia would be in peril. And right now, it looked very much like he was going to.

19

Sophronia sat at her desk, biting her nails.

There was no use pretending that she was going to look at the packet of submissions that had arrived from Portland last week and was collecting dust on her desk. Concentrating would be an exercise in futility; her night had been sleepless, alternating between thrilling memories of Mr. Stone's soft lips on hers, and terror every time the wind scratched a branch against the window. But the longer she sat lost in her thoughts, the closer the walls pushed in around her, and the tighter her chest squeezed.

Helen was muttering her charms and drifting through the house in a cloud of sage smoke. "I have to go out," she said abruptly, cutting Helen off in the middle of a spell.

"Go out?" The sage dropped to Helen's side. She looked aghast at the suggestion. "Sophy, you can't even think of going out. I can make the house safe again, but it will take time. As for a protection charm, I still need clove and—"

Sophronia stopped her with an impatient flutter of her hand. She was so tired of magic that served no purpose other than giving Helen a sense of importance. "Someone was in my *home* last night," she said, standing and tucking the wretched note into her reticule. "I have to let the constable know."

This was partly true. She had every intention of notifying the constable, but she also knew that it was unlikely he would do anything to help her. He certainly hadn't been concerned enough to protect her when the town turned against her after Nathaniel's death. No, her real reason was much less altruistic; she wanted to see Mr. Stone again. He had confided in her about his past, shown himself to be trustworthy, and now it was her turn to do the same.

Gabriel stood in the damp hall of the old courthouse that served as both town hall and jailhouse, waiting for the constable who he had been assured would be back from a late lunch any moment.

After he'd read Tom's letter last night, he'd gone into the sitting room and found another letter waiting for him on the mantel. This one had been decidedly less friendly than Tom's. It hadn't been signed, but Gabriel didn't need a signature to know who it was from.

Eventually, the constable came bustling in the door, his complexion florid, crumbs from his lunch still dusting his lips. "Mr. Stone, good to see you again." He stuck out a clammy hand that lay limp in Gabriel's when they shook. "I heard you were looking for me. How may I be of service?"

Gabriel considered the man who had not seen fit to investigate anything that had occurred in the town up until this point. "I've received a threatening letter."

The constable's brows furrowed as Gabriel handed him the note. "I see, I see. And when did you receive this?"

"Last night. It was on my mantel when I came home."

The constable's lips moved as he read the letter to himself. Looking up, he gave Gabriel a not very subtle up-and-down assessment. "You'll excuse my saying so, Mr. Stone, but you're a...sizable man, and I hardly think there is anyone in Pale Harbor who would be fool enough to cross you. I shouldn't give it much thought if I were you."

Gabriel just stared at him, caught between the old shame of his ungainly size and wanting to use that size to land a blow that the constable wouldn't soon forget. But he was spared the need to decide when the door pushed open and Mrs. Carver stepped inside.

She was headed for the constable with single-minded determination, but when she saw Gabriel she stopped short, her lips pursing in surprise. "Mr. Stone," she said, her expression softening and sending warmth flooding through his body.

Constable Morris gave her a curt nod of his head. "Mrs. Carver, to what do I owe the pleasure?" His tone indicated that he considered her visit anything but. "I don't suppose you've received a *mysterious* letter, as well?" He gave Gabriel a wink, as if it were all part of some joke that they were both in on.

Mrs. Carver looked between him and Gabriel, her face registering surprise. "Yes," she said, producing a piece of paper from her reticule. "That is exactly why I'm here."

With a weary sigh, the constable took it from her. After he'd read it, he handed it back to her with a shrug. "Begging your pardon, ma'am, but I think it's safe to assume that this is the work of some young scamp. It's no secret that some of the children in town hold a special fascination with you."

Gabriel felt her stiffen beside him and resisted the urge to take the little man and shake him by the collar for his insolence. Anger flared in her eyes, and something told him that her usual facade of patience and grace was growing thin.

"Thank you, Constable," he said, swiftly taking her by the elbow before she could say anything she might regret. "I'll see Mrs. Carver home."

She looked as if she wanted to argue, but he pressed his fingers into her arm. "Not worth it," he whispered in her ear as he guided her to the door.

When they were outside, Mrs. Carver pulled her arm from his grasp with a peevish look. "What was that about?"

"He's not going to help us," Gabriel said. "But you didn't really think he would, did you?"

Her shoulders slumped. It was mizzling on the town green, the ocean breeze snatching at her dark hair and blowing it across her face. He resisted the urge to reach out and tuck it behind her ear. "No, I didn't. I only thought that someone ought to know." She bit at her lip before meeting his gaze. "You got one, too. What does yours say?"

Gabriel handed her the note. He'd already memorized the nonsense lines. "From nothing I have built my throne in this kingdom by the sea, and I am death and death becomes me. I look gigantically down, and see that unworthy are you and she."

Grimacing, she handed it back to him. "The rhyming scheme is atrocious, and it's not just referencing one of Mr. Poe's poems, it's downright derivative... I've read something almost exactly like this."

"You recognize it?" He was impressed; after reading and rereading it last night, he hadn't been able to make heads nor tails of it.

"I can't recall the name of the poem, but I don't believe it ends happily. Here," she said, handing him the note from her reticule. "This was left in my parlor."

Gabriel read it, then read it again as tiny raindrops soaked into the paper, smearing the words. Anger simmered through him. "This is my fault," he said shortly.

She looked up at him in surprise. "What are you talking about?"

"Someone has noticed the time we've spent together, Mrs. Carver," he said, drawing his hand through his wet hair. "This is not the idle play of children. This is serious."

"Helen says the very same thing."

He couldn't believe he was saying it. "Helen is right."

With a huff she turned her face away, and stared off across the miserable town green. "Constable Morris is an idiot."

Gabriel couldn't argue with that. He hated seeing her upset, hated knowing how impotent she must feel for her charges to be dismissed out of hand. "Come on," he said suddenly. "Let's get out of here."

"I don't want to go home yet," she protested.

Turning his collar up against the rain, he raised a brow at her in challenge. "Who said anything about going home?"

By the time they had reached the top of the hill behind Castle Carver, Mrs. Carver's half-quirked smile had returned, and she was in high color. "Truly," she said, inhaling deeply, "I don't think there is any air so fresh and good as this."

The rain was still hanging in a mist about them, gilding her wool cloak with a mantle of droplets. But the rain didn't seem to bother her, and it would have taken a monsoon for Gabriel to deny her anything she wanted.

He watched her from the corner of his eye as she lowered herself down on the natural dip facing the harbor, heedless of the damp grass. As he sat down beside her, he let his sleeve just brush the edge of her cloak. How much closer he wanted to get to her. He couldn't stop reliving the memory of her supple lips under his, and he willed her to lean over and draw her finger down his chest again, making him dizzy with hunger for her.

Instead, she turned her head toward him on the grass, her gaze wistful. "What is Concord like?"

She could have asked him absolutely anything in that moment, and he would have answered her. If she wanted to know about Concord, he would paint her the most detailed picture he could muster, never mind the pain that it caused him.

In his mind's eye, he was standing on the old footbridge with Anna pale and drawn by his side, tossing pinecones into the water and watching them bob away. Then he was thinking of the animated discussions that took place in the tavern amid wood smoke and beer and oysters. "It can be a tranquil place, but there's an energy to it, too, because it is full of so many brilliant minds and new ideas. It's very picturesque, and folks from Boston will come in the autumn just to rusticate and to see the leaves change color."

Giving a satisfied sigh as if this was just what she wanted to hear, Mrs. Carver closed her eyes. "Sometimes I feel as if I've been there already from reading Thoreau and Hawthorne. Do you miss it?"

With the harbor shrouded in lavender fog and Mrs. Carver beside him, it was impossible to wish he were anywhere else. "I used to. But not anymore."

"It is no small thing to move to a new place and bring nothing with you but a dream and a trunk."

He shifted slightly, so that he was propped on one elbow and could gaze at her. With her eyes closed and her bonnet pushed back off her temples, her face was a serene mask. He wanted to know everything about her, what experiences had shaped her into the extraordinary woman she was. He wanted to know how she had gotten the scar running down her cheek, the laughter that had contributed to the fine lines at the corners of her eyes.

"You aren't from Pale Harbor. How did you come to be here?"

She gave a little laugh, her eyelids fluttering open. "What gave me away? My accent?"

"Something I heard around town."

"Whatever stories you've heard about me, I assure you, the truth is much more mundane. I came from New York on my marriage to Nathaniel."

New York was a rapidly expanding metropolis, full of opera houses, literary circles and theaters. It seemed a poor trade to live there and then come to sleepy Pale Harbor. His surprise must have registered on his face, because she said, "Is it really so hard to picture?"

"A little."

"Nathaniel came to New York looking for investors, and we met at a dinner my father hosted. Nathaniel was dignified and handsome, completely different from anything I was expecting a businessman from a small town in Maine to be. I was seventeen and tired of living what I saw as a constraining life—decadent, yes, but always under the thumb of some nursemaid or governess. I don't know why I thought marriage would be different, but when Nathaniel proposed after our whirlwind courtship and asked me to come back to Pale Harbor with him, I didn't hesitate in my answer."

She gave him a sidelong look. "All the money is mine, did you know that? Nathaniel's coffers were empty, which is why he went to New York in the first place, and in marrying me he got quite a nice settlement from my father. Despite their hatred of me, I get the impression that people here think I ought to marry again—to one of them, I presume—so that the town can enjoy my wealth." She paused, the hint of a sad smile playing on her lips. "Funny how money has the power to erase everything from prejudice to contempt."

His chest twisted with jealousy at the idea of her marrying anyone else, let alone one of the unworthy townspeople.

"Anyhow, I fell in love with Pale Harbor. It's so different from New York, which felt like it was choking all the air, the life out of me. So congested and busy... I could never find myself within the roads and sewers and coal fires of the city." Her silver eyes grew distant. "I am small within nature, but I fit in there. The breeze on my skin reminds me that I am part of something larger than myself, something grander and more beautiful than the dramas of humankind."

Gabriel was transfixed, unable to take his gaze off her. "You sound like a transcendentalist."

Pink touched her damp cheeks and she looked away, as if she had forgotten that she had an audience. "So, we have both found a haven here," was all she said in answer.

"I suppose we have." He paused. "Will you stay?" The thought of losing her was excruciating, but the thought of her being in danger was even more unbearable.

"Where else would I go?"

Away with me. Somewhere far away. But he had no money to whisk her away, and he couldn't ask her to finance such a harebrained scheme. Besides, he had come for Anna. To flee now would be a betrayal of the highest order.

They lapsed into silence. She was plucking up dead clover blooms and tossing them to the wind. Then she gave a heavy sigh. "I had better return soon."

He could hear the rest of her unsaid words: *to Helen*. She was moving to get to her feet but he jumped up first, offering her his hands. He pulled her up, and before she could step away he gathered her into his embrace. She caught her breath as she landed against his chest, and the warmth of her skin radiated through even her sodden dress, making him burn with an aching need. "When can I see you again?"

The laugh she gave in answer was small, but there was a hint of strain in it. "I've not even left yet."

It didn't matter. Every moment that she wasn't in his arms felt wrong, empty. "Sophronia." He'd never used her Christian name before, but it slipped from his mouth as smooth and rich as velvet. Her bonnet had come off, hanging by its ribbon around her neck, and he breathed in the scent of her hair, feeling her tremble under his touch.

"I can't."

"Why not?" But he already knew the answer.

"Mr. Stone," she pleaded. "You know that Helen could discover us."

"Gabriel," he corrected. He wanted to hear her say his name again. "And what does Helen matter? She's loyal to the bone. She wouldn't give us away."

She pressed her lips and looked away. He took her by the chin, gently, bringing her gaze back to meet his. Her silver eyes flashed. "You don't… Never mind, I can't explain it."

With a sigh, Gabriel dropped his hand. "Very well." There was something she wasn't telling him. He wouldn't push her, but it cut him to the core.

20

Another note. Cold sweat beaded down Sophronia's neck as Helen handed it to her at her desk the next day. Setting aside her tea, she studied the envelope, knowing that she should open it, but paralyzed by the thought of what she would find inside. The penmanship was not that of the recent threats, but nor did she recognize it as belonging to anyone she knew, either. Taking a deep breath, she forced herself to quickly tear it open.

Her fear evaporated as she scanned to the bottom and saw it was signed *G. Stone*. A smile tugged at her lips. He wanted to see her again.

It had cost her everything to pull away from the refuge of his chest and leave him on the hill the other day. Every fiber in her body had cried out to stay, to let her lips find his again, but her mind had won out. Becoming involved with him simply wasn't an option, for so many reasons: Helen finding out, the town turning against Mr. Stone—and then, of course, there was her past. It seemed that she was forever destined to be chained to her history, to pay for it over and over.

But she was weak, and she wanted, needed, to see him

again. As she continued reading, her smile faded when she saw his proposed rendezvous point: the cemetery, in the Carver plot, no less.

There were a hundred secluded spots in Pale Harbor that would have been more appropriate for a clandestine meeting, so why on earth would he choose the cemetery? Perhaps he wanted to know if she still mourned for her husband the way he mourned for his wife? Or perhaps he finally would ask her what had really happened on that fateful night four years ago. He had been gentle with her thus far, but his patience must have been wearing thin.

A thought struck her: What if the note was not from Mr. Stone at all? What if it was her tormentor luring her there for some nefarious reason? And again, why the cemetery? She sat, paralyzed, her desire to see Mr. Stone warring with her fear of the unknown. If it was truly from him, then she would be granted one more chance to feel the thrill of his touch. If it was from her tormentor, then perhaps she would be able to finally face him and put an end to this once and for all.

In the end, the promise was greater than the fear. Armed with a kitchen knife concealed in her skirt, Sophronia set off for the cemetery.

Sophronia didn't seek absolution, or at least that's what she told herself when she found her fingers curled around the wrought-iron gate of the ancient burying ground. She was not the one who had once held a hot poker to Nathaniel's arm, threatening to brand him if he didn't submit to her perverse whims. She was not the one, who, in a fog of brandy and anger, had taken a knife to his cheek, paring him as neatly as a piece of ripe fruit. She was not the one who had degraded him in a thousand little ways, day in and day out. Spending time with Mr. Stone had brought these and a host of other memories to the surface, memories she had worked hard to keep pushed down for years.

If Nathaniel had dropped dead of a heart attack or drowned by accident in the bath after one too many drinks, she would have done her duty and publicly mourned, all the while inwardly celebrating. But his death had not been a natural failing of his body, nor yet an accident. He was dead because of her.

Did Helen feel the same crushing sense of guilt? Did she also breathe easier without Nathaniel around, and, at the realization, catch her breath a hundred times a day as if he might still materialize from the shadows?

With a resolved sigh, Sophronia pushed open the gate and slipped into the old burying ground nestled beside the harbor.

Wet leaves clung to her boots as she picked her way through the weather-beaten stones. The last time she had come here had been the day they buried Nathaniel. It had been an early spring afternoon and beautiful, but the colors of the floral wreaths had been too vivid, the chorus of the birds too boisterous for such an occasion. She was burying not just the man who had drained all the joy from her, but the only woman she could ever remember being. It was as much a funeral for her as it had been for him, a punctuation mark on an era.

With every step toward the Carver plot, her skin grew clammier, her heart heavier. Mr. Stone would not have asked to meet her in this godforsaken place; she was certain of it.

In death, as in life, Nathaniel had insisted on being set apart from, above, the other citizens of Pale Harbor. The crypt took advantage of the small, natural hill in the middle of the cemetery and was enclosed by a wrought-iron gate and fencing. An obscenely large cenotaph thrust up from the ground, proclaiming his sense of importance.

She didn't need to be in front of the stone to know what it said. The words had branded themselves onto her mind years ago.

In Memory of
Nathaniel Hubert Carver
1798-1841
Esteemed gentleman &
Beloved husband
"The righteous shall go into Life eternal"

There was plenty of room on the cenotaph for her name, her dates. When would they be? What would be said about her, and who would be the one to say it? But it was not the prospect of death that sent a shiver of dread down her spine, but the thought of spending an eternity slumbering beside Nathaniel.

"Mr. Stone? Are you there?"

The only response was the rasping of a crow on a branch far above her. She hadn't really expected him to be here, yet the absoluteness of her vulnerability, her isolation, suddenly became real. Swallowing, she took a step closer to the cenotaph, looking around the side.

"I received your note," she said loudly, unable to keep her voice from wavering. "What do you want?"

She held her breath, her body tensing. But there was no answer. This had been a mistake. What had she been thinking coming here? A fantastic terror filled her as she clutched handfuls of her skirts and hastily retreated to the gate. She stumbled, and in the process her foot kicked aside something yielding and organic.

Her first thought was it was a dead animal, a rat perhaps, or even another bird. Had her tormentor really lured her here just to leave another one for her to find? What if it was still alive, though, like the raven? Crouching, she peered closer at the indistinct pink shape. It couldn't possibly be what she thought it was. She recoiled, waves of nausea overcoming her. *Oh, God, it was.*

Gabriel had only just sat down at his desk when there was a frantic knock at his door. He'd been planning a sermon, a real one. This wasn't going to be some tepid plagiarism of other men's work; this was going to be a revelation. He would capture the feeling that enveloped him when he was with Mrs. Carver, find the right words and illuminate the darkest crevices of the universe. But every time he meditated on her smile or the gentle warmth of her touch, his thoughts wandered to decidedly less holy topics.

Pushing aside his papers, Gabriel looked up to see Fanny leading the hack driver Reuben Reese into the room. "Mr. Stone?"

Gabriel was on his feet in an instant. He'd spoken to Mr. Reese only once before—on the night Garrett Hawkins died—but he struck Gabriel as a levelheaded and self-possessed man. So when he saw the knit in Mr. Reese's brow and the tightness with which he gripped his hat, Gabriel knew there was cause for alarm and in his gut he knew what it was about. "Is it Mrs. Carver…is she all right?"

Mr. Reese gave a tight nod. "She's safe, but you'd better come quickly. I've already sent the constable on ahead."

If the constable had dragged himself out from behind his desk, then it had to be no small matter. Gabriel tamped this down along with his other swirling thoughts as he sprang into Mr. Reese's hack, and they flew through the town.

The wheels had hardly come to a stop when Gabriel hopped down. They were in front of the cemetery. "She's in there?"

Mr. Reese didn't say anything, just led him to the center of the cemetery where a barren elm tree stood above a shaded cenotaph and crypt.

He hardly noticed the constable standing beside the wrought-iron fence as Gabriel rushed to Mrs. Carver. "Sophronia," he said as he crouched beside her and took her face in his hands. "Are you all right?"

She looked up at him with glazed eyes. She was pale, and her skin was clammy under his touch. "I...I think they meant to frighten me to death," she said with a shaky laugh.

"What happened?" There was no evidence of violence on her, thank God, and the cemetery was quiet except for the sound of a slight breeze through the branches above them.

"I've never seen anything like it," the constable said before Mrs. Carver could answer, pushing his thinning brown hair back and shaking his head. "I've lived in Pale Harbor my whole life, and I've never seen the likes of this before."

Gabriel wanted to shake him by the shoulders and tell him if he'd bothered to stick his head outside once in a while, he would have long ago realized that something was afoot in the town.

Once he'd made sure that Mrs. Carver wasn't in any danger of fainting, he stood back up and glanced around the forlorn gravesite. "And what would that be, exactly?"

The constable didn't say anything, just peeled back a cloth Gabriel hadn't noticed on the ground and then stood back.

Mrs. Carver's tremulous voice came from behind him. "Is... is it human?"

The heart was too large to be human—cow, maybe? pig?—but it was bloody and fresh, a network of ruby-red veins running through it. Some of the tension that had knotted in Gabriel's shoulders softened. Disgusting, yes, and awful, but the heart belonged to an animal, not a person.

He shook his head. "No, not human." She let out a long breath of relief. Little wonder she had been shaken; she'd thought that someone had left a human heart, and that meant she'd thought there was a body somewhere.

As he was about to stand up, there was a break in the clouds, sending a brief shaft of sickly sunlight through the branches. "Wait, what's that?"

A glint of something metal shone through the blood, and when he leaned closer to inspect the heart, a faint ticking sound met his ears. Mr. Reese and the constable gathered closer.

"What the devil?" the constable muttered.

Cautiously, Gabriel reached out and slipped his fingers into the cold, wet muscle until he had purchase on what felt like a chain. It came away little by little until the chain was free of the heart, coming out with a nauseating slurp. Behind him, he heard Mrs. Carver stifle a cry.

"His watch." Her voice was little more than a tremor. "That's Nathaniel's watch, but it's missing the fob."

Gabriel shared a look with the constable, who was holding a handkerchief up to his suddenly pale face. "Why in God's name would someone put your husband's watch in a heart?"

Her fingers fluttered at her chest and she swallowed hard. "Not why...*how*. Nathaniel was buried with that watch."

As the horrible implication took root, all sets of eyes went to the crypt. "They must have..." The constable's words trailed off, the meaning too terrible to voice.

Sophronia turned a shade paler and murmured something that Gabriel couldn't make out. "What was that?" he asked, lowering his ear closer to her.

"'The Tell-Tale Heart,'" she murmured, hardly any louder. "It's another Poe story. A murderer conceals the heart of his victim beneath his floorboards, but it still beats, reminding him of his crime until it drives him mad." Her frank silver eyes met Gabriel's, the resignation in them nearly making him wince. "Whoever has done this thinks me Nathaniel's murderer."

With a sigh, Gabriel dropped the bloody cloth back down over the heart. "Who in the hell would do such a thing?" he muttered as he stood up.

She looked up at him, and despite her red eyes, there was a hint of grim irony in her words. "Do I know who would go to the trouble of exhuming my husband, winding his watch, and then leading me to his grave and leaving a bloody heart for me to find? No, I really haven't a clue."

But Gabriel had an idea of who might do such a thing. There was one man who had not just access to all the crypts, but the church, as well. A man who was so mild-mannered and unassuming that Gabriel had all but dismissed him out of hand as a possible suspect. A man named Lewis.

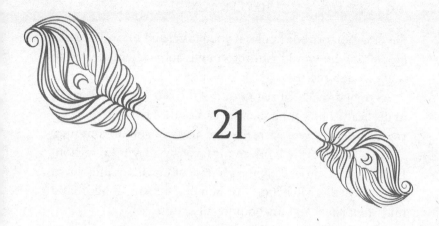

21

"Well? Where to?"

After he'd seen Mrs. Carver safely home and promised to return the next day to see how she was recovering, Gabriel had gone back to the waiting hack, lost in his swirling thoughts until Mr. Reese's impatient voice cut through the silence. He was standing at the door, looking at Gabriel expectantly.

"I'm not sure," he murmured. Lewis hadn't been at the cemetery, and besides the church, Gabriel hadn't the faintest clue where to look for him. "Where do you think I might find Ezekiel Lewis at this time of day?"

"Mr. Stone," the driver said with no small amount of irritation. "How would I know the whereabouts of the man any more than you? You tell me where you want me to take you, and I take you there. That is my only job. And," he added, glancing longingly down the drive, "the missus has a pot of beans and ham hocks waiting at home, and God have mercy if I'm late and it gets cold. So, tell me where you want me to take you or use your God-given legs."

"Of course," Gabriel murmured, chastised. "Take me in

the direction of your house, if you please, and I'll walk back."
Hopefully, he would run into Lewis somewhere along the
way through town.

As they drove, Gabriel spun out the case for Lewis's guilt
in his head. The young man's access to the church and crypts
was damning. Lewis seemed good-natured and unassuming,
but that could easily work in his favor by allaying suspicion.
By the time Gabriel caught a glimpse of Lewis coming down
the road with a satchel on his shoulder, he had all but found
him completely and unconditionally guilty.

Gabriel called out to Mr. Reese and the carriage came to
a stop. When he'd paid and sent Mr. Reese on his way, Gabriel jammed his hands in his pockets and watched as Lewis
approached.

The road was empty of traffic, and for a moment Gabriel
wondered if confronting him in such a remote area was a wise
course of action.

Lewis had put the satchel down to rest, but straightened
when he caught sight of Gabriel, giving him a wave. Gabriel's
blood boiled as he caught a snatch of Lewis's tuneless whistling,
saw the spring in his step. The man walked as if he hadn't a
care in the world, as if he hadn't been plotting the most das-
tardly ways in which to torment Mrs. Carver.

"Mr. Stone!" he called out. "How are you this afternoon?"

Gabriel gave him a curt nod. "Lewis," he said.

"I was just on my way back from the blacksmith," Lewis
said as they drew closer. He opened the satchel to give Gabriel a peek inside at a jumble of tools. "Had to get my pick
sharpened before it's needed for the winter."

Gabriel didn't say anything, unsure of what Lewis was talking about, but not liking the look of the sharp and gleaming
objects. He raised a brow in question.

"The earth here turns hard as stone in the winter, and unless folks want a body sitting in their barn for months till a thaw, easiest thing to do is break up the ground," Lewis explained.

Gabriel grimaced; the old tool would also make a formidable weapon. "You have keys to the crypts, do you not?"

Lewis looked slightly taken aback by the directness of the question, but nodded. "That's right." Reaching into his coat pocket, he produced a heavy ring of keys. "That's most of the crypts except some of the oldest—no one really needs to get into those anyway." He gave Gabriel a curious look. "Did… did you need something with one of them? I wasn't planning to go to the cemetery today, but I can take you if you want."

Ignoring the question, Gabriel continued. "So, you would be able to get into the Carver crypt, for example."

A faint line formed on Lewis's brow. "Yes," he said. "Though I've no reason to go in there. Mr. Carver has been buried these four years, and aside from Mrs. Carver someday, there's no one else in Pale Harbor with a claim on that crypt."

Gabriel fought back the sudden stab of nausea at Lewis's glib reference to Mrs. Carver's mortality. It was becoming clear that Lewis wasn't going to make this easy for him. He would have to take another tack. "I don't suppose you heard about what was found in the cemetery today."

The line on Lewis's brow deepened. "Can't say that I did. What was it?"

"Someone divested the late Mr. Carver of his pocket watch, which was buried with him, and left it in a cow's heart for Mrs. Carver to find."

Lewis took an unsteady step back. "A…a heart?"

"Where were you this morning around eleven?"

Pure panic flashed across Lewis's face as he realized where this line of questioning was going. "You can't possibly think…" He trailed off, working his cap nervously in his hands.

Gabriel didn't want to think Lewis was guilty. The man

had been nothing but kind and helpful since Gabriel had arrived in Pale Harbor that first miserable night. What's more, the man wasn't overly bright, and had a nervous constitution; for him to carry off such disturbing deeds and then act so bewildered and innocent was deeply unsettling.

"You have access to both the church and the Carver crypt, so…" Gabriel let his meaning hang heavy in the air between them.

"I—I would never! On my honor, I would never tamper with a body or rob a grave."

"Where were you at eleven o'clock?" Gabriel ground out again.

Suddenly, Lewis's face brightened. "I was in Harpersville all morning." He lifted the satchel and shook it, as if the jangling tools could corroborate everything he said. "You can ask anyone at the shop, or the blacksmith John Boyle."

A spark of relief kindled in Gabriel's chest, but just as quickly it dimmed. Just because Lewis had an alibi for that morning didn't mean he hadn't done it. The heart had been fresh, but it could have also been left out last night, the cold preserving it. Or—good God—what if he had an accomplice? "What about the first of October?" he asked, thinking of the cat manikin.

"I—I don't rightly know. That was weeks ago."

Lewis looked just as terrified of Gabriel as the night that they'd first met in the church. Good. For once Gabriel was glad of his size, of his ability to intimidate. "All right," he said. "I'll be looking into your whereabouts. In the meantime, don't even think about leaving Pale Harbor."

After he released Lewis and watched him practically run back toward town, Gabriel turned his collar up and started slowly walking back to the cottage.

The late-afternoon sun shafted down through the bare

branches above as the familiar scent of wood smoke and brine followed him down the road. Gabriel wondered what Pale Harbor would look like in the spring. Would this nightmare be over by then? Would he and Mrs. Carver walk down this very road, arm in arm, and laugh about what had occurred? Or was there even more sorrow on the horizon?

Sophronia watched from the window as the hack sat in the drive before Mr. Reese finally climbed up and gave a light flick of the reins, and the chestnut horse bore them away, out of sight.

Helen had tried to tempt Sophronia into staying downstairs with hot tea and all manner of cakes, but the thought of eating anything turned Sophronia's stomach. When she had finally managed to assuage Helen of her immediate fear that she might faint, she went to her room, took out the list she had started the night Mr. Stone had brought news of the cat manikin to her, and carefully added two more items.

October 19—note in the house, Mr. Stone also receives note
October 21—heart (cemetery)

She had looked up the poem from which Mr. Stone's latest note had been derived—"The City in the Sea." But it told her nothing new, and it seemed tame and mild when compared to the bloody cow's heart. When she thought of someone breaking into the crypt and extracting Nathaniel's watch from his corpse…well, it was beyond the pale. Someone had opened a sealed casket, rifled through the clothes of a dead man and stolen his most personal item. All for the purpose of terrifying her.

Looking over the list in its entirety, Sophronia's heart sank. She had no answers, no revelations. What horrors would she add to the list in the coming days and weeks? When would it end, and at what cost?

When Gabriel arrived at Castle Carver the next day, he found Mrs. Carver sitting in the parlor, dressed in a silk day dress of tender green, her raven hair twined neatly at the nape of her neck. She might have looked like the gentle first days of spring were it not for the dark smudges under her eyes, the haunted pallor to her cheeks.

Mrs. Carver's smile when she saw him was thin but genuine, and his heart did a little kick. Helen had grudgingly admitted him into the house, and was now knitting in the corner, glaring at Gabriel over her knitting needles.

"I came," he said stupidly.

"I see that."

He flicked a glance at Helen and cleared his throat. "You'll be glad to hear that your...that Mr. Carver's pocket watch has been reunited with him."

"Oh," she said faintly. "I am relieved."

They immediately lapsed into silence, the only sounds the clacking of Helen's needles and the ticking of the mantel clock. Mrs. Carver sat stock-still, her hands clasped in her lap, the only sign of her discomfort a tightness around her mouth.

Aware that Helen was listening to every word that he said, Gabriel kept his tone neutral, his voice low. "I spoke with Lewis yesterday."

"Lewis? Whatever for?" But even as she spoke, Gabriel could see understanding dawning in her quick eyes. "What did he say?"

"He claims that he was in Harpersville at the time of...of the incident in the cemetery."

Mrs. Carver gave him a keen look. "But you don't believe him."

"I don't know what to believe. It would be incredibly convenient for him to be out of town, but even if he was and his whereabouts can be corroborated, it doesn't mean he didn't have an accomplice or go about it in some different way."

The words were barely out of his mouth when Mrs. Carver was rising, her eyes flinty with determination. "There's only one way to know for certain. We go to Harpersville."

The coach ride to Harpersville had been painfully awkward, with Helen insisting that she act as chaperone, and alternating between fussing over Mrs. Carver and chastising her for undertaking such a scheme at such short notice. The trip was made further uncomfortable by the fact that every time the coach went over a rut, Mrs. Carver's skirts jostled, brushing against his legs and making him prickle with desire.

The carriage had barely come to a stop when Gabriel threw open the door and hopped down into the cold, fresh air. Taking a moment to compose himself, he turned back and helped Mrs. Carver down. Helen refused his hand with a scowl.

"Goodness," Mrs. Carver murmured. "I never thought of Pale Harbor as cosmopolitan, but..." She trailed off, and Gabriel followed her gaze. Boasting only a handful of cottages and a church smaller than his, it was barely more than a village, flanked by muddy grazing fields on one side and a meandering river on the other.

"Aye, he was here," the blacksmith told them when they'd followed the smell of smoke and the clanging of metal. "I sharpened a pick ax and number of other tools for him. He comes about once a year as I offer a fair price and my work is good and clean."

Relief and disappointment shot through Gabriel. He hadn't wanted it to be Lewis, but then again, who *did* he want it to be? At least he would have had his man, and they could take the next step of seeing this matter laid to rest.

"So he was here," Helen said as they made their way back to the waiting coach. "There could have been any number of ways the scoundrel could have still done it."

Gabriel wasn't so sure. It was true that Lewis might have an accomplice, but if that were the case, then Lewis almost certainly wouldn't be the mastermind behind the whole plot, and they would be looking for a second suspect anyway. "Or perhaps we're following the wrong trail."

"Of course we aren't. The man is a weasel, pretending to be simple and all the while contriving the most disgusting plots."

"You seem certain it was Lewis," Gabriel said, growing irritated that Helen had so insinuated herself into the matter.

Helen gave him a sharp look. "And you seem quite ready to take his word as gospel truth."

"But we've just received proof that—"

"Please!"

The word cut through the argument, and Gabriel realized that he and Helen had been carrying on while Mrs. Carver had stopped some paces back and was standing in the road.

"Please, stop arguing." She had a hand to her temple, and was looking very pale.

"Sophy? Are you all right?"

"It's just a headache," she said. "I'm sure it will pass."

But Helen was at her side in an instant, taking her by the arm and tutting like a mother hen. "This was a mistake. You shouldn't have made such a strenuous journey. Come, let's get you back to the carriage."

Gabriel trailed helplessly behind them, acutely aware that he could do nothing to help, that it wasn't his place. Perhaps Helen was right, and he should have considered Mrs. Carver's constitution, unused to travel as she was, when they'd decided to make this trip.

"Really, it will pass," Mrs. Carver was saying, but Helen didn't heed her weak protests as she ushered her up and into the carriage.

If the ride to Harpersville had been awkward, the return home was downright painful. Gabriel watched as Mrs. Carver tried to close her eyes and rest her head against the squabs, while Helen ceaselessly worried over her. "Poor dear," she crooned. "When we return, I'll make you some of that tea with the honey and licorice that you like so much, and I will prepare a warming pan for your bed. All you must do is change and slip into bed and then rest."

As Helen continued in her fussing, and Mrs. Carver continued insisting that she would be fine, an unwelcome truth dawned on him: so long as Mrs. Carver was in distress, Helen was useful. She had a purpose.

At Castle Carver, Mrs. Carver insisted that Gabriel come in and warm himself in front of the fire before he returned home. They sat in awkward silence in the parlor, Helen resuming her knitting and shooting dark looks at Gabriel over her needles.

He couldn't talk to her like this. He couldn't say the things he needed to say, not with Helen sitting there like a slavering guard dog.

Mercifully, Mrs. Carver seemed to sense the same thing. "Do you know, I think I would like that tea after all. Helen, would you be a dear and brew me some?"

Helen all but jumped out of her seat to fetch it. No sooner was she out the door than Gabriel went to Mrs. Carver. Kneeling beside her, he took her hand and pressed it to his lips, relishing the flutter of pulse that ran beneath her warm skin.

Finding himself alone with her made him bold, and he took her hand, running his fingers over the smooth inside of her wrist. "Are you all right?"

Her hand lingered in his grasp before she gently withdrew it and began twining her fingers together in her lap. "I've been better," she said.

A great chasm threatened to open between them if they could not speak frankly. He didn't know how long Helen would be gone, and as soon as she came back, his chance to say what he needed to say would be lost. But he was mesmerized by her tapered fingertips, imagining them running through his hair at the nape of his neck the way they had when he and Mrs. Carver had shared their first kiss.

Looking up, he caught her studying his face. "You'd better just have out with it, whatever it is," she said.

Rocking back on his heels, Gabriel tented his fingers together, not meeting her eye. He took a deep breath. What he was about to say gave him no pleasure, but for her sake it needed to be said. "I think you need to consider that the person behind everything is very possibly Helen."

There was no one else it could be; no one else that had such intimate knowledge and access to the house. But more importantly, there was no one else who stood to benefit from keeping Mrs. Carver frightened, keeping her at home.

No one except Helen.

His words washed over her like a wave. Sophronia stilled her hands, quashing down her own ugly suspicions that had started to bloom ever since finding the note in the parlor.

Glancing at the open door, she lowered her voice. "You can't possibly think it was Helen," she hissed. "Why, I love her dearly, but she simply doesn't have the imagination for such a thing. Besides, what on earth would be the point?"

She said the words as much to comfort herself as to convince Mr. Stone. He frowned, the intensity of his gaze making her shift a little in her seat. "What do you know about Helen, about her past?"

Frightfully little. Hazarding a glance at the doorway again, Sophronia tried to remember what Helen had told her of her history. She knew that Helen had suffered abuse at the hands of her husband before he'd left her in the poorhouse. She knew that Helen had no children and no family. Helen had once mentioned a farm in Vermont, but Sophronia wasn't sure how she had eventually ended up in New York.

She huffed and sat back into the pillows, unwilling to admit how little she knew. "I don't think it fair that you throw such accusations at her. You're like a child, vying for my attention."

Mr. Stone didn't say anything to this, but the slightest flush of pink crept up from his collar. So he *was* jealous. She might have told him that it was a fine thing for him to accuse Helen, when he himself had lied about his identity and his past. Who was he to lecture her on misplacing her trust?

They fell into silence, Sophronia running her finger absently over the smooth surface of her brooch as her thoughts spun away in a thousand directions at once. When Helen had given it to her, Sophronia had been so quick to forgive, so eager to have things go back to the way they had been between them. Was that what Helen had wanted all along? Would she go to lengths greater than the gift of an expensive bauble to make certain that nothing changed, that Sophronia never left? No, it was ridiculous. Just like the day of their fight, Sophronia was being too hasty with her judgment.

Mr. Stone's voice cut into her thoughts, firm but sympathetic. "I don't want you staying here with her, Sophronia. It isn't safe."

"Isn't safe," she echoed. She could have laughed; if only he

knew. The whole situation was preposterous. It was just a case
of another man trying to assert his authority and ownership
over her. Well, she was a free widow now, and she didn't have
to put up with it. "Helen would never hurt me."

He took a long breath. "Perhaps not hurt you, but I don't
think she wants to see you free, or with me, either."

Sophronia stared at him, dumbfounded. Then incredulity
turned to anger. How dare he. How dare he sweep into her
life, dazzling her and chipping away her defenses, and then
turn around and point his finger at her dearest friend.

"All this started before you came to town," she said, aware
that her tone was veering into petulance. "You must hold
yourself in high esteem indeed if you believe Helen would go
to such lengths to keep us apart."

She expected him to look hurt, angry even. But the look
in his eyes was worse, so much worse. It was resignation, as if
she had just confirmed what he had always suspected.

It couldn't be helped. How could she bear it if it was Helen?
It wasn't Mr. Stone's fault that he had given voice to suspicions that had been simmering in her own mind for weeks.
She needed him to leave, right now. She needed to salvage
any shred of normalcy and safety.

Sophronia rose and stood stiffly by the window. "If you
don't mind, I have work to do, and I feel another headache
coming on."

From the corner of her eye, she saw Mr. Stone open his
mouth as if he were going to say something, but just then
Helen swept in with the tea.

"Mr. Stone was just leaving," Sophronia said, trying to rein
in the tremble in her voice.

Giving her a curt nod, he rose and pulled his hat brim
down low over his eyes. When he had gone, Sophronia stood
paralyzed by the window, watching as Helen poured out tea

for the two of them. No, Helen didn't have the imagination, and Sophronia could only assume she didn't have the inclination, either. And thinking her capable of murder, well...it was simply impossible.

Except that it wasn't.

But that was different, Sophronia told herself. What had happened that night four years ago was very, very different. Between the two of them, Sophronia was the murderess.

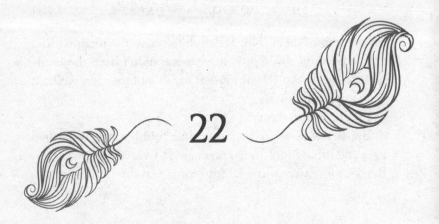

22

The woman was a fool, as stubborn as an ox, and Gabriel could not stop thinking about her.

It was his fault. He cursed himself for the umpteenth time as he stormed back home. He'd scared her off when he knew how unreasonably loyal she was to Helen. How could Mrs. Carver live in the same house as her? How could she be so close to her, yet so blind to Helen's true designs? If only she would be reasonable and... His thoughts hit a wall. And what? Run into Gabriel's arms? They had shared a few conversations and a kiss. He held no sway over her.

His only consolation was that he did not think it likely that Helen would harm her. Not physically, in any case. Helen had worked for her for years; if she wished harm upon her mistress, she certainly could have done it by now. So what was the purpose of all this? To keep Mrs. Carver scared?

Gabriel had barely climbed his front steps when the sound of wheels struggling through the mud cut through his churning thoughts. In all the chaos of recent weeks, he had nearly forgotten that Tom was due for his long-promised visit.

The carriage came to a lurching stop and the door was

flung open. The familiar rumpled figure of a darkly tanned man hopped down, neatly landing in the drive.

"Gabe," Tom said with a grin, striding over and clasping him by the shoulders. "God, it's good to see you."

As he clapped Tom on the back, Gabriel was nearly overcome by emotion. He swallowed the deep sense of relief. It was so good to see a familiar face. A face from before all this mess. "Welcome to Pale Harbor."

Anxieties fell away as they went inside, Tom filling the modest cottage with his easy good humor and exuberant laughter. As usual, he was without hat and coat, and his fair hair was charmingly tousled, a deadly combination that always made him popular with ladies. He gave an appreciative whistle as Gabriel led him into the parlor, which had benefited enormously from Fanny's attentions. "Not bad, Gabe. Not bad at all."

Fanny, hearing their voices, rushed out from the kitchen, brushing her hands against her apron. "Should I help with the trunks?"

Before Gabriel could answer, Tom stopped short. "Gabriel," he said with a broad smile, his gaze trained on Fanny, "you didn't tell me that you kept a goddess in your employ." He gave her a wink, sending her into a blushing rapture.

Gabriel cleared his throat. "Thank you, Fanny, but Tom and I can manage the trunk. Could you bring us some coffee, please?"

Nodding eagerly, Fanny dipped an unnecessary curtsy and then ran back to the kitchen.

"Behave yourself," Gabriel murmured into his friend's ear as he bent to carry the trunk.

It took both of them wrestling with the trunk to get it upstairs. Tom gave Gabriel a sheepish grin as they paused midway to collect their breaths. "Sorry, old friend," he said. "Wasn't quite sure what to pack."

Balancing the trunk on his thigh, Gabriel wiped his perspiring forehead on the back of his sleeve. "It's Pale Harbor," he said. "I doubt you'll find occasion to wear even half of what you've brought." They hefted it up and managed to get it straight back into the bedroom in one last go.

"Yes, well, having never been to Pale Harbor, I had no idea what to expect," Tom said. "From your letters, I gather that it's not quite as bucolic as it seems?"

Gabriel gave a snort. "That's a conversation that calls for a drink."

"Well, then?"

They headed downstairs, where Tom threw himself in a chair with a contented groan. "God, coming up the coast by water is one thing, but the rail and coach is another entirely. Feels as if my back is going to snap from all the bumping and jolting."

Fanny brought in a tray with cups of hot coffee, little buttered buns and a garnish of fresh mint, which Gabriel couldn't help but notice she had never done for him before. When she was still lingering after setting it down, Gabriel cleared his throat. "Thank you, Fanny. Why don't you take the rest of the day off?"

She didn't look as pleased as he had expected. "Are you sure? I can stay and make another batch of fresh buns for you and Mr…" She trailed off, looking at Tom with coquettish expectation.

"Ellroy," he said with the easy grin that spelled trouble for young women. "You can call me Tom."

"Tom," she said with a dreamy sigh.

Gabriel took quick action, rising from his seat and guiding her by the elbow to the door. "Thank you, Fanny," he said pointedly.

Flushing, she dropped another deep curtsy. When she was gone, Tom raised a brow.

"She's a good girl and don't you dare get any ideas," Gabriel said.

Tom held up his palms in submission. "Wouldn't dream of it."

They finished their coffee, and then Gabriel poured out two whiskeys. They drank in companionable silence until Tom put his cup down with a gratified sigh. "So, how goes the proselytizing?"

Gabriel groaned. "You know that's not what I do."

"I know very little of what you do, thanks to your maddeningly short letters," Tom said. "You're going to have to enlighten me, because I can't for a minute understand to what end all this playacting is for."

Gabriel swirled his whiskey side to side before downing it in one gulp. "I wonder the same thing myself."

It felt strange to let his guard down for once. With Tom, he wasn't Reverend Stone, transcendentalist minister to a small town. He wasn't responsible for protecting Mrs. Carver. He was just Gabe. Lost, bereaved, perpetually hopeless Gabe.

Tom didn't say anything, just studied him with unnerving interest. "And how is our mysterious merry widow?"

"Not so mysterious anymore," Gabriel said. He felt like a schoolboy, the way his stomach warmed at her mention. But then it soured when he remembered Helen and the wedge she was driving between them, the danger she posed.

"But perhaps you don't like what you've found?" Tom asked, misinterpreting Gabriel's darkened expression.

Gabriel shook his head. "No, it's not that." He plucked

at a loose thread on his cuff. "I...I have feelings for her," he blurted out.

Tom blinked at him and then took a long, slow drink. "We've come a fair way from suspecting her of murder, I see."

"I shouldn't have written that." He was ashamed to have fallen under the sway of gossip. She was no more a murderer than he was, and she had weathered such accusations with grace and resolve.

"But?" Tom said, sensing Gabriel's unspoken hesitation.

Gabriel looked down at the empty glass in his hand. "But I don't think there's a future for us. Besides," he said, hastily pushing aside the emotion welling in his throat, "there is still Anna. I couldn't possibly think of..." He trailed off. What a bastard he was.

Tom was silent for a moment. "I'd like to meet her," he finally said.

Gabriel looked up sharply. "Why?" he asked, suspicious.

"Why not? Your letters may be short, but her name makes frequent appearances. I'm curious."

Would she even want to see Gabriel again after he'd accused Helen? She'd made it clear that not only did she not believe him, but that she was angry he could even make such an accusation. But perhaps this could be his chance to make things right with her. With Tom there, some of the pressure would be taken off Gabriel, and if anyone could charm one out of a dark mood, it was Tom.

The next day an invitation was sent to Castle Carver, and the answer returned so quickly that there was no time for reservations or second-guessing himself. Mrs. Carver would dine with them that night. Gabriel hoped, desperately, that Mrs. Carver would not assume that Helen had been invited, too.

Gabriel sent Fanny out with a shopping list and instructions to go to the Marshalls' house to see if their cook could be spared for a few hours that evening. He paced about the small house, making sure that the dining room was in order, dusting off ancient bottles of wine from the cellar and shaving himself so close that he nicked his chin, twice. He would pay good money to know what Mrs. Carver was thinking; she had so clearly been angry with him, and yet she had accepted his invitation straightaway.

Tom watched the preparations unfold with an amused smile that quickly turned incredulous. "You don't just have feelings for her," he said, "you're completely smitten. My God, are you sure you want her to meet me after all?"

Shrugging off the truth in his friend's words, Gabriel uncorked a bottle of brandy and took out two glasses. "If you look at me like that any more, I might start to regret it."

They sat in the small parlor, throwing back brandies and swapping stories from their days in the navy. He was happy to let Tom do most of the talking, and they were laughing loudly when Tom suddenly stopped midsentence, lowering his glass and gazing past Gabriel's shoulder.

Gabriel turned around, and there she was. Fanny must have let her in before leaving. For someone who rarely left her house, Mrs. Carver had certainly made an art of making an entrance.

He opened his mouth, but found his throat suddenly dry, his breathing ragged. He shot out of his seat. "You came," he said in a hoarse whisper.

"Gabe!" his friend exclaimed. "Where are your manners?" Standing, he gave Mrs. Carver a neat bow. "Please don't tell me he's always like that?"

She smiled indulgently at Gabriel before turning back to Tom. "I'm afraid so. He's an absolute beast," she said, silver eyes sparkling. "Whenever I go anywhere, rather than welcoming me, he gawps and acts as if I had just alighted from the sky!" Holding out her hand, she said, "Sophronia Carver."

Tom took the proffered hand and imparted a kiss above the glove. "Tom Ellroy," he said. "I've heard much about you from Gabriel, but even he did an inadequate job preparing me for just how beautiful you are."

Mrs. Carver blushed deeply, and Gabriel cursed himself and his slow tongue. "Tom is a flatterer," he said at last, coming out of his stupor. Then, realizing his blunder, hastened to add, "But in this case I can't fault him." Mrs. Carver smiled at him, warmly, he thought. Perhaps he had not fallen completely from her good graces.

They sat down to the meal prepared by the Marshalls' cook. In his old waistcoat and rough trousers, Gabriel felt shabby and underdressed compared to Tom. And, of course, Mrs. Carver was resplendent in a dress of the deepest turquoise, cut simply and flattering to her elegant figure. He wondered how many gowns she had, how she decided which one to wear each day. He wondered how the frock would look pooled on his bedroom floor, her naked body emerging from it like Venus from the clamshell. Shifting in his chair, he clenched his jaw and willed himself to focus on something else.

Tom sparkled, as he always did when in the company of a beautiful woman. Gabriel might have been jealous, but he couldn't help but be grateful to Tom for keeping the conversation flowing smoothly, because as usual, Mrs. Carver's presence seemed to have stolen all his words away.

"Gabe tells me that Pale Harbor has had some unusual occurrences lately. Occultists, is it?"

Gabriel stifled a groan. Tom was never one to tiptoe lightly around taboo subjects.

Mrs. Carver took a long drink from her glass, not meeting Tom's eye. "That's right," she said.

When she didn't offer any more information, Tom tried again. "Gabriel wouldn't give me any of the details, except to say that it was all very unusual, and the authorities are baffled." He looked to Mrs. Carver and then Gabriel, expectant.

Gabriel cleared his throat into his napkin. The last thing Mrs. Carver would want to do would be to recount the horrors that had been plaguing her. "The details are inconsequential."

Tom looked disappointed. "You thought it consequential enough to include in your letters."

"It's the fancy of children, bored with the constraints of our small town and lack of culture," Mrs. Carver said in a breezy voice. "I am sure it is the same phenomenon that swept Salem all those years ago. Girls feeling as if they have no control over their lives act out, hoping to cause a reaction. I can hardly blame them… Pale Harbor must be a dreadful place to be a child."

Tom put down his fork and looked between them, as if sensing some unspoken disagreement. "Why does no one speak with these young people? Why is it allowed to continue unchecked?"

Mrs. Carver shrugged her shoulders and took a delicate sip of wine. "I suppose you would have to ask their parents."

Gabriel held his tongue. He thought of the Marshall twins and the other children of Pale Harbor. Mrs. Carver was allowing herself to believe in a delusion if she really thought such small children could be responsible for all of this.

"Surely there are police here, or some other authority that could intervene?"

Sighing, Mrs. Carver pushed some chicken around her plate. "Has Mr. Stone told you about my reputation around town?"

Tom made a show of blustering that he had no idea what she was talking about, and Mrs. Carver gave him one of her neat, disarming smiles. "Of course he has." Then, with a deftness that spoke to her upbringing in New York high society, Mrs. Carver turned the conversation away from her troubles toward the national obsession with the compositions of Franz Liszt.

"The man is a genius with the pianoforte, but I can't help being somewhat disturbed by the cult of admirers that has sprung up around him. Women falling over themselves just for a scrap of his handkerchief or a broken string from an instrument he played upon." She shook her head. "It's amazing how people can lose all reason in the worship of an idol."

"You say you enjoy his music. Does that mean you play yourself?" Tom asked.

"Only a little, and not very well. Helen is the real musician."

"Helen?"

Mrs. Carver colored a little and shifted her gaze down to her plate. "My house servant."

Tom raised a brow. "Your servant is a prodigy at the piano! My word, how lucky you are. It's all I can do to get my shirts pressed once a week. I would love to hear her play sometime." Tom chattered on, oblivious to the heavy curtain of silence that had fallen at the mention of Helen.

Gabriel studied Mrs. Carver as she half-heartedly picked at her meal, the candlelight dancing off the soft planes of her face. How he wished he could take back his words about Helen. He would do anything to see Mrs. Carver happy, even if that meant shielding her from an ugly truth. But more than that, he would do anything to keep her safe.

Dinner couldn't end soon enough.

"Did you walk?"

After dinner was finished, Gabriel had excused himself and left Tom with a sherry by the fire while he accompanied Mrs. Carver outside.

"I took a hack, but I rather fancy stretching my legs."

"Will you allow me to walk you back, then?"

She looked like she wanted to say no, so Gabriel hurried on before she could. "I know you don't need an escort, but it would put my mind at ease. Please." The unspoken words, *There is someone out there who wishes you harm,* hung between them.

She pressed her lips together but nodded her consent.

The crisp evening air wrapped itself around them as Mrs. Carver glided out into the gloaming, her turquoise gown and gray cloak blending into the mist. She looked over her shoulder at him, making sure he was falling into step beside her, and then began walking at a furious clip.

He should apologize. Shouldn't he? He'd upset her, accused her dear friend of the terrible crimes that were plaguing her and then asked her to dinner, only to have his friend interrogate her. But then again, he'd spoken nothing more than the truth. Helen had every motive and opportunity, and Mrs. Carver was being willfully blind.

He gathered his resolve and jogged to catch up to her. But just as he was opening his mouth, Mrs. Carver said, "Tom is lovely. You're lucky to have such a friend."

He frowned, thrown off by her sudden enthusiasm. "Yes," he said carefully, "I count myself as such."

She hurried on. "I would love to talk with him again. He must have so many stories from his time in the navy. Pale Harbor used to be full of mariners and sea captains, each with stories and goods from all corners of the world. Of course, that was before my time, but I've heard—"

"Sophronia." He stopped her with a hand on her arm, and the rest of her words died away. Her pale face looked up at him through the dusk. "I feel that—"

She shook her head. "Please, don't. Let's not speak of it. Let's just go on as we did before."

But he could not go on as he had before. He could barely go on now. "Before we kissed? Or before I suggested Helen's guilt?" Even in the darkness, he could feel the heat rising to her cheeks.

They had slowed until they were standing in the middle of the road, facing each other with naught but the mist between them. "Oh, Gabriel," she said on the back of a sigh. "I don't know."

She'd used his name only once before, and longing ran through him like a current. Unable to stop himself, he reached out and took her gloved hands in his own. When she didn't pull away, he brought her closer to him, until she was only a hairbreadth away and he could smell her sweet rosewater scent. "Am I the only one that feels this?" He took her hand and placed it flush against his chest.

She wouldn't meet his eye, but she shook her head. "No, you aren't the only one," she whispered.

His heart leaped into his throat. "Then what is it?" he pressed. He could feel the wall she had built up around herself starting to quake and sway. How he wanted to see it come crumbling down, and how he wanted to be the one who caught her and held her close when it did.

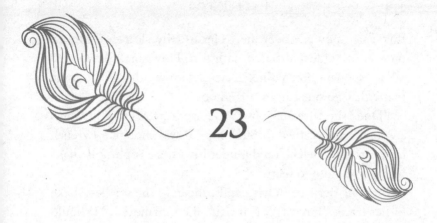

23

A carriage clattered past them, spraying mud and pebbles up in its wake. It wasn't safe for them to be walking in the middle of the road without so much as a lantern, so Gabriel took Mrs. Carver by the elbow and led her to the sandy path that ran along the harbor. Her body was shaking under his touch, and he peered at her closer in the dark to see that her face had gone as white as the moon.

"What is it?"

She shook her head. "It's just, that carriage, the way it was driving reminded me of…" She trailed off, staring at the receding hack. Then, as if coming back to herself, she gave him a pathetic smile. "It's nothing."

It definitely was not nothing. They sat on an old bench overlooking the harbor, the cold stone biting through his trousers. "Will you tell me?" He wasn't sure if he was asking about her reaction to the carriage, or her reluctance to speak her mind about her feelings. It didn't matter; he would take whatever she chose to give him.

Mrs. Carver took a long, shuddering sigh, her shoulders sagging. "You think me free, but I am a prisoner. Helen has this, this…power…over me." Her usually clear eyes looked up at him, wide and flared with fear. How small she looked all of a sudden, how vulnerable. "She knows things about me that…that no one can ever find out."

"Does she threaten you?" Gabriel's protective instincts awakened and seethed through him. It was enough to wrench his heart that Helen could render his strong Sophronia shaking and so close to tears.

Burying her face in her hands, she gave the smallest shake of her head. "I'm sorry, Gabriel," she murmured. "I should never have kissed you, made you think that we could be together. It will only lead to trouble."

His heart twisted, but her words made him only more determined to fight for her. "You have nothing to be sorry for," he reassured her, placing his hand on her arm. Her skin radiated heat through her cloak, and he longed to take her up in his embrace and smooth all her misery away. Longed to fill her with joy. She hadn't stopped shaking since the carriage had careened past them, her body seeming to have shrunk in on itself.

There was something about the carriage, something to do with all of this. Taking her chin in his hand, he gently tilted her gaze up to meet his. Her eyes were wide and glassy with horror. "Sophronia?" he asked. "What happened?"

Nathaniel had been drinking; it always started with drinking. She had tried to keep her gaze trained on her embroidery, to avoid his eye and therefore his attention at all costs. "We're going to the Crawfords' for a business dinner in Portland," he'd said. "Get dressed and try to make yourself presentable."

Nodding, she had risen and put away her embroidery. She didn't want to sit through a mind-numbingly boring dinner at the Crawfords', but going out was safer because it meant that

Nathaniel would be on good behavior. "I'll need to make sure Helen has pressed my blue silk. It was in a trunk all winter."

There must have been something in her tone that he didn't like, because he stopped in the doorway, looking back at her over his shoulder. He had been having crippling headaches for weeks, and his temper had been shorter than usual. And then it happened in a flash, as it always did, him coming at her fast—so fast, how did he move so fast when he was with drink?—and she on her feet with her arm protectively in front of her face. It was like trying to shield herself from a tumbling boulder with a veil of lace.

He always started out small, a punishment for an indiscretion on her part; a slap across the cheek for looking at him with her "accusing" eyes, a chokehold when she spoke out of turn. It was a test to see if she would fight back. She was quiet, always quiet; she had long since learned that to resist only made it worse. But that night she cried out. Later, she wouldn't remember why she'd cried out when so many times she had bit her tongue until it bled. When the next blow came, it knocked her so that she could hardly stay standing, a blinding pain radiating from her cheek that made her see stars.

As quickly as the storm had blown in, it ceased. Nathaniel had straightened his cravat and regarded Sophronia with cold distaste.

Just then Helen brought in a tray with a brandy snifter. She must have heard the fight. She shot a glance at Sophronia, a silent understanding passing between the two women. Helen knew better than to say anything out of place when Nathaniel was in one of his moods.

"Your brandy, sir."

Usually the butler brought Nathaniel his drinks, but Larson must have been busy somewhere else in the house. It didn't matter to Nathaniel what nameless face hovered behind the tray anyway; he snatched the snifter up and drained it in one gulp.

"I've called for the carriage. We leave in half an hour."

Dinner with the stodgy Crawfords had been uneventful. Sophronia had powdered her face until she was as bleached as flour, and the bruise no longer showed. She kept her gaze trained on her plate, making polite comments or deferring to Nathaniel when the conversation required it.

It had been the carriage ride back when the tenuous strands of her life began to snap apart.

Nathaniel had brought a stack of bills and correspondence with him—he hated wasting time that could be spent on business— and was methodically opening them with his ivory letter opener and muttering over the contents. How he could see anything in the dim light of the carriage was beyond her, but she was just glad that he was occupied with something besides her.

Just as the rhythm of the carriage was lulling her to sleep, Nathaniel let out a sharp cry. Her eyes flew open to find him clutching his middle, his face going a startling shade of green as the letter opener clattered to the floor.

Sophronia shrank back into her velvet cloak, wary of his outburst. "Are you all right?"

"My stomach." Doubling over, he let out a pungent belch and groaned. She turned away, wishing it was warm enough to open the window and get some fresh air.

When she looked back, it was to find her husband studying her with icy malice. *"You."* He spat the single word. A nervous, dangerous energy radiated from him; he was like a desperate animal in a cage. She inched farther away from him on the seat. "What? Nathaniel, what are you—"

But she didn't have a chance to finish. He lunged at her,

rocking the carriage and coming down on her, hard. It was all she could do not to fly onto the floor.

His breath was putrid, and with more than just the effects of an evening of eating fish and drinking strong wine. He was struggling to get his hands up around her throat, but there was something wrong with him. His fingers were clumsy, his movements jerky and unnatural. She groped blindly on the floor for something, anything. Out of the corner of her eye, she caught a flash of metal glinting in the passing moonlight. Nathaniel's letter opener. Her hand closed around it.

His breathing was raspy and labored. "I'll...kill...you." Fingers scratched and struggled at her throat, his feverish body pinning her down, his fingers finding purchase around her neck and tightening.

What had she done to him to incur this sort of wrath? Her vision was going fuzzy at the edges, her head light. Panic rose in her throat, and some primal instinct told her that if she didn't act then, she would perish. With all the strength she could muster, she drew the letter opener back and then plunged it up into Nathaniel's chest.

The hands around her neck loosened, and Nathaniel jerked back. Their eyes met, his wide with shock. Slowly, he looked down at the ivory handle sticking out of his lavishly embroidered waistcoat.

Had she done that? He opened his mouth as if to speak, but only an indignant sputter came out. Then his body went slack, and he slumped against her.

Something wet trickled down her wrist. She stared at her shaking hands as if they belonged to someone else. Blood. Her heartbeat thundered in her ears as the carriage continued rumbling along as if nothing had happened. But something *had* happened: she had killed her husband. And soon they would be home.

Numbness swept through her, and she felt as if she were looking at herself from afar. She was a murderer. A refrain of *You killed him! You killed him!* ran through her head, followed by a slow, quiet chant of *You're free! You're free!*

But when they arrived at Castle Carver she would be found out and her freedom from Nathaniel would be short-lived. One look at her and the coachman would see her guilt writ large and bloody on her. She had to act, and she had to act fast.

The carriage was traveling at a good clip, and every rut and bump jostled Nathaniel a little further off her. Gathering all her strength, she propped Nathaniel's body upright against the door, his head lolling to the side like a marionette. How could this be real? Her neck still smarted from his hands around it, and now he was limp and lifeless.

Taking a deep breath, she grasped the letter opener with her slippery hands, and pulled until it dislodged with a great spurt of blood. Then she reached over her husband's corpse and closed her shaking fingers around the door handle. She pushed. Nathaniel was bigger than her, but he was by no means a large man. So when he didn't budge at first, she felt pure, hot panic. She gave another push, and another, until finally his arm swung out into the open air, and the rest of his body followed.

In the end she did not have to feign her shock. Seeing him hit the ground and roll as if he were no more than a sack of potatoes was enough to tear a convincing scream from her throat.

The carriage came to a shuddering halt. This was it; there was no time to spare. Before the coachman had a chance to jump down, Sophronia tumbled out of the carriage and raced down the dark road to where Nathaniel's body lay. She threw herself on top of him, sobbing, the blood on her gown mingling with the fresh blood that flowed onto the dirt. The fall from the carriage had caused a wound to open on his scalp, and she hoped desperately that the coachman would not be able to tell where on Nathaniel's body the blood was coming from.

Footsteps pounded toward her, and then the coachman was towering above her. "Sweet Jesus." He crossed himself. "Mrs. Carver? What's happened?"

Rocking back on her heels, she looked up at the worried face in the moonlight. "He...he had too much to drink, and..." Her mouth went dry. *Say the words. It's just a little lie and this can all go away.* "He stood up and stumbled into the door and it fell open. I couldn't stop him! I don't know what came over him."

She knew what it looked like. She was covered in blood, and a dark stain was spreading in the road. But the coachman must have been in as much shock as her, and his only concern was getting Nathaniel to Castle Carver.

He somehow managed to heft Nathaniel's body back into the carriage and drove them home at breakneck speed. He must have thought there was hope yet for Nathaniel to live, but Sophronia had known the moment the letter opener slid out that he was dead. *The letter opener.* She groped about on the dark and bloody seat until her hands met the sticky ivory, and slipped the letter opener into her reticule.

Helen met them in the drive with a lantern, as if she had been expecting them. She took control, instructing the coachman to lay Nathaniel out in his study and to fetch fresh linens and boiled water.

As soon as the door clicked shut behind him, Sophronia crumpled onto the floor, great gasping breaths wrenching from deep within her chest. What was happening to her? How could the death of a man who had delighted in her torment pull such raw emotion from her hollow body?

Helen had been remarkably calm throughout everything,

and it was only when she cut away Nathaniel's waistcoat and shirt that her face had registered any kind of emotion.

"Good God, Mrs. Carver. What did you do?" Her voice had been quiet, reverent almost, as she took in the ragged puncture in Nathaniel's chest.

But there was no time to explain, to tell her that it had all been done in defense of her own body. The coachman had returned with the water, and he was joined in the doorway by Garrett, and Larson the butler. Helen hastily closed Nathaniel's shirt, but not before Larson's gray brows had shot up at the sight. "I'm sending for a physician," he said, turning.

Sophronia's gaze flew to Helen. All it would take was a cursory examination to see that Nathaniel had died from a stab wound and not a fall. The doctor couldn't come.

Helen was already three steps ahead of her. "There is no need," she said in a tone that was both sorrowful and matter-of-fact. "Look." Taking a small mirror from Nathaniel's desk, she held it beneath his nose to show that it didn't fog. "He's passed."

Silence shrouded the room. Sophronia dared not breathe, lest her breath somehow resurrect him.

Removing his hat, the coachman placed it over his chest in a sign of respect. "God bless him," he said gruffly. "I'll send for the undertaker in the morning."

Larson remained stony-faced, but there was something in his eyes that frightened Sophronia to her core. He suspected her. He stood, unmoving, for an unnervingly long time, until Helen spoke. "I'll sit up with him tonight, and make sure that he is cleaned and prepared for the morning."

Because of her unmarried status and austere disposition—not to mention her knowledge of herbs—Helen was often called to lay out and prepare bodies in Pale Harbor, so it only made sense that she would do so now for her own employer. This seemed to placate Larson, and he gave Helen a stiff nod.

After the servants had left, Helen moved briskly and efficiently, removing Nathaniel's boots and clothing. Sophronia watched with glazed eyes as Helen began washing the body of the man who could never hurt her again.

"What...what is that?" she asked as Helen produced a small leather pouch and proceeded to take out what looked like bundles of dried plants.

Without pausing from her work, Helen began stripping leaves from one of the bundles and laying them out in neat piles on Nathaniel's desk. "Mullein. It helps guide the spirit to the afterlife." She paused, looking up at Sophronia. "Not that the bastard deserves it, but it will ensure that his spirit does not come back."

Sophronia watched in stunned silence as her maidservant of over five years performed what was undeniably witchcraft. Had Helen been practicing in secret this whole time? Had she cast other spells, other charms since she had lived at Castle Carver? The irony was not lost on her that it was only the second most unbelievable thing that had happened that night.

"May I?"

The question pulled Sophronia out of her daze. She looked up to find Helen standing beside her with a smoldering piece of...something in her hand. It looked like a bit of wood, or a plant stem. "It's a protection spell." She must have caught Sophronia's hesitation, because she added, "It will help keep you safe should you fall under suspicion."

With a stiff nod, she allowed Helen to dot her temple with the ashes and mutter some words over her she couldn't quite catch. Sophronia didn't believe in charms and potions, but there was something comforting about the idea of an intangible shield of protection. Maybe she could leave the nightmare of this evening behind her. With Nathaniel gone, maybe she would finally be safe.

When Helen's words died away, Sophronia opened her eyes. She didn't feel any different. "How does it work?"

"That is not for you to worry about." Then the corners of Helen's mouth turned down. "You had better go upstairs and clean up." She nodded at her mistress's blood-soaked dress.

Sophronia knew that while she could change her gown, she could never wash Nathaniel's blood from her hands. But she nodded and rose to leave. The sooner she could get out of the stuffy room with Nathaniel's lifeless body lying prostrate and accusing on the sofa, the better.

But before she had even reached the door, Helen called out and stopped her. "Sophronia? This is our secret now." Helen gestured to the herbs on the table behind her. "All of it."

It was the first time Helen had ever referred to her by her Christian name. It was also the first time Sophronia had really looked at her servant, saw her as more than just an act of charity. The tables were turned, and Helen had been the one to save her. Nothing would ever be the same again.

A gust of salt air pulled Sophronia back into the present, scattering the wretched memories out into the ocean.

"The rumors are true. I did kill him." Her words turned to vapor in the cold air. "I killed my husband."

She watched Gabriel, waiting for him to recoil in disgust. But all he said was, "Oh, Sophy," and, lacing his arms around her, pulled her into his embrace. "There now." The deep timbre of his voice vibrated through her. Her instinct was to pull away, to leave him there on that cold bench in the night and flee back to the safety of her life with Helen.

But her body knew better, and she pressed her head against his chest. Why hadn't she trusted him to understand sooner?

She tucked her head under his chin; they fit together like a key slotting into a lock. If she could only melt into him, safe and secure, and never come out.

Finally, she pulled away, placing her hands on his chest and looking up at him. "But do you see? Helen and I, we are in it together. We swore to each other that we would never tell another living soul, and now I've broken that promise. I've betrayed the person who gave me a new life."

He frowned. "It doesn't seem like much of a life if you're shackled to her. Surely she doesn't expect you to sacrifice your happiness in the name of gratitude?"

Sophronia worried at her lip, ignoring his question. "You still think her capable of tormenting me?"

Gabriel did not say anything for a moment as he gazed out over the misty expanse of water. "No," he finally admitted. "What she did for you…" He trailed off before shaking his head and adding, "I don't think she would hurt you, but I do think the hold she has on you is…unhealthy."

"She needs me," Sophronia said weakly.

"She needs you," he echoed. Gabriel stared at her, his expression a mixture of disbelief and disappointment. "It seems she's more than capable of taking care of herself. Sophronia, I need you."

She caught her breath at his words, and her stomach blossomed with warmth. But then just as quickly it turned ice-cold.

A tidal wave of words built up in her throat, but when she opened her mouth, they all died away. Why couldn't she say anything? How many times had she cursed her cowardice, wishing that she would find not only happiness, but the bravery to recognize and embrace it? And now that happiness was in front of her, declaring itself, she couldn't bring herself to let down her defenses.

The moonlight cast his handsome face in profile as he regarded her with wistful eyes. "I was hoping to hear that you needed me, too," he said quietly.

Her heart sped up in her chest. Of course she needed him. She was driven to distraction thinking about him every day, her body aching for his touch every night. But she wasn't brave like him, and she couldn't bring herself to admit it. She was furious at her own impotence. If she could have lashed out at Nathaniel for making her weak or Helen for making her scared, she would have. But there was only Gabriel with her on the lonely bluff, so it was he who bore the brunt of her anger.

"Do you think that it's been easy living in self-imprisonment all these years? I want to die of boredom, but at least I have some measure of freedom as a widow, and won't throw it away on the trifling feelings of the first man who comes along and fancies himself in love."

She caught a brief flash of something dark in his eyes before the moon slid behind a cloud and obscured his face. When he spoke again, his tone was low and chilly, and she immediately regretted her outburst. "Let me be very clear—my feelings for you are *not* trifling."

His words lanced right through her unworthy heart. It took everything in her not to surrender to him. How easy it would be, but it would be later that she would pay the price. "It wouldn't be fair. Not to me, not to Helen and not to you. I can't give you what you want."

Gabriel stood up abruptly, and the wind that he had been blocking wrapped around her with full force. Pushing his hands through his hair, he let out a tortured curse before whirling back around to face her. "You build up these walls yourself! Do you really think that anyone is completely free of obligations? You cannot claim to love someone and then say that you aren't willing to take the risk to act on it."

Her words slipped out fast and cold before she could stop herself. "I never said I loved you."

He stared at her, stunned. What was wrong with her? How could she say such a terrible thing? As soon as she said it, she knew she could not deny her feelings. She loved Gabriel with a ferocity that shook her to her very bones. She loved the reticent minister who believed more in the beauty of a painting than the words of the sermons he preached every week. She loved the man who tried to hide the brilliant passion inside him that couldn't help but shine through. And that was exactly why it was so important that she spared him from the crushing tedium and desolation of her life. Perhaps Nathaniel had been right: she was frigid and unlovable.

She swallowed and looked away into the blackness of the night. "I'm sorry," she managed to say in a whisper. She could justify her words all she wanted, saying that they'd had only a few conversations, a kiss and a dance, but it was an insult to him and to herself to deny what they both knew simmered between them.

The night air grew colder, sharper. A fine mist settled around them, soaking through her cloak and into her skin.

"You're freezing," Gabriel said, his voice distant and hoarser than usual. "I'm taking you home."

"Gabriel." Her chest ached with sorrow and want. "Truly, I'm sorry. It's just—"

He stopped her with an impatient shake of his head. "There's nothing to apologize for. I misread the signs. It would hardly be the first time," he added under his breath.

He extended his hand to help her up from the bench, but directed his unfocused gaze past her shoulder. Her heart sank;

he wouldn't even look at her. If the night had been cold before, the air around him now was downright glacial.

She pressed her hand into his, but once she was standing, she couldn't bring herself to let him go. His familiar smell of warm sandalwood and whiskey wrapped around her, making her dizzy with longing. She wanted to sink into the oblivion of his warmth, to let him take her under completely and never surface again. Helen's disapproving face faded from her mind, as did her constant reminders that it was the two of them against the world. Nathaniel's cold eyes, the stomach-knotting fear that his footsteps had instilled in her... It all evaporated. There was only Gabriel, and her body's desperate plea to surrender.

Standing on her toes, she hesitantly closed the small distance between them. Her eyes grew heavy as their lips met, a drowsy haze descending over her.

"Sophronia." His voice was tortured as he gently broke the kiss. "Don't tease me. I can't..." He trailed off.

"I'm not," she whispered. "I would never."

He searched her face, and whatever he saw there must have convinced him, because he took her by the shoulders and returned the kiss. It would have been a rough, possessive gesture had his fingertips not stolen up to her cheeks, caressing her as if she were made from the most delicate porcelain. She arched into him as he cupped her breast with one hand, the other snaking around her to grasp her from behind. A low moan caught in his throat, and it was like a switch had been thrown: what had started as a slow, probing kiss now turned into something hungry and desperate.

It wasn't enough. She needed to be closer to him, so much closer. She needed to let him in completely; there could be no halfway. As if thinking the same thing, he rucked up her skirt and petticoats until frigid air hit her bare flesh. She hardly noticed it. Through the rough fabric of his trousers, she could feel him straining against her belly.

She let out a whimper, and his hand stilled in its exploration of her thigh. "Do you want this?" he asked, his voice low and tentative. "Tell me you want this or I'll stop."

"Don't stop, please," she managed to gasp. His hand was a deliciously warm contrast to the cold air pricking at her skin.

"Thank God." He threw his coat on the ground, plucked her off her feet and gently laid her down.

Sophronia's mind was wonderfully tranquil as he lowered himself between her thighs. When was the last time she had felt this at peace? The weight of him was exquisite. Liquid warmth pooled in her stomach as he settled against her.

He hesitated. *Why was he hesitating?* "Are you sure? You deserve—"

Reaching up, she took his face in her hands and looked straight into his eyes. "I need you. *Now.*"

His pupils flared with desire, and in one glorious moment he was inside her. She cried out at the delicious sensation of being stretched, filled completely.

He stilled, and for a terrible moment she thought he was going to stop, to withdraw and leave her aching and empty. "Oh, God, did I hurt you?"

Tears pricked her eyes and she couldn't help but smile. "No," she said in a whisper. "It's just…you're perfect. Don't stop."

At her words he let out a low moan, and then he was moving steady and powerfully inside her. No matter how deep he thrust, she couldn't get enough of him, and she arched her hips to meet him. Pebbles and dead grass stabbed at her through the coat, but she wouldn't have traded this moment with Gabriel on the ground for all the feather beds in the world.

His thrusts came harder and faster until she reached a dizzying peak of pleasure, and they came crashing down together.

Languid and spent, they lay entangled on his coat. He brushed her temple with a kiss. Nuzzling closer into his chest, she laid her palm over the taut muscle that sheathed his heart. They were custodians of each other's fragile hopes now; she had never been more vulnerable, and yet she had never felt safer.

24

"You're back."

Sophronia nearly shot out of her skin at the disembodied voice in the shadowed hall. When she saw that it was only Helen standing at the foot of the spiral staircase, she let out a gasp of relief.

"What on earth are you doing awake? You scared me half to death." She kept her voice even, but her fingers were shaking as she removed her cloak and hung it up. Her braids were loose and tangled despite her efforts to pin them back into their style, and she was grateful for the darkness obscuring the evidence of her transgression.

Stepping out of the shadows, Helen took up the lamp from the sideboard. The flickering light threw her face into sharp relief, deepening the furrow between her brows and the downturn of her lips. "I was worried when you still weren't home by eleven. I went out to find you."

Sophronia's heart stopped. Went out to find her? Had Helen followed her to Gabriel's? Followed her afterward? Could she have… Oh, God, could she have *seen* them? Her throat went tight at the thought.

"Well, here I am," Sophronia said, moving to brush past her and go upstairs. Her legs were still unsteady, her heart racing in exhilaration at what had transpired on the bluff.

But Helen didn't budge, and stopped her with a surprisingly firm hand to her arm. "You told him."

Heat rushed to Sophronia's face, and she stumbled at the bottom step. Helen knew. She knew that Sophronia had betrayed her secret, knew that Sophronia had lain with the minister out in the open like some common harlot. And yet, she couldn't seem to shore up any regret. "And you followed me? For shame."

"You don't deny it?"

"Oh, so what if I did!" She yanked herself out of Helen's grasp. "I can't carry it around anymore. It's killing me. What happened that night has kept my heart in fetters these four years. I trust Gabriel. He won't betray me. Us," she quickly amended.

Picking up her skirts, she walked quickly up the stairs. In a moment, the sound of footsteps followed her. "Sophy, wait."

Something in Helen's voice stopped her. With a sigh, Sophronia turned around on the landing. "I'm tired. We can talk about it tomorrow. You needn't worry, though, this doesn't change anything between us."

Helen made no move to leave. The air around them was close and warm, charged with an uneasy energy.

"Oh, but it changes *everything*." Helen's voice came out in a cool, dangerous hiss that Sophronia hardly recognized. "You think you carry a heavy burden, but you have no idea the things I've done for you, the lengths I've gone to protect you, both from that monster and from the people of this town."

"Please, not tonight," she said, the joy at the time she had just spent with Gabriel draining from her. She was too tired for this, and as she turned to go down the hall to bed, she remembered with chagrin how staunchly she had defended Helen to Gabriel. She was struck by a sudden, perverse impulse, though she knew it would only anger Helen. Just as she was about to the turn the knob to her room, she paused, looking back at her in the dark hall. "Do you really believe your herbs and charms count as protection?"

Helen didn't move, and for a moment Sophronia thought that she hadn't heard. But then she was sweeping down the hall, stopping just short of the door, so close that she could see Helen's dark pupils glinting. "And do you really believe that you were strong enough to bring Nathaniel down yourself?"

Dumbfounded, Sophronia just blinked at her. A memory flashed through her mind from the night of the carriage ride, the way Nathaniel had practically fallen onto the letter opener. She wet her lips. "What...what are you talking about?"

Crossing her arms, Helen surveyed her with a mixture of pity and exasperation. "He would have killed you, Sophronia. Anyone could see that he was getting worse, his outbursts more violent. You were in no position to defend yourself."

"Helen," she repeated slowly, "what are you talking about?"

Helen's look hardened. "I poisoned him, for weeks. Slowly, and just a little bit at a time. I knew the right herbs that would make the poison build up in his body. I gave him the fatal dose the night of the Crawfords' dinner, and poured the rest into his flask. You might have plunged the knife into him, but he was already weak and dying."

The world spun out from under Sophronia's feet. She leaned against the wall for support, her mind reeling. "You...you *poisoned* him?"

All these years, Helen had let her believe that she, Sophronia, was solely responsible for Nathaniel's death. All these years, she had made Sophronia feel indebted to her for her role in covering up Nathaniel's death. All these years, she had let Sophronia carry the guilt, the fear of being found out. But Sophronia hadn't been responsible, not completely. "How could you do such a thing?"

"How could I not! You're too soft, too delicate. I never thought when you returned that night that he would have been covered in blood from a stab wound. The poison would have finished him discreetly, and no one would have ever known the cause."

Somehow, beyond her anger and horror at what Helen had done, Sophronia felt a pang of regret. She could have been rid of Nathaniel without so much as shedding a drop of blood by her own hand. She swallowed, pushing the unwelcome thought away. "I never asked for your help."

"You didn't need to. I saw how it was with him, how frightened you were."

"Of course I was frightened of him!" The words exploded out of her. They felt good, cathartic. "He was a horrible man who traded in fear to get what he wanted." An awful thought dawned on her. "But that was never what it was really about, was it?"

Helen's expression grew wary. "What do you mean? Of course it was."

"Mr. Stone is all the things that Nathaniel was not—good and kind, gentle. But you still hate him, can't even bring yourself to look at him when he calls. Don't tell me that you were driven purely by the urge to protect me. Gabriel offers me no threat and yet you—"

Helen stopped her with a panicked hand to her arm. "Do you love him? Does he love you?"

The question caught Sophronia off guard. She pulled her arm away. "I don't see what business it is of yours."

Taking her by the shoulders, Helen was peering at her with frantic eyes. "Just tell me. Yes or no."

She pushed away. "So what if I do! I love Gabriel, and he loves me, as well." The words should have made her heart light, should have been pure joy to utter, but Helen had pried them from her with all the force of a rusty shovel.

"Then it is done," Helen said in a whisper.

"What are you talking about?"

"The spell, the protection spell. It's broken."

Not this again. Sophronia let out an exasperated huff. She just wanted to go to bed, to luxuriate in her night with Gabriel while the memories were still fresh. "Your spells never worked," she said. "I was content to let you believe that the salt circles, the smudged herbs really worked, and I even let myself believe it, too. But there is no such thing as magic, and you no more helped me by pretending otherwise than you did by poisoning Nathaniel."

Helen was cradling her temples in her hands, shaking her head like a little child. "No, no, no," she said, with a moan of despair. "You never noticed it because it was working. So long as you loved me best, you were safe."

The clock struck the hour, and Sophronia started as twelve emphatic chimes rang out. Helen, her friend, her only friend, had cast a spell on her. Never mind that spells weren't real; she had sought to keep Sophronia bound to her by some dark force.

"I can't… I can't talk to you right now," Sophronia said, pushing past her into her bedchamber. She closed the door behind her, leaning her head back against the heavy wood and wishing that she had never visited that godforsaken poorhouse.

Gabriel watched the darkness of the winding drive swallow up Sophronia's figure before he finally turned to walk slowly back home. He had begged her to come back to his cottage, to spend the night safe in his arms, the town's gossip be damned. But she had insisted on returning to Castle Carver, saying that Helen would be beside herself with worry. It stung that even after she had entrusted her confession to him, she still wanted to run to Helen.

Mist turned to rain, cold little needles slicing into his skin. His body might have been drowsy and satisfied, but his mind reeled with fresh memories of Sophronia on the bluff, her body soft and yielding under his. She made him feel as if he were the only man in the world when she looked up at him, and God knew she was the only woman in the world for him.

Anna. Her name floated into his mind, and he cursed himself. He could not forget her; yet what was worse was that she always came as an afterthought, compounding his guilt with a deep sense of shame.

Damn. *Damn.* He'd let desire cloud his mind, and now he'd all but broken his vow to Anna. Some part of him had been glad that Sophronia had the good sense to rebuff his advances at first, and he'd been ready to accept her choice. But when she had surprised him by kissing him, he'd been powerless to resist.

Tom would set him right. But then he groaned inwardly; he'd sworn to Sophronia that he would not tell another living soul her secret. And what did he think of the truth, now that it was finally laid before him like a feast for the eating? Her husband had been despicable, the worst sort of man. The kind of man who was charming and wealthy and could have had anything he wanted. The vilest, weakest kind of man who only wanted a pretty wife, someone to take the brunt of his frustration and wrath.

Gabriel was just turning down the path when a noise through the trees stopped him. He turned around, peering into the darkness. "Who's there?"

The only answering sound was the wind licking around him, scattering paper-dry leaves across the path.

It had probably been a fox or some other nocturnal creature, but it reminded him that the nights were still fraught with danger here. Shoving his hands in his coat pockets, he picked up his pace. He should have insisted Sophronia come home with him, her stubbornness be damned. He had meant what he said about Helen earlier; if she had kept Sophronia's secret and protected her all these years, then it was unlikely she was responsible for tormenting her mistress. But that meant that the actual culprit was still somewhere out there, and Gabriel was no closer to discovering the person's identity. Sophronia was still at risk.

"So," Tom said casually as they strolled to the church the next morning, "when will we be graced with the lovely Mrs. Carver's presence again?"

Gabriel frowned, idly thrashing a stick at dead bushes along the path. What *would* happen now? Just because Sophronia had shared her body with him didn't mean that she would deign to be his wife. Would she stay at Castle Carver with Helen, only venturing out on occasion to rendezvous with him? Or would she come to her senses and sever him from her completely? The thought was unbearable.

Tom stopped and took Gabriel by the arm. "Gabe?" he said with a searching look. "What happened last night?"

A schoolboy impulse made him want to crow a little, but what had happened between him and Sophronia had been so much more than the stuff of schoolyard tattle. It had been like coming home, an affirmation of every feeling that had smoldered in his chest since he met her. Clearing his throat, he plowed on ahead. "Nothing. I walked Mrs. Carver home."

Tom matched his brisk pace. "You were gone for three hours."

Scowling, he threw Tom an impatient look. "Something happened that shouldn't have happened, and I'm too much of a rotter to regret it."

"Is that so?" Tom paused, tipping his hat to two elderly women passing in the opposite direction. "Seems to me that if you don't regret it, there's no use in blaming yourself. What's done is done and you might as well be glad of it."

Gabriel didn't say anything, just continued thwapping his stick and letting his thoughts run around him in circles.

Tom let out a sigh. "You deserve some happiness, Gabe. Don't make it harder for yourself than it has to be."

"If it were up to me, I would marry the woman and take her far away from here. But it's not up to me."

Wasn't that one of the reasons why he loved Sophronia, that she was her own woman? How could he demand that she give up her independence for him? And yet, she wasn't free. She had said herself that she felt like a prisoner in her own home. Perhaps he could talk to Helen, try to reason with her and convince her that Sophronia needed his protection, but he knew that Sophronia would be furious if he interfered. He gave his stick a good thwack against an obliging tree trunk, cracking it in half.

He didn't need to look at Tom to feel his incredulous gaze. "I never thought I'd see the day," Tom said. "Gabriel Stone in love again and with a mind to take a new wife. I expect we'll see pigs fly next."

"Oh, don't get too excited," Gabriel muttered. "Even if she would have me, I'm not free to marry."

Tom raised a brow. "Oh? Have I missed something? Are you betrothed to someone else, married already, perhaps?"

"You know what I mean, Tom."

"No indeed, I confess I don't. But please, enlighten me."

"Anna," Gabriel said. "I can't… I couldn't do that to her."

This silenced Tom, and for a time they walked without speaking. Finally, Tom said, "You don't really feel that way, do you?"

"Of course I do," Gabriel said roughly. "After she came back to me, I promised her I would be a better man. I can't break that promise now that she is dead, and dead because of me, no less."

Tom's look softened. "Women die in childbed all the time, Gabe. It's tragic and cruel, but you can't blame yourself."

Gabriel shrugged off his words. "I got her with child and she died. I don't see how anyone else could be to blame."

As they walked, he replayed the events of the previous night in his head. He should have been feeling as light as a feather. It was a beautiful fall day, crisp and bright, with a sky as sharply blue as crystal. The same blue as Anna's eyes. It was a moment before he realized that Tom had fallen behind as he plowed ahead.

"My God, man." Tom jogged to catch up with him and took him by the arm. "Gabriel, I…"

Gabriel tugged his arm away. "Just leave it."

Tom was staring intently at him. "Gabe," he said, clearing his throat, "There's something you should know. Something about Anna that—"

"Wait." Gabriel came to an abrupt halt. There was something down off the side of the road, in the brush. A sick feeling of dread came over him. "Do you see that?"

Squinting, Tom followed his line of sight. He sucked in his breath. "Is that…?"

The men looked at each other and then broke out into a sprint, scrambling down to where the body lay.

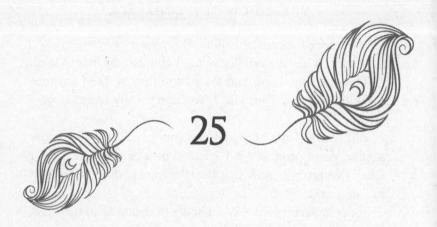

25

Sophronia had no stomach for work. Every time she sat down, her thoughts turned to Helen's revelation and what it meant. Helen had killed Nathaniel. Well, not quite, but Sophronia certainly never would have needed to draw the letter opener on him if it hadn't been for Helen's poisoning. Everything about their friendship had been built on a lie.

And then there was Gabriel. Sophronia drifted about the house in a languid haze, desperately trying to re-create the previous night in her mind. Standing in the upstairs window, she stared out at the misty harbor. It had been only one day, but already she felt deprived from the lack of Gabriel's touch, and the air around her body was strangely empty and cold. He had somehow become as familiar to her as her own skin. She had let him in completely—body and soul, secrets and all—and for the first time in years, she felt an intoxicating sense of freedom.

Had she truly ever feared the townspeople and what they would think of her? In the afterglow of what she had shared with Gabriel, it seemed so silly now. Why had she let her fear dictate her life for so long? It was as if she had been under a fairy-tale enchantment these past years, and it had taken a night of passion to break the spell. Grimly, she thought of Helen, how she'd claimed that she'd put a spell on Sophronia for so many years.

Sighing, she pulled her shawl tighter to keep out the creeping November chill. Work couldn't be put off forever. Reluctantly, she went back downstairs, hoping to avoid Helen, and made herself a cup of tea to take to her desk. A letter from the Portland office had arrived that morning, full of bland praise for the batch of stories she had sent them last month. All very nice, but her publisher, Mr. Wilmot, wondered if she could send another Poe story. He was keen to point out that Mr. Carver had been able to secure stories from the notoriously fickle author. Or, if not Poe, could she find something equally chilling? She had briefly considered sending him one of Jasper Gibbs's dreadful stories, only to realize that she had thrown most of his submissions out, and that any others had probably been lost when Duchess had spilled ink on her desk.

If she had no stomach for work, she certainly had no stomach for Mr. Poe's morbid stories, which had seeped into the fabric of her life. Casting the letter onto her desk, Sophronia tapped her pen and stared out the window at Helen, who was walking back and forth outside the carriage house, the raven perched on her wrist. She could just make out Helen's lips moving, as if she were conferring with the bird, and the raven cocked its head in turn, as if it were listening. In her black homespun dress and severe, braided bun, Helen looked every inch the formidable witch.

Duchess jumped up on the desk to join her, watching the scene from the window. "It seems that I've been replaced," Sophronia murmured as she absently scratched behind the cat's ears. "By a bird, no less."

She and Helen had avoided each other that morning, and

when they did cross paths it was tense, their words to each other few and cold. What could they say? Sophronia had kept their secret all these years, only to tell Gabriel in a fit of passion, and then find out that the truth was not at all what she had thought.

Footsteps on the front path drew her out of her melancholy reverie. She arranged her face into a bland mask, fortifying herself for another tense encounter with Helen.

Then she caught the sound of male voices accompanying the footsteps. It wasn't Helen. Sophronia shot up, disrupting Duchess and sending her hiding under the sofa. Her heart leaped to her throat as she hurried to the door, and she felt her cheeks go hot in guilty anticipation. "Gabriel?"

But then his voice was joined by someone else's. She opened the door, finding Gabriel with his fist raised, ready to knock.

She stepped back, deflated. Gabriel stood flanked by Mr. Ellroy and Constable Morris. His gaze met hers briefly, something like an apology flashing in his eyes.

It was the constable who spoke first. "Mrs. Carver," he said by way of greeting.

Sophronia stood with her hand on the doorjamb, too surprised by the unlikely trio to say anything.

The constable cleared his throat. "May we come inside?"

"I...excuse me, but what is this concerning?" Something in the gravity of the constable's voice—and the way no one would meet her eyes—made her uneasy. "Have you found who was responsible for disturbing my husband's grave?"

The men shared a glance. "No, ma'am, I'm afraid not," the constable said. "This concerns another matter."

She tried to catch Gabriel's eye again, but he was looking past her sightlessly into the hall. Her skin prickled. What had happened since last night? Why wouldn't he look at her? Suddenly, the constable wanting to speak with her was the least of her worries. But there was no way to speak to Gabriel alone and quell her fears, so she just nodded.

"Very well," she said, standing back and admitting them inside.

When Gabriel stepped in, he paused next to her as if he would bend and whisper something in her ear. He looked worried, his shoulders hunched into his too-tight coat, his usually full lips pressed thin. She couldn't help her eyes fluttering closed, his nearness making her restless despite her misgivings. But he didn't say anything, and then they were moving into the parlor.

"Will you take anything to drink?" she asked. The men shook their heads.

Should she ask them to sit down? It was unbearable, the way that none of them would look her in the face. "Well, perhaps you had just better be out with it and tell me why you're here," she said, struggling to keep her voice light and accommodating.

The constable, whose gaze had been wandering over the furnishings and paintings on the walls, leaned against the back of the sofa and locked eyes with her. "There's been a murder."

"Oh, no," Sophronia said faintly. Her mind raced. Why were they here, telling her? She had no family in town, and Helen was safe in the carriage house. How could this concern her? "How terrible. Who?"

"Jonas Peckham."

She frowned, racking her brain, trying to place the familiar name. "What, not old Jonas?" She knew of his drunken misadventures as related to her by Helen, but she'd be hard-pressed to say whether she'd ever even met the man. "What happened?"

"His throat was slit," Gabriel said, a note of apology in his voice, as if he would spare her from the gruesome revelation.

"That's...that's awful, but I wasn't acquainted with him," she said. "I'm afraid I can't be of any help to you."

But the men didn't budge. The constable was scratching at a shaving scab on his chin, Mr. Ellroy was pointedly looking out the window with his hands clasped behind his back and Gabriel was still maddeningly distant.

"The murder occurred last night." At the constable's words, Gabriel colored, so faintly that she was sure she was the only one to see it. Last night, while they were surrendering to their deepest desires on the bluff, a killer had slipped unnoticed through the town and taken the life of an innocent man. Her stomach turned over.

"I see, but how does that concern me?" But one look at the constable's grim expression confirmed her worst fears.

Her knees went weak and she had to reach out behind her, gripping the arm of a chair. Nathaniel's stupid, empty chair. Gabriel took a step forward as if he might try to steady her, but he stopped short.

She had an alibi, but to admit that she was with Gabriel in the middle of the night, alone... Well, that would hardly be any better in the eyes of the constable.

The spell. Helen's wretched spell. Could it have been real after all? Was it coincidence that as soon as Helen said it was broken that a murder charge would be laid at her doorstep? Sophronia pushed the ridiculous idea away.

Finally, Gabriel met her gaze and his look hit her like a blow. He was thinking the same thing she was: that to admit that they were together would only serve to harm her. But did he agree? Did he think less of her now that she had lain with him? Instinctively her fingers went to her scar. Men hurt you, that's what they did. It might not be with a knife, but they would leave their mark one way or the other. At least the scar was proof that Nathaniel had come and gone, that she had survived him; what would Gabriel leave her with, other than more crippling self-doubt?

"Perhaps you could explain this, Mrs. Carver," the constable said, producing a scrap of white fabric.

Sophronia looked between the constable's outstretched hand and Gabriel. He winced.

Confused, she took the proffered linen. It was stained with blood, but then she saw why they had brought it and her heart sank.

She stared in horror at the familiar handkerchief with the neatly embroidered initials and violets. A little project she had done years ago to help the endless hours pass. How had it found its way out of the house? How had it found its way to Jonas Peckham, for that matter? She couldn't even remember the last time she'd seen it.

"Those are your initials, aren't they, Mrs. Carver?"

S.L.C. Sophronia Lee Carver. Her mouth had gone so dry that she could only stare at it in dumb disbelief.

"Don't be ridiculous," Mr. Ellroy said, clearly impatient. He had taken off his coat and was pacing restlessly about the room. "Initials are hardly proof of murder."

Biting her lip, Sophronia dropped her gaze, wishing that she could prove Mr. Ellroy right. When she looked up, she found Gabriel studying her with an unreadable expression.

"Of course it's not," he said, finally breaking his silence. "Mrs. Carver," he said, his gruff voice softened with concern, "tell Constable Morris that it doesn't belong to you, and then he can leave. This is just a formality."

Heat flooded her face, and she shook her head, words choking in her throat.

"Sophronia?" he repeated in a whisper, his hazel eyes filled with questions.

"It's mine."

★ ★ ★

The clock struck three. Sophronia sank down onto the sofa, Gabriel at her side. "Where...where was it?"

"On the body," Gabriel said, hoping to spare her as many of the grizzly details as possible. There had been no mistaking the cause of death, and it certainly hadn't been an accident this time. They had found Jonas's throat slit end to end like a grotesque grin, his face painted red with his own blood. Gabriel had no doubt that there was some connection to Poe.

"I—I don't know how it got there," Sophronia said, looking up between him and Tom. The earnest supplication in her eyes was heartbreaking. "I haven't seen this for months. I'd assumed it had gone missing in the wash."

The silence of the parlor pressed in around them. It killed him not to be able to gather her up in his arms. If he had felt the urge to whisk her away at the funeral or the ball from the animosity of the townspeople, it was physically painful to watch her suffer now. She sat there in her blue silk dress, her slender neck bowed and vulnerable. She must think him the worst sort of man for taking her roughly on the ground last night and now hardly able to meet her eye.

Raking his hand through his hair, he let out a long breath. God help him for what he was about to say. He would either damn her further or absolve her, but not without significant repercussions. "She was with me last night."

Tom politely cleared his throat and turned away, making a show of examining one of the paintings on the wall. Color flamed up the sides of the constable's neck, as he snapped his gaze from Gabriel to Sophronia. He was looking at her with something between contempt and fear, and Gabriel knew that no matter the damage to her reputation, it was far better to admit that they were together than for her to be implicated in this mess.

"I see," Constable Morris said in clipped tones. "You might have told me that sooner."

Gabriel didn't say anything.

Tom finally turned from the painting and spoke up. "I can vouch that they were together. Gabriel walked Mrs. Carver home after a late supper at his house. Left me alone to drink sherry in the parlor for hours until I realized he wasn't coming back."

Gabriel shot him a sharp look, but all he got was a shrug and a hint of Tom's crooked grin in return.

The constable let out a huff. "That still doesn't explain the handkerchief, or how it came to be on the body of a dead man."

Unable to keep the irritation from creeping into his voice, Gabriel fisted his hands at his sides, lest he become tempted to wipe the smug look from the constable's face. "It's clear that someone is trying to malign Mrs. Carver, to scare her. You can't think it a coincidence that her husband's watch was dug up for her to come upon, and then a handkerchief with her initials on it would be found on a body. Why would she do such a thing herself?"

The constable ignored this. "Mrs. Carver, I would recommend that you not go anywhere for a while until this matter has been looked into further. I'll need to consult the magistrate and possibly send for a detective from Portland."

To her credit, Sophronia didn't seem perturbed by the demand. If anything, there was a hint of weary amusement in her eyes. "I assure you, Constable, I am not given to sudden flights."

"Humph." He narrowed his eyes, as if suspicious that he was the butt of some joke he didn't understand.

A knock at the door saved Gabriel from having to intervene. The constable looked from Sophronia out to the hall. "Stay here," he ordered.

Sophronia wound her hands in her lap, and Gabriel had to force himself not to reach out and take them in his own. She was handling herself with her usual easy grace and dignity, but tight lines around her mouth and the heaviness of her eyes betrayed the toll it was taking on her.

A moment later, Fanny was cautiously coming into the parlor with the constable at her back. The girl shot Gabriel a questioning look.

"Fanny," Sophronia said with a strained smile. "I'm afraid you find us quite in disarray. I've not had the chance to gather the linens yet."

Fanny frowned, her eyes full of questions, but she nodded. "I can fetch them. It's no trouble."

The linens. In a flash, it all made sense how the handkerchief had gotten out of the house. Could the girl really have been so careless to lose something she'd been paid to mend? Gabriel knew that Fanny took her work seriously and was nothing if not fastidious. But the alternative was that she had taken it on purpose, even had something to do with this nasty business.

He saw Sophronia catch her breath as if she had had the same thought. "Would you mind very much coming back tomorrow? I have some old frocks that I'd like to go through first. I'm so sorry you had to come out here for nothing," she added.

"Oh," Fanny said, flicking her glance around to the men. Gabriel prayed that the constable would not realize what Sophronia surely had: that Fanny had access to her personal effects and could have easily taken the handkerchief. The evidence might absolve Sophronia in the eyes of a just man, but Gabriel did not trust that Constable Morris was just.

The constable watched with hard eyes as Fanny nodded her understanding and left.

As if sensing that Gabriel needed to talk to Sophronia alone, Tom gave an overloud yawn. "You'll excuse me, but I'm dead tired. I think I'll escort Miss Gibbs home and then retire, if you have no further need of me."

Gabriel shot him a grateful look and the constable waved him off. "Go, go. Though I'd ask you also not to leave town until this business is straightened out."

After Tom had left, Gabriel turned his attention to Constable Morris. It had been torture to be so close to Sophronia and not be able to touch her, to comfort her. Now he wasn't sure how much longer he could contain himself. "Constable," he said. "If you've no more questions for Mrs. Carver—"

Constable Morris interrupted him in a rare display of decisive authority. "I'll decide when the questioning is finished."

With held breath, they waited for him to continue his interrogation. But it seemed that he was done anyway. With an irritated glance at the clock, the constable cleared his throat. "It's later than I realized. I should be going."

Gabriel exhaled.

"Remember," the constable said, narrowing his eyes at Sophronia, "no leaving Pale Harbor."

She nodded. His look lingered on them for a moment longer. Then he said good evening and touched his hat to them, finally leaving her and Gabriel alone.

26

The door had barely clicked shut when Gabriel crouched before Sophronia and took her hands in his. "Are you all right?" he asked, searching her pale face.

She was trembling. "I…I think so, yes. I wasn't expecting to be accused of murder today."

His heart squeezed. "Sophy, I'm so sorry," he said, aware that the words were completely inadequate. "Tom and I came across the body and sent for the constable. He found the handkerchief and…well, I was hoping it wasn't yours. He would have come regardless, and I thought it better if I were here when that happened."

Her hands had stopped trembling, but they were still so cold. "I'm sure I cannot fault the constable for doing his job, even if he does seem only lately to have taken an interest in it." Her lips curved up in a small smile, but it did not warm her face. Then she dropped her gaze to her lap. "I…I thought that you were upset with me. That you regretted what happened between us last night."

Her voice was small, like a child's. She looked at him from

under shy lashes, but he just sat there, stupidly staring at her. "Angry with you?"

"I know that men... That is, it's been my experience that sometimes the act of..." She seemed to be fumbling for the right words. "...of lovemaking, can change the way in which a man perceives the lady afterward. Perhaps it is regret, or contempt. I'm not sure what it is exactly, only that it is never the same between them again."

Gabriel didn't say anything, didn't move. That such a spirited, beautiful woman could even think of herself in such a way made him white-hot with rage. Rage for the man who had used her so ill, who had taught her that she was anything less than precious. Taking her face in his hands, he skimmed the soft skin of her jaw with his thumb. "You've done nothing wrong. Never, *never* apologize for the love inside of you. Last night was..." He trailed off. Last night he had felt a connection with someone that he had never felt before. It was more than he and Anna had shared, more than her ghost could ever give him. "It was incredible."

The clouds passed from her silver eyes, leaving them sparkling and clear. Her shoulders sagged in relief. "Truly?"

He nodded.

Color touched her cheeks. "I can't stop thinking about it. I wish—" She broke off, her gaze darting to the doorway and then the window. "I wish we could truly be alone."

The words tripped off her lips, and his loins tightened at just the suggestion. If he could have taken her then and there, he would have, and murder be damned. But she was still shaken, and God knew Helen was probably skulking about somewhere.

"Let me fetch you a glass of water," he said, abruptly standing. It was as much for her as it was for him to gather himself. When he returned, she was sitting with her usual regal posture, but there was still a faint line of worry on her temple. "Thank you." She took a sip and put the glass down, shaking her head. "I simply cannot accept that Fanny has anything to do with this."

Gabriel carefully sat across from her and waited for her to continue. She was lost in thought, her slender fingers nervously turning the glass around in her hands.

"I've known her for years, and she's sweet through and through and completely artless."

Sighing, he pressed the heels of his hands into his eyes until his vision swam with stars. Christ, what a mess. There was no rhyme or reason to any of it, and each new clue, each new horror, only brought more questions. "You didn't ask the details of the death," he finally said.

Sophronia spoke slowly, as if choosing her words with great care. "I can't say I wish to know, but I suppose it would be better if I did. Tell me."

He hated having to shatter what little innocence she had left, but she knew more about Poe than he did, and would recognize if there was some meaning in the blood on Jonas's face. "His throat was slit, ear to ear."

A little noise of shock escaped her lips, but she didn't say anything as he continued.

"I'm afraid that's not all." He paused, searching for the right words to describe the gruesome scene that had met him and Tom in the brush that morning. "His face was covered in blood, almost as if it had been...as if it had been painted with it."

He had expected her to recoil in shock, or that she would need a few moments to process this, but instead she simply sat there, her expression growing almost thoughtful. "Painted in blood?" She frowned. "I take it this means you think the killer is the same person who has been responsible for the notes and the other…gifts." She shook her head and gave him a helpless look. "I'm afraid it doesn't sound familiar."

Gabriel let out a breath. Did it even matter if there was some significance to the blood on the dead man's face? All of the connections to Poe they had discovered had gotten them no closer to learning the identity of the perpetrator. But suddenly Sophronia sat up straighter, as if she'd just thought of something, then sprang out of her seat and rushed to her desk where she rifled through a pile of magazines.

She flipped through one before holding it up for him to see. "'The Masque of the Red Death,'" she said with a note of pride. "I remember seeing this one when we first went through all the magazines. No one's face is painted in blood, per se, but Death comes to visit a masquerade ball at an abbey where the rich people of the town have barricaded themselves against the plague. He moves about the abbey in a red mask, killing all the wealthy guests." Sophronia drummed her fingers against the magazine, thinking. "The killer may have been trying to emulate that in his own clumsy way."

They both sat in silence, Sophronia no doubt thinking the same thing he was: how morbid it was to reduce a man's life to nothing more than a clue in a riddle. Up until now the ravens and the cat manikin and heart had been unsettling, the notes vaguely threatening. But now a man was dead, and the culprit had shown himself to have no qualms about taking a human life.

"We need to find out who is after you, Sophy," Gabriel said. "This—" he broke off, gesturing vaguely toward the window and the town beyond "—is only getting worse, and it could be anyone."

She nodded, but the furrow in her brow only deepened. "Yes," she said faintly. Her expression was faraway, distracted. "Yes," she repeated. "It could be anyone."

★ ★ ★

When Gabriel left, he took the little remaining daylight with him, leaving Sophronia alone with her thoughts. The weight that had briefly felt as if it had been lifted from her shoulders came rushing back. Standing to stretch, she went to the windows and drew the curtains against the descending dusk. The room was growing cold, and she realized that Helen had not put coals in the grate as she usually did.

Footsteps clipped along in the hallway and then Helen appeared, as if summoned by her brooding thoughts. "I saw the constable was here," she said without preamble. "What did he want?"

Sophronia kneeled at the grate, taking her time scooping the coals. Was Helen frightened that her involvement in Nathaniel's death would finally come to light? Would she sacrifice Sophronia for her own freedom if it came to that? "There was a murder."

Rising, she wiped off her sooty hands. "Jonas Peckham," she added before Helen could ask who.

"Well?" Helen said, lowering herself carefully into a chair and folding her hands in her lap. "What is it to us?"

"What is it to us?" Sophronia echoed in amazement. "You must know that they suspect me. First it was Nathaniel's watch, and now this. They think I am some sort of...of witch...and take unnatural pleasure from tampering with the citizens of Pale Harbor."

Helen gave her an impatient scowl, glossing over the accusation. "And they're all damned fools. You're not capable of killing a fly, let alone a grown man."

It might have been a compliment or an insult the way she said it. Either way, the words took on new meaning in the light of Helen's gruesome revelation. "They found my handkerchief on the body," Sophronia said, studying Helen's expression carefully.

Helen's dark eyes widened almost imperceptibly. "How is that possible?"

"I thought I lost it weeks ago after it never came back with the mending. It could have fallen out anywhere along the way when Fanny took the linens, but I didn't think anything of it at the time." Fanny did the laundry in the big soapstone tub in the kitchen, but she often took pieces home with her for additional mending. A little handkerchief could have easily slipped out of her basket along the way.

Helen gave her an incredulous look. "Fell out and found its way to a dead Jonas Peckham?"

A knock at the door saved Sophronia from having to respond. She stood and gave a heavy sigh. "The constable must have forgotten something." All she wanted to do was escape to her bed for an early night. She was beyond exhausted, and feared that she would not be able to put on a show of confidence and grace much longer today.

Pausing before she opened the front door, she took a deep breath, smoothed down her skirts and pasted a bland smile on her face. "Constable," she said, opening the door. "I—"

Her hand dropped, and the door swung the rest of the way open. There was only yawning darkness.

She caught her breath, looking down the misty path. A white envelope lay neatly on the top step, a small stone on top of it to keep the wind from gusting it away. It was just like the night of the candles. Her face grew hot, her neck prickled. With the light of the hall spilling out into the night, someone could be hiding only steps away, watching her.

Heart pounding, she grabbed the note, slammed the door shut and bolted it against the darkness. Helen had come up

behind her, and watched silently as Sophronia slowly unfolded the note.

Her whole body was tensed, her hands shaking. There was
nothing she wanted less than to know what this letter said.
She forced herself to read it anyway. "You shall know what
it is to be hunted."

Another sermon, another funeral.

Would facing this congregation be any easier than the first
time? Gabriel wondered as he looked out over the pews packed
with worried faces. These were not the curious people who
had come only weeks before to gawk at the new minister
from Concord; these were frightened, confused people looking for answers.

Gabriel gripped the wooden pulpit. He had not been able
to sit down the previous evening and craft any sort of appropriate eulogy. His mind had been too full of Sophronia and
her predicament, too tortured by thoughts of how much he
wanted her. And that was to say nothing of the fact that he
didn't know the first thing about Mr. Peckham or how to best
remember his life. Any attempt at a eulogy would be hollow,
trite. Now, as he gazed out over his congregation, he realized it didn't matter. There were no words that would honor
Jonas Peckham more than promising swift action to find his
killer. He could only wonder if one of the familiar faces that
looked back at him belonged to the murderer.

Before he could think better of it, Gabriel blurted out, "I
vow to find who has done this and bring him to justice."

Drooping bonnets snapped to attention, and there were
murmurs of surprise. Bolstered by this, he continued. "Someone in this town thinks to bring us to our knees in fear. But
I am here to say that they will not succeed." If he could have
gathered up Sophronia into his arms, shielding her from ac-

cusations and proving her innocent, he would have. But this was the next best option.

Or so he thought. Just then a man in the back piped up. "Oh? And what if it's that woman? Will you still be so keen to see justice done when it's someone you take a special interest in? Don't think we haven't seen you going up there every chance you get."

Jesus Christ, didn't anyone have anything better to do in this town than spy and gossip? A growl built deep in the back of Gabriel's throat, but he quashed it down and took a deep breath. "*Whoever* it is," he said. "There can only be one truth, and it will come to light."

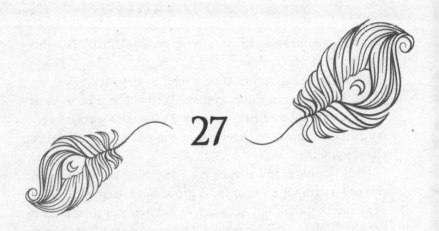

27

Gabriel and Tom sat silently in the cottage parlor, Tom with a newspaper in his hand, and Gabriel trying to come up with some scrap of truth to pass off as a sermon that week. Jonas Peckham's funeral service had almost been a stay of execution in having to deliver a true sermon, and he dreaded a return to the transcendentalism he was supposed to be preaching. What was the point anymore? Was it still worth continuing with this charade? Sophronia knew the truth, and the rest of Pale Harbor could not have cared less if he shut his doors. Nonetheless, some perverse sense of duty—whether it was to Anna's memory or his own refusal to admit defeat—compelled him to try.

Across the room, it seemed Tom was having an equally hard time concentrating. He was fidgeting in his chair, snapping the newspaper open and shut, crossing his legs and uncrossing them. Gabriel was just about to propose a trip to the tavern when Tom finally spoke up.

"There's something you need to know."

The quiet force in Tom's voice made Gabriel look up and set aside his work. He sat back in his chair and crossed his ankles, waiting for Tom to have out with it.

Pushing his hand through his overlong hair, Tom gave him a look that was half-sheepish, half-apologetic. "There's no good way to say this."

Gabriel had known Tom for years, and couldn't remember the last time he'd seen him so flustered and at a loss for words. Uneasiness crept over him. "Go on."

It was a long, stretched out moment before Tom finally spoke again. His words dropped into the room, heavy and lethal.

"Anna was not faithful to you."

Gabriel didn't move as time ground to a halt completely. Then, all at once, blood rushed to his head and he felt as if he were going to pass out. He *knew* that Anna had been unfaithful before she came back to him—all of Concord had known—so why was Tom bringing this up now? Why was he forcing Gabriel to relive the embarrassment, the hurt, the betrayal?

He curled his fingers around the arms of his chair, fingernails digging into the wood. "I know that," he ground out. "You know that I know that. I took her back and endeavored to be a better man, one worthy of keeping her."

"That was not the end of it, Gabe," Tom said quietly.

His heart began speeding up. Gabriel could hardly force the word out between his clenched jaws. *"What."*

Tom looked as miserable as Gabriel felt. "Anna was going to come to Pale Harbor with Joshua Whipple."

Gabriel wet his dry lips with his tongue, staring at his distorted reflection in the window. It couldn't be true. And yet, what reason had she given him to trust her, other than she knew he was like a dog, loyal even to the hand that struck him?

"It's very likely the baby was Whipple's," Tom finished, his voice full of pity.

How could Tom know that? Had Anna confided in him? An even worse thought scuttled through his mind... Oh,

God, had everyone known? Gabriel stared at the man he had thought was his closest friend, a fresh wave of betrayal curling around him.

Gabriel had molded himself into a different man for her. A man who trekked across New England and came to rest in an obscure little town. A man who preached words and ideals that were as empty to him as the supposed love of his wife. And for what? The memory of a woman who had lied to him, betrayed him?

It was too much. Gabriel exploded out of his chair, grabbing fistfuls of Tom's collar and throwing him up against the wall. Plaster crumbled in a cloud around them. "Why are you telling me this? What right have you to drag her name through the mud! How *dare* you."

Tom was lean, but he was strong and capable. He could have easily unhanded Gabriel, but he did not fight back. It was only when the haze of anger cleared long enough for Gabriel to realize what he was doing that he let go. He pulled away from Tom, more disgusted with himself for his own violent outburst than he was at his friend's betrayal.

"How dare I?" Tom looked at him in disbelief, his hair rumpled and his necktie askew. "Good God, man. How could I not tell you? You obviously love your Mrs. Carver, but you're too paralyzed by guilt to pursue her, and all from some misguided sense of duty to your dead wife! A wife who, I might add, found comfort in the arms of another man not once, but twice, *and* probably carried his child."

Gabriel ran the back of his sleeve across his perspiring temples, the flush of anger gradually receding. Tom was right; Gabriel knew he was. Yet it didn't make it any easier to accept.

"How do you know?" he asked gruffly.

"She didn't exactly go to great lengths to hide it, Gabe." Tom paused, as if waiting for Gabriel to say something. When he didn't, he sighed and went on. "She and Whipple...the night of the town assembly, they were dancing and carrying on. I saw them slip outside together, and when I followed them..." He trailed off, then shook his head. Gabriel knew Tom was trying to spare him the details. "She begged me not to tell you. Whether it was right or wrong, I promised her that I wouldn't. She said that it was a mistake, that it wouldn't happen again. When it came down to it, I couldn't bear the thought of being the one to break your heart."

All the air had gone out of the room, the small sounds of the coal fire and the ticking clock amplified in the stillness. Anna had been unfaithful to him right under his nose, and Tom had known all along.

Tom's voice softened. "What happened to Anna was a terrible, sad thing. The love you felt for her was real and true, whether she returned all of it or not. But you cannot live your life under all this guilt." He paused. "I see the way you look at Mrs. Carver. I've not been lucky enough to find someone like that, but what you feel for her gives me hope. You owe yourself happiness, Gabe."

It was as if he had been wearing an iron yoke all these years, and now that it had come free of his shoulders, Gabriel felt clean and cold and light. He should have been outraged that Anna had lied to him, but how could he be angry at a ghost? She had not been happy, and he couldn't fault her for seeing a chance at happiness and snatching at it, even if it had come at the cost of his.

Gabriel sat down hard on the sofa, and Tom perched himself next to him. "I was a fool." Holding his pounding temples in his hands, Gabriel let out a weighty breath.

"Come now," Tom said, some of his characteristic good humor returning. "You may be foulmouthed, stubborn and utterly hopeless when it comes to current fashion, but 'fool' is being rather hard on yourself."

Gabriel offered him a sardonic look, but his heart was fit to burst with gratitude for his old friend. "And you're perceptive as ever, damn you."

"Come on, let's have a drink."

Pouring out two healthy glasses of whiskey, Tom handed him one and they settled in for an evening of reminiscing and old navy stories. Though Gabriel laughed along with Tom and put in a word at the right times, his mind was far away.

Because the question remained: Gabriel might be free to love Sophronia, but would she even have him in return?

Sarah Burns was at her wits' end.

The twins had gotten a new paint set for their birthday—probably in the vain hope that a genteel hobby would help them develop into accomplished young ladies—and they had promptly proceeded to grind up the pigments to smear on each other's faces, leaving a huge mess on the carpet in the front parlor. A huge mess for which Sarah was now responsible. Had Mrs. Marshall disciplined them? No, of course she had not; she was no doubt in her bed with one of her "headaches" that always seemed to coincide with the twins' mischief.

To make matters worse, Miss Harriett was staying with the family for the winter holidays. Sarah couldn't stand the preening young woman with her airs and pretensions, always ordering Sarah about as if she was her personal lady-in-waiting.

Rocking back on her heels, Sarah paused in her scrubbing of the carpet and wiped at her perspiring brow. The fumes from the vinegar and bleach were making her light-headed, and she could practically hear Mrs. Marshall complaining about the smell, never mind that she would have complained a hundred times more about the stain. With a heavy sigh, Sarah clambered to her feet and opened the windows, letting in a rush of cold air.

But if it wasn't one thing, it was another. The stain was gone, but by the time the smell had dissipated the room would be freezing. Taking up the tinderbox, Sarah scratched up a flame and threw it into the grate.

No sooner had she wiped her sooty hands on her apron than smoke began backing up and filling the room. Oh, if one of the twins had closed the flue as a prank again, she was going to wring her little neck.

It was too smoky to check, but it had been open last night when the family had gathered for hot drinks and a game of cards in the parlor. That was odd. And they'd had the chimney swept only last month; it shouldn't have been in need of another cleaning already. With a corner of her apron over her mouth in one hand and a pair of iron fire tongs in her other, Sarah knelt and began poking blindly up into the fuming chimney.

Resistance met the tongs almost immediately. Whatever it was didn't feel like the simple accumulation of soot; this was…large.

"Devil racoons," she muttered, getting a better angle with the tongs. The nasty creatures occasionally found their way inside, and now one had gone and gotten itself stuck and died. It was a wonder they hadn't smelled it before.

With one good wrench of the tongs, Sarah was finally able to get purchase and she felt the blockage come loose.

Swatting away the plume of smoke and sparks, Sarah coughed and squinted to see what she had dislodged. Whatever had fallen out of the chimney was bigger than a racoon. Much, much bigger.

When the smoke had finally cleared, Sarah crept closer,

her apron still over her mouth, and the last thing she saw before fainting dead away was the upside down, charred visage of her mistress.

The day after Tom's revelation, Gabriel found himself walking to nowhere in particular, trying to clear his head. The farther he walked in the cold, clean air, the more he saw Anna's transgressions cast in a sorrowful light, rather than an unforgiveable one. Oh, Anna. How could he have been so blind to her unhappiness? How could he have tried to keep her when she so obviously yearned to fly free? He could no more fault her than one would fault a wild creature for trying to escape its cage.

As Gabriel wandered through the center of town, he found himself on the road to the Marshalls'. The air hung heavy with the smell of smoke here. Not the pleasant wood smoke that usually permeated Pale Harbor, but something acrid that made Gabriel's eyes water.

A man ran past him, nearly bowling Gabriel over. "Sorry, Reverend. Fire at the Marshall place—they need all hands to form a bucket chain."

Quickening his step and shaking off his reveries, Gabriel followed the man until they'd reached the end of the street. There were no flames, only a thick smoke that threatened to blot out the sky. Several people were clustered about, and Gabriel saw Manuel pacing the perimeter of the yard, scratching his head. "We were going to form a bucket line, but there doesn't seem to be any fire," Manuel said when he noticed Gabriel had come up.

"Do you know if the family is inside?"

Manuel opened his mouth, but before he could say anything, there was a commotion at the door and a young woman came spilling out in a frenzy of blackened skirts and wildly waving arms. Soot smudged her face and her hair had escaped her cap, but Gabriel recognized her as the Marshalls' house-maid. Before he knew what was happening, she was collaps-ing in a hysterical heap into his arms.

"It weren't a racoon!" she said between great racking sobs. "Oh, but it were the most horrible thing I ever seen!"

Sensing something more than just a fire was afoot, everyone gathered around her, craning their heads to get a better look.

Gabriel gestured for them to give her space. "Easy now. Are you hurt?"

But the girl didn't seem to hear him. "I saw her myself. Came crashing out of the chimney in a great dusty heap, she did."

Gabriel shot Manuel a startled look. "Go and make sure the rest of the family is out of the house."

Manuel nodded and ran up the porch and disappeared into the smoky doorway.

Taking the girl gently by the shoulders, Gabriel peered into her red-rimmed eyes. "Who did you see? What are you talking about?"

She noisily snuffled back her tears. "Oh, Mr. Stone," she said in a tremulous voice. "It were Mrs. Marshall, stuffed up the chimney as if she weren't nothing more than a sack of flour!"

"She...what?"

Surely he'd heard her wrong. But just then Manuel ran back out of the house, his brown skin coated gray with ash. He shook his head. "No sign of the family," he said. "But there's...that is...it's Mrs. Marshall." He took a deep breath before meeting Gabriel's eye. "She's in the hearth. Dead."

The girl had been telling the truth. Gabriel dropped his hands from her shoulders and stepped back, absorbing the sheer horror of this. How did a grown woman end up in a chimney?

Had she been cleaning it and gotten stuck? But Mrs. Marshall would have hired a chimney sweep; there was no reason for her to be anywhere near that chimney. *Oh, God.* Not unless she was already dead, and someone had hidden her body there.

It could be no coincidence that Jonas Peckham had been murdered two days ago, and now Mrs. Marshall was dead as a result of foul play. Gabriel cursed under his breath. If there was a connection between a Poe story and her body being shoved into a chimney, then Gabriel really didn't give a damn. The connections told them nothing, shed no light on the perpetrator; they only served to distract, to frighten. Gabriel had had enough. Because if the killer had gone after Mrs. Marshall in her own home, what was to keep him from pursuing Sophronia next? He thought again of Mr. Marshall's name on their list. Surely he would not have killed his own wife? Sitting at their dinner table, he had found them warm and solicitous to one another, a well-matched couple. But then again, how much did he really know about them? How much did he really know about what went on behind closed doors in this town?

28

A low, expectant thrum of voices and nervous energy filled the church that night. Mothers and fathers, afraid to leave their children at home, clutched their sleepy offspring by the wrists. Eyes were bloodshot, and lips pressed tight as neighbors exchanged weary nods of greeting and recognition.

News of Mrs. Marshall's grizzly death had spread like wildfire through the small town. Unlike Jonas, who had been viewed as a harmless drunkard at best and a public nuisance at worst, Mrs. Marshall had been a well-bred lady from a prominent family. If Jonas's killer had decided to go after her, who might be next? Death had cast its sickly pall over the town, and nothing was certain anymore.

Gabriel and Tom stood to the side of the pulpit where the constable was running a hand through his thinning hair, eyeing the restless townspeople as if they were a pack of hungry wolves. Gabriel scanned the crowd, but there was no sign of Sophronia. Good. It was better that she stay out of the public eye. The last thing he wanted was for her to put herself in danger if the meeting turned ugly or violent. Still, he had not seen her since Tom's revelation, and he was nearly dizzy at the prospect that the next time he saw her, she could be his.

Throwing a harried look at the unruly crowd, Constable Morris rapped his fist against the pulpit. "All right, let's come to order." He rapped again louder, and gradually the murmurs and private conversations fell to a hush.

"I know that everyone is anxious to see justice done, and I want to assure the good people of Pale Harbor that everything is under control. We're not going to stand by while our citizens are murdered in cold blood. To that end," he said, flicking a nervous glance at his audience, "we might consider a town-wide curfew."

As expected, this was met by thunderous grumbling, mostly by men who liked to frequent the Chestnut of an evening.

The constable lifted his palms in a placating gesture. "It's for our own safety. Why deliver ourselves up into his hands?"

"You speak as if the killer is a man," shouted one particularly disgruntled gentleman, "when we all know perfectly well it's most likely a woman." He jutted his chin over his shoulder to the back of the church.

At this, all heads swiveled to the back. Gabriel followed their gaze to find Sophronia standing against the wall, Helen stationed beside her. She must have slipped in after the meeting had started, forgoing her usual dramatic entrances. Her face paled at the accusation, but she did not flinch.

Gabriel grit his teeth, preparing to step in, should the anger in the crowd simmer over into something dangerous. But the constable was already calling for order. "All right, all right, that's enough," he said, uncomfortably clearing his throat. "While no one can be ruled out at present, I won't have this turn into a circus of accusations."

The murmuring died down, and when Gabriel glanced back at Sophronia, it was to find that she was already gone. His first instinct was to chase after her, make certain that she went home where she would be safe. As if sensing his impulse, Tom laid a hand on Gabriel's sleeve, imparting a silent warning for him to stay. Grudgingly, Gabriel clenched his fists at his sides and forced himself to wait until the meeting was over.

"Now," Morris continued, finally finding his footing, "as darkness falls around six o'clock, a curfew of eight o'clock should be more than reasonable. We may have to ask Portland to send a detective or two down to—"

But the rest of his sentence was lost in a roar of outrage. People were exploding out of their seats, yelling over each other as if he'd suggested that they cede the town to the Queen of England.

"I think I speak for everyone here when I say we don't want, and we certainly don't need, some detective from Lewiston or Portland coming and sticking their noses in our business!" exclaimed a woman holding a sleeping babe on her hip. "Clara Marshall—God rest her soul—was killed in her own home! What good would a curfew have done for *her*, the poor soul."

A murmur of approval for this speech rippled through the crowd, heads nodding in agreement. Morris opened his mouth, but bolstered by the support, the woman continued. "What right do they have to come in and police us, poking about, asking questions?"

More murmurs and a "Hear, hear."

After much slamming of his fist on the pulpit, the red-faced constable was finally able to cut through the rabble. "What if it's you next? Or your child? We simply don't have the resources to deal with this sort of thing."

But they weren't having it. Manuel stood up. "Well," he said, hooking his thumbs through his belt loops, "maybe someone else from Pale Harbor ought to have a go at it if our own constable lacks the means."

"Maybe we need a new constable!" someone else piped up.

All the color drained from Constable Morris's face as the idea went around the room, gathering steam like an out of control locomotive.

"All right, that's enough." Gabriel's voice boomed off the walls. When the worst of the clamor had died down, he yielded the floor to Constable Morris, who gave him a weary nod of thanks.

"Then it's decided," the constable said in a voice that was equal parts exasperation and relief. "Curfew starts tonight. Anyone found out past eight gets to spend the rest of their night as my guest."

The meeting broke up, and Gabriel cut a hasty retreat through the crush of bodies to the door, only to be intercepted by Harriet Wiggins.

"Mr. Stone," she said. "Oh, but I'm glad to see you. Uncle is beside himself with grief, and Sarah is so addle-brained that she can't even speak. Cook ran off in hysterics and hasn't come back! We are practically starving, and that's to say nothing of the state of the house."

He was not in the mood for Miss Wiggins's theatrics, but he watched her carefully for any sign that something more than just undependable servants might be amiss at the Marshall household.

But she was the same as always: flighty and coquettish, even under such circumstances. She wrapped her hands around his arm and pulled herself close to him, the miasma of her perfume making him light-headed. "How very brave you are to see that this criminal is brought to justice."

"It's nothing," he said, not out of some sort of misplaced humility, but because his mind was already far away from promises of justice and the clutches of Miss Wiggins. He craned his head above the tall feathers of her bonnet, trying desperately to catch a glimpse of Sophronia.

"Oh, come now, it's not nothing!" Miss Wiggins squeezed his arm tighter. "Even our constable is not prepared to deal with anything other than the occasional drunkard. And," she said, "you must have noticed that Pale Harbor has a shortage of young, able-bodied men."

Extracting his arm, Gabriel put as much space between them as possible. "I...have to go. Please, give your uncle my condolences and let him know that I'll endeavor to visit him soon."

Miss Wiggins opened her mouth to object, but Gabriel was already bolting for the door.

Sophronia was standing under the old elm tree across the road when he finally broke away from the church. She looked so small in her fur-lined cloak, the craggy tree branches hovering menacingly above her. Helen, thank God, was nowhere to be seen.

Without waiting to see if anyone was watching, Gabriel crossed to her and folded her into his arms, inhaling her scent, as sweet and fresh as a spring breeze. "Are you all right?"

"Yes," came the muffled reply from his chest, but there was a slight hitch in her voice. He held her out at arm's length, surveying her face in the moonlight.

She gave him a weak smile. "Truly, I just needed some air. I sent Helen home so I could wait for you."

He bit back a curse. She shouldn't have come, but now that she was here he was terribly glad. "I'm sorry you had to hear that."

"Everyone is so on edge, so consumed with fear." She looked back at the church, where the last people were trailing off into the night, and shook her head. "It's even worse than when Nathaniel died."

"Hopefully, the curfew will be the end of it." But Gabriel himself didn't have much faith in his words. Something had gripped the town, and it would take much more than a curfew and a few policemen from Portland to curb the perpetrator of that darkness.

Reaching out, she gently smoothed down his wrinkled waistcoat. Her hand lingered on his chest, her warmth and scent sending a surge of desire through him. But before he could lean down and kiss her, she pulled her hand back and pursed her lips. "I…" She started to say something but broke off, shaking her head. "Gabriel," she said, "you were right."

He raised his brows, not following her line of thought. "Oh?"

She was biting her lip, looking everywhere but at him. "Helen…" she began, and then trailed off again.

"What about Helen?"

"Never mind. It's just that I think that I am very tired."

Of course she was, and it was no wonder. "Let me walk you home," he offered.

She shook her head, impatient. "No, that isn't what I mean. I'm tired of playacting and being bright and proper. I'm tired of denying myself my heart's dearest desire, and I am tired of fearing what will happen if I should get it."

Something in his chest tightened. She'd given herself to him, but he had not been free to accept her, not completely. But now something had changed, and with Tom's revelation about Anna, well, there was nothing to stand between them.

Her words fell into the cold night air, and Sophronia rushed on before her nerve abandoned her.

"I thought that my safety, tucked away in my house with Helen, was happiness. I thought that because I was free from

Nathaniel, that meant that I was free from sorrow. But I am not free, and I am not happy. I know that you had a wife, and that you loved her very much…" She paused, swallowing. She was making a hash of it. "I just wanted to tell you that you were right the other night when you said that love is meaningless without taking the risk to act on it. I'm ready to take that risk, even if it means losing everything I've known these past years."

Gabriel blinked at her in the dark. Rain was starting to spit down on them, and she shivered in her cloak. "Please say something," she whispered.

But he didn't utter a word. Instead, he pulled her to him, his hazel eyes dark and flared with desire. Her body met the length of him, and she let out a shuddering sigh. How perfectly they fit together. There was no need for words when she was ensconced in his solid warmth.

His mouth joined with hers, hard and urgent, then softened when she parted her lips to him. She could feel his arousal against her abdomen and the knowledge that he wanted her as badly as she wanted him was nearly her undoing.

It would be so easy to let herself give way to desire here in the night again. But there was too much to be done first, too much at stake. She had to clear herself of the cloud of accusations, had to make sure the right killer was found and brought to justice. She pulled back, her legs shaking and her heart beating in triple time.

"What is it? When can I see you again?"

Meeting his confused gaze, she offered him a rueful smile. "Soon. There is one thing I must do first."

That night, after Helen had gone to bed and the house was still, Sophronia pushed all the furniture out of the center of the parlor. She changed into her dressing gown, made herself a cup of tea and then settled in for a long night.

She wanted to be with Gabriel. Oh, how she wanted to be with him. But she could not go to him frightened and unsure of her motives or her freedom. If they were to be together, then she must know that she went freely, and not because she was driven by danger into his arms. And that meant finding some answers, once and for all.

Outside, the autumn rain pelted against the windows, the wind rattling the shutters. Sophronia took out all the threatening notes she had been carefully keeping in a locked drawer of her desk, and a stack of blank correspondence paper. She found the paper on which she and Gabriel had written the chronology of the notes, and began going through it again, adding the deaths of Jonas Peckham and Mrs. Marshall. She omitted Garrett's death, as it seemed very likely it had indeed been an unfortunate accident.

Helen had told her of Mrs. Marshall's gruesome end after learning about it in town. As soon as she had mentioned where the body had been found, and in what manner, Sophronia had recognized the connection to Mr. Poe's story 'The Murders in the Rue Morgue.' It had been ages since she'd read it, but a detail such as a body stuffed into a chimney tended to imprint itself on one's memory.

But the fact remained: it didn't tell her anything, or at least, it didn't tell her anything she didn't already know. Undeterred, she went through the stack of magazines and newspapers, making a note on her list of when each Poe story had been published. With a sigh, she studied the list. There was no pattern, no great moment of clarity. If anything, she was more confused than ever. The notes had clearly targeted her, referencing Nathaniel's death and her past. But now two people were dead; surely they had not been killed because of her? She felt sick at the thought. Jonas had been found with her handkerchief on his body, and the note that she received the day of his murder implied that the killer had every intention of making sure that she was blamed for the death. Was there some message in Mrs. Marshall's death meant for her, as well?

Her legs were going fuzzy with pins and needles, the rough wool of the carpet biting into her palms. Standing, she closed her eyes and stretched. Perhaps she was going about this all the wrong way, looking for clues and connections where there weren't any. She crumpled up the sheet of paper and took out a fresh one. Then she began a new list of men, women and youth in Pale Harbor. The perpetrator had to be physically strong to have slain Jonas and Mrs. Marshall. They had to be able to read and write, and what's more, be familiar with Mr. Poe's stories, which were serialized in the papers each week. They had to hate Sophronia with an intensity that went beyond common disdain.

Was there anyone in town who had been particularly fond of Nathaniel? Who would have felt his death more keenly than everyone else? Everyone certainly admired him in the way one admires a charismatic, wealthy man, but he had no close friends, or even family that she knew of. His parents had both died long before he had married Sophronia, and the only relative he ever spoke of was an estranged older brother who had died in the war in 1812.

But all her mind kept coming back to was, why now? Nathaniel had been dead these past four years. Had someone been plotting this since his death, waiting to set in motion a chain of events meant to punish Sophronia? Perhaps this person's hatred for her had nothing to do with Nathaniel at all. But then, what was their motive?

Sophronia looked at her list and began crossing out names,

starting with the most obvious. It could not have been Gabriel because he was with her the night Jonas was murdered, and he had not even arrived in Pale Harbor when the ravens had started coming. It could not have been his friend Tom Ellroy for the same reason. It could not have been Lewis, as they'd already established—unless he had an accomplice.

There was one name she could not cross out, though it broke her heart. The person had access to Castle Carver. Though not large in stature, the suspect was lean and strong. And, as Sophronia now knew, she had been lied to by omission all these years.

She circled the name, and then, in a fit of regret, violently crossed out the entire paper before crumpling it and throwing it across the room.

As much as it sickened and saddened her, she had to admit that Gabriel had been right; there was a very good chance that it was Helen.

She sat down on the sofa, her head light, her body far away. There were people in the world like Nathaniel who were evil and who delighted in showing their true colors. They were terrifying, but at least one knew what to expect from such a person, could gird themselves against cruelty. But what of someone like Helen? Someone who was not only kind, but let it be known time and again that she would do anything to protect her friend? Someone who had insinuated herself into every aspect of one's life? How could she protect herself from someone like that?

Sophronia awoke on the sofa with a crick in her neck and a vague sense of unease. She blinked, jumbled furniture and a mess of papers before her slowly coming into focus.

"Sophy?" The voice startled her the rest of the way awake.

Looking up, she saw Helen crouched beside her with a steaming cup of tea in her hand.

"I must have dozed off last night," she murmured.

"I can see that," Helen said with a frown. "What were you doing?"

The fog of sleep cleared and Sophronia remembered her list, the crossed-out names. Getting up, she hastily swept up her papers and forced a smile. "I had a fancy that I might do a little investigating into Mrs. Marshall's death, but I'm afraid I'm no closer than I was yesterday and have only a sore neck to show for it."

Her heart beat fast and erratic as Helen placed the cup on the side table and helped her back onto the sofa. "I don't think you should take this into your own hands," Helen said. "You'll only upset yourself. The best thing you can do is stay put in the house."

She was silent as she watched Helen bustle about the room, setting the furniture to rights. "Perhaps you're right," she finally forced herself to say, trying to keep her voice steady.

All those years she had shared a roof with Nathaniel, Sophronia had known what it was to fear a man, to know that he could kill her if the drink was strong and his mood bitter. Helen had been Safe, a steady beacon in troubled waters. But good Lord, she had *admitted* to poisoning Nathaniel; what else might she be capable of?

When the last chair was back in place, Helen straightened. "Oh, I nearly forgot," she said, reaching into her apron pocket and producing a little envelope. "This came for you."

Sophronia opened it and read the scant lines.

To the fair water you must go;
With rocks and ice so cold below.
Hasten there anon, and all shall you know.

If she was understanding the rather poorly constructed poem correctly, the note's author wanted her to go to the bluff.

Sophronia hazarded a glance at Helen, who was watching her with sharp eyes. Her pulse raced, but she made an effort to appear impassive. Nothing must change between them. Helen must not know that Sophronia suspected her.

"What does it say?"

Sophronia folded it back up and slipped it under the collar of her bodice. "It's an invitation from Mr. Stone for supper this evening."

Helen studied her, and Sophronia felt her face grow warm. Had Helen written the note herself? Was this Helen's way of testing her?

"I think I'll dress and then leave early," she said. "I'll be back well before curfew."

Helen didn't say anything, didn't even make a move to stop her. She was sitting in her usual chair, hands on the arms, watching her with unnerving intensity. Sophronia was almost to the door when Helen spoke. "You're acting strangely."

Turning, Sophronia wet her lips and forced a tight smile. "Am I? I suppose I'm tired. All the upheaval, it's—" She broke off. "I daresay some fresh air will clear my head and wake me up."

Helen nodded, and Sophronia was aware of her eyes on her back as she left the room. Her legs shook as she forced herself to take the stairs, all the while wondering if she was walking right into some trap. But there was only one way to know for once and for all if it was Helen or not, and Sophronia intended to prove it.

Sophronia walked briskly away from Castle Carver, then picked up her pace, nearly tripping on her hem. Her breath came out in furious bursts. This was madness. She could very well be offering herself up to the hands of a killer. She curled her fingers into her reticule, reassuring herself that the knife she had smuggled from the kitchen before she left was still there.

Dark clouds gathered above her, and soon the fine mist turned to rain. She reached for her hood, before remembering that she'd forgone it in her haste to leave. Well, it hardly mattered now.

Her feet carried her as if beyond her control, mud splashing up the back of her legs, the steady rain soaking her skirts. She glanced about her, half-expecting to see Helen's silhouette passing her behind the trees, racing to reach the bluff before Sophronia. Did Helen relish the hunt? Did leaving notes and animals and cryptic messages excite her? Nathaniel had taken a perverse pleasure in Sophronia's suffering; was Helen the same way? After all, she saw the effect of the threats on Sophronia every day. What had ever happened to it being the two of them against the world? All these years she had thought them friends, sisters almost, and all that time, Helen had been playing a game of cat and mouse. Now, she looked back on the past as if it were a foggy dream, not knowing what had been real and what had not.

Soon she found herself on the bluff overlooking the harbor, the smell of wood smoke and salt air filling her lungs. There was no one there.

She took a few deep breaths and gradually her heart slowed its frantic pace. Kicking a pebble off the steep embankment, she listened to it tinkle down into the water. Then she froze, hearing the sound of footsteps behind her.

Someone was already here, and she was trapped against the sheer drop to the water. Suddenly, the knife in her reticule seemed foolish and useless.

Her heart plummeted, her body stilled. Slowly, she forced herself to turn around, and her breath caught in her throat. "Oh," she said in a choked whisper. "It's you."

29

Tom was already at the breakfast table the next morning when Gabriel staggered in, bleary and ill-rested. Without a word, he slid into his seat and sat there, too preoccupied to do anything but stare at his empty plate.

He hadn't liked the look in Sophronia's eye the night before. Whatever it was she thought she had to do, she was determined, and Gabriel had a sickening feeling he knew what it was.

Tom put down the newspaper he had been reading. "Good God, you look like you could use a drink." He pushed the tin coffeepot across the table. "Better drink up."

Grunting, Gabriel poured himself a cup of thick, strong coffee. If he had only been able to figure out who was behind all the death, the notes, the strange occurrences, then Sophronia wouldn't be taking matters into her own hands. Why hadn't he done anything before? Why had he let it reach a breaking point before taking any kind of meaningful action? His body ached for her like a hunger that could not be sated, a thirst that he had no power to slake. If he could only slip his arms around her, feel the warmth of her small back beneath his fingertips. And this was why he never accomplished anything; all it took was one stray thought about her, and all his concentration fled.

Ignoring Tom's curious gaze, he drained his coffee dregs and poured out another mug. "Where's Fanny?"

"She went to buy eggs for a custard." Tom leaned back in his chair, lacing his hands behind his head. "That girl is a genius in the kitchen. A man could get used to being this well fed."

"Wouldn't have thought her your type," Gabriel said carefully, watching his friend from over the rim of his mug. He felt protective of sweet, capable Fanny, and while he loved Tom dearly, he knew his friend was anything but steady when it came to women.

"You'd have thought wrong," Tom said.

Before Gabriel could address the dangerously dreamy look in his friend's eyes, the back door slammed, and then light footsteps were clipping down the hall.

"That must be her now," Tom said, quickly pushing back his hair and affecting a casually languid posture. "What?" he said innocently when Gabriel rolled his eyes.

A moment later Fanny ran in, red-faced and panting. A wicker egg basket dangled from her elbow, empty.

Tom put his cup down, his charming smile melting away. "Fanny? What's wrong?"

She looked between the two men, and the raw panic that Gabriel saw in her eyes made his heart lurch. "What is it?"

She opened her mouth, but no sound came out.

"Fanny?" Tom was taking her gently by the shoulders and guiding her to his chair. "Come, sit down. Can you tell us what's happened?"

The girl's voice was little more than a croak. "It…it's Mrs. Carver. She—"

"What?" Gabriel was already up, striding to the door and grabbing his coat. "Where is she? What's happened?"

Fanny wrung her hands miserably. "She...she's dead," she said in a choked sob. "Oh, God. They found her down by the harbor and..."

Fanny might have gone on speaking, but Gabriel couldn't hear her. The coat slipped from his fingers, falling to the floor. His ears were ringing. It was impossible. She couldn't be dead; they had spoken last night; he had held her in his arms. How could he have let her go back to Castle Carver alone? Had the murderer taken advantage of the two women alone in the house? Or had it been Helen all along? Bile rose in his throat.

"What happened, Fanny?" Tom was crouched in front of her, his expression gentle yet urgent. "How do you know she's dead? What have you heard?"

Fanny snuffled back her tears. "I don't rightly know, only Mr. Marshall is saying it's the killer again and..." She trailed off, looking at Gabriel and then to Tom, unsure if she should go on. Tom nodded. "A fisherman found her down by the bluff. She's still there, I think," she added with a quiet hiccup.

The color drained from Tom's face, and he swallowed. "Still there?"

Before Fanny could say anything else, Gabriel was slinging his coat on. This couldn't be happening. He was back in the tiny kitchen in Concord, downing whiskey while the doctor explained to him that they couldn't staunch the flow of blood, that Anna was never going to rise from the childbed again. He was helpless, impotent to save the people he loved.

Tom intercepted him by the arm at the doorway. "I don't think you should go, Gabe. She might be...that is, you might not want to see her like this. I'll go and send word for you when—"

Violently shrugging off his hand, Gabriel pushed past him.

"They've left her lying down there like a piece of garbage, goddamn them," he snarled. "I'll be damned if I let her stay there a moment longer."

Tom opened his mouth, but as if thinking better of whatever he was about to say, closed it again and gave Fanny a tight nod. "Thank you, Fanny. You'd best stay here."

But Fanny wiped away the last of her tears and stood up. "I'm coming with you."

The rain made the way muddy and slippery, and more than once Fanny stumbled, Tom stopping to help her back up. Gabriel hardy noticed them, running as fast as he could until the trees gave way and ship masts were visible in the harbor.

A group of coated backs greeted them at the edge of the bluff, collars turned up against the wind and boots muddied. The faces were vaguely familiar—there were Lewis and Manuel—but they might have been strangers from another country for all Gabriel cared.

He pushed past them. He had to see her for himself, or else he wouldn't be able to accept that this nightmare was real. Someone put out an arm to stop him, but he elbowed it aside and stood teetering on the edge of the steep embankment, looking down.

There she was, just as Fanny said, on a bed of seaweed and mud. She looked like a broken doll, her arms flung out and her purple dress spread about her like a silken tide. The whole way there he had hoped, prayed, that it was all a mistake, a terrible joke, even. But there she was, a vulgar testament to the cruelty of death.

"Oh, God." Gabriel stumbled down the muddy embankment, half sliding and nearly losing his balance. When he reached the bottom, he gathered her up in his arms, pressing her damp head to his chest.

She was so small, so light and so cold. He took one of her hands in his own, as if trying to rub life itself back into her. "Sophy." His voice cracked. Last night he hadn't wanted to let her go, almost as if his body had known what his mind had not: that he would never hold her alive again.

How could he have ever thought that he had grasped enlightenment? How could he have even briefly believed that love was some grand, unifying force? He was a peddler of lies. There was no light, no undercurrent of good permeating the universe. Life was random, cruel and bitterly unfair.

"G-Gabriel?"

The word was so soft, so faint that he was sure he'd imagined it. The wind was whipping off the harbor, carrying with it the cries of gulls. But there it was again, this time followed by the slightest touch of a cold finger on his neck.

Slowly, afraid that his mind was playing a terrible trick on him, he pulled back and looked down at her. A trace of pink as delicate as the first spring apple blossoms touched her cheeks.

"Tom!" he yelled over his shoulder, shrugging his coat off, ecstasy ebbing through him. "Come quick!"

Above him, Tom jumped to attention and scrambled down, while Gabriel wrapped his coat around Sophronia's cold, trembling body.

"Gabriel…"

"Don't try to speak. I'm going to get you out of here."

She was alive and that was all that mattered, but as he tucked the coat tighter around her, he could see the extent of her injuries. Purple marks in the shape of fingers ringed her neck. He burned with rage at the thought of hands wrapped around her, choking the life out of her. Even though he was as gentle as he could be when he began to lift her, she let out a whimper so pathetic that it cracked his heart in two. "There now, my love," he said in soothing tones. "There now, you're safe. I have you."

A moment later Tom was beside him, sharp eyes taking in Sophronia's injuries. "Right," he said with a brisk nod. "Let's get her up."

As carefully as if they were carrying an infant, they got her off the ground, Gabriel cradling her in his arms while Tom climbed up ahead, testing footholds in the slippery dirt. The meandering path from the docks would have been easier going, but up the embankment was faster, and every moment she was exposed to the elements put her in greater danger.

At the top Tom cleared away the encroaching circle of curious onlookers. "Is there a physician where we can take her?"

"No!" The force of his voice cut through the murmurs. "She's coming home with me," Gabriel said roughly. He was not about to let her out of his sight.

Tom nodded. "All right then, that's enough gawking," he said to the crowd. "If you want to be of some use, someone fetch a physician and send him to the minister's cottage. Bunch of vultures," he muttered as he and Fanny fell into brisk step beside his friend.

As Gabriel wound through the foggy town, his mind was strangely light and empty. All his fears, all the darkest directions that his thoughts ever took had come to fruition, and yet Sophronia's heart was still beating and, in that moment, that was enough.

He was so lost in a cloud of his own euphoria and grief, he was practically on top of Mr. Marshall before he saw him hurrying through the mist from the other direction.

"Gabriel! I was just at your house looking for you. I—I'm afraid I bring the most tragic of news. Mrs. Carver has—" His words trailed off and his face blanched when he saw Gabriel and who he carried in his arms.

"Afraid what? That she died?" Gabriel snapped. "There's no time to waste, out of my way." He pushed past the dumb-struck Mr. Marshall, and Sophronia let out a moan at the jostling movement.

Mr. Marshall's mustache curved around his open mouth. "She...she's alive?"

"Yes, she's alive, no thanks to you. How quick you were to leave her for dead." Remembering the question of Mr. Marshall's possible involvement, Gabriel's suspicions snapped back to life. "And just what were you doing on the bluff anyway?"

To his credit, Mr. Marshall looked horrified. "Good God, man, we never would have left her if we knew. She looked so..." He trailed off at Gabriel's stony expression and opened his mouth to try again. "I was overseeing an incoming shipment with Manuel and Jasper when we saw her. I told Jasper to send for the constable while I went to fetch you."

Gabriel could have cuffed the bastard against the side of his head. How could he have left her there, dead or not?

"All right, Gabe," Tom said with a firm hand on his back. "There will be time for this later."

Gabriel was about to shrug Tom off and demand that Mr. Marshall answer for his callous actions, but he thought better of it. Mr. Marshall may have been hasty in his decision to leave Sophronia there, but he was also a man in deep mourning for his wife. Besides, how would an argument help Sophronia now?

Gabriel gave him a clipped nod and carried Sophronia the rest of the way back to his house, where she belonged.

Gabriel lay looking up at the unfamiliar ceiling in the spare bedchamber, his eyes gummy and unable to close. He could hear the surgeon moving about the next room, giving orders to Fanny, who, unlike him, had been permitted to stay with Sophronia.

Before the surgeon had banished him, he'd assured Gabriel that most of her wounds were superficial. But she had looked so fragile tucked into his bed, her bruised arms laid outside the quilt. What if his rejoicing at finding her alive was short-lived, and she would not recover after all? He couldn't lose her, not again.

A sharp knock at the door cut through his tumultuous thoughts. Springing to his feet, he stumbled to the door and threw it open. "Yes? Is she all right?"

It was the surgeon, Tom a respectful distance behind him. There was a smattering of blood on the surgeon's white smock. Seeing his expression, the older man hurried to reassure Gabriel. "I bled her, and that is what you see. It was imperative to drain the ill humors before they spread. She's resting now."

The surgeon was still talking, but Gabriel couldn't hear him. Sophronia would be all right. Pure, dizzying relief filled him. He slumped his forehead against his arm on the door frame, suddenly drained of energy.

"I believe that she is through the worst of it. I set her ankle and dressed her bruises with poultices. The only concern now is to watch for infection." He paused, arching a meaningful brow. "She is very lucky, all things considered."

The surgeon was still talking, giving directions for some sort of broth that was to be fed to her twice a day, but it was all just background noise to Gabriel.

Tom caught his dazed look. "Go on," he said, squeezing Gabriel's shoulder. "I'll finish up here."

Too grateful for words, Gabriel barely managed a nod before bolting to his bedchamber where Sophronia lay.

The fire had been banked up and was crackling away, the

room warm and cozy. He had no sooner set foot inside when a stirring came from the corner.

"Oh! I didn't mean to startle you." It was Fanny, uncurling herself from a chair next to the bed. "Dr. Jameson said she was out of danger, but I didn't want to leave her alone, not even for a minute." She yawned and looked around, blinking. "Must have dozed off."

He relaxed, but just a little. Whoever had done this to Sophronia was still out there, and although she was safest with him, he didn't for a second trust that she was out of danger.

Glancing at the dark windows, he realized that it was probably well past curfew, and he couldn't send Fanny back home. "Why don't you sleep here tonight? You can make up a bed on the sofa."

She nodded and moved to the door, but he stopped her with a hand to her arm and gave her a gentle squeeze. "Thank you, Fanny, for everything today. You were very brave."

In the firelight, Fanny flushed pink and gave him a bob of her head before leaving him alone with Sophronia.

Taking up Fanny's chair, Gabriel clasped the hand that lay outside the quilt. It was small and warm, and he had never felt anything so wonderful. "My love," he murmured. "I'm so sorry. This is all my fault. I never should have let you go."

She looked so peaceful, the faint light of the fire flickering across her features. To think that he might have been gazing at her in a coffin instead of his bed. He shuddered and held tighter to her hand. Someone had done this to his beautiful Sophronia, and someone would pay.

She hadn't realized she had been in the dark until her heavy eyelids squinted open, and dim light seeped in. Everything was far away and indistinct, as if she were on the edge of a very long, very elaborate dream, and was not quite ready to wake up. But what had the dream been about?

Her throat was sore, and there was a dull pain that seemed to pulse in time with her heart, coursing through her entire body. She winced.

She wasn't in Castle Carver with her bed's lavish tester and purple curtains, and she wasn't alone. From somewhere just beyond her vision came a light snore.

Turning her head as much as her stiff neck would allow, her gaze fell on Gabriel, slumped over in a chair, chin in hand. A sliver of a memory flashed through her mind, as blinding and ephemeral as the tail of a comet. They had been kissing, Gabriel looking down at her with utter adoration. But the face in front of her now was drawn and ashen, the heavy eyelids smudged dark. How long had she been here, and what had happened to transform his boyish face into one so weary and careworn?

He must have felt her gaze on him, because he opened his eyes, starting a little to find her awake. A slow smile tugged at his lips, lighting up his tired face. "Welcome back," he said, his smile permeating his husky words. "How do you feel?"

"Awful," she said, though she couldn't help the answering tug of her own lips. If she could only wake up to that smile every day of her life, she would be the happiest woman in the world. But there was a heaviness pressing around the edges of her mind, threatening to dash all her dreams. "Where am I?"

He was stroking back her hair, but at her question he paused, his smile turning sly. "My bed."

"Oh!" She darted her glance as much as she could into the shadowy recesses of the small bedchamber. She had often wondered about this room, thought about the time that Gabriel spent here when he was not with her. This was where he slept, where he returned at night and dreamed or read, or sat staring out his window. Question after question bubbled up in her mind, not least of which was how she had come to be here, feeling like she'd been trampled by a herd of wild horses.

As if reading her thoughts, his expression grew grave and he swallowed. "You were found by the harbor, at the bottom of the embankment." His words came out low and rough, barely more than a hoarse whisper. "You looked..." He cleared his throat, as if trying to overcome some great emotion lodged there. "You were so cold. We thought you were dead."

"Dead?" Her voice cracked on the word and she felt dizzy. She didn't remember being near the harbor. She didn't remember how she'd gotten there, or why she would have been there at all. She certainly didn't remember anything that would have resulted in her near death.

"I don't suppose you remember anything about what happened?"

Sophronia closed her eyes, trying to grab at any snippet of memory. She remembered being with Gabriel under the elm tree after the town assembly. She'd gone home, then spent the night making lists and spreading papers out all around her. Fear had hung over her head, but also determination. There had been a name, and reading it had sent despair spiraling through her. The next morning she'd told Helen she had to go somewhere, to meet someone. There had been something different about Helen, but she couldn't remember what. Then she'd left, walking out into the windy, rainy day with determination in her step and a mission in her mind. But after that, nothing. Opening her eyes, she shook her head. "I'm sorry."

"Don't be sorry." Gabriel gave her the ghost of a smile, but she could see the disappointment in his eyes.

"What did the surgeon say?" Every part of her body ached, as if the intangible dread in her mind had taken on a physical form and was coursing through her veins.

Gabriel looked uneasy. "Someone tried to strangle you. They must have thought they'd succeeded, and then pushed you over the embankment." His voice was low, with an edge of anger that sent a chill through her body, though she knew it was not directed at her. "When I think how close you were..." He trailed off, his jaw clenching so tightly that she thought he might crack a tooth.

Sophronia looked down at her hands, still raw and covered in scratches, testaments to a fight she didn't remember.

The silence that lapped back up around them was too strained, too heavy, for the ordeal they had gone through. They should have been in each other's arms; they should have been reveling in their togetherness and making plans for the future. Closing her eyes, Sophronia let out a weary breath.

Her eyes flew open. A detail had unfolded in her mind, but not about the fight.

Gabriel's gaze went feverishly bright. "What is it?"

She flicked her tongue over her dry lips, trying to put words to the alarming image she had remembered. "I—I do remember something, but...but it can't be right."

Moving to the edge of his seat, he took her hands. Warmth ran through her, and suddenly everything else seemed inconsequential. All she wanted to do was stay in this bed with him beside her forever. "What is it? Anything could help." His voice was gentle and calm, but there was something desperate in his eyes, his jaw still tight.

She dropped her gaze, afraid that what she was about to tell him would only act as tinder to the smoldering flame she saw behind his eyes. "I remember..." She cleared her throat, trying to dislodge the words. "That is, I was arguing."

"Arguing?"

"I don't know what it was about. I just remember being on

the bluff and arguing. Our voices were raised, and they put their hand on my arm. I pulled away."

His hands tightened around hers, his breath warm on her cheek. "With who, Sophy?"

She swallowed, staring at their entwined fingers. Even as she lay in bed weak and injured, saying the name felt like a fresh blow. Then she raised her eyes to Gabriel's, and whispered, "Helen."

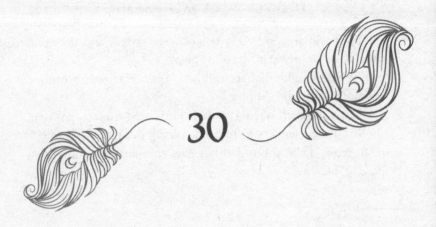

30

Blood pounded hot and fast in Gabriel's ears. So it had been Helen. Every suspicion, every hair-raising instinct had been correct. Sophronia's embroidered handkerchief that had been found at the scene of the murder had been Helen trying to throw suspicion onto her. Who else would have had access to it? The note left in the house, the dead birds. She could have easily hired some boy from the town to deliver them to the front step on her behalf. And all for what? Trying to scare her beloved mistress into staying with her? Had she decided that if she couldn't have Sophronia, then no one could? Goddamn him, he should have gotten Sophronia out of that house when he'd had the chance.

A soft voice broke into his violent thoughts. He looked up to find Sophronia watching him with a furrowed brow. "Did you say something?" he asked.

The furrow deepened. "I said, don't do anything you'll regret. Anything I would regret. Please."

He held her searching gaze, not saying anything. She asked too much of him; how could he not punish the person who had tormented her all these months, who had left her for dead?

He looked away, studying the flames licking in the grate. "Of course," he murmured.

He could still feel her eyes boring into him, imploring him not to give into his most primitive desire for vengeance. Standing, he brushed her warm temple with a kiss. "You should rest. If you need anything, just call for Fanny."

Sophronia nodded, but just as he was turning away she caught his hand. "Please, Gabriel," she said. "You must promise me that you won't do anything rash. I know that Helen…" She swallowed, a cloud of dark emotion rushing across her face. "Please, I don't want to see her hurt."

Gently removing her hand, he pressed it with a kiss and gave her a weak smile. "Try to get some sleep, my love."

Tom had fallen asleep at the kitchen table, his head cradled on his arms, but he sat up with a groggy yawn when Gabriel came in. "How is she?"

Without answering, Gabriel set glasses on the table and poured two fingers of whiskey into each. He tilted his glass back and drained it in one swallow. "Tired, weak and confused." He paused, trying to push the image of her lying at the bottom of the embankment out of his mind. "But talking."

"Well, that's good news, then!" Tom studied him as Gabriel poured out another drink. "Isn't it?"

"What? Oh, yes. She's incredibly lucky. I'm lucky. I…" Gabriel put down the glass and scrubbed a weary hand over his face. "She remembers, Tom," he said quietly. "Not what happened, exactly, but who it was."

"Well?"

"Who do you think?" He tossed back the rest of his whiskey and gave Tom a jaded look. "We're going to go pay Miss Helen a visit."

★ ★ ★

Gabriel pushed aside the pang of guilt at leaving Sophronia as he and Tom made their way to Castle Carver. She'd be safe at his house; he'd given Fanny orders to lock the doors behind them. He had been careful not to make any promises he couldn't keep, but so long as Helen was skulking about, Sophronia wouldn't be safe. He had no choice but to see that she paid for what she had done.

The house loomed above them, silent and dark. Without Sophronia inside, it was a dreary, sinister place, the turret making it look more prison than castle.

Gabriel was just about to knock when Tom caught his wrist and stayed his hand. "Gabe," he said, forcing Gabriel to meet his eye. "What's the plan here?"

Bristling, he yanked away. "Plan? The plan is to confront that woman and make her pay for what she's done."

Tom's expression told Gabriel just what he thought of this course of action. "I understand you want to avenge Mrs. Carver, but she deserves better than vigilante justice. Besides," Tom said, brushing a piece of lint from his frock coat with a frown, "she's a woman. You can't very well give her a thrashing."

Tom was right, which only irritated him more. "Fine," he ground out. "I'll just talk to her."

"Good." Tom gave him a tight smile, then rapped at the door.

They stood waiting, Gabriel hardly breathing, his muscles coiled in anticipation. He gave the door another knock. When there was still no answer, he glanced around the abandoned yard. "She might be in the carriage house."

Just as they were about to step off the porch, there was the muffled fall of footsteps. When the door swung open, Helen's hopeful gaze landed on the men before pinching in distaste. "Oh," she said. "It's you. What do you want?"

"To talk." He had to use every ounce of self-control to conceal his bubbling malice.

Tom shot him a warning look. "May we come in?"

Helen looked as if she wanted to shut the door in their faces, but she stepped back to admit them inside.

Without a word or a backward glance, she led them to the parlor. Her black dress swished primly side to side, her shoulders straight, back erect. She must have thought herself so clever to have deceived them for so long. Gabriel's fingers twitched at his sides; all it would take was one push to send her sprawling to the floor, just as she had done to Sophronia. As if sensing his thoughts, Helen gave him a sharp glance over her shoulder.

When they reached the parlor, she seated herself on the sofa as if she were a highborn gentlewoman and they lowly servants. Had this been her plot all along? Get rid of Sophronia and install herself as mistress of the house?

Helen gazed up at them with open contempt. "Well?"

"I think you know why we're here," said Gabriel, returning her stare in equal measure.

Helen gave an irritated cluck. "No, I do not. I suppose you're sniffing around, looking for Sophronia." She raised a brow as if challenging him to deny it. "She's not here."

Tom opened his mouth to say something, but Gabriel stopped him with a swift look. He wasn't about to let Helen know exactly how much they knew, yet. "Do you have any idea where she's gone?" Inside, his blood was boiling, but two could play Helen's game of feigned innocence.

"I thought she was with you. Clearly I was mistaken."

"Don't play stupid, Mrs…" He trailed off, realizing he knew nothing about this woman other than her first name.

She scowled. "Mrs. Douglas. And I assure you, I am not playing at anything. Sophronia told me that she received a dinner invitation from you and was going to *your* house," she said.

"I sent her no such invitation," Gabriel said coldly.

For a moment Helen's mask slipped, her face registering surprise. Then she composed herself and the look vanished. "What are you talking about?"

It was all he could do to not take her by the shoulders and shake the truth out of her. Tom hastily interceded. "Why don't you tell us what happened yesterday." His voice was silky smooth, the voice that Gabriel had heard him use many a time on shore leave with a young lady.

Helen glared at him, but must have decided that answering his question would be less odious than being subjected to Gabriel's angry scrutiny.

She gave a little nod before saying, "Sophronia was acting strangely. She told me she received a dinner invitation from Mr. Stone, but I didn't like the idea of her going out by herself. I ran to catch up with her and found her on the bluff, just standing there." Helen bit at her lip, her gaze dropping to her lap. "She was acting so strangely," she said again. "There was something almost wild in her eyes, and I asked her if she wouldn't come back home with me. She refused, but the more I tried to reason with her the more hysterical she became. I didn't want to force her, so I left her there."

As far as alibis went, it was flimsy in the extreme. She was admitting to being with Sophronia on the bluff, to arguing. "You didn't have a fight?"

Helen swiftly looked away. "No, not a fight. We've had plenty of those. This was more of a…heated disagreement."

Lies. Helen was playing him for a fool. Unable to contain himself any longer, Gabriel stormed to the sofa, towering over her. "You're lying! The things you did to her… I saw the marks myself. And after all she has done for you," he said in disgust. Oh, how he wanted to see Helen thin and shivering behind iron bars, or, better yet, shackled to a transport ship bound somewhere far away where she would live out her days performing hard labor. Anything to get this deceitful, dangerous woman away from Sophronia.

"Steady on," Tom murmured.

Breathing hard, Gabriel came back to himself. Helen was sitting stock-still, her slightly raised brows the only indication that she had registered his outburst. Reluctantly, Gabriel stepped back. His heart was racing, his blood hot. He'd never felt such blinding anger before.

"You said something about marks." She flicked a glance between him and Tom. "Is she all right?"

"Sophronia was attacked, brutally. She's safe now, and resting," Gabriel said in clipped tones. "But you already knew that, didn't you?"

The color drained from her face. She looked genuinely surprised, shocked even. But if he had learned anything by now, it was that Helen was not as innocent as she appeared.

She whispered something so low that Gabriel couldn't make it out, except that it sounded like "the spell." Then she slumped back into her seat, staring past them out the window. "I never should have left her there by herself."

Tom sat down next to Helen and crossed his legs, reclining as if they were old friends. "There, now," he said in his usual easy way. "Why don't you tell me what all this is about. We all care about Mrs. Carver, and only want to do right by her, don't we?"

To Gabriel's surprise, Helen nodded, as meekly as a child, her severe expression softening into distress. "It wasn't the first time I followed her, and she was angry that I wouldn't trust her to go out by herself." At this, the corners of her mouth twitched downward, her throat working compulsively as if trying to tamp down some unpleasant emotion. "I should've insisted. I should've made her see sense and come back home with me. Please," she said, her eyes bright and searching as she looked between the two men. "What happened to her? Where is she?"

Tom caught his eye, and Gabriel's heart sank. Tom believed her.

"Excuse us for a moment," he said roughly to Helen, motioning for Tom to follow him out into the hallway.

"Don't tell me you're falling for her act," Gabriel hissed once they were out of earshot.

"She's telling the truth. Did you see her face when you said that Mrs. Carver had been attacked? She was horrified."

Rubbing at his dry eyes, Gabriel bit back a curse. He was so tired. At the very least, he had expected Tom to back him up. "You don't know her as I do," he said stubbornly.

"Are you sure you're not bringing your history with her to bear on this? I've never met her before in my life, and I can tell you, that woman is telling the truth."

Gabriel glanced over his shoulder into the parlor where Helen was staring out the window, her foot tapping nervously. He couldn't believe she was completely innocent, but Tom clearly did, and if he was going to ferret out the truth, he would need his friend's support.

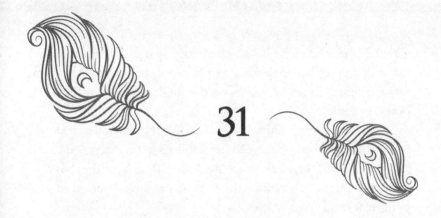

31

Sophronia had been drifting in and out of a light sleep when the murmur of voices floated up from downstairs. Her entire body throbbed, but it was her throat that felt as if it were on fire. She thought about calling for Fanny to bring her a glass of water, but when she opened her mouth found she was too parched for more than a whisper to come out.

Her conversation with Gabriel seemed faraway and dreamlike. None of it could be true, could it? Helen couldn't have tried to kill her; she had taken it upon herself to protect Sophronia all these years, so why would she want her dead? Maybe her fall had been an accident. They had been arguing and it could have become heated, Sophronia losing her balance and tumbling down the steep embankment. But then why would Helen just leave her there? And what about the finger marks on her throat?

There were so many questions, so much that didn't make sense. But first, she needed something to drink. With no small effort, she pushed the heavy quilt off and gathered her strength to stand. She hadn't paid much attention to the room as she drifted through her pain and groggy memories, but now, as she stood on shaking legs, Sophronia took in the details of Gabriel's bedchamber. It was small and sparsely furnished, the only sign of his presence a pair of wool socks drying before the grate, a stack of papers on the small desk, and a half-burned candle.

Shrugging into a comfortably worn dressing gown that had been left by the bed, she forced her stiff legs to limp across the cold wood floor. Her ankle throbbed beneath its bandage, but she gritted her teeth against the pain as she forced herself to put one foot in front of the other.

The voices grew louder as she slowly descended into the parlor. At the sound of the creaking floorboards, Fanny looked up and jumped out of her seat. "Sophy!" she cried in equal parts surprise and dismay. "What are you doing out of bed?"

"I was thirsty and thought a walk to get some water might do me good."

She must have looked even worse than she felt, because Fanny darted to her side, lacing her arm about her waist and helping to maneuver her down onto the sofa. "You should have called me," she reprimanded.

Sophronia's head was pounding. "Yes, perhaps you're right," she murmured as she allowed herself to be fussed over. "Where is Gabriel?"

"He and Mr. Ellroy went out for a walk."

Frowning, Sophronia glanced about the small parlor. "I thought I heard you talking to someone. I must have imagined it."

Fanny turned around, revealing Jasper leaning against the door frame and watching them with shrewd, assessing eyes. Dressed in oilskin pants and a roughly patched coat, he looked as if he'd just come from the docks.

"Oh, just Jasper," Fanny said as she unfolded a quilt across Sophronia's lap. "He stopped by for coffee."

Taking out a watch from his pocket, Jasper glanced at the time before pushing off from the door frame. "I have to get back to work," he said.

"Oh, but you only just came!" Fanny said, her lip in a pout. "You've been so busy lately that I feel I never see you anymore. At least stay for some supper."

"I can scrounge something up at home."

Disappointment was palpable on Fanny's face, but she smiled. "All right then, suit yourself."

Jasper allowed Fanny to stand on her toes and give him a peck on the cheek before he snapped his watch shut and placed it back in his pocket. It was a slow, deliberate movement, as if he were an actor performing on a stage.

Sophronia's heart stopped in her chest. Suddenly, her sore throat was a distant burning, the pain in her ankle fading away. The only thing she could see was the gold watch fob hanging from Jasper's grubby shirt pocket. She knew that watch fob.

Before she could tear her gaze away, Jasper caught her staring, his sharp eyes flaring like a wolf scenting prey. "Mrs. Carver," he said with a slow curl of his wide lips, "Fanny tells me you took a nasty tumble and can't remember a thing."

After they'd left Helen with strict orders not to come near Sophronia, Gabriel and Tom slowly walked back to the cottage.

"Mrs. Carver was right," Tom said softly as they made their way down the quiet road. "Helen isn't capable of these brutal acts. She's frightfully devoted to her mistress, and she's not a murderer."

Gabriel didn't say anything. He still wasn't convinced of her innocence. Even if she hadn't attacked Sophronia, she might as well have, arguing with her and then leaving her out there by herself while a killer prowled.

"I say, that fellow's in a hurry, isn't he?"

Gabriel looked up to see Mr. Reese's hack come careening toward them at breakneck speed. It was all they could do to jump back into the brush to avoid being trampled.

The hack flew by in a spray of gravel and mud, thundering hoofbeats echoing through the still November air. "You would think we were in Boston with drivers like that," Tom grumbled as he brushed dirt from his buff trousers. "With any luck, Fanny will be able to get the mud out before it stains if we get home soon."

Gabriel watched the hack disappear around the turn. The thought of returning to Sophronia with more questions than answers made him feel sick.

"Forget about the trousers," he said suddenly. "Come on."

Tom looked up, frowning. "Where are we going?"

"To find some goddamn answers."

As soon as Jasper left, Sophronia told Fanny that she had made a mistake in coming downstairs and she was going back to bed to rest. It wasn't a lie, but it wasn't the entire truth, either. She needed time to herself. She needed time to think.

That had been Nathaniel's watch fob; she knew it without a shadow of a doubt. As she gingerly climbed back up the stairs with Fanny hovering at her elbow, her stomach churned with a growing sense of dread.

Sophronia eased onto the bed, every bone in her body raw with pain. She closed her eyes and forced her aching head to focus. Well, there were lots of reasons he could have had it, weren't there? Whoever had stolen Nathaniel's watch and chain to put in the heart could have discarded the fob or pawned it. Jasper might have simply come upon it. She hardly knew anything about him, other than that he worked at the docks and had no family except Fanny. Yes, he disliked Soph-

ronia by all accounts, but he was hardly singular in that regard in Pale Harbor.

Unable to find rest, Sophronia got back up, breathing heavily and trying not to focus on the pain radiating from her
ankle, and then eased herself down at Gabriel's small wood
desk. His sermon notes sat in an endearingly jumbled pile, and
something familiar nagged at the back of her mind, something
she had seen in a stack of papers like that.

Stories, horrible stories. Jasper had submitted his, and she
had rejected them roundly. But that hadn't stopped him from
sending more and more until she finally resorted to throwing
them straight into the fire.

Gooseflesh sprang up along her arms. Jasper. She had not
been able to cross out his name on her list, but nor had he
stood out in any way among the handful of other names. Now
everything was falling into place. How could she not have
seen it sooner?

She should wait for Gabriel to come home, tell him her
suspicions. But Jasper knew she was here, and he knew that
Gabriel was not. Would he come back to finish what he had
started? Surely he wouldn't try anything so long as his sister
was here? He had wanted her to see that watch fob, she was
sure of it. She gripped the edge of the desk with sweating
hands, her mind racing. She had to get back to Castle Carver,
to tell Gabriel that he was wrong about Helen, that it had been
Jasper all this time. Gabriel had told Fanny he was going for a
walk, but she didn't for one minute believe he had gone anywhere but to confront Helen. She had seen the look in his eye,
and it had been nothing short of murderous.

She had to stop him from whatever he thought to do. Sophronia had unwittingly put Helen in danger. Walking there in
her condition was out of the question, but neither could she

send a note with Fanny. What if the girl read it, warned her brother?

So moments later, to Fanny's dismay and disbelief, Sophronia hobbled back into the parlor and asked her to send for Mr. Reese.

"You can't possibly think of leaving! The doctor said you must rest, and Mr. Stone gave me strict orders that you were not to be disturbed. I don't think he'll like it if you—"

Sophronia stopped her. "Just send for the carriage. Now."

Fanny must have run the entire way, because she was back within a quarter of an hour with Mr. Reese's hack. Sophronia was ready, the dressing gown cinched tightly around her shift and petticoats, her boot painstakingly laced over her swollen ankle. She must have looked like death personified, but she pulled herself up tall, and in a clipped voice, she ordered Fanny to stay at the cottage while she was gone.

Fanny's face fell. "But Sophy, Mr. Stone wouldn't want you to go alone. Of course I should come. What's going on anyway?"

A terrible thought flitted through Sophronia's mind as she watched her young friend plead her case: Was Fanny complicit in her brother's crimes? Did she know what he had done, or—God forbid—had she even helped him? She had access to Sophronia's house; she could have taken the handkerchief. The very thought made her sick.

She chose her words carefully; Fanny must not know that Sophronia had any suspicions about her and her brother. "Helen is at home. I'll be fine. Besides," she added, "Mr. Stone and Mr. Ellroy will be returning from their walk soon, and I'm sure they'd appreciate a nice hot drink."

Fanny looked like she wanted to argue, but Mr. Reese was already at the door. Leaning against him, Sophronia let him help her to the carriage, and then they were flying to Castle Carver.

★ ★ ★

Declaring his need for answers was proving to be much easier than actually finding them. Gabriel and Tom had spoken with at least a dozen people, and the only consensus they had reached was that no one had been up on the bluff the previous day, and no one remembered seeing anything otherwise out of the ordinary.

After a particularly disheartening conversation with Mr. Marshall, who was convinced that it had all been an accident due to muddy conditions, Gabriel was beginning to make peace with the fact that they were going to return home empty-handed. They were just standing to leave when Mr. Marshall stopped them.

"I suppose you'll want to speak to Harriet?" Mr. Marshall paused, gazing out into the hall. "She's been such a help since Clara...since..." He made a valiant effort at clearing his throat, but Gabriel could see his eyes swimming with tears. Sympathy shot through him; whoever had done this to Sophronia had left her with her life, whether they'd meant to or not. Clara Marshall had not been so lucky.

The last person Gabriel wanted to see at the moment was the flirtatious Miss Wiggins, but he would not be able to face Sophronia if he had left even a single stone unturned.

She was sent for, and as soon as she stepped into the parlor and saw Gabriel, her face lit up. "Mr. Stone! I was wondering when you would call." Her gaze slid to Tom. "And I see you've brought a friend!" She offered Tom her gloved hand, which he obliged with a chaste kiss.

"I'm afraid we're not calling on pleasure," Tom interjected for Gabriel. "We've come to ask you some questions."

Her smile slipped. "Oh?"

"Mrs. Carver was attacked yesterday, we believe by the same person responsible for your aunt's death," Gabriel said without preamble. There was no time to waste; every moment that he was out searching for the perpetrator was a moment that Sophronia was alone. In his bed. The thought simultaneously electrified him and made his stomach knot with worry. "Were you near the harbor yesterday or did you see anything suspicious?"

"Suspicious?" She gave a little frown, thinking. "Yesterday I was shopping for fabric for a new gown. The annual Christmas festival and dance is just around the corner, you know," she said with a meaningful look at Gabriel.

Sidestepping her snare, he crossed his arms. Civility was getting him nowhere. "You've never liked Mrs. Carver, have you?"

Her blue eyes widened, and she looked between the two men as if they were joking. When she found only grim expressions in answer, she held an affronted hand to the lace at her chest. "You think *I* had something to do with this? I assure you, if that woman found herself the victim of an attack, then I can only assume she had it coming to her."

"Enough!" Gabriel slammed his palms down on a rickety side table, sending a porcelain statuette of a shepherdess quivering from the force. "You've always been jealous of her. Perhaps you thought to get rid of her."

Of course the petite Miss Wiggins never could have done any real harm to Sophronia, and of course she wouldn't have been able to stuff her aunt's ample body up the chimney, but he was tired of her simpering and her vicious tongue. Sophronia had nearly died, and all Miss Wiggins cared about was spreading slander.

Her mouth dropped open. "I have never been so insulted in my life. And to think I would have let you court me!"

Gabriel let out a snort of derision. "*Court* you!"

"Gabe," Tom said, tugging at his sleeve. "I think it's time to go."

Just then, Mr. Marshall wandered back into the room, pipe in hand. "What's going on? I heard shouting. Harriet, are you all right?"

"Oh, Uncle Horace," she said in a sob. She ran to him in a flutter of lace petticoats, throwing her arms around him. "Mr. Stone is being horrid, accusing me of…of *attacking* Mrs. Carver! As if I could ever hurt a fly!"

Mr. Marshall's gaze snapped to Gabriel, the pipe frozen halfway to his lips. "Is this true?"

"I'm so sorry for any distress we may have caused," Tom said, swiftly taking Gabriel by the arm. "We were just leaving."

Gabriel yanked his arm back, nearly sending the shepherdess flying off the table completely. If he was going back home without any answers, then he was sure as hell going to have his say first. "Your niece is just as guilty as the murderer, spreading rumors and fanning the flames of hatred in Pale Harbor."

Mr. Marshall's whiskered face reddened. "How dare you, sir! This is a house in mourning! And to think I took you under my wing, gave you every opportunity to succeed in Pale Harbor."

Miss Wiggins was quietly sobbing against her uncle's chest, but Gabriel was sure he saw her flash him a sly look at this.

What a waste of time. He could have been with Sophronia, making sure that she was safe and comfortable, and instead, he was chasing flimsy hunches and letting Miss Wiggins rile him up. "Come on," he bit out at Tom. "Let's go."

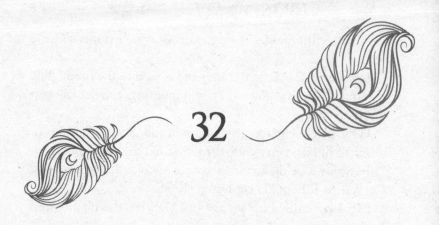

32

"Helen, are you home?"

Sophronia stood in the front hall, bracing herself against the banister to collect her breath. She'd sent Mr. Reese away, sure that she would find Gabriel and Mr. Ellroy inside. But there was no sign of them. What if she was too late? What if Gabriel had come and gone, having visited some terrible vengeance on Helen?

"Helen?" When there was still no answer, she made her way painstakingly to the parlor, leaning heavily against the wall and pausing frequently to rest her throbbing ankle.

Her desk was just as she'd left it, stacked with papers and packages that Garrett had never had the chance to send to Portland. Nothing was out of place, and there was no sign of violence or a struggle. She let out a slow, shaky breath.

"Your minister and his friend were just here."

She jumped at the sound of Helen's voice. "Oh, you gave me a fright."

Though she had no reason to fear her now that she knew the truth about Jasper, Sophronia couldn't help the lingering vestige of mistrust she felt. After all, even if Helen was not responsible, she had still lied to her all these years, had poisoned a man and let Sophronia carry the guilt alone. Sophronia wasn't just hurt, she was angry, too. Angry that Helen had made a fool of her, had kept Sophronia in her thrall, playing the part of her savior.

"They accused me of all sorts of vile things," Helen said in cold tones.

Unable to meet her eye, Sophronia began leafing through the papers on her desk. She couldn't tell Helen that until just an hour ago, she had shared Gabriel's suspicions. When she didn't say anything, Helen took a few hesitant steps into the room, her face drawn with worry. "He said you were attacked."

The evidence she needed to condemn Jasper was somewhere in that stack of papers. She only had to find it, but Helen was hovering, waiting for her to say something. She drew in a shaky breath. "Yes, I was. But I'll be fine. I just need to find something."

Coming the rest of the way into the room, Helen blanched when she saw Sophronia's neck. "Sophy! Are you sure you should be out of bed? Come," she said, moving to take her by the arm, "we must get you upstairs. I'll make you a compress and brew up a tisane."

But there was no time for Helen's coddling or hysterics. She needed to find Jasper's stories and show them to Gabriel and the constable. "No!" she said with more force than was strictly necessary. "No, there's too much to be done. I need to find something. It's important. It's…" She trailed off.

Drawing back, Helen's hand flew to her mouth. "You *know*," she said. "You know who it is."

Sophronia stopped, her fingers on the papers. Should she tell Helen her suspicions? She had been wrong before and look where that had gotten her. But, perhaps worse, what if she was right? Gabriel had gone off without her knowledge or permission to confront Helen on her behalf; what if Helen took equal measures upon herself and decided to exact retribution on Jasper?

Resuming her rifling, she shook her head. "I have my suspicions."

Helen didn't say anything as Sophronia continued her search. It was growing difficult to concentrate with the pain in her ankle building, her throat so raw that her eyes were starting to water.

"For God's sake," Helen said roughly. "You're fit to pitch over. Sit down and tell me what you're looking for."

Sophronia was about to protest, but the promise of sitting down and closing her eyes was too hard to resist. "Jasper Gibbs," she said, sinking gratefully onto the sofa.

If the name shocked Helen, she gave no indication of it. "I never liked him," she muttered as she took up the stack where Sophronia had left off.

A sharp, icy rain was picking up outside, the wind throwing it in gusts against the windowpanes. It was the kind of day in which Sophronia used to revel, a day where there was nothing tempting in the world outside and she was content to curl up by the fire with a cup of tea and a good book. But now the tempestuous weather only served to heighten the growing dread in her gut.

Suddenly, Helen froze. Sophronia watched her as she sucked in her breath, her eyes hurriedly scanning a thick packet of pages.

"What is it?"

Wordlessly, Helen handed her the packet. There it was, right on the first page: Jasper Gibbs. She flipped through it, her fingers barely able to match the frantic pace of her eyes. She remembered his first submissions, gruesome stories that seemed to serve no purpose beyond instilling disgust and horror in the reader. After she'd gently rejected them, he'd sent more, and eventually most of them had found their way into the rubbish or the fire. But not this one. This one had slipped through the cracks.

It was violent, graphically so. The story followed a young man, Tucker, who had been wronged by a woman; something about being jilted at the altar for another man, and ended with the protagonist exacting revenge not only on the woman, but on the man she loved by killing him while she was forced to watch.

Sophronia shoved the paper away from her, wishing she could banish the words from her mind. Closing her eyes, she took a deep breath and leaned her head back. It was Jasper. It had to be Jasper.

"I'll kill him," Helen said softly.

Sophronia's eyes flew open. "You will do no such thing." There had been enough violence, enough misplaced revenge.

Helen wasn't listening. She was staring at the rain out the window, her knuckles white as she wound her hands together. "Sophronia, there is something I must tell you, I—"

But before she could finish, a desperate banging came from the front door.

"She went *where*?" Gabriel's words came out in a roar.

Fanny was twisting her hands together over and over in front of her apron, looking like she wished she could melt into the floorboards. "She insisted on going! I couldn't very well force her to stay. I think she just wanted to go home."

Good God, how did she even have the strength to walk downstairs, let alone make the journey to Castle Carver? He would have been in awe of her fortitude if he weren't so damned sick with worry.

"All right, Gabe, no need to shout," Tom said with a reassuring smile at Fanny. "She'll be safe enough at Castle Carver. Helen won't harm her."

Gabriel forced himself to breathe. Tom might have thought Helen innocent, but he still wasn't so sure. Scraping his hand through his hair, he looked around the kitchen, half-expecting Sophronia to materialize from the walls. How could he fail her so spectacularly and so often?

"We have to go back."

Before he had even had a chance to convince Tom to put his hat back on, there was a knock at the door.

It was a young boy, holding a note out in one hand, the other open waiting for a coin. Tom paid him and sent him on his way while Gabriel tore the envelope open.

"There, now," Tom said, clapping him on the back. "She's written you to tell you she's safe and sound."

Gabriel didn't say anything as he unfolded the note and scanned the brief lines. Blood began thundering in his ears. He should have been stunned, but somehow, as soon as Fanny told him that Sophronia had left, he'd known that something was very, very wrong.

"What? What is it?"

His throat was dry and his voice hoarse. "They have Sophronia."

Sophronia made to get up, but Helen stopped her with a stern look and a hand to her shoulder. "You stay right there."

Too tired to argue, Sophronia allowed her to answer the door. With any luck it would be Gabriel, and with a little more luck he wouldn't be *too* angry with her for absconding from his house.

But when Helen returned, she was alone, a note in her hand. If she never saw one of those blasted envelopes again, it would be too soon.

"A messenger boy brought it," Helen told her. "He ran off before I could ask him who it was from." Sophronia nodded, giving her permission to read it aloud.

"'So, we are strangers no more. If my company alone is not enough to entice you, then allow me to sweeten my proposition. I have Gabriel Stone at the old lighthouse. Come, and come alone, or your beloved hack of a minister will be the next to find himself under my blade.'"

Anger seethed through Sophronia, starting in her fingers and boiling up to her throbbing temple. She knew it was Jasper, and the coward *knew* she knew. And now he had the nerve, after months of terrorizing her and spilling blood in Pale Harbor, to demand this of her.

She took the note and crumpled it. She had thought herself clever the other day when she went with her little knife to face her tormentor on the bluff, but now all her bravado had fled. Jasper had Gabriel; he had already killed two people, and Sophronia didn't for a minute believe that he would have any qualms about killing another.

The old, overwhelming paralysis overtook her. She could stay in the house, and she would be safe there. Gabriel would not want her to come; she could almost hear his rough voice chastising her for even thinking about it, could see his intense hazel eyes narrowing in warning.

Rain was coming down in sheets, the heavens building walls of water to keep her inside. But the longer she sat there ruminating on her fear, on Gabriel's danger, the clearer it became what she had to do.

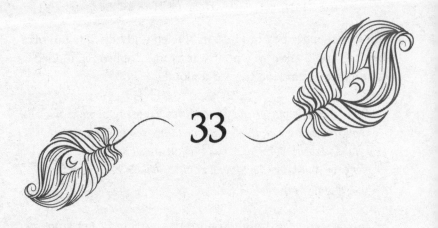

33

Mindless of the pelting rain, Gabriel hurtled out of the house with Tom hot on his heels. This couldn't be happening. He'd had her, and now she had slipped through his fingers into danger again.

The note said that she was at the bluff, but they were barely to the turn in the road when a young man came sprinting toward them, his bright red hair a startling flame against the dead trees. Stopping just short of them, Jasper doubled over to catch his breath.

"It's Mrs. Carver," he said between gasps. "Something terrible has happened."

Gabriel's body went rigid, the cold air in his lungs turning to ice. He was too late. This time there would be no miracle, this time the universe would have its final laugh at his expense.

Tom, thankfully, suffered no such paralysis. "Where is she?" he asked sharply.

"On the bluff. I think she's hurt."

Hurt, but alive then. Gabriel's breath escaped in a hiss. They started to follow him, but Jasper turned and shook his head at Tom. "No, you go tell the constable, and have him bring some men," he said. "I'll take Mr. Stone. I know a route that will take us there quicker."

Tom shot Gabriel a questioning look. "You'd better do as he says," Gabriel told him. They would need reinforcements, but he had to get to Sophronia as quickly as possible.

Wind licked at Gabriel's collar and raindrops rolled down his cheeks as Jasper, clearly no longer winded, ran ahead and urged him to keep up.

The path Jasper led him on was narrow and winding, overgrown with trees so thick they might as well have been in a tunnel. Gabriel had never been this way before, but he was sure that it was leading them farther out of town, not to the bluff. He called to Jasper, but the young man was too far ahead, and the wind only carried off his words.

When the path widened they emerged not on the bluff, but past the other side of town. The old lighthouse that Sophronia had pointed out to him sat stoic in its desuetude above a rocky beach.

"Just a little farther, up there," Jasper said, pointing to the lighthouse when Gabriel finally caught up with him. The old lighthouse was perched above the violent water on a sheer cliff of rock and scrub grass. Waves crashed daringly close, and a veil of mist obscured the top. How many ships had looked to it as a guiding light, giving them comfort in the dark? There was nothing comforting about it now, though.

"You said she was at the harbor, at the bluff there."

Jasper furrowed his brow, pushing wet hair out of his eyes. "Did I? I meant the rocks."

Uneasiness curled through him. How had Jasper come across her here? And how the hell had Sophronia gotten up there with her injuries, for that matter?

And then a terrible, cold realization sank through his body. It was Jasper. It had always been Jasper. He looked at the young man waiting for him, hands on hips, to follow. If Tom were here, they could have taken Jasper down together, and then gone to the lighthouse. But Gabriel couldn't risk Sophronia being up there, hurt and alone, and so he had no choice but to follow him.

Skirting the dilapidated keeper's cottage, Jasper led him to the peeling red door of the lighthouse. It groaned open, and Jasper stood back to let Gabriel pass. "She's up at the top, hurry," he said, pointing up the rickety iron steps.

Gabriel rushed in. The door slammed shut behind him as he raced up the never-ending spiraling stairs. He would kill Jasper for this. By the time he reached the top, he was nauseous, out of breath and in a frenzy of worry. He peered through the thick gray light of the lantern room. "Sophronia?"

A prickling feeling started at the back of his neck, working its way down his body. She wasn't here. Deep down, he'd known as soon as he'd seen the lighthouse that she wouldn't be. Just as he was turning to go back down and confront Jasper, there was a flash of red hair out of the corner of his vision, and then everything went black.

Sophronia was out of breath and ached from head to toe by the time they reached the road that led to the old lighthouse. If she'd had time and had been prepared, she would have taken a pair of Nathaniel's old trousers. As it was, she constantly had to fight with her damp and heavy petticoats, not to mention her injured ankle, exhausting herself twice over. Plowing ahead in her sensible wool dress, Helen did not seem the least bit spent.

"A moment," Sophronia called out. She hadn't even tried to dissuade Helen from coming with her, and for once, Helen hadn't tried to talk her out of going. "I cannot protect you without the spell, but at least I can make sure that you are not alone, that no harm comes to you if I can help it," she had told Sophronia. Even with her friend's betrayal still hanging over her, she was bone-deep grateful for the support. Given time, perhaps she could come to forgive Helen for taking Nathaniel's death into her own hands, for deceiving her all these years. Perhaps.

Catching her breath against a tree, she took stock of their position. Jasper had chosen a clever place for their meeting, she had to concede that much to him; he would have a nearly panoramic view from the top, and she was at his mercy, as only one path led to the lighthouse.

But perhaps she could leverage that to their advantage. He would be expecting her to come from the road, to walk straight through the front door, leaving her vulnerable to an ambush. He would not be expecting her to come from the rocky beach below the lighthouse. And he certainly would not expect her to have Helen with her.

The only problem was, the same reason Jasper wouldn't be expecting her from the rocks was why it would be nearly impossible to accomplish: they would have to scale the rocks farther down the beach, make their way across to the lighthouse and then climb back up. She was not dressed for it, and she was still weak from her ordeal, her ankle inflamed and throbbing, her body aching with fatigue. But there was no other option. He had Gabriel.

She took one last giant gulp of cold, damp air before gathering her muddy petticoats and summoning her remaining resolve. "Come," she told Helen. "We're going down."

The world was spinning.

Gabriel felt as if he were back in the navy on a storm-tossed ship, listing side to side. Cracking his eyes open, he saw he was in a small, circular room cast in heavy shadows. His mouth tasted metallic, and when his vision focused enough, he saw blood on his chest. He tried to stand, but his hands were bound and laced around some sort of pole or beam behind him. Panic rising, he gave a violent twist of his shoulders to shrug out of the ties, but they held fast, and only gave him rope-burn for his trouble.

"Good, you're awake," came a voice. "I wouldn't waste your time trying to slip your bindings. I know how to tie a fast knot."

It took Gabriel a moment to bring the speaker's face into focus. Red hair and freckles, a wide, downturned mouth. Jasper leaned casually against the iron stair rail, knife in hand, watching him with dispassionate eyes. "Everything will go much more smoothly if you're awake."

He opened his mouth to speak, but his throat was as dry as cotton. "Sophronia," he managed to ground out. "Where is she?"

Jasper's lips twisted into a scowl. "She's not here. You're even stupider than you look."

Closing his eyes, Gabriel leaned his throbbing head back against the beam. He *was* stupid. It had all been a ruse, and he'd walked right into Jasper's trap. How had he never considered that Fanny's brother could be responsible? He hated Sophronia, had practically pushed her over at the ball, and would have been able to steal the handkerchief from Fanny's mending basket to frame her.

"Where is she?" he rasped again.

"Oh, she's coming. And when she gets here, we'll all have a nice chat, and then I'll see the scales tipped even between us."

Gabriel didn't know what he was talking about, but it didn't matter. He had to think fast, to get out of here before Sophronia walked into the same trap. If he could only get Jasper to come close enough, he was confident he could give him a good knock with his head. "Water," he said. "I need water."

Jasper gave him a long, hard look before stalking to the corner where a tin water pitcher and cup stood on an upturned crate. Just how often did he come here? How long had he been planning this?

But then, standing a good three paces away, Jasper tossed the water directly into Gabriel's face.

He was already soaking wet from the rain, so Jasper's infantile gesture made little difference to him. It was the fact that he didn't get close enough for Gabriel to land a blow that incensed him. Gabriel spat. "Why Mrs. Carver?" he asked. "What has she ever done to you? Don't tell me you believe the nonsense that she's a witch who can summon demons from the woods."

Jasper scoffed, pitching the tin cup off the wall and watching it clatter down the spiral steps. "Don't tell *me* that you didn't know she was responsible for her husband's death."

Gabriel didn't say anything. Like most people in Pale Harbor, Jasper wasn't wrong when he said that Sophronia had killed her husband, but he was far from knowing the whole truth. Besides, like everyone else, Jasper had only his suspicions and prejudices. "What do you know about her husband?" he finally asked.

"What do *I* know?" Jasper gave him an incredulous look. "You really are that stupid."

If he couldn't incapacitate Jasper, then the next best thing was to keep him talking, to keep him distracted. With any luck, Tom would figure out where they'd gone and come with reinforcements soon, hopefully before Sophronia did. "Why don't you enlighten me?"

As if reading his thoughts, a slow, terrible smile spread across

Jasper's face. "Why don't we wait for Mrs. Carver? She will have received my invitation and should be here any moment."

If there was one thing of which Gabriel was certain, it was that Sophronia would have more sense than himself. She wouldn't so easily fall into Jasper's trap. Besides, she was still weak and recovering; he could only pray her injuries alone would prevent her from coming.

"She's injured, she won't come," Gabriel said. "But you already know that, don't you? You're the one who pushed her off the bluff." He paused, desperately wondering if Jasper had meant to kill her and failed that day, or if injuring her had been all part of some greater plan. He dared not ask.

Jasper's expression turned stormy, and he began to pace. "Oh, she'll come. For you."

Gabriel's heart sank. He was right. If Sophronia came, it would be because of him and him alone. Why had he ever allowed himself to become involved with her? Hadn't he learned anything from Anna? The people he loved always ended up hurt because of him. But it was too late for regrets now; his only option was to keep Jasper talking and hope that Sophronia stayed far away.

"Tell me now. I want to know how you managed all this. It must have taken a long time to write all the notes, to figure out just what would scare Mrs. Carver the most."

Jasper gave him a long, assessing look. He was obviously bursting to crow about his ghastly achievements. Gabriel decided to give him one more nudge. "All the references to Poe's stories were very clever. How did you think of them?"

"I know what you're trying to do."

Gabriel played innocent. "Oh? And what's that?"

"You're trying to flatter me," Jasper said with a black look. "It won't work."

Gabriel shrugged as much as his bonds would allow, and silence fell over them. The lighthouse shuddered and creaked in the unforgiving wind. Pacing the small turret, Jasper twirled his knife, catching it neatly. "Nathaniel Carver was our father," he said out of nowhere. He cocked his head, watching for Gabriel's reaction. "There, you didn't expect that, did you?"

Gabriel's mind raced. "Does Sophronia know that you and Fanny are her husband's children?"

The look of satisfaction faded, and Jasper scowled. "No, because she could never be bothered to meet us."

Nothing about what Jasper was saying made sense. Sophronia had clearly met both of them, and if her husband had children, she would have wanted to know. Before Gabriel could ask what the hell he was talking about, Jasper continued.

"Our mother was a whore," he said dispassionately. "She died from a disease of her trade, leaving Fanny and I to fend for ourselves when we were only twelve years old. But before she died, she told me who our father was. We were living in New York, and I scraped together enough money to buy Fanny and I passage all the way to this pitiful little town. When we got here, I went straight to Castle Carver. The servant wouldn't let me in, but my father came to the door. He told me that he would gladly take us in, except that his new wife wouldn't want sniveling little children of questionable birth in the house. Then he shut the door in my face."

Defending Sophronia would only anger Jasper, so he kept his mouth clamped shut, but he knew in his heart of hearts that Sophronia never would have turned a young boy away from her door.

"No, she couldn't take *us* in, her husband's own flesh and blood, but she took in Helen, a complete stranger and charity case."

Jasper's face had taken on a childlike expression as he told his story, but now it hardened, his voice becoming rough. "If it hadn't been for that bitch, my father would have recognized us as his children and given us his name. Everything would have been different. I wouldn't have to work on the docks unloading stinking nets of fish, and Fanny would have grown up a lady, instead of being forced to launder for a stepmother who refused to accept us."

"That's a sad story, Jasper," Gabriel said evenly. "Does Fanny know that Nathaniel Carver was your father?"

At Fanny's name, something warm flickered in Jasper's eyes. Then just as quickly, it passed. "No," he said curtly. "When we moved, I told Fanny it was because of better opportunities up north. It only would have served to hurt her if she knew the truth."

Fanny wasn't involved then, thank God; Sophronia would have been heartbroken. "But you can't blame Mrs. Carver for your father's callousness."

"No?" Jasper's expression had turned venomous. "But I can blame her for ruining my chances at a literary career. She got her hands on my father's magazine, that conniving, murderous bitch. I might have made a living writing if it had been left to me. I was forced to submit my stories to her as if I were any other common writer, and she had the nerve to reject them!" He kicked over the crate on which he'd been sitting, sending it scraping across the floor. "She works my sister like a slave. She calls her a friend, but who would make their friend sweat over a steaming tub of lye for them? If she wanted to help us, she could have gotten my stories published. God knows why my father left her the magazine. I wouldn't be surprised if she forced him to change his will before she killed him." He paused, crossing his arms like a sulky child. "I'm as good as Poe, you know, better, even. My stories go beyond anything you've ever read before."

Jasper's delusions of grandeur were nearly as frightening

as they were laughable. "Is that why you left the ravens, the one-eyed cat dummy? To prove that you could be like him?"

"Everyone loves Poe. Mrs. Carver was so keen to publish his stories and not mine, I thought she might like to have a taste of them in real life."

Pushing aside his revulsion, Gabriel pressed him further. "What about the bones and animal remains in the church and around town? The Marshalls said someone found a crude doll stuffed into the hole of a tree. Was that you, as well? You knew Mrs. Carver didn't leave the house and would never see them, so why go to the trouble?"

Jasper was staring out the window. His breath came out in an annoyed huff, fogging the glass. "Not everything is meant for the public. A writer doesn't share his first draft with the world. Some of the other things like the doll..." He trailed off, shrugging. "Thought it might be fun to stir up the town a little. The animal remains were meant to go in the belfry," he said. When Gabriel didn't say anything in response, Jasper's tone turned incredulous. "Don't tell me you never read 'The Devil in the Belfry'?"

"I'm afraid I missed that one."

Jasper shook his head in disgust. "Poe is an orphan, too, just like me. At least *he* had the benefit of an education... Do you know how I learned to write? I taught myself. I read everything I could get my hands on. But it took years of practice. It was the same for punishing Mrs. Carver—I needed practice. I never killed a man before, but practice makes perfect, doesn't it?"

"Is that why you waited until now? Four years after your father's death?"

"She kept rejecting my stories and I needed practice, time," was all Jasper said.

The young man was disturbed in ways he couldn't even

fathom. Gabriel's revulsion must have shown on his face, because Jasper rounded on him, clutching his knife and waving it so close to his face that Gabriel could feel the air quiver.

"What? Do you think you're better than me?" Jasper trailed the knife down Gabriel's cheek, the cold steel making his hair stand on end. Gabriel refused to give him the satisfaction of flinching. "You hide behind your fancy tracts and letters, pretending to be a godly man, an *enlightened* man, but I see the animal gleam in your eyes. Sophronia Carver will watch you die, painfully, slowly, and once you're gone, there will be no one left to protect her. She will get what she so long has avoided—punishment. And I'll be famous for writing the entire story."

Gabriel could only stare at him. Jasper's anger and hatred for Sophronia transcended his supposed grief for his own father. There was only one thing more dangerous than a man not in control of his anger: a man driven by revenge.

34

The wind whipped her hair and snapped at her numb cheeks. Sophronia had barely scaled down the first slippery rock and she was already questioning her plan. Her ankle screamed in pain with every jarring step. The bandage bunched out of her boot, leaving her skin raw and exposed, and she had to rely on Helen to steady her. Below her, angry waves crashed on the rocks. The tide was coming in.

When was the last time she had been so tested? Had she ever been? Her fear of Nathaniel had caused her to retreat into herself, to build up a wall and hide away. But she could not hide from this, not if she wanted to ever see Gabriel again. She bitterly thought back to the day she had tried to leave the grounds of Castle Carver to go to Gabriel's church, only to be thwarted by her own doubts and fears. Now she was scaling down slick, wet rocks with an injured ankle in the middle of a storm like some sort of heroine from a gothic novel.

Her good foot slipped out from under her, and her stomach dropped as she quickly shifted weight. Pain lanced up her leg. Helen shot out her hand and steadied her by the waist. "This was a bad idea," she muttered.

The sharp movement sent Helen's cloak billowing back, revealing a pistol strapped to her waist.

"Where did you get that?"

Helen glanced down, as if she had completely forgotten about the firearm. "From his desk."

Sophronia opened her mouth to ask Helen what she had been thinking, but then clamped it shut. She hadn't even known that Nathaniel had kept a pistol, but now that she saw the heavy silver and mahogany weapon, she was glad that Helen had brought it. Whatever awaited them in the lighthouse, she only prayed they would not need it.

There was a leak in the old lighthouse roof, and the steady drum of dripping water made time feel stretched out and unbearably slow. Despite Gabriel's best efforts at keeping Jasper talking, he had gone back to sitting on the crate, anxiously tapping the knife handle against the palm of his hand. Every now and then he would spring up to look out the window, and then mutter a curse. For all of Jasper's scheming and impatience, Sophronia was still not here. *Good girl*, he thought. *Stay far away.*

"Are you sure she's coming?" Gabriel couldn't help asking in a mocking tone.

Jasper scowled. "She's coming. I have what she wants."

A dull thud sounded outside, cutting off the rest of Jasper's words and sending him flying to the window. Gabriel's gut clenched, but it had come from the rocks, not the road. It was probably just a gull disoriented from the storm.

When the noise didn't come again, Jasper reluctantly turned away. But no sooner had he sat back down than there was another thud, this one closer. Much closer.

Even with Helen helping her, Sophronia's palms were raw and bloody, and her body ached with fatigue by the time they reached the rocks directly below the lighthouse.

"Look." Sophronia followed Helen's finger, which pointed to where a dangerously rusted handrail and a staircase ran from the ground all the way to the top. After scaling rocks for what seemed like hours, it would be a downright luxury to climb it.

When they reached the top, they found the stairs ended in a narrow walkway that circled the outside of the lantern room. Sophronia collapsed on the solid wood in a puddle of aching muscles and relief, but when she chanced a look down, her head went light. They were such a very long way up, with nothing but rocks and waves below.

Helen crouched beneath one of the large windows, peering over the ledge. "Jasper has a knife. I can only see Mr. Stone's legs...he's behind something."

Sophronia's heart dropped into her stomach at the thought of Gabriel bound and beaten, all because of her. They had come this far, but she wasn't sure she had the strength to find out if he was unharmed, or God forbid, dead. Before terror could bubble up in her throat, Helen squared her shoulders, taking control.

"I have the gun," she said. "I go first."

Before Sophronia knew what was happening, Helen was putting her shoulder against the old door and bursting into the lantern room.

There was a scuffle as Jasper realized what was happening and scrambled to his feet, lunging at her from across the room. But it was Helen who was up first, the victor, with her pistol pointed at him. "Drop the knife, Jasper," she ordered in a voice that was so low and deadly that Sophronia couldn't help but shiver.

Taking a deep breath, she pushed aside the pain throbbing through her body, the fear that Gabriel might not be all right. She mustered all her strength, sent up a silent prayer to the universe, and then it was her turn to push forward into the room.

★ ★ ★

It all happened in a flash. Jasper had been sitting there twirling his knife and catching it over and over again, and then the door exploded inward, followed by a cloud of black skirts.

Stunned, Gabriel watched as Jasper jerked back in surprise. He stumbled close enough to Gabriel that he was able to kick his leg out, tripping Jasper the rest of the way and sending his knife clattering to the floor. The black skirts settled, and then Helen was standing there, training an ancient-looking pistol at Jasper.

Jasper's hands shot up, palms open in surrender. "What the hell are you doing here?"

It was only Helen. Closing his eyes, Gabriel leaned his head back against the beam as relief rode through his body. Sophronia was nowhere to be seen.

The knife had landed just short of Gabriel's feet. If he could just stretch his legs a little more, he could pull it back toward him. But before he could try, there was movement at the platform door.

Oh, no. God, no. Gabriel watched in horror as Sophronia pushed open the protesting door, swaying on her feet, her face twisted in pain. She had come after all. Gabriel's heart lurched; he had never felt so powerless.

Jasper made a move for the knife, and in response, Helen cocked the pistol. "Don't move."

"Gabriel." Sophronia was crawling on hands and knees to him, her face a ghastly shade of gray. "Are you all right?"

"I'm fine," he said. "You shouldn't have come." But he couldn't help the gratitude welling inside him; despite everything that should have stopped her, she had come for him.

"These ropes say differently," she said as she grabbed Jasper's knife off the floor and began sawing at his bonds.

"I see you received my invitation," Jasper said, craning

his neck to see past Helen. He spoke as calmly as if he were hosting a dinner party and not holding people hostage in an abandoned lighthouse. "Though it wasn't supposed to include any guests."

Sophronia didn't respond as she continued cutting at the ropes with shaking hands.

Helen kept her pistol trained on Jasper, who looked suspiciously unruffled. "Going to have your guard dog kill me?" he called to Sophronia. "You always were a coward... Hiding in your house, refusing to face the consequences of your actions."

"Be quiet," Helen growled.

"No," Sophronia said with quiet force from her seat on the floor. "Helen will not shoot you, and certainly not at my direction. You are coming back with us and will answer to the highest court in Maine for what you have done."

"Sophronia," Gabriel murmured in warning. "Don't say anything. It's not worth it."

This seemed to amuse Jasper, because he raised one brow and gave a snort. "You still don't understand, do you?"

"I understand that you are a small man, someone so petty that he would wreak havoc on this town, murder people, all because his horrid stories weren't printed." She gave a hard swallow as if the words she were about to say would cost her dearly. "Does your sister know? How could you do this to Fanny?"

The amusement faded from Jasper's face, and his eyes flashed with anger. "You think that's all this is?"

She had sawed the ropes just enough for Gabriel to snap them the rest of the way off. In an instant he was on his feet, bringing Sophronia with him and spinning her so that his body blocked her from Helen and Jasper. He would be damned if that pistol went off anywhere near her.

His legs were numb from sitting so long, his wrists chafed,

but feeling her in his arms and smelling her familiar scent brought the world back into balance. "The little bastard is your stepson," he said, wishing he could spare her the hurt and confusion that the revelation would cause.

"Don't use that word," Jasper ground out.

Gabriel could feel her stiffen.

"I...what? But how can that be?"

"Oh, don't play stupid," Jasper spat. "You knew he had children, and you didn't want him to take us in."

"I never knew," she said. "Nathaniel never even mentioned that he had been married before."

Jasper's face went red, his nostrils flaring. "He wasn't married," he ground out.

"Why didn't you say anything? Why didn't you come to me? Why all of this?"

"I did come, you bitch! I came and was turned away at the door."

"And I'm telling you that I never knew!"

Gabriel squeezed her arm. He was relieved down to his bones that whatever physical toll coming here had taken on her, her spirit was still high, but the argument was serving no purpose now but to rile Jasper.

"Leave it," he said gently. "I've already had the full account, and he's stark raving mad." He gave Helen a nod. "Let's take him back." As long as they kept the gun on him, they could march him right into town and put this whole bloody mess to rest.

Returning his nod, Helen and Gabriel moved in unison to take Jasper by the elbows.

But before Gabriel could reach him, Jasper violently pulled back. "That's where you're wrong."

In the time it took him to blink, Jasper made a grab for the pistol, catching Helen off guard. In one swift motion he had seized it and backhanded it across her skull. She fell back with a sickening crack. A cry choked from Sophronia's lips as Helen crumpled to the ground.

This couldn't be happening.

Helen lay motionless, a thin stream of blood trickling from her head onto the dusty floor. The only movement in the room came from the cold air pushing its way in from the window, tugging at Helen's dark hair.

Gabriel was sizing up his chances of rushing Jasper; she could feel it in his coiled muscles, pressed tight against her. Looking up, she gave him an almost imperceptible shake of the head. She didn't need him escalating the situation even further, riling Jasper up. What if he shot Gabriel?

"Who should go first, I wonder?" Jasper said with a cock of his head, swinging the pistol between Gabriel and Helen's prostrate body on the floor. "Which one do you love more? Who will be the most painful to watch die?"

"No one needs to die," Sophronia murmured. "What is this really about, Jasper? You never knew your father. You can't pretend that you had a great love for him. It's the stories, isn't it? You're angry that I didn't publish your stories."

Gabriel's arms tightened around her in warning.

"You still don't understand, do you?" Jasper's green eyes had gone wild. "You took *everything* from me. It would have all been so different for Fanny and me if we'd had Nathaniel Carver for a father. I would be an acclaimed writer, and Fanny would never have to do laundry again. She could marry a gentleman."

His brotherly concern was almost touching. Almost. Having read his disturbing stories, though, Sophronia very much doubted that they would have ever been published, distinguished father or no. "You would be more like Poe, your idol?"

"Shut up about Poe!" The force of Jasper's voice reverberated off the old walls, warring with the wind whistling in through the broken window. "He's a hack! Don't you see? Everyone loves him, but his stories aren't any more original than mine." He took a deep breath. "Now," he said, his voice eerily calm and level, "I want to know how my father died. I heard it was a carriage accident, but the old butler from Castle Carver told me that he had his suspicions. What did you do to him?"

Sophronia winced. She held no love for Nathaniel, but the man had been poisoned, stabbed and dumped from a carriage. She really had no idea which of these had actually stopped his cold heart from beating. "It was a carriage accident, Jasper."

He stared at her, silent anger radiating from him like a coal fire. When he spoke again, his voice was a low, snake-like hiss. "Even now, you refuse to tell me the truth. You have to choose."

She could feel Gabriel's body tense ever so slightly next to her. Helen was still on the floor, the gash on her head oozing blood. She needed help, and soon.

"You know that you won't escape from this, don't you?" Gabriel said. "It doesn't matter if you kill Helen or me first. Mrs. Carver will see you brought to justice for what you've done."

Jasper raised a brow. "Do you really think me so stupid? There will be no witnesses," he said with a malicious glimmer of triumph in his eye as he shifted his gaze to Sophronia. "I won't shoot you with a pistol here. No, that was never my original plan. You will watch your friend and your lover die, and then I will take my time, carving you up, making sure you suffer just as surely as my father suffered at your hands."

But before he could utter another vile word, there was a flash of black out of the corner of her vision. Helen had staggered to her feet and lunged at Jasper, her hands at his neck as the gun clattered to the floor.

And then it happened. Jasper broke free, taking a giant step backward that nearly threw him off balance before charging right at Sophronia with his hands outstretched. She shrank into Gabriel's chest as he twisted around so that his back would take the brunt of the impact.

It never came. The last thing she saw before Gabriel pressed her face into his chest was Helen and Jasper, tangled together as they hurtled toward the sea-facing window. Jasper let out a sickening shriek, there was a shattering of glass, and then there was only the mournful wind and faraway crashing of waves.

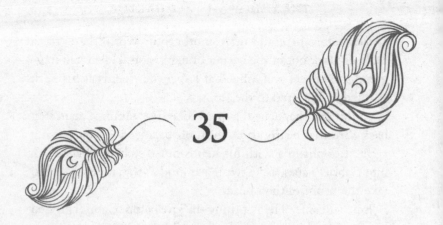

35

The flowers she had brought last week were already brown and bitten with frost. How different the cemetery was from the spring day when she had buried Nathaniel. What a different sort of sadness carved out space in Sophronia's heart now. Sinking to the grave, she gently laid down a fresh bouquet of violets.

"I think you truly did care about me, in your own way," she whispered to the frozen patch of dirt. When Helen had told her of the poisoning, the binding spell, all Sophronia had felt was a doleful sense of betrayal. But for all the lies and bad feelings, there had been years of cherished memories, too. Helen had been the mother she'd never known, the sister she'd never had. They had shared a home, a reputation and all the hours of their days, and now she was gone, her life given so that Sophronia might live. Her last, defiant act of protection.

When she was ready to rise, a strong hand gripped her gently, helping her to her feet. She knew that Gabriel didn't like her outside in the cold while she was still recovering, but she couldn't be smothered anymore, not even in the name of affection.

"Do you want to wait for Fanny?" he asked.

She nodded. Glancing across the old cemetery, Sophronia watched as Tom tucked Fanny under his arm with a tender, protective kiss to the top of her head. The young woman's face was pale and splotchy, but she at least stood without swaying now. The week before, when Fanny had learned the fate of her brother, what he had done and who their father had been, Sophronia had been afraid that the young woman would never recover. But she had surprised them with her resilience and shocked them further when she accepted a proposal of marriage from Tom Ellroy. It seemed that within all the horror of the past weeks, Sophronia had missed the romance blossoming right in front of her. "I'm glad they have each other," she said.

"Me, too." Gabriel followed her gaze, shaking his head in disbelief. "I never thought I would see Tom settled, but he couldn't have found someone more suited to him than Fanny."

The relief that Sophronia had felt when she learned that Fanny was completely innocent of her brother's crimes had been so profound that she'd nearly wept with joy. Her instincts and her capacity to trust... They were not broken. Nathaniel and Helen had made her question her judgment of character, made her wonder if there was something implicitly wrong about her that made her such easy prey to those who would deceive her. But they had not broken her completely. Indeed, they had only made her stronger.

A few moments later, the couple turned from the grave at the edge of the cemetery and joined them.

"For all his unhappiness, he loved you very much," Sophronia said softly, taking Fanny's hand in her own. "You were the best part of his life."

Fanny nodded, sniffing back errant tears. "I know. I just wish that had been enough for him."

It made Sophronia's heart ache to see such sorrow in her

friend's eyes, to know that whatever chaos Jasper had wreaked on Sophronia's life, he had inflicted the same tenfold on his own sister.

Tom stamped his feet against the cold. "Our ship leaves for London tomorrow, so I suppose this is goodbye."

"Only until Rome," Gabriel said. "We'll see you there in April."

Sophronia kissed Fanny's wet cheeks and embraced Tom. "Take good care of her."

Looking down at Fanny, Tom smiled. "I will."

After they'd seen Tom and Fanny off in a carriage, Sophronia and Gabriel turned toward Castle Carver. They had their own packing to do. They would get married abroad, travel and see some of the world outside the foggy confines of Pale Harbor.

As they walked, Sophronia couldn't help but steal glances at her beautiful fiancé. There had been no hesitation, no question in her mind when he'd asked her to marry him. She'd been sitting wrapped in a quilt before the fire, dutifully recuperating with a book and a cup of tea and her foot propped up on a stool. She had barely noticed that Gabriel had stopped studying the paintings on the wall and was nervously hovering near her.

"Sophy," he said.

She looked up from her book, nearly dropping it in surprise. Balanced on one knee, he looked like a medieval knight prostrating himself before his lady.

"Mr. Stone," she said, addressing him formally with the sole purpose of needling him. "What on earth are you doing down there?"

He shot her a dangerous look full of warning and heat. "I'm trying to propose to you, goddamn it."

She'd known as soon as she'd seen him on one knee, of

course, the question burning in his eyes, but her stomach still dipped at his words. Putting her book aside, she folded her hands neatly in her lap. "Oh, well, by all means. Please, continue."

"Sophronia." He swallowed compulsively, gazing up at her from under thick, dark lashes with such tender earnestness that she could hardly breathe. "Would you...that is..." Clearing his throat, he took her hands in his. "Would you do me the great honor of marrying me?"

As soon as he'd gotten the words out, she was throwing herself into his arms, mindless of the pain in her ankle and the upturning of her chair. He caught her up, his strong, safe arms encircling her.

There was no fear, no invisible bonds that made her say yes, only the exuberance of her heart, the certainty that she no more wanted to go through life without him by her side than she did continue in her Safety: alive but not feeling, loving but not acting.

Now, as they walked through town, her arm laced through his and her feet hardly touching the ground, Pale Harbor itself became a bride in a beautiful wedding gown of fog and mist. A few people offered them clipped nods of the head as they passed. Even with Jasper's death and the subsequent truth coming to light, she was still greeted with chilly reserve and lingering suspicion. She sighed. "I suppose I will never be greatly liked here."

Guiding her around a patch of ice in the road, Gabriel glanced down at her. "We don't need to stay, not if you don't want to."

"No, I belong here. *We* belong here. Besides," she said, "there's your church."

"Ah, right. That." He was quiet as they crunched through the thin snow. She waited, feeling the tension in the cold air around him. When he spoke again, it was as if he were weighing his every word.

"I think it's time for me to step down as minister. It was someone else's dream, and I don't honor her by lying and pretending to preach what I myself don't believe. I'm also miserable at writing sermons," he added with a grunt.

She let this sink in. An idea had been germinating in her mind, and now it unfurled its petals with perfect clarity. "You know," she said slowly, "I've always had a fancy to write my own stories. I read so many that I'm sure I could be passing good at it." She had never said the words aloud, but as she spoke them a feeling of rightness came over her. "If I had someone to read the magazine's submissions, I might have time to pen something of my own."

Writing stories would mean she could banish her demons to the page, render them harmless in black and white. Once set in ink, perhaps they could no longer haunt her. Chancing a sidelong glance at him, she held her breath and waited for his reaction.

He nodded thoughtfully, and then flashed her a shy but brilliant grin. "You would be a good writer," he said, his tone so confident that she had no choice but to believe him. "I'd like to read your stories, and if taking on the submissions would let you do that, then nothing would give me greater pleasure."

Some of the coldness that had settled in her chest after the past week thawed, and she began to feel real hope for the future. She leaned into him, and they finished the walk in comfortable silence.

Castle Carver stood waiting for them, a looming outpost of memories. Inside, the house seemed emptier, as if robbed of some vital force. Sophronia had always considered it a quiet, lonely place, but now Helen's absence made her realize just how much a part of the house she had been. The pianoforte was dusty, the kitchen cold and dark. There was no brisk swish of skirts in the hallway, no tuneless humming as Helen drifted about the house, tending to the lamps. Perhaps she was seeing everything through the rosy lens of nostalgia, but would she still have wished for change if she'd known it would come at such a high price?

"There's one thing we must do before we leave," she said, taking Gabriel by the hand and leading him out to the carriage house.

It had been nearly five years since she had been inside it, but with Gabriel by her side, she opened the door and stepped in as if it were any other building, as if the carriage that still resided there was no more than a skeleton, a dull echo of the terror of that night long ago.

The raven sat on its perch in an old stall that had been converted to a still room, dried herbs hanging from the rafters and neat rows of glass bottles lined up on a shelf. It appraised them with cautious black eyes as Sophronia reached out a tentative hand. To Gabriel's surprise, it climbed on as obediently as if it were a tame dove.

"Helen nursed it back to health after it was left injured on the steps," she explained. Running her fingers over the bird's feathered head, she looked up at him with a shy, excited smile. "It's so much softer than I imagined it would be."

He followed her as she carefully brought the raven outside. How he had come to hate the sight of the carrion birds and the death and terror that seemed to follow in their wake in Pale Harbor. But now all he saw was a stately creature, gentle and intelligent, despite its grim appearance.

When the raven began dancing impatiently on her wrist, Sophronia raised her hand, tossing it up into the sky. For a moment it bobbed, as if unused to its own weight, but then it righted itself, its powerful wings propelling it higher until the fog swallowed it up.

Gabriel's arm found its way around her waist, and he pulled her close. "Are you sure you don't want to move into the cottage with me?" He would happily live in Castle Carver with her—he would happily live in a shack with her, for that matter—but he couldn't imagine she would want to stay, not after everything that had transpired there.

Her lips pursed in thought, and then she shook her head. "I thought I couldn't be content here, but now I realize I would only be unhappy if I were alone with the ghosts. I won't be alone, and my soul has grown stronger." She met his gaze with her frank silver eyes, her small gloved hand tightening around his. "It is not a cage, but a branch. And every bird needs a sturdy branch from which to take wing."

As if in echo to this revelation, from the bleak December dusk rang the far-off cry of a raven.

★ ★ ★ ★ ★

AUTHOR NOTE

Thanks to a wealth of revolutionary thinkers, writers, poets and philosophers, Concord, Massachusetts, was a vibrant center of transcendentalist thought in the early to mid-nineteenth century. Gabriel would have been neighbors with the Alcotts, walked through the woods that inspired Henry David Thoreau and gone to lectures by Ralph Waldo Emerson. Today, you can visit many transcendental sites of significance in Concord, such as the Olde Manse where Nathaniel Hawthorne and his wife Sophia Peabody lived, the "author's ridge" in Sleepy Hollow Cemetery (the final resting place of authors Louisa May Alcott, Ralph Waldo Emerson, Nathaniel Hawthorne and Henry David Thoreau), and Walden Pond.

Although Castle Carver and its environs are fictional, I did draw on aspects of the historic house of Castle Tucker in Wiscasset, Maine. You can tour Castle Tucker and see the grand windows overlooking the Sheepscot River, climb the spiral staircase and experience the sweeping beauty of midcoast Maine.

While his celebrity may not have reached the level of hysteria surrounding Hungarian composer Liszt (the "Lisztomania" that Sophronia touches on), Edgar Allan Poe enjoyed a certain level of fame and notoriety during his lifetime as an author (largely due to his wildly popular poem "The Raven"). He was also a literary critic, lecturer, and campaigned for better wages and reforming the magazine industry. When he died at the age of forty in 1849, he left behind an unpublished manuscript simply titled "The Light-House." Narrated by the newly arrived lighthouse keeper through his journal entries, the story chronicles the keeper's growing anxiety and dread at his isolation on the island, eventually becoming paranoid that nothing is safe or as it seems. The entries are few and brief, until the last entry is left completely blank, so ending both the story and Edgar Allan Poe's brilliant and tumultuous career. Poe died under fittingly mysterious circumstances: on October 3, 1849, he was found in Baltimore, stumbling through the streets in a confused and fevered state, wearing someone else's clothing. He died a few days later, on October 7, and the actual cause of his death remains unknown.

ACKNOWLEDGMENTS

Thank you to Jane at Historic New England for giving me the opportunity to explore Castle Tucker, and who was so generous with her time answering my questions. While the Castle Carver of my story grew into a very different place, I could not have created it without such a solid historical foundation.

My critique partners Trish and Jeannie for all their support, and for reading very early, very messy drafts, and cheering me on to the end.

My deepest gratitude goes to Graydon House and the team at Harlequin for giving my dark stories such a wonderful home. I am incredibly humbled to get to work with a team of really amazing women. My editor, Brittany Lavery, who champions my vision and helps me shape my stories into the books of my dreams. Lisa Wray for her indefatigable enthusiasm in promoting my work and finding such amazing opportunities for me. Pam Osti for her brilliant marketing work. Sarah Goodey for her warmth and enthusiasm, and for bringing my books to the UK. A big thank-you to the rest of the HQ team in London and all their efforts on my behalf.

Thanks to my agent, Jane Dystel, for her fierce advocacy and Miriam Goderich for her reading and feedback. I would not be where I am today if not for both of them believing in me.

And finally, my heartfelt thanks to everyone who read, reviewed, borrowed, bought, recommended, or supported my first book, *The Witch of Willow Hall*, in any way, and the booksellers and librarians who hosted me for events and signings: you're the reason I get to keep doing this, and I'm so humbled and grateful. Special thanks also to the Bookstagrammers and the book bloggers who featured my book, and who are so integral to the writing community.